BREAKING THE LAW OF ATTRACTION

ZENNA BOWEN

Copyright Page

Unfolding himself from the chair behind the desk, he straightened, stretching both arms, and back. Should a casual observer have been present in the room, they may have feared for the safety of the central light fitting. They could not know that this man was aware, with utter precision, of his reach in any direction. They would, however, have been aware of the precision pressing of his crisp white shirt. This was in perfect contrast to his dark skin, sharply punctuated by collar and cuffs.

He sat once more, bending over files which he annotated in quick succession. Thus the secretary was greeted by a view of the top of his head as she entered, after her quick tap on the door. The close-cropped, tightly curled hair was replaced by the dark brown eyes lifted in question.

"Some cheques for you to sign, Monsieur du Blez, and I've had a call from Simpson and Drewett. They're stuck in traffic and likely to be a few minutes late for their appointment. Is that going to be a problem?"

Already one long arm was reaching out for the mouse, attention transferred to the monitor. "Another client straight afterwards. Cottonwood? Oh, the new case. Remember anything about that Maureen?" He signed the cheques, passing them back as he looked for her answer.

"Sounded quite straightforward, I think. Just a small affair, freelance business."

"Fine. When they arrive, warn the first two I have another meeting after them."

"Yes M. du Blez."

He smiled as she departed. Maureen was the other crucial element to this business, the first, of course, being himself. A good secretary was worth the proverbial weight in gold. Efficient; trustworthy; implacable and plain. The last two qualities were both very useful. They prevented the clients either bullying or flirting their way into special treatment, and him from being waylaid into activities that might make work less organised. Not that he tended to lack discipline in his professional conduct. The present junior, Justine, had brains, which was the essential part, but also an appearance sufficient to render many men lax in propriety. However, trainee solicitors came and went. He would have no trouble resisting her allure for whatever allotted time she was here. Secretaries, on the other hand, tended to be more permanent fixtures. Maureen was ideal. The first two ladies he had tried in the post had insisted on calling him Mister Dooblez. A travesty further compounded by the rolling Bristol accent. He wouldn't stand for that. He might be prepared to live and work in England, but not to have his name anglicised.

He worked on, quietly filling the time left fallow by the late arrival of his current appointment. Suddenly tired of marking files, he pushed himself from the desk and walked over to the window, looking down into the street below. Familiar scenes. Very familiar, bordering on dull in fact. Maybe he should go home for a visit, remind himself why he preferred voluntary exile. Things had definitely felt a little stale recently; he could do with some diversion. Not yet though, that was his desk-phone, probably Simpson and Drewett arriving.

Down in the street, so recently scanned, one thing was not functioning with the calm normality of everyday routine. A woman was changing direction, for the third time now, and muttering under her breath. She had left plenty of time to find the address and arrive calm and composed, or so she had thought. The numbering on Whiteladies Road did not seem to proceed in anything like a logical manner. Inevitably, she had started to trot along, doubled back, and then hurried on at an even faster pace in her original direction. She felt sweat breaking out under her hairline and at the back of her neck. She told herself she was bound to find the place any moment, and then she would feel a fool for panicking and arriving in a humid heap. If she was honest, which she generally was when by herself, some of the panic was due to the actual appointment. She never enjoyed being in a situation where she

4

felt at an intellectual disadvantage. Not that her intellect was particularly faulty, but appointments happened with people who had specialist training, like solicitors. She felt they were possibly the most intimidating of professional consultants, and with the least excuse. They weren't even like doctors, who obviously required technical knowledge, and lots of it. In their case, a certain degree of superciliousness could be forgiven. But solicitors, they only dealt in words! It should, she was adamant, be possible to understand what they did, and make sense of what they said and wrote. It just didn't seem to work though. She suspected them of wilful obstruction, a smoke and mirrors trick with the English language; that was unpardonable. She looked again at the piece of paper in her hand. Any horrors she had about the lack of meaningful communication between professional and client were not helped by the name written there: Monsieur F. du Blez. She could imagine his thin moustache, wide nostrils and condescending expression. Ugh, why had she made this appointment? No, it was no use, she needed to consult an expert, just find the place and get on with it. Of course, she had forgotten the 'A' after the number. There it was, between the spartan but exorbitant hi-fi shop, and the Talon Talent nail bar. There was an entry buzzer at the front door, which when released gave straight onto a flight of stairs. She climbed, and arrived, still with five minutes to spare, at a further door into what turned out to be a plush suite of offices. The reception desk, all pale wood and matte silver metal, was manned by a short but no less impressive woman. Lucy thought, from her face, that she could not be many years older than herself. Had she known the exact number, her mortification would have increased to the intolerable. Lucy, unaware of the mere half-decade difference, was concluding that their tastes differed even more widely than their ages. She looked down at the grey hair, apparently recently set at the hairdresser's, the large spectacles, the pale pink twin-set above the charcoal skirt, and hoped fervently that she would never reach that stage.

"I should just take a seat Mrs. Cottonwood. He's still with another client. I'm sure he won't be long."

Lucy sat down, removing her linen jacket to aid necessary cooling, and the receptionist turned back to her keyboard.

After a few moments, someone else appeared from whom Lucy felt an equal separation. A fashionably dressed younger woman emerged from a door off to Lucy's left. She was carrying a large bundle of files.

"Maureen, did M. du Blez tell you what other files I should go through before the meeting tomorrow?"

"Erm, no Justine, he's not mentioned that."

"Well, I've searched this lot, not really anything relevant. Would you be a sweetie and check that out with him for me please? I've skipped lunch to finish these, if I don't go out and find sustenance I'm going to keel over, I swear. I'll be back in twenty minutes."

With that the files were dumped on Maureen's desk, and the high black heels tip-tapped off down the stairs. Lucy looked again at her watch, the only thing in the place which was offering any feeling of affinity.

Just then the door in front of her opened and two men emerged. They nodded to the receptionist as they left; she was already speaking into the desk 'phone. She rose.

"I'll just be one moment with M. du Blez, Mrs. Cottonwood. We won't keep you."

Lucy shrugged, no reply was needed.

It was literally only seconds later that Maureen emerged and holding the door back with one hand for Lucy, said "M. du Blez will see you now."

Whatever she had been expecting, it wasn't this. Suddenly she could hear the voices of tall, graceful women, the replies from men with regal bearing and the laughter of wide-eyed children. Was it just those voices from her memory, or had he spoken? He extended his hand and she turned her attention to the long, almost delicate fingers and the exquisite gradation of colour across the nail-beds. Now there was something worth drawing! His raised eyebrows finally gave Lucy the clue that she had been staring, possibly with her mouth open, that could be believed. She hurried to grasp the hand he offered and stammered a hello.

He shook her hand very formally and gave a slight bow of the head as he said, "Madame."

She was still staring at him and finally ventured softly, "Somali?"

He smiled, breaking the formal set of his expression, "My mother is Somali, my father French. You probably guessed that from the name. You know Somalia?"

"I was there some years ago. They are a striking people, very graceful, I can't forget them."

"I have only been once, for a brief visit. Maman was quite young when she left there." He held out the elegant hand she had just shaken towards a chair, "Please, take a seat."

She sat down, unable to stop observing him. She noticed that his hair was the sort Somalis would describe as soft type. He smiled again and leaned forward slightly, "How can I help you?"

"Right," said Lucy, trying to shake herself into work mode, "It's a question of intellectual property. Sorry, of course it is; that's your specialist area."

Again, a slight incline of the head, an economy of movement, indicating acquiescence and inviting her to continue.

"I work as a web site designer, freelance. About two months ago I was asked to do some work for a local limousine hire company. The owner, Les Wilson, said he had recently expanded into that area of transport and wanted a web-site for it. He asked me to submit a few outline designs for a small fee. He said he was asking a couple of other designers to do the same and he would choose one to work with. I tried to decline, that isn't normally how I take on a brief. I advised him to go for one of the template web-sites you can get; that would have been perfectly adequate. Anyway, he was very persistent, said he was considering having other material designed too and wanted it all to match. He kept badgering me and I said yes to shut him up really. After a couple of weeks my work was returned, with the fee, and I was told he had decided to use another designer."

She paused, as if checking she hadn't left anything important out so far, before continuing. "Three weeks ago I saw their new web site; it bears a remarkable similarity to what I sent in. He denies it, of course, saying it was coincidence; my designs merely had elements in common with the other material they received and went on to use. It's clearly nonsense and I'm not happy about it."

He had remained motionless during her explanation, now he leaned forward, elbows on the desk, hands thrown upwards, questioning, "Do you have any material to show me?"

She bent down to the briefcase at her feet, and pulled out a thin file which she passed across to him.

It was her turn to sit in silence as he turned over the loose sheets of paper, looking at each one slowly, and then putting some side by side for comparison. He turned to his computer and tapped keys briefly, narrowing his eyes at what came up in front of him.

"Can you give me a couple of web-sites you have designed please?"

She gave him two web addresses, which he accessed and scanned quickly.

"I think this looks straightforward. The button icons are clearly characteristic of your work. Also, there is very little change from these drafts you've shown me."

She snorted, "It looks like some schoolkid has cut and pasted my mock-ups you mean!"

He gave her a brief smile, eyes flicking across to her from the screen, "Something like that yes. I take it this client of yours did not impress you with his artistic appreciation."

"No, he seemed a bit dense and unimaginative, except for imagining he could get away with this."

"How did you find out about it?"

"Chance. A friend was looking to hire a limo for her son's eighteenth birthday. I remembered this lot and looked it up for her. I wasn't too pleased when I saw the site; I don't want people thinking I'm responsible for a bad job like that."

"Well, providing, of course, you have your computer records intact and can make them available to me, we should have a very straightforward case here." She nodded. "Good. Can you e-mail them to me tomorrow? Yes? Excellent, we can start on this straightaway, my clerk Justine will get the preparatory work done."

She sat still for a moment, waiting for the next comment, but there didn't seem to be one. Her voice came out sharply, "Great. Is that it?"

He shrugged. "It looks like a simple case. That does not mean it will necessarily be quick. We will accuse them. They will deny it. We will write threatening letters. Their solicitors will reply threatening us. We will write again showing that we have proof and demanding substantial compensation. They will reply suggesting we meet to discuss the issue. Several dates will be suggested; finally one will be agreed upon, weeks ahead. We will show them the proof; they will argue it is insufficient. Then they will go away to consider the case before writing to suggest a compromise solution. There may well be several rounds of letters before an agreement is reached which does not satisfy either party. You will receive some money and my bill, which no doubt will horrify you. You pay me, we shake hands and you go away with the rest of your settlement. Do you doubt any of this?"

She sat for a moment, stunned, not so much by the résumé, which she did not doubt, but by the honesty of the man in giving it.

"Are you saying I'm wasting my time?"

"Non. Not at all. You cannot let these people cheat you. You will not receive as much as you wish financially, but they will know they cannot disregard the law, and that you are vigilant. That is part of the result you want, no?"

"Yes, it is," she said, amused by both his unexpected candour and his strengthening accent as he warmed to his theme.

He smiled broadly, his teeth so white against the ... what colour exactly was his skin? Actually, it almost had a bloom on it, as if it was fine suede, but his hand had been very smooth, and that ....oops! He was speaking again. Really, she needed to concentrate; he would get a totally wrong impression if she carried on like this.

"Is that not so?"

"I'm sorry?" she shook her head slightly, trying to recapture the sentences that had sailed past her ears and failed to connect with her mind. He must think she was an idiot.

"Many people are frightened of legal matters, I see this all the time. But I am not the monster. I can help you, so you will feel better."

He was beaming at her now, and looking rather pleased with himself. She was still wondering what she had missed in the conversation to have got to this point. She settled for a smile and a nod, hoping she wasn't fuelling some peculiar ego-trip.

He stood, "Very well, here is my e-mail address, send the computer files tomorrow, we will start the game rolling."

"Ball," she said automatically.

"Hein?"

"Start the ball rolling. Or get the game under way. One or the other."

He looked mystified, then his brow cleared. "Of course. Forgive me, even now your English phrases get the better of me, there are so many."

He reached out and shook her hand again. Yes definitely very smooth skin, but it was a firm grip; that was a relief, how she hated limp handshakes.

He continued to look at the papers in front of him. Something was jingling a little bell in his mind, waking him up to something. Suddenly he leapt from the chair and put his head round the door. Good, she was still in the reception area, putting on her jacket.

"Actually, Madame Cottonwood?"

She turned, "Yes?"

"Could you send also some more examples of work you have done for other companies, and their web addresses? That would be very helpful to me."

"Yes, of course."

He closed the door again, shutting her off from view and returned to his desk, where he sat for a few moments in thought. That had been a surprise. He had expected nothing of the sort. Very few people ever recognised a particular origin for his features. Was that why she stared so much? He had been on the point of concluding that she was terrified by the combination of a large black man and the legal profession, he'd seen it often enough. And on top of that she'd been completely overt in her dissatisfaction with the formal process on offer. Not too terrified to voice her disdain. He liked that, when his first impressions were wrong. She was not the mouse he had taken her for. No, much more the household cat, soft and furry but suddenly claws out, small and sharp. Her clothes were smart, but not chic; slightly younger styles than he would have expected from the lack of attempt to cover the grey which dusted her brown hair, or the sparse make-up she wore. He flipped open the cover of the file, which Maureen had started prior to her arrival. Her date of birth made her mid-forties, a few years older than him. He would have guessed slightly younger. Was his idea a good one? Perhaps. He particularly liked the way her eyes changed as her focus shifted. Grey-blue when she had stared at him for so long, tawny flecks firing at her amusement over his explanation. Yes, it was worth following up. He would do something about that.

Back at home, in her study, she was berating herself for her lack of concentration in front of the solicitor. While it was on her mind, she turned to the computer and sent off the files he had requested. At least she had listened for that bit, and could show him that she wasn't totally scatterbrained by getting them to him promptly. She sat in front of the screen but for a while was lost in her recollection of the interview. Why was the colour of his skin so difficult to describe? She had worked in graphics and design for many years, she even still painted occasionally, but she knew it would take her a long time to get that particular shade right. His skin was not just brown, or even black, but with a distinct grey or taupe cast to it. No, more sort of coffee with a hint of - no, that was wrong too. Never mind, she hadn't seen anything like it for twenty-five years and it had taken her breath away. Extremely fine bone structure; wide forehead, high cheek bones, nose long and lips bordering on narrow; together they had spirited her back in time, and left her feeling disorientated with her present world. She still had all the sketches. She must let Mark know that she had followed his recommendation. And Tom would find it interesting, something to write in the next e-mail. That lightened her thinking, news had been sparse lately and they had never been the type of couple that rambled on endlessly with romantic prose to each other. She was aware that the only way to make him feel still part of life at home was to share the minutiae of unimportant things that occurred from day to day. But they rapidly became about as interesting as a note to the milkman. At least he would be glad to know she was getting the copyright issue dealt with and, like her, interested by the Somali connection, however slight.

Her thoughts continued in this random fashion for some time then she put on more music and contemplated the idea of proper work. The design for the kindergarten needed to be finished off. Happy thoughts were required for this, she decided, and made herself a cup of tea.

The telephone was jammed between his chin and shoulder; he was scribbling something on a pad while he listened to the ringing.

"Helloo," the voice sounded like it had been interrupted from some other pastime.

"Ah, good morning, Madame Cottonwood, this is Monsieur du Blez. I was wondering if you might have any free time today and be able to see me?" There was silence on the other end, had the connection failed? "Madame?"

"Yes, yes of course. Sorry, didn't expect to hear from you so soon after your warning yesterday. When were you thinking? I'll see if I'm free."

He was sure she could arrange her day to suit herself; she worked from home after all. "Well, I was wondering about lunch-time, say one o'clock?"

"Yes, I can do that."

He could hear the surprise in her voice, but did nothing to dispel it. "Excellent. Do you know Hubert's Bistro? It is just off the main road, on the right hand side below the shopping arcade, further down from my office."

The voice now held audible notes of confusion, "Yes, I think so."

"Good, I will see you there at one. But could I take your mobile number? Just in case I am delayed with another client, then I can let you know."

"Er, yes, hang on a second."

He could hear scrabbling at the other end. She was obviously one of those people who never remembered their own number. Eventually she returned and read it off to him.

"Thank you, I will see you later."

He was smiling broadly to himself. He had no way of knowing, but his guess at the look of blank incomprehension his call had left on her face was completely correct.

2

As she walked down the road, the same one that yesterday she had been trotting hurriedly up, she found herself feeling more and more confused about this. Why did he want to meet her at a café instead of the office? She shrugged, telling herself she would find out in a few minutes. It was just past the hour as she pushed open the door and went in. Looking around she could see no sign of the solicitor, nor much in the way of empty seats. She felt very hesitant; the man behind the bar was watching her, as though she had no right to be in here. Just then her mobile beeped and she pulled it from her bag to retrieve the text message. It read 'Sorry to keep you. On my way. FdB'

"Can I help you madame?"

She jumped, unaware that the waiter had approached her.

"I was looking for a table, I'm waiting for my. . ."

She hesitated, about to say solicitor, but that seemed like unnecessary detail.

"For someone," she finished.

"I am sorry, but we are busy, there are no empty tables at the moment."

She nodded and turned to leave; annoyed she'd been landed with a problem she hadn't asked for. Just then the solicitor in question came through the door.

"Good day madame. Ah, bonjour Hubert, ça va?"

"Bonjour mon ami!"

She stood by and watched as they babbled at each other, seeming to use their hands as much as their mouths. She wondered vaguely what French sign language would look like. Next thing, they were being shown to a table at the back of the room, set into an alcove and partly hidden from the rest of the diners.

As they were seated, the waiter leant over her shoulder, making her jump again, "My apologies madame, I did not realise you were with M du Blez."

He handed her a menu and left.

She sat regarding him with marginally flared nostrils, feeling again at a disadvantage in a setting that was familiar to him but alien to her.

"Shall I order for you?" he asked.

"No thank you," she said tartly.

He raised his eyes to look at her, but she had lowered hers to the menu, which was all in French. The corner of his mouth curled up in a slight smile as he regarded the stern set of her face.

He did not bother to even glance at his own menu, he would ask Hubert for what he liked anyway, but he took pleasure in watching her expressions while she pondered. After a brief pause she looked up and nodded to him. The waiter came back and they ordered.

"Would you care for wine?" he asked.

Lucy declined, requesting sparkling water instead

When they had been left in peace once more he spoke.

"I apologise madame, not just for being late, but for not explaining myself on the 'phone earlier. I have not asked to see you about the case you brought to me. That is why I asked you to lunch. There is something I wanted to discuss with you in a more leisurely fashion."

"Oh?" she said, shifting in her seat, and a faint look of alarm registering momentarily on her face.

"Yes, I have been looking at your designs and I would like to ask you to do some work for me."

She was quiet for a moment. "What kind of work?"

"Your usual," he laughed. "These days even dull solicitors have web-sites. The current one we have is dreadful. Justine, my assistant, has been pleading with me to get it updated. I like your designs; I thought you could produce something a bit more fresh and interesting for us."

"I see," she leant forward, elbow on the table, chin in hand and fingers over her mouth. She smiled slightly behind her fingertips.

He smiled back, "What did you think I was going to ask for?"

"I had no idea," she said tilting her other hand out in a gesture of incomprehension, perhaps it was catching.

"I see. I must have made you very uncomfortable, my apologies once more."

Now that she had a grasp of the situation, Lucy started to relax. She began asking him questions about what he needed for the web-site, which he did his best to answer. She explained they would need to have a closer look at various options to define the brief better and he was content with that. They had just started discussing the kind of designs he was interested in when the food arrived, and they continued to talk over the meal.

Once the plates were removed, he commented that there was more to this than he had thought. She nodded.

"Yes, but that's true of everything, isn't it? The more you start to look into something the more you realise there is to know. Everyone else's job sounds easy until you try to do it. We just don't observe well, not until there is a reason to look."

"But you do observe, that is why you produce good designs?"

She shrugged her shoulders, "It would be nice to think so."

"Mais oui, certainement."

She smiled, "Vous êtes trop gentil."

He grinned broadly, "Please Madame Cottonwood, tu not vous."

"In that case, if we are dispensing with formalities, Monsieur le Notaire, you had better call me Lucy. Madame Cottonwood does seem a terrible mouthful."

Now it was his turn to look uncomfortable, and her eyebrows met in a frown of interrogation.

He sighed, looking down at the table, "And my name is Farine."

"Farine?" she asked, making sure she had heard correctly. He nodded.

"Farine du Blez?"

Again he nodded, "Oui."

"Clearly there's a story there, do I get the chance to hear it?"

He raised his hand to Hubert, "Very well, but only over a decent cup of coffee."

He settled back in his seat, and crossed his long legs. Obviously the story too was going to be of some length.

"My father is French as you know; he was in the army in the sixties. For a while he was stationed near to Somalia, in a very small country called Djibouti. The army were there overseeing many things in preparation for independence. As always, there were different factions, and the potential for terrorist acts. One night there was an incident, my father's unit were involved in capturing and disarming what was thought to be a group of militants. It turned out to be not insurgents but people traffickers. A group of about twelve young women, mainly from Somalia, were being taken through the capital to be shipped on to various locations."

The coffee arrived, and they settled themselves comfortably again.

"So, the soldiers found themselves with a few criminals and a large group of frightened girls. My mother was young and very beautiful. My father was very lonely, a long way from home. She was, of course, very grateful for being rescued. By the time his tour of duty was finished, she was also very pregnant. He married her there, so she could legally come to France, but had to arrange passage for her on a cargo ship to Marseille while he went home on a troop carrier. When he met her again, the boat had been delayed, and she was too close to her time to complete the journey to her new home. I arrived two days after she landed in Marseille. Typically, my father got supremely drunk in celebration of my birth. Knowing my father, I can assure you he would have been incapacitated for days. He sent her to register me; I was to be called Fabian, after my grandfather. Her French was quite minimal at that point, I leave you to imagine what my parents had spent their time doing in their months together, but obviously it wasn't language practice. There was some confusion with the officier de l'etat civil, the registrar. He probably thought she was just a poor immigrant trying to give her child a French-sounding name. When she brought the birth certificate back to my father, I was Farine du Blez. French bureaucracy, as you must know, is infamous, I was stuck with it."

She put her hand over her mouth to hide the smirk on her face before she asked, "Is any of that really true?"

He looked thoroughly offended, "Of course! What do you think I am? This is my history. It is certainly the story my parents tell. I have my suspicions that my mother was somewhat intoxicated at the time too, but she denies it strenuously."

She bit her lip, "Don't be cross; it just sounds far too exciting to be true. It certainly gives you a memorable name. Does it cause you many problems?"

"In this country, not so many. A lot of people don't speak French anyway so it means nothing to them. Of course in France it raises eyebrows," he shrugged looking away briefly, "but I'm used to it by now. Between that and being the first black child at the village school, it made my youth interesting. Whichever way you look at it, I'm an oddity. It's best to learn to deal with it quickly."

"Well, I'm absolutely delighted to have met someone called Farine du Blez!"

"Will you work for him?"

"Yes, of course. If you can afford me" she produced a gentler copy of his autocratic stare from the previous day.

He threw back his head and laughed. "Touché. I can see I will have to draw up a contract very carefully for this. When shall I see you again?"

She went back to professional mode, "Well, really we need to nail down the technical bits of the web-site you need. That would be best done at your office, you'll need to look at some examples online and choose what features you want. After that, probably a couple of meetings about a week apart, although I could e-mail you a lot of it, and you can just say which designs you like for the different bits. It shouldn't take

18

too long, depending on how good you are at making up your mind."

He shook his head, "Choosing designs? I am terrible. But for you, I will try to observe well."

"Right, so when do you want me to come to the office?"

"Ah yes, I do not carry my appointment book to lunch, can I get my secretary to call you this afternoon? How long will we need?"

"It can take an hour, or even two. Let's say an hour. We'll just have to book another session if we don't get it finished. Is that okay? Now let's settle up."

"Please, madame, I invited you. I am a gentleman."

He straightened out his body, she had forgotten, as they sat, just how tall he was.

She looked up at him and gave him a warm smile.

"Well, thank you for lunch, and thank you for the work."

She held out her hand, he shook it once more.

"Madame." He did the quaint little bow of the head as he murmured this, and she wanted to laugh, but didn't dare. She had never met anybody quite so determinedly French.

Running up the stairs, she felt very cheerful at the prospect of the next hour. He was undeniably good company; it should make working through all the usual practicalities a bit livelier for her.

"Good morning," she directed her bright greeting to Maureen and the desk.

"Oh good morning Mrs. Cottonwood, please take a seat. M du Blez has someone with him."

"Thank you, I know I'm a bit early."

"That's quite alright, in fact that's rather helpful. Justine has asked for a word with you before you go in to M du Blez, I'll just let her know you're here."

Lucy pulled a face to herself, wondering what this was about, but Justine appeared almost immediately, so she did not have to wonder long. Today Justine had on red high heels, which won Lucy's admiration just for her ability to walk in them without falling over. They shook hands and sat down.

"I hope you don't mind, I wanted a quick word about the web-site. I can see why M du Blez chose you; you've produced some very clean attractive sites."

Lucy felt she was being buttered up and was interested in what would come next. Her eyebrows rose slightly in response as she waited for Justine to continue.

"I thought it might be good to let you know that the boss can be a bit old fashioned. You know, tend to go for something a bit staid. It would be good to direct him towards the modern I feel.

"Well, I'm sorry, all I can do is produce designs for him to view. He is the client; the choice is up to him."

"Oh, absolutely. Of course." Justine was nodding vehemently. "It would just be good, you know, to give him options including the modern, and er, maybe point out what is the current type of thing people choose. That's all, just so he knows."

Lucy returned the glittering smile before reiterating her point, "Presumably he's asked me because he likes the kind of design I do. It's his decision."

Justine nodded again, defeated, or at least deflected, for the moment, "Okay then. I'll let you get on with it."

She went back to her office, and Lucy again raised her eyebrows, this time at Maureen, who had obviously heard it all.

Maureen appeared delighted at the opportunity to confide in Lucy. "I don't know, these youngsters, eh? She's a nice girl, but she acts like M du Blez is out of the last century!"

Lucy couldn't help thinking that he was, and they certainly both were, even the stylish Justine. But she refrained from saying it. Perhaps Maureen had an even further distant epoch in mind.

"She probably thinks he's going to choose coats of arms and things. As if he would! I don't know what his family crest is like, but he never flaunts it or anything. You know? That he's a Count?"

A quiet voice inside Lucy's head started asking her to double check and make sure she hadn't fallen down a rabbit hole recently. She looked round in case there was a half-formed cat anywhere, smiling at her. No, definitely not. She looked back at Maureen. "Pardon?"

"He's a Count. M du Blez is the Comte d'Ambouzac. He has a château in the South of France."

"Then what's he doing soliciting in England?" Something had definitely fallen out the wrong way there, but she wasn't going back to pick it up when there was something more crucial to pursue here, "Are you telling me he's French nobility?"

Maureen nodded, and Lucy felt herself deflate like a perished balloon. Oh really! She had just got over her automatic distrust of solicitors and decided she liked the guy, along with his ridiculous name.

"It's quite tragic actually." Maureen was clearly not finished with the confidences, and Lucy wasn't sure why she qualified to get them all. The recently raised eyebrows were regretted, but the secretary was already leaning across her desk and dropping her voice even further.

"I think it's because of his wife. She's disappeared you know."

Lucy shook her head in disbelief. They had moved from children's classic to gothic novel in one smooth step.

"Yes, every so often M du Blez gets a report that she's been seen somewhere and he rushes off to try and find her. She's been missing for years. Very sad."

Lucy wasn't sure whether a response was needed here and she certainly couldn't think of a sensible one. She settled for "Mmm," and hoped that conveyed an appropriate amount of feigned sympathy.

"I suppose she could have gone mad. I mean, that's quite common in these noble families. Isn't it? All that inbreeding."

Lucy felt that things were getting beyond her and looked around again in the hope that someone else might arrive, perhaps she could ask Justine to come back, but Maureen was still speaking.

"I expect he works to take his mind off her."

She was spared the ordeal of fabricating another response; at that moment the door ahead of her opened and Farine emerged with a thick-set man. They shook hands and he departed.

Farine turned to Lucy, "I'm so sorry to have kept you waiting again. I seem to be making a habit of it. Please come in."

In his office Farine asked her how they needed to arrange things. She sat them both on his side of the desk and started tapping away at the keyboard to bring up the site she wanted. She was working swiftly through the different options for pages of the web-site. He felt like he was being whisked along and said so.

"Sorry, I'll start again. I was trying not to take up too much of your time."

"Lucy, you are annoyed with me. I cannot throw out a client because he talks on. I was not very late."

"Of course not, no, that's fine."

"Then what is the matter? Please tell me."

"I told you, I'm just trying to be concise. I know you're busy."

She was aware that her voice and bearing were huffy. They had no business to be. He may or may not be a Count and he didn't have to explain it to her either way.

"I'm sorry. I didn't mean to be brusque. Let's just start again and you say if there's anything you don't understand."

"No. I don't want to start until I know what is wrong. You are apologising to me, but you are the one who is offended. Why?"

She stared at the screen, as though it might produce some guidance for her. It remained steadfast in portraying the information she had already requested of it. She pulled a face, even this failed to make it offer her anything different. And her delaying tactics had not helped; she still wasn't sure what to say. She was aware of his stare as he waited for a reply. She aimed her gaze just over his left shoulder.

"I didn't know you were a Count." It sounded very lame as a reason to be offended.

He groaned slightly. "Maureen has been talking to you."

"Does she make it up?"

"No, it is true; I am le Comte d'Ambouzac, for what it's worth."

"What does that mean?"

"It is a title, but very little else. We have the remains of an estate. The nobles they did not behead, the French crippled by economics, very much like your country."

"Except we didn't bother with the beheading part."

"True. Anyway, I told you a little bit about my parents. I didn't tell you that my father joined the army to get away from my grandmother. She was trying to get some money back into the family and wanted to marry him off to a wealthy woman with her eye on a title. Can you imagine the reception they got when my father turned up with a black child-bride and the infant of their union? Grandmother was furious. She tried to get the marriage annulled, me declared illegitimate, anything to save the du Blez family from this disgrace, and certain poverty. Now you know."

"This is the second fantastic tale you've told me about yourself. Can all this really be true? Perhaps you're just inventing an interesting background, I can understand that some people do, but I don't want to hear lies."

"It is true, but I don't usually tell clients all of this. It has nothing to do with how well I do my job. And why does it bother you?"

"I hate pretence. I mean in the people I deal with, I want to know if I can trust them. I came to you because I've just clashed with one guy who's a cheat, not much help if you're a sham in your own right, is it?"

He shrugged, "Yes, I can see that would matter to you. I can't see that I needed to give you my pedigree though. I work with lots of people who know nothing about me being a Count. You don't normally ask the life history of people you work with, do you?"

She was flustered, and tried shrugging it off, "Well, if I'm honest it shouldn't matter, but it does. And if we're considering life histories, you told me a lot about yourself last time I saw you, but not this. It was a bit of a shock."

"Because you find I am not quite the person you thought I was?"

"Yes, that's right. I'm sorry, I know it's none of my business at all, but it threw me. I don't know if that makes sense?"

"Yes, I think so. Besides, you do not like to feel inferior to people, and you think because I have a title I will look down on you."

"I don't care about your bloody title!"

She reddened at her own outburst and his consequent flash of amusement.

"If you did not care, surely you would not be annoyed?" His tone slid suddenly from calm probing to slicing accusation, still politely delivered, "So you are not prejudiced against me because I am black, or because I have a joke for a name, but because I am from a noble family. I'm sure that's culturally more acceptable. No doubt you English will have a phrase for it."

"Inverted snobbery. And you French can be supercilious enough without a title!" Her own brief hubris had given her the mettle to find a riposte, but the content of his challenge was working its way into her brain and she picked up her repentant state accordingly.

"Do you get a lot of that? Of prejudice, people underestimating you?"

"It happens, sometimes. I have been successful in different things; that tends to offset it."

She reflected on the momentary attack she'd experienced; she could imagine anyone who did underestimate him soon regretted it. She'd come to the right man after all, and a small smile was allowed onto her face. Les Wilson watch out!

"I'm sorry, and I mean it. We all have prejudices we're not aware of until something crashes into them. Actually, being totally honest, I wasn't keen to meet you in the first place because you were French. Having got over that hurdle, to find out you're some kind of lord was too much."

He shook his head in disbelief, "Well, I can see you like to be on certain ground, I'm sorry my origins make you feel unsure. I can't help where I was born, any more than you can. If you want to know what it's like, it's more of a nuisance than a privilege. Now, is there anything else you want to check out about me before we get some work done?"

"Well how about he disappearing wife?"

"Ah, now I am ashamed. She is not exactly real. You catch me in a lie there."

"Why?"

He did one of his Gallic shrugs, "It was true once. I married when I was twenty. After two years she ran away. But I have neglected to tell Maureen that I found her again within three months, with another man. We divorced. However, it is useful to have an excuse to go off on long weekends occasionally. Maureen is sympathetic, which she probably wouldn't be if she knew I was away enjoying myself. Also, I think I am safer if Maureen believes I am married still. She would probably vet all my clients for a suitable match. Being a Count is romantic enough, from her point of view, without being a single one.

Lucy finally let go of all her qualms, "You've got a Bunbury!"

"I'm sorry, I have a what?"

"A Bunbury, a useful but imaginary reason to disappear every so often. You know, The Importance of Being Earnest."

"Comment?"

"A play by Oscar Wilde. Have you not heard of it?"

"Ah, yes. Oscar Wilde. I remember. You are not offended with me then?"

"It's far too funny to be offensive. I think you are a bad influence on me, though. How are we going to get on with this web-site if you keep having all these exotic bits of your life interrupting us?"

"I can think of nothing else which should arise for now."

"Right, that's reassuring, is it? For now?"

She turned back and grimaced at the monitor. Setting the conversation aside, she started a more leisurely tour through the main features, trying to explain the differences it made to the overall way the web-site would work. After a while she glanced at her watch.

"I think that's enough today. You won't be able to remember it if I do too much. You've probably already forgotten what things you need to choose between so far."

"Not at all, there is nothing wrong with my memory and I have made notes."

She looked across to the notepad and saw small neat writing carefully set out, summarising all the salient points. Maybe neat writing was essential for being a Count. And she wasn't sure why she didn't find it irritating when he made these slightly arrogant statements, possibly because she was finding it so hard to take him seriously anyway. She shrugged then smiled to herself. How many Counts had she met? None previously. Perhaps this was par for the course.

"What is amusing you?"

"Just you, you're different. I'll give you that."

"Is that good or bad?"

"Oh good, definitely. Once I've got over being frightened of it, I enjoy different."

"Well, as we are on friendly terms again, why not come and have some lunch with me? Surely we have earned a little rest from all this planning?"

3

They left the office chatting about one or two of the considerations that needed to be taken into account before they could move any further on the project. As they reached the café, he turned to her.

"Okay, that's the end of work for now. And we have discussed me quite enough for today; tell me about your life."

She made a kind of strangled noise before replying. "Well, there isn't a lot to tell. I'm a pretty boring person really. Very ordinary life compared to yours I'm afraid."

"I don't want you to compare it to mine. I want you to tell me about it."

"Okay. I was born in the north of England, which is probably why I am so blunt. My parents were ordinary working class people who were delighted when I got the chance to go to university. I did art but swapped to graphic design, which led to a few jobs over the years with advertising agencies. I married Tom when I was twenty-two. He's a few years older than me. We have two children, Jennifer who works near here and Nick who is still at university. When the kids went to school I taught graphics for a while in college. That gave me the chance to get computer savvy, graphics is largely computer driven these days, and a few years ago I went freelance as a designer. That's about it."

They were eating some olives and bread, he was already halfway down a glass of red wine, she had mineral water again.

"I don't understand. What is blunt? That is the opposite of sharp, no?"

She looked at him for a moment, then her eyes widened. "Oh I see, sorry. Blunt is also when you speak too honestly, you just say it, without tact or thought. It's very much a northern thing; here in the south they are more polite, which often means not telling you the truth."

"I detect a theme here," he said smiling, "you must be honest, and people must be honest with you."

"Yes, I guess that's true. I mean, I suppose we're all polite rather than honest sometimes. There isn't always the time to work it all out, is there? I recognise politeness is a social necessity but I use it less frequently than some people."

"I like that, yes. I agree with you. But I don't think you speak without thought."

"Well, I can do, sometimes."

"What does your husband do? Is he a designer too?"

"No, he's a logistics expert. He worked for a big company for a number of years, planning the supply and transport for new sites in different parts of the world. He took early retirement last year; he wanted to do some different things. Right now he's on a six-month trip to Tanzania, helping a charity to reorganise its bases in several countries. They've had to pull out of some areas because of fighting and they need to re-assess their resources and capabilities."

"That sounds very interesting. Did you not want to go with him?"

She seemed to have drifted away during her last answer, it took her a moment to engage with this last question. Whatever she'd been thinking, she wiped it off her mind as she applied the smile to accompany her reply.

"The charity can't afford to send me too, and I can't afford to ditch my freelance work for that long. I may get out there for a couple of weeks part way through his stint, or at the end. Depends how much work I get, and how much I earn!"

"Ah, then we are helping you, good. So he is in Africa now, and you said you have been in Somalia, when was that?"

"After university, I did a voluntary spell out with a relief agency. You'd call it a gap year now. That's where I met Tom, he was in charge of logistics on the ground. They were trying to repatriate a lot of the Somali refugees who had been displaced at that time. There had been several waves of fighting and fleeing the country. We were involved in distributing basic farming implements to start off people who had gone back to their homes."

"Not such a boring life as you pretended."

"Well, it's not as exciting as being a Count. Why did you choose to come and work here, instead of staying at your estate?"

"Several reasons, not least being I represent an odd sort of Count."

"I couldn't say, not knowing any others I have no idea what a normal Count is. Why would you be so odd?"

He laughed, "You are being very insouciant. How many black Counts do you think there are in France?"

"I hadn't thought about it. I mean there are quite a lot of black people in France, from all the ex-colonies and that. It never occurred to me to wonder whether any of them were part of the nobility."

"Well, not everyone is like you. Of all the black people in France, most are in the big cities; very few would be lords of small country châteaux."

"No, I suppose not. Who looks after the estate now then?"

"I have lots of brothers and sisters. My parents continued their relationship as they started it. Several of them run the château and the land."

"Isn't that a bit odd, them running it all for you?"

He shrugged, "No, they run it for themselves, not me. They live there; they drink the wine, and eat the produce. Where else would they go?"

"Hmm. I guess as long as it works that's all to the good. But what about your parents? If you hold the title now, your father must be dead."

"Yes, that is so. My grandfather was aware the family money was dwindling; he used almost the last to send me to university. He always stood by my parents and he was very fond of me. He said I would be Comte one day, my birth could not be denied and he did everything he could to equip me for it. He died during my time in Paris, and obviously my father inherited. He was an alcoholic by then, and had the good grace to drink himself to death two years later."

"Did he make life miserable for your mother? With his drinking?"

"No, they adored each other till the day he died. I meant because of the money. What little there was left, my father was drinking away. Any more and my mother would have had to return to her original occupation!" She looked at him, eyes very wide. "Oh come along, Lucy, I told you she was being trafficked through Djibouti. What do you think she was being used for? She was sold into the sex-trade."

"It doesn't sound like the sort of thing you talk to your children about!"

"No, it isn't. But we know. At least she escaped, the vast majority do not."

"Did it happen a lot? The trafficking out there I mean?"

"All the time. I went out there for a short spell after I qualified. It was certainly still going on then. Trafficking is the only means of productivity in the country. What do you think of that as a statistic? I tried to work as a human-rights lawyer," he paused peering down at the table for a moment. "I'm ashamed to say I didn't last long. The corruption and hopelessness were overwhelming."

She could understand anyone's horror at the disgusting trade, to know it had affected someone in your own family was unimaginable. She asked softly, "How old was she then? You described her as a child-bride."

"Well, she claims she was sixteen when she met my father. I'm sure that was so the marriage was legal; I think she was probably about fifteen when I was born."

"What a life! And then she was left with no money, a château and numerous children to look after."

"Yes, seven, but three of us were in our twenties by then. Apart from the fact that he drank the money away, my father was no use for earning it. My mother, on the other hand is a very practical woman, and brought her children up to be likewise. Francine, the oldest girl learned to manage the vineyards, Henri my next brother is turning the estate into a tourist attraction, Tomas my younger brother is an art dealer, and the other three girls all have useful skills like book-keeping or cooking. I am the one with the education and the sophistication, and all I am useful for is keeping out of the way and practising law."

"Why don't you practise law in France? I find it easy to imagine you in court taking ground away from an opponent, like you did with me earlier."

He checked her face, no animosity. "It would appeal in some ways, but the legal system in France is different; we have an inquisitorial system, not adversarial like yours. No, I prefer to be an unremarkable, but well-paid solicitor in chilly Britain."

Suddenly he raised his finger and pointed at her, "You are very wicked; we are talking about me again. We are supposed to be talking about you. Now that you know all these terrible dark secrets of mine, I insist I know something about you."

She pulled her mouth to one side and screwed up her nose. "I haven't a clue what to tell you. I honestly can't think of anything interesting,"

"Okay, I will ask you questions, but you have to answer honestly."

"Thought we'd sorted that one!"

"Wait and see. You keep having water at lunch, do you not drink alcohol?"

"Oh yes, I drink wine." He smiled. "Soft Australian reds, mostly." His expression changed to one of horror. "But I don't drink at lunch-time; it sends me to sleep for the afternoon. And as for champagne, I like them fruity, which means only the cheaper ones."

He shook his head, "Very honest, no politeness there. What about music, what do you like?"

"Ooh, difficult. Lots of old rock classics, some jazz, even some of the modern stuff like techno-jazz; it's useful having kids for that. Not rap, not shrieking females, not disjointed stuff like Mahler."

"So you think Mahler is disjointed, and other classical?"

A shrug, "I like some, but I'm not very educated about it, I tend get bored with it quickly. It needs to be melodic, and not dreary." There was a pause. "Is the test finished? Do I pass?"

"You are very opinionated."

She nodded, "Definitely."

"What about your marriage? Are you happy?"

She raised her eyebrows at him and waited briefly before replying, "Yes, Tom is a good man, we've been very happy together."

There was a moment's silence, during which she tried not to frown at his last question. Perhaps she thought that was too inquisitive. He was unconcerned anyway.

"What would you most like to do that you haven't done yet?"

She groaned, "I hate those questions, my mind just goes blank. I'm sure there are things I'd like to do, but I don't know what they are. Yes, I know one. I'd like to fly in a private jet to Reykjavik and have dinner in Perlan, the revolving restaurant, and then see the Northern Lights before flying home."

"Why?"

"Well, I have been there; it's one of my favourite places. I haven't seen the Northern Lights though. And the private jet thing is just ridiculous luxury, wouldn't actually do it, but it's a dream."

"I have never been to Iceland. Do you think I should go?"

"Certainly. There's so much geology for a start, and the people are very practical."

"Hm. Interesting, an artist that likes geology. That must be unusual."

"I wouldn't have thought so; surely artists often start with the beauty of the natural world around them. Geological structures and forms are often very architectural I think, well, other way round I suppose. Anyway, Iceland is a good place to see some of it."

"You make it sound appealing, but you cheated with your answer. I said something you haven't done yet."

"I haven't done the private jet bit or the Northern Lights, doesn't that count?"

"Okay, I will let you keep that answer, if you will let me come with you in the jet."

She smiled at that and then they just sat for a while. The silence didn't feel uncomfortable, but then Lucy looked at her watch.

"Good grief, look at the time! I need to go. I bet you've got clients too."

He looked at his own watch and swore mildly. They got up and left quickly, as they parted he said, "I will call you!"

"Yes, I can't get on with the web-site till you do."

Early the following week, Lucy sat at her computer, grumbling under her breath. She turned to a pad and pencil on the desk and scribbled a few notes, then sat back and pushed both hands through her hair. She stared at the screen for several minutes, eyes slowly losing focus. "It's no good!" She got up, stretched and walked round the room. She sat down again, pulling her work diary across to her, and frowned as she flicked back and forth across two pages. She sighed and picked up the telephone.

"Oh, hello. This is Mrs. Cottonwood. Yes, I need to speak to M. du Blez about the web-site. Mm hm, I thought that was likely to be the case. Could you ask him to ring me when he can please? Yes, that would be great. Thanks then. Bye."

She turned back to the computer, but after another two minutes insulted it heartily and went off to make another cup of tea. She took her mug into the garden, perhaps a wander round the plants for a few minutes would loosen her mind up a bit. She could do with a bit of de-stressing. When she finished her drink, she walked back to the kitchen and heard the 'phone ringing from inside. She trotted through and snatched it up. "Hello?"

"Ah good, you are there. I thought I had missed you."

"Oh hi, Farine. Sorry, I'd just popped out to the garden."

"So, what is the problem?"

"Right. Is there a terrific hurry for the web-site?"

"No, why?"

"Well, I've got deadlines for three clients in the next fortnight, and one of them has just changed their mind about what they want. I'm going round in circles trying to re-invent it. Sorry, that's not your problem. What I meant was: if there's no hurry I won't start yours for the next two weeks. But please say if that's a nuisance, it isn't your fault this has happened."

"No, of course. Take your time. There is no hurry."

"That's very decent of you. I appreciate your patience. I'll call you in a fortnight, shall I, and you can let me know your decisions?"

There was silence on the other end of the line.

"Farine, is there a difficulty with that?" Still silence. "Farine, are you there?"

"Oui. Yes, sorry, I am here."

"What is it?"

"I was thinking that would mean no more little chats for a while. Can we not meet for a coffee or something?"

"What, you mean just socially?"

"Yes, is that alright? Surely you must stop work sometimes?"

It was her turn to pause before replying, "Yes, I manage to do that, just occasionally! Alright then, let's have a coffee soon."

"Good. The client I have last thing today may not take very long. Why don't we meet about five, at the café on the downs if you like?"

"Oh! This afternoon? Well I suppose that would be okay. It would give me something to work towards I guess. Maybe it would help me to crack this annoying problem if I know I can escape afterwards."

"Excellent. I will see you then."

She put the 'phone down and sat back in front of the screen, bringing it back to life but it was a few moments before she began to engage with the images there.

The study was getting hot with the afternoon sun, but she was making good progress, so she angled the blinds a bit more and opened every window. After another hour of furious tapping and clicking, she sat back and scanned through it all with a grim smile on her face.

"Eat your heart out Mr. Featherstone! If you don't like this baby, you can stick it where the sun don't shine."

Suddenly she remembered about the arrangement with Farine and looked at her watch, thinking she would have to run. No, that was fine; it was actually earlier than it felt. Good, she had time to take a bit of a walk on the downs before she met him. She checked once more that all the changes in the files had been saved, closed the windows and blinds, and got ready to leave the house.

She loved summer, being able to walk out without a coat or a jumper. She picked up the essential mobile, keys and money from the shelf where she routinely left them and stowed them in the small, bright fabric rucksack Jenny had brought her back from Peru. She enjoyed walking so much more with her hands and arms free.

Half an hour's good walking made her feel much better; widening her physical horizons always lifted her spirits. She was still early but she felt distinctly ready for a drink, so she headed over to the café. There was hardly anyone left there. She got a coffee and sat out in the sun, enjoying the feeling of having the space all to herself. She slouched back in the chair, putting her feet up on the base of the table. They had music playing inside the café, and without the chatter of other customers, it was just loud enough here to wash over her. She had finished her coffee and a song started that she remembered. She closed her eyes and tipped her face up to the sun, absent-mindedly singing along quietly. It was so relaxing to feel warm and let the song run her mind along for a while.

" ...If I could blink, if I could breathe, if I could get my legs to move, well this could be the day that I get this girl to love me..."

"This is one of the songs you like?"

Her eyes flew open and she sat up straight, cheeks turning pink.

"Do you always creep up on people like that?"

"Only when the opportunity presents itself. What is the song?"

4

He removed his jacket and tie. As he sat down, he rolled his shirt-sleeves up. Clearly he too was enjoying the chance to finish work and enjoy the sun.

"Oh, it's by a band called Phantom Planet, one of Nick's CDs. He used to play it a lot when it came out. I always liked it. I think he was crazy about some girl in his class at the time, so I heard it often!"

"Yes, you looked happy singing it. I see you have already had a coffee. I thought I was early."

"Well, you are, but I was earlier still. And I'm more than happy to have another drink. No, I'll go," she said waving him back into his seat as he made to rise. "I suppose you want espresso?"

"I'd rather have a pastis to be honest, but I think coffee is all I will get here."

"Yes, I think it is," she smiled down at him. As she turned away she felt vaguely guilty for how much she enjoyed looking at his skin. His bare arms fascinated her and she wanted to draw them, or better still run her hands over them before setting pencil to paper. That caused a mental version of a rap across her own knuckles, after which she was purposefully very polite to the girl at the till to compensate.

She brought the coffees back and as she sat down he asked about the client that had caused the current difficulty with her work. She laughed and gave him a description of the dithering Mr. Featherstone and an account of her own, private but impolite, reactions.

"Yes, I know what you mean. This last man today, he always goes round and round the same points with me, as if he cannot believe I meant what I said the first time. I have worked out that it varies between three and five times I have to say anything to him. But I am not allowed to tell him he is an idiot. Now, when I see him I give him twice as long as anyone else. It means I get to charge him twice as much, some comfort for me."

"But he didn't keep you this afternoon?"

"No, thankfully it was the end of the business and there was not a lot to deal with. I hoped he would not need the full time and I was right. We all got to leave early. What about your awkward customer? Will you make him pay for being a nuisance?"

"The quotes I give are for the job completed, so I don't charge by the minute like you."

He looked up at this barbed comment, but saw her eyes smiling at him over the rim of her cup and relaxed. Then he shook his head.

"You should charge him more; he has given you extra work."

"Well it is a bit difficult. Because clients can't see exactly what they will be getting, they often need me to make changes as we go along. That's expected. Usually though, they have some idea of what they want and communicate that, if only roughly. This man, however, is hopeless! He's changed his mind quite radically about how he wants it to look. We had a fairly heated discussion and I said I would do this one major overhaul; any other changes will have to be minor. I think I'll get my solicitor on to him if he tries anything else. Although I have to be careful not to ask him anything twice or I get charged extra." She was smirking somewhat across the table at him now.

"You keep making fun of me today! And you are allowed to ask twice, I only charge extra for three times or more. Anyway, I can see I must be careful too, or I might end up suing myself for being an awkward customer and not knowing what I want."

"I can't imagine that. You seem very self-assured all the time." Suddenly her expression changed and she leaned forward. "I hadn't thought though, should I be doing your web-site? I mean is that not a conflict of interest or something?"

He laughed, "Don't be silly. There is no problem."

They had long since finished their coffees and the waitress came out to collect the empties with a severe expression on her face.

"Oops, time to go, I think we're holding them up," she said, getting to her feet.

They crossed the road and strolled back towards the town. He had his jacket hooked on his finger over his shoulder and was looking round across the open green space and towards the gorge.

"It will be a warm, pleasant evening I think. They are so rare here, I do miss that. Would you like to have a walk with me? We could have glass of wine or something to eat afterwards, would you care for that?"

She seemed hesitant and a quick kaleidoscope of emotions flickered across her face.

He stopped and turned towards her, "What is the matter?"

She shrugged slightly and looked awkward. "We seem to be spending an increasing amount of time together that's nothing to do with web-sites or suing people."

"Am I keeping you from something?"

She shook her head but made no further comment. He reached out his hand and placed it gently on her arm above the elbow. "I thought we were becoming friends. Is that not what friends do, spend time together?" She looked up into his face, as if she was checking for something but she didn't say what. "I know I must be different to your other friends, but you said you like that, when you get over being frightened. Have you not got beyond being frightened of me yet?"

She smiled and looked down at the ground before raising her eyes to his again. "I'm not entirely sure I'll ever get over being a bit scared of you. Partly because you seem to remember absolutely everything I've said."

"Well, to be a solicitor you have to have a mind that remembers things, whether written or spoken. So be careful what you say to me."

"You'll take it down and use it in evidence I suppose."

"Yes, precisely. Never say to me something you don't mean."

"That's scary territory again, particularly if I'm meant to be a friend."

He nodded thoughtfully, "Yes, you are right. You see, I need you as my friend to stop me being a cold-hearted solicitor. You will be a good influence on me with your honest and direct opinions."

He had turned, and, with his hand still on her arm, steered her forwards to resume their journey.

"I need to go and get rid of the suit, not the best clothing for a walk. Why don't you come with me? My flat is only a few minutes from here, then we can go straight on."

"I don't seem to have a choice! Is this a route march?"

"Sorry, I forget my legs are much longer than yours, I will slow down. But seriously, do you think I am bullying you, do you not wish to come?"

"No, you're not bullying me. I think I'll cope but I'm reserving the right to scream and run if I can't."

"That is fair. It is also an incentive for me not to be too terrifying, hein?"

She thought his apartment was predictably gorgeous. Very modern, completely done out with wood floors and everywhere painted white. There was a balcony from the lounge, edged with frosted glass panels, and it gave onto glorious views down across the city and to the river. It was beautiful. During the ten minutes he took to shower, she reflected it was a fitting home for him. Some women would find him immensely attractive; others would consider him far too tall and thin. As far as she was concerned, he was artistically fascinating. And beautiful; he was one of only very few such men she'd seen in the flesh. She had always thought that getting to know one of them would prove a huge disappointment.

He reappeared, "Okay, I'm ready now, let's go."

As they left the apartment and set off walking, she was aware once more of how he used a touch on the elbow or a hand lightly on the back of her waist to direct her. It reminded her of something, or someone maybe, but she couldn't place it. It certainly wasn't unpleasant. Finally she decided it made her feel looked after. Interesting, was that something she was in need of?

They had walked and talked and finally eaten. Now they sat finishing their wine, looking around them at the people coming into the restaurant in the next wave of customers. They were discussing whether or not to stay for a coffee, when a woman passing the table stopped.

"Farine! Long time no see darling!"

He stood and greeted her French style, kissing both cheeks, then shook hands with her companion. Lucy watched in fascination. The woman had a deep resonant voice, long wavy dark hair and a flamboyant dress style. Her associate seemed pale and insubstantial by comparison. He too was tall but, unlike Farine, his slender frame looked merely thin, rather than athletic. Even his hair, fair and wispy, seemed a token sketching in. Suddenly she realised they had turned expectantly to her and were obviously waiting for introductions to be completed. She looked up to Farine with something close to panic in her eyes. He gave her a slow smile, and reached out his hand to draw her to her feet.

"Yes, this is my friend Lucy, she is very artistic. She is designing my new web-site. Lucy, this is Vanessa and Carl."

They shook hands and made remarks as though they were thrilled to be making each other's acquaintance. At least Vanessa did, Lucy said virtually nothing. After another few exchanges, mainly between Farine and Vanessa, she and her water-colour companion moved on to their table, Farine and Lucy left by unspoken agreement.

Outside in the street it was still not dark and Lucy felt glad to be out of the confines of the restaurant. She couldn't help thinking that the radiant Vanessa was more the sort of person Farine would normally be seen with.

"You have not asked me about the people we met."

"I have no intention of being nosey. Your friends are not my concern." She was annoyed with herself; that had sounded haughty, and she hadn't intended to be. She tried again. "I mean, oh no, never mind. I'm too tired to say it right."

He laughed, "You are automatically afraid of people who you think may be better than you in some way. I tell you, you have more brains than either of them. They are good musicians though. Vanessa plays violin, and Carl plays bassoon."

She couldn't think of anything to say, so she just nodded.

"Are you really tired?"

"Yes," she said producing a yawn as if to verify it, "I was up early to tackle Mr. Featherstone's little problem and I guess I was at it pretty intensely for quite a while."

"Okay, then I will walk you home. I don't want to be responsible for ruining your work tomorrow."

As they got to the top of the street and crossed over, he automatically moved behind her, again steering her into place on his other side with one hand. Suddenly she remembered. "That's it, of course!"

"What are you talking about?"

"The way you do that, keep changing sides with me. To make sure you're against the street or protect me or something. It reminds me of my brother-in-law. He always said something about keeping his sword arm free."

"Oh, did he fence too?"

She stopped dead in her tracks and he nearly trod on her. "Oh don't tell me you fence!"

"Yes, I was going to ask you how you knew."

"I didn't, and no my brother-in-law is not a swordsman. It was just something he used to say about being a gentleman, always protecting the lady he was with."

"Ah, I see. Yes of course a gentleman protects his lady. Can we move on? We are somewhat in the way."

They set off again. "So really, you do sword-fighting?"

"Well, I fence. But don't think of it as an old-fashioned sword-fight. I was in the national Olympic team for a few years. I won a silver medal one time, it should have been gold, but. . ." he trailed off with a shrug.

Lucy felt she had nothing left to say. She was beginning to think the gothic novel had taken over her life but wasn't sure if she could explain that adequately. They walked on for a while in silence before curiosity got the better of her.

"Do you still do the fencing?"

"Yes. I stopped for a while, but I really missed it. A few years ago I discovered there is a good team at the university here, and they are happy to have a few veterans along, so I get plenty of practice now."

"Why did you say it's not like real sword-fighting?"

"It's all electronic; the blades don't even have points. And the technique is very different to duelling. Even the sabre, my weapon, became scored electronically in the late eighties, the foil and the epée much longer than that. What about you, do you have a sport?"

"No, I run, well, jog several times a week. That's just to keep fit though. I've never been any good at sport. How did you get into fencing?"

"My grandfather, he started to teach me when I was a child. It seemed I had a talent for getting into fights of one sort or another. His view was that it might as well have a purpose. Actually he was a great swordsman in his prime, so I suppose it was the obvious thing for him to try me with a blade. He was delighted that I had a natural ability for it; I think perhaps it had been a sadness to him that my father never took to it. Maybe I made up for it. It was a shame that he did not see me win my medal though, he would have been very proud. My nephew, Etienne, he shows promise. I keep saying I will give him some tuition when I go home. But I have not visited for a while. I think he is tired of waiting."

"Well, what about the rest of the family? Did none of your brothers and sisters take it up?"

"Not really, I mean most of them have had lessons at some time, mainly from me or my grandfather when he was alive. But none of them have shown any talent. Only Etienne, he is Henri's boy; I get on very well with him. He is at that age where he argues with his father a lot, and an uncle seems more interesting than a parent. Besides, having been a good swordsman, he sees in me something he wants."

She found it fascinating that the normal British mode of self-effacement never came in to play with Farine. If he thought he was good at something, he said so, and that was that.

"Do you get involved coaching the team here?"

"Not officially, but if the team have an event coming up, they will ring sometimes and ask for an extra practice session. It makes us older men feel useful!"

"Are you past your best then, as a swordsman?"

"Ah, now I see this northern influence you tried to explain. Alas. Yes, I am not as fast as I used to be, but I don't admit that to everyone. My reflexes are still good, that's why I keep it up, and of course I have much experience."

Suddenly the whole evening seemed to have become a surreal whirl of duelling Counts and French noble families. She felt herself being spun off with the centrifugal force of it, her head spinning in accordance. "Verry well, D'Artagnan, I weell take you into ma serveece."

"What are you talking about? And why the terrible French accent?"

She was giggling and shaking her head, "Sorry, combination of too much wine and being tired. Just ignore me, I'll soon go away."

"Sometimes, I think you do not act your age."

"Ah, probably true. Sorry squire, I'll be sober next time I see you, promise."

"No, I am relieved. It was not a complaint. I think it is good that we have fun."

She stopped, "Okay, this is where I live. Thanks for the ride, sir knight." She wobbled slightly.

"My God, you are drunk, how is that possible?"

"No, I'm overtired. I tend to get slightly hysterical at this point. Don't worry, I'll be fine."

"Ok, but take care. Bonsoir." With that he kissed her on both cheeks and walked away.

"Absolutely fine, stop fussing."

She was on the telephone next lunch-time.

"You don't want to meet me because you are embarrassed about last night."

"No, I don't want to meet you because I have a shed-load of work to do. That and I'm just a tiny little bit embarrassed about last night, okay?"

"At least you are being honest."

She was thinking that if he could see her red face at the moment he would re-assess the honesty rating. She wasn't sure she could remember all the stupid things she'd been saying, and the ones she could sounded vacuous now.

"Yes and I honestly have loads to do. So thanks, but no thanks."

"Okay. But will you ring me when you have some time? Use my mobile; it will be better than the office line."

"Sure," it came out with an audible lack of conviction, and she felt a pang of guilt when the response was a wounded silence at the other end. "Look, it probably won't be for a couple of days. But towards the end of the week I promise I'll be in touch."

"Okay then, I'll leave you in peace. Au revoir."

She came off the 'phone and made a slight grimace. This was feeling distinctly scary. For all their talk of friendship last night, the whole thing seemed to have 'dates' stamped all over it. A couple of days without any contact could only be a good thing.

She paced backwards and forwards for a short interlude, trying to put it all to the back of her mind, but it was very reluctant to leave its place in the limelight of her thinking. Finally she settled down and was able to tackle the pile of work again; at least it was a dull and drizzly day so she couldn't be seduced away by the weather this afternoon.

'You would have told me off a treat. Or possibly laughed till you cried. Anyway, the whole evening was so ridiculous, I wondered if I'd dreamt it. What do you think? Am I being disgraceful touring the locale with a posh French Count in my free time? Do you suppose he's genuine? It would be just like me to make a friend of some slightly lunatic foreigner, and have to explain him to Jen for the next three weeks. Except I can't imagine anybody of that ilk making it to solicitorhood. I hope he's got all his qualifications in order for dealing with my case anyway.

I forgot to tell you last time, I ran into Guy. He's missing you, says he has nobody to go for a pint with at the moment. Did you know Rich was over in Ireland? His mother is very unwell apparently.

Talking of which, have you got over that sickness bug properly now? I really think you should see a doctor if it goes on any longer.'

She paused and took a mouthful of tea, wondering what other bits of news she needed to tell him. Being able to access e-mails fairly regularly; it meant they could keep up to date with these small inconsequential things that long-married people liked to discuss. Hopefully some of his friends would remember to e-mail too. Well, she'd better finish this off and get back to gainful employment.

By Thursday she had accomplished a satisfactory amount of the workload, and she found herself picking up her mobile on and off through the morning, but then putting it down again. She had half expected Farine to ring, technically, the 'couple of days' she had specified had now transpired. It was something of a relief that he hadn't called; better that he was waiting for her to make contact. But should she? Obviously, she had promised. Would that be encouraging him in something she didn't really want to continue though? What did she want? Both excellent questions. He was delightful company, very charming, very good looking. That was a distinct problem right there. And he scared her, but wasn't that part of the charm? She sighed, and looked at the 'phone again. He couldn't be much more different to Tom. Ah yes, Tom. A quick frown of annoyance passed across her face. She was feeling fed up with his absence again today, it was becoming tiresome. Not surprising she was tempted to take up the offer of a new friend like Farine. He was certainly a change. And he was sophisticated and moved in circles that encompassed people like the Magnificent Vanessa.

Did he want just friendship, or more? There were probably plenty of women who were after him for his body, not that she knew of course, but it was very likely. What if he was one of those dreadful men who just made conquests of every woman they met? That was stupid, Count of Monte Cristo or not, he acted every inch a gentleman and she would have felt something negative, she was sure. How about a message then? She was more comfortable with that than a call. Yes, a text was the answer. She tried several, deciding finally that 'work going well, how are you' was safe enough. He could reply to that with no commitment expected. He was probably in a meeting anyway. Well done then, now back to work.

Twenty minutes later her mobile went off and she dropped it in shock, before being able to answer it. "Hi there."

"Hello Lucy. Can you hear me okay? I am rushing down the street."

"Yes, I can hear you. What's the matter?"

"I have meetings all day and they are already running late. I was looking forward to lunch perhaps, but I will not be able to now. I am sorry."

"No problem, don't worry about it."

"But this week has been very dull. Why don't you come and have dinner with me tonight? Properly, not like the other evening."

"I don't know. I have no plans yet, but you don't have to take me out."

"I know I don't have to, but it would be pleasant. If it bothers you, we can discuss the web-site for half of the time."

"Not necessary, I'm sure I can cope with just dinner and no work.

"Good. I'll 'phone and book a table. I'll let you know where and when."

"Okay, that's fine."

The restaurant was decorated to give the feel of a private house, the space organised into a series of small inter-connected rooms. Presumably, and believably, this reflected its origins. Velvet covered chairs surrounded intimate tables, an arrangement that made it hard for the gathering of large groups. A Victorian fireplace, thankfully not over-ornate, was currently home to a large bowl of simple summer flowers in place of a warming fire. It was topped by a mantelpiece, on which sat a selection of china ornaments. These were doubled in number by the large mirror behind them, possibly a genuine relic of the days the place had been a dwelling. It's silvering was decaying in random patches, causing diners to appear afflicted with some strange disease, infection dependent entirely on seating position. Lucy could imagine people either loved or hated the genteel but faded opulence of the atmosphere. Her judgement would be reserved until dinner had been presented.

They were shown to a table by the window. Farine was to be the one who could view the whole room, half directly, and the half behind him by means of the pock-marked mirror. Iced water was brought immediately; Lucy gratefully accepted a glass while she contemplated the menu.

"Something's pleased you, I'm glad to note." Farine was smiling, obviously waiting for her to share whatever small delight she was enjoying.

"You'll think it's a very odd point to notice, or take pleasure in."

"I'm intrigued all the more. Now you have to tell me."

"Their menu. I don't mean what's on it. I mean the card they've used and the font, just the way it's been put together. Classy, it says good taste and quality."

"I see. And most of the clientele would notice or not?"

Her eyes flashed up to his from the item under scrutiny, "Did you?"

"Touché, madame." He closed his eyes, the wide smile slowly relaxing, a small frown taking its place. "Not consciously, but the card in the fingers feels substantial, a slight texture to it." He opened his eyes again, looking back to her in query, "Is that what you mean?"

She nodded, "Yes, and the fact that you register it unconsciously means they've done the job well. They don't shout how good they are, we all know real quality speaks for itself. Let's hope the food is on a par."

With that they turned their attention to the contents of their menus, taking a little while to discuss and make sure they selected different dishes.

They were a good way through the main course, Farine had just remonstrated with her for reaching across to his plate and helping herself to a taste of his meal. This resulted in a pause and a lively debate on what constituted good eating etiquette.

"You're French! You can't possibly object to me enjoying the food."

"Yes, enjoying your food, not stealing mine."

She pushed her plate forward, "It's a swap, you're welcome to try some of this."

He gave an exaggerated sigh and shrugged acceptance, about to extend his fork. Suddenly his eyes were drawn beyond the plate, beyond Lucy, and to something over her shoulder and further up the room. Lucy disciplined herself not to turn and identify the cause of this distraction. In all likelihood it would be who, rather than what. And judging by the way his teeth had come together behind slightly parted lips, and the fact that his eyelids had dropped, slightly hooded, she was guessing it was someone he was not pleased to see.

5

She murmured softly, "You look ridiculous with your fork in mid-air. Especially as you're gritting your teeth. If you don't want them to notice you, I suggest you involve yourself with the food again. Either yours or mine."

He said nothing but tilted his face down and followed her advice. She assumed the source of his discomfort was coming closer, she could certainly hear the waiter's voice and that of another man approaching. As they passed, she did what she could to gather any information, difficult with only back-views to consider. What she could see was a tall man in a suit, well-cut, but the grey fabric a little too shiny for her taste. He possessed thick straight, dark hair and had his hand on the back of his companion, a girl almost as tall as himself. Some of her height was due to the heels she was wearing, but that still left an appreciable length accounted for by legs. And good legs they were, which was just as well considering the slit in her skirt which allowed a section of bronzed thigh to flash as she strode by.

They were shown to a table at the end of the room, against the far wall. This meant Lucy was able to get a much better view, just of the woman, the waiter being in front of her escort. Golden seemed to sum her up. The bronze of her skin seemed to be very uniform and extensive. Her hair was blonde, and even her dress was a pale gold, though there wasn't a great deal of it. Apart from the stiffly straight set of her hair, Lucy could imagine her as an Amazon. She looked strong and healthy, which Lucy felt she should admire, but somehow couldn't.

Taking her eyes away from the unexpected floor show to check up on Farine, she found him making use of the large mirror to do exactly what she'd just done.

"So? Impressed? She's quite a looker, do you know her?"

"No, it is her friend that I have met before, but some time ago. I don't think I've ever seen her."

"I'm sure you'd remember. I imagine men generally take a good long look at all that."

He put a hand up to his face, smile still visible over the finger his chin rested against, "You disapprove of her?"

"I can't, given that I don't know anything about her. I'm just jealous."

"What? Because she is younger than you and has a body she likes to display?"

"Because she's younger than me and has a body worth displaying!"

He took a sip of his wine, "You still disapprove though. I saw your face as you observed her, definitely disapproval."

She sighed, reaching for her own glass, "True, I like to think I observe objectively, but it's hard not to make judgements from what we see."

"And they are?"

"That she's very aware of her looks and likes to use them. I should have no cause to be jealous of such a two-dimensional female, should I?"

His eyes went straight back to the mirror, "I don't think you can describe her as two-dimensional!"

"Idiot! I didn't mean in the sense of flat. I meant lack of personality or intelligence. But that's a judgement I have no right to make. She could be a nuclear physicist for all I know, or work as a doctor in Papua New Guinea most of the year. Somehow we assume not though, am I right?"

He inclined his head slowly, "I have to confess you are."

"You see, the curse of good looks. Thankfully, I don't have to bear it."

"You're hardly an unattractive woman!"

She was nonplussed for a moment, "Well, no, I'm not ugly. But I'm not, I mean, I've never been, it. . ." her hand was flapping in a weak attempt to direct her thoughts into order. The waiter materialised at her side just then and received a soft blow on his waistcoat. She was rendered helpless by the combination of mirth and embarrassment, leaving Farine to apologise and order some desserts. When they were left in peace once again, she appeared over the top of her hand, still trying to quell her laughter.

"I know why you keep asking for my company."

50

"Indeed, you are by far the most entertaining person in the vicinity. Life would be very dull without you."

The laughter stopped of its own accord and she looked down into her wine glass instead. She wasn't sure what to say next, but that became irrelevant. A table next to the couple of their interest emptied, and Farine now looked up to the mirror with an entirely different expression on his face. Lucy shifted slightly to one side and was able to peruse the man Farine was viewing in reflection.

She spoke very softly, "Why don't you like him?"

"So, you're observing me as well as him."

"Of course, quite easy from my seat. And you haven't answered my question."

"You answer mine first. What do you conclude form your observations?"

Her eyes went back to the subject of their discussion, interrupted briefly by the arrival of dessert. In between slow mouthfuls of sweet, she gave her assessment.

"He too likes to show off his looks, although he thinks of himself as charming rather than just handsome. I'm sure a lot of women find the startling green eyes and floppy dark hair over them quite attractive. I think I'm prejudiced against green eyes, though I don't know why. For me, his nose is too narrow and his chin too sharp."

"I have a narrow nose!"

"Yes, but yours isn't pointed like that. It's hard to describe, but his is one of those faces that will get more like a crescent moon as he ages. The chin will stick forward and the nose will seem longer and sharper still."

"You're terrifying! I didn't know you could predict the future."

"Just lived long enough to have seen faces change with time, that's all. Anyway, we're discussing mystery man. He also likes to show off his money, he keeps looking at his watch and he lifts up his hands a lot so we can see how much gold is on them. He laughs rather too loudly at his own jokes; I can hear him from here. He's expecting to be admired, but I'm not sure there isn't something of a challenge about it. He keeps checking everyone round him, almost as if he's daring them not to like him. How am I doing?"

"I can't disagree. But my dislike is from experience, rather than a personality sketch." He had returned his attention to Lucy, face still serious.

"Well, what has he done? Not pay his bill or something?"

Farine looked away, momentarily uncomfortable, "You're asking me to break client confidentiality."

"Yeah, so? You know you want to tell me. I won't blab, scouts honour."

"Were you ever in the scouts?"

"Certainly not, now get on with it."

He took a moment to compose himself, "He came to me over a copyright issue."

"That must have been a surprise."

"Do you want to hear this?" She nodded, cheerfully unrepentant. "He worked for a firm which published greetings cards. They discovered a small company were producing cards very similar to a range their own designers had come up with. They brought along examples, and they were right, they had a good case."

"Was this guy the designer?"

"No. Something in the administration, he and the designer came to see me together first of all, but after that I just dealt with him. His name is Chris Brogan."

"Irish?"

"Possibly, he has an accent I find difficult when he is agitated."

"I'm guessing that means you witnessed him in agitated mode."

"Yes, part of why I prefer not to deal with him again."

"Did you not win, does he blame you?"

"On the contrary. We had a very strong case, the smaller firm admitted liability and we agreed compensation, it never came to court."

"So what stirred him up?"

"When I gave my opinion on the strength of the case, he wanted to demand a ridiculous sum of money. I outlined what was considered normal and appropriate, he wasn't very happy with me. By his own admission, he wanted to cause the other firm as much damage as possible, though he phrased it somewhat differently."

She was quiet for a few seconds, watching him again. "You didn't like him because he wanted to hurt the other person, instead of wanting justice."

"I suppose so. I can understand anger when someone has damaged you, but the law is about redress, not vengeance. And no-one had hurt him personally. It wasn't even his company then."

"Then? So it is now?"

"I don't know the details. I read about it in the paper some time ago, I just recognised the name of the company because I'd worked with them. They went into liquidation, owing a lot of money, obviously. Then they did a phoenix."

"What does that mean?"

"A new company rises from the ashes of the old. It's a way to lose the debts and start again."

"Is this legal?"

"Perfectly, providing the directors have no personal liability. Assets are usually disposed of quietly beforehand, though that part is not legal. A token effort is made at paying creditors from what remains. Then someone buys the failed company at rock-bottom price and can start trading again immediately. It's often a family or management buy out. The latter in this case, Chris Brogan bought it and started again. That's all I know, his name stuck in my mind for the reasons I told you."

"I'm guessing you wouldn't want to do business with him."

"Let's just say I won't be ordering the practice Christmas cards from him."

The waiter came to clear the plates and they asked for the bill. As they rose to leave, they were spotted and hailed loudly by Brogan, making it impossible to ignore. Rather than cause a stir, they went across, at least to lower the volume for everyone else. Brogan was on his feet and acting like a long-lost friend to Farine, who by contrast was trying to muster the swiftest of polite greetings followed by farewells.

"You know I'm running the old business, do you?"

"Yes, I read it in the paper, congratulations."

"Oh aye, and warranted. I have a chain of shops as well now. Done away with all that old-fashioned wholesale supply. Stock-control system and everything, direct to outlet. It's the way forward, you know. You'll take a drink with me?"

Lucy had been expecting the soft lilt of a southern Irish voice; instead the harsher accent of Belfast hit her ears. Tamed, but not banished. She was relieved that Farine was making credible apologies; she didn't think she wanted to hear every detail of this success story.

"Ah well, next time eh? I'll probably run into you again, I'm in this area more often now. I've just opened my latest shop, here in Clifton. Not too exclusive for Chris Brogan now, I'll have you know."

He accompanied this parting shop with a poke in the ribs to Farine. She had never seen his face so still and calm, yet somehow she felt the waves of animosity flow out from him. There was no time to wonder what he would do, he seemed to be shaking hands with the other man warmly, even grasping his elbow as he steered him back into his seat and took his leave. Before she drew breath he had turned her and they were leaving.

Outside it was two minutes before he slowed enough for her to keep up.

"Sorry, that wasn't very polite of me. I hope you weren't too embarrassed."

"What did you do? You just seemed to shake his hand, but his face was all twisting up. Was it a Vulcan death grip or something?"

"I have no idea what you're talking about. I simply got us out of there as quickly as I could."

"Don't come that with me. You did something to him, what?"

He stopped, looking down at his feet, "I just applied a little pressure, not enough to damage him, just enough to make him sit down and shut up."

"Can you teach me?"

He laughed and draped his arm round her shoulders as they turned to wander on.

"Lucy, you really are a lot of fun to be with. I wasn't just flattering you before. You know, you can share my expensive dinners any time you like."

She couldn't think of any witty replies to that. It left her glowing with pride, and queasy with something that felt a lot like guilt at the same time.

6

Pulling back the curtains, Lucy was pleased to see that the cloud of the last two days had dissipated, and that a bright morning was waiting for her. She pottered through her usual rituals and then took breakfast out into the garden. This was one of those unremarkable pleasures that never failed to lift her day, like flowers in a room. She sat on the bench near the house and surveyed the scene before her as she sipped and munched. She was making a mental list of the jobs that would need doing over the weekend. She sighed, looking after the garden was normally a joy, rather than a duty, but with Tom away she had to admit the balance had tipped somewhat towards the latter. Thinking of Tom led her to remembering the e-mail she had sent him last night. He had been so amused to discover she had become friends with a solicitor, that he had wanted her to tell him all about it. So she had, well, she'd tried. She found that she was happy to report the facts, but was screening her thoughts and feelings for 'unsuitable' material. Just how honest should one be with a husband about how good looking you thought another man was? She'd tried to make light of it all, and hoped her accounts would entertain him, but what might he be reading between the lines? It was too tricky a question to formulate any reliable answers, and she gave it up, succumbing instead to the dead-heading that called.

Having done the rounds of the day-lilies, numerous, and the roses, sparse, and then been sidetracked into pulling out some weeds at the front of the bed before they set seed, she decided she'd better get ready. Somehow she had agreed to meeting up with Farine again for a coffee this morning. His plea of 'nice and relaxed, no work to worry about on Saturday' had won the argument she'd been conducting in her head at the time. She hadn't even thought where she would choose for coffee yet. In fact now she thought about it, she couldn't remember the names of any of the cafés, she needed to go there and have a look.

While she was walking, a pub that boasted a terrace looking out over the gorge came to mind. That would do. She sent a text with directions, and they both turned into the street at the same time.

"Good morning how are you?"

"Fine, it's such a lovely day. Did you get your court appearance in the end?"

"Ah yes, satisfactorily concluded, thank you."

They found a table on the terrace, and ordered coffee. He was wearing shorts again, and some sort of flip-flops, although the word didn't do them justice, they were a lot more expensive looking than the flimsy rubbery things. As he crossed one elegant leg over the other, she gazed at the line of his bare shin curving into a slender foot, flip-flop dangling, and her fingers itched for a pencil. Fortunately the coffee arrived and she had something to do with her hands as a displacement.

"What did you do last night? Out clubbing?" He was unusually quiet, and she tried teasing to spur him into life. Instead he answered with a serious tone.

"I don't go to clubs, much. I prefer conversation to gyration, although I have nothing against dancing.

"Oh, I like the 'much' in that sentence! You only go when you're on the prowl for a pick-up, do you?"

"No, I generally find women in quieter places, wine-bars, concerts, that sort of thing. Where do you go to pick up men?"

Her nostrils narrowed and she took a sharp breath in, but saw the curve of his mouth not quite hidden by the hand his face leant on. She shook her head. "I know what you're doing." One raised eyebrow invited explanation. "You're provoking me to see what comes out. You want to know what I'm made of."

"Of course, and to see if you are as honest as you claim."

"What are you getting at there?"

"You said you like different, but you're struggling with this – us spending time together – because you think it's outré. You were so uncomfortable at the restaurant, when I said something that wasn't even halfway to a compliment." He sat back suddenly, letting his eyes wander over the gorge before them, "But I shouldn't be surprised, a lot of British women do that."

"Yeah well, we don't get the practice."

His eyes swept back, "I could give you some!" A broad smile followed swiftly, "You see, straightaway you're ill at ease. Why don't you admit it? You like us being together but you're worried about exactly what kind of man I am, and what people may think."

She picked up her spoon, pointing it at him before plunging it in the coffee. "That's hardly surprising! The way you dealt with that guy the other evening is cause enough for some concern."

"It was nothing. Between the fencing and my father, I learnt how to take care of myself, that's all.

"Well if he's the vindictive type, was it a good idea to use some old army moves on him?"

"Hardly military tactics! I just squeezed his hand a little bit, thumb in the back here;" he pointed, "he would think it was an accident due to how we were standing." She was extremely quiet, regarding him with a stare he wasn't sure was an admiring one. "So now you think I'm an unsavoury character, and you disapprove of me." His jaw tensed and his eyes flicked to and fro rapidly across the gorge opposite.

"I didn't say that."

"But you're thinking it!"

"Oh, so you're a mind-reader as well, are you? With that and my ability to see the future we should make a formidable team."

His face came back to hers once more, eyes dancing this time, "Yes, I think so. You judge me worth forming some sort of alliance with then?"

She put her cup down, "I thought we'd decided the other evening that judging anyone was a risky business."

"Nevertheless, judgements have to be made, all the time. Do I trust this person enough to do business with them? To look after my children or to operate on me?"

"Let them represent me legally, or even have coffee with them and allow them to become my friend?"

He smiled, "Precisely. You can check my credentials as a solicitor, but not as a companion. Head cannot govern heart for everything. Gut instinct has to deal with quite a lot."

"I agree, but your instincts are not as divorced from reason as you might like to think." She continued over his surprise. "They have discovered, researchers that is, that you pick up micro-signals from expressions and body language. These are processed incredibly fast and come together to make your gut-reaction. Most people who lie, give off these tiny signals with no idea they're doing it. We detect them unconsciously. Some people are better detectors than others."

His silence was broken by a quiet question, "Where did you get this?"

"Just New Scientist, I read it sometimes."

Suddenly he tipped his head back, laughing. "You are formidable on your own, you don't need me. I thought you liked my company because it scared you a little. I'm beginning to think I'm the one who should be afraid. And your ability to predict the future; is that also explained by scientific analysis? You haven't told me about this."

"That's what you said when I made a comment about Brogan's face."

"Oh yes, so I did. And what micro-signals did he emit?"

"I told you, it's at a subliminal level, so I wouldn't know. But his legs are too short, definitely dodgy."

"What?" he asked, dazed.

"Tall men whose legs are unusually short for their bodies, often have criminal tendencies."

"Now you're making this up!"

"No, New Scientist again. I'm not sure what the proportions have to be, and it's only a tendency. All these things have to be taken carefully. I'm not being entirely serious, but I didn't like the fact that his height is mainly in his body."

"Thank goodness my legs are uncommonly long! I must be very honest."

"I'm sure it's not a linear relationship. But maybe that's why I deem it safe to spend more time with you than I should."

"Go on then, what do you see as the future for our friendship?"

She toyed with the spoon on the edge of the saucer for a moment. "It means trouble for someone, certainly."

"Really? Who and why?"

"Well, Les Wilson for a start! At least I hope so. Providing you haven't forgotten there's a case to pursue."

He had laughed again, now he calmed to answer her, "No, don't worry. I warned you, it takes weeks before anything happens. You're not seeing that clearly then?"

She smiled now, shaking her head. "No, relax, I can't actually see the future. Sometimes I disturb people though. I have a tendency to ask questions that ferret their own way into their minds, or I put my finger on something that's a problem they didn't realise they had. I think it can be a bit spooky for them."

"You mean that don't you?" She nodded. "No explanation? No-one been to interview you and run tests?"

She shrugged, "Maybe it's just the micro-signals. Maybe I really am a prophet. So you could be right, you might need to be afraid."

"I'll take the chance. But if that's the case, you should know whether or not this friendship will work."

"Oh it will work! The omens, or possibly the micro-signals, are good. However, I'm a creature of reason, indulge me and tell me more about your background."

"Only if I can get another coffee." He paused to wave at the waitress. That attended to he sat back again, "What do you want to know?"

"How about all these brothers and sisters. Tell me about them."

"There are seven of us all together. Francine is about a year younger than me, she is Catholic, we fight a lot, because we are close in age I think, and similar. Then Henri about two years below me, he thinks he should have been Count really. I think that's why he changed from being a Moslem to a Catholic when he was sixteen. He and I fight a lot too. Then Sylvie, she's four years after me, Catholic again. We are very

60

close. Four years after her came Violette, she is Moslem, then Tomas two years below her, Catholic; and finally three years later Suzette who is Moslem. That is it."

"What's with all the Catholic-Moslem-Catholic thing?" she asked laughing.

"Well, of course my father was Catholic, but Maman is Moslem. I was brought up as both, but they realised it wasn't very practical, so they took it in turns after me."

"How on earth can you be both Moslem and Catholic? Doesn't that cause a bit of confusion?"

He shrugged and smiled, "No, I'm used to it. If something happens I can say 'it is the will of Allah', then if I feel guilty about it I can go to confession. I don't worry."

She was genuinely shocked, and seemed lost for any comment.

"Do you think it strange then?"

"Yes I certainly do. I can't imagine that, well, only if neither of them really mean anything to you."

"So, you are not religious?"

"I hope not! I hate religion." She said that more vehemently than she'd intended. "Sorry, I mean the rules and regulations thing. I haven't got a problem with faith."

"Do you have faith in anything?"

"Yes, I'm a Christian, but I don't like being signed up to something with a label beyond that. I think God's real, and I want to know what he's like. Theology is important, up to a point but I don't think it can ever be right. If God exists then he's infinite. No set of human thoughts is going to cover it really." She looked up, realising he might have glazed over at this point and stopped. "Sorry again, getting on my soap-box a bit there. Shut me up by all means."

"No, I like to see you talk about something that matters to you. You are more alive when you talk with passion."

"That's what I don't understand. If you are a Catholic and believe what you hear there, how can you be happy in the mosque? Or vice versa? Surely you can't be passionate about either."

"No, not passionate, that's true. But I've always taken some comfort in both places. I just accept that God is big, and maybe Catholics see some things, Moslems other things."

"Same God, different interpretation?"

He nodded, "Perhaps." After a moment he spoke again quietly, "Besides, if people get too passionate about it they seem to become militant."

She snorted, "I'm afraid I can't subscribe to the view that God is responsible for war, to me that's completely specious. I think it's entirely people. Humans bend anything. All the structures and rules that we know as religion are designed to keep one group in power and everybody else under the thumb. They're also very handy as an excuse to hate somebody else."

"All as bad as each other?"

"Yes, pretty good evidence for fallen humanity."

"So you don't think God can be found in a mosque or a church?"

"Yes I do, but he can't be defined or contained by them. The people who run them often seem to think their opinions are more important than his."

"And you do know what his opinions are?"

She laughed, "Oh yes, I'm aware that as soon as humans start talking about God, arrogance comes right in. That's what I'm trying to say. People who genuinely believe something is right, have to be careful not to create a rigid system but keep open. Having to do certain things and trying to not do things wrong is mostly motivated by fear, and I think God is very much about love."

"Most religions would say that."

"Yes, but then they end up making a list of things you have to tick off to earn your brownie points. I mean, I find myself doing that, it's the human condition, but then I have to go back to concepts like grace and mercy and get my head straightened out. You know, not worry about ticking boxes."

"I don't think that's true."

She looked taken aback. "Why?"

"Because we've already seen that you do worry about doing things that may be questionable. I am the one who is relaxed about how I live."

She smiled slowly, "Well, I am very responsible, being right can be a concern. But I would like to break out of rule-driven thinking and become more than I am now. Be a bit more adventurous in what I do. "

He stood up and took her hand, pulling her to her feet too.

"Where are we going?"

"I thought we might go and find some rules to break."

Before she had time to complain, they were heading through the streets. He was towing her slightly in his wake, forcing her to trot to keep up with him. She didn't seem to have the option of slowing down as he was still holding on to her hand firmly. She tried asking a question, but the combination of breathing hard and trailing behind him rendered it ineffective. Thankfully, after some way, they reached a busy road, and had to wait briefly for the traffic before they could move on. She took her chance.

"What are we doing exactly?"

"Ah, exactly, I do not know. Not yet."

"Well how about generally then? Could you divulge that?"

"You said you wanted to break out of thinking by rules, we are seizing the moment. We are going to find something we would like to do that makes us leave the rules behind."

"I see; just any rules randomly? Or do you have some specific ones in mind?"

To her chagrin they were by now already halfway across the road and into their pursuit of the unknown again, so this last question was lost to his ears, apparently.

She was left with thinking, which was progressing along the lines of: 'opened my big mouth and put my foot in it' swiftly followed by 'what the hell have I got myself into now?' neither of which were any comfort.

They turned a corner and into one of the shopping streets. At least they had to slow down a bit here, too much pedestrian traffic this time to keep up their previous rate of progress, which was something of a relief. She decided to capitalise on this and purposefully tried to slow her pace further, looking into the shop windows as they passed. She sensed his irritation at her impedance and when he frowned at her she cocked her head slightly and asked "Is it a rule that we have to rush swiftly off to find rules to break? If so, I feel duty bound to break it."

"Hah, very clever, but you are getting cold feet. You now wish you hadn't said something I could act on."

"Well, it's a bit difficult when I don't know what it is I'm expected to do."

"It would not be an adventure would it, if you knew what you were doing?" He bent his head closer to her, "Don't forget, you enjoy different when you have got over your fear."

She groaned "Not that one again. And now I've just given you more ammunition to torment me with!"

He produced a slightly wolfish smile, but then shook his head, "I won't torment you."

"We'll see, but could you at least let me get my breath back?"

He inclined his head, "I forget you have such little legs and must move slowly."

"Hey! I'm the one from the north!"

He did then let them wander rather than rush, and they relaxed into chatting a little more. She stopped suddenly at a gallery window, forcing him to step back towards her and find out what she had seen.

"Look! They've got some new Sandy Winston pictures. I love her work!"

The annoyance he felt at her delay drained out of him as he watched her face come alive, eyes devouring the paintings in the window. She absorbed one and then another, eyelids rising or dropping, sometimes angling her head to change the way the light fell on it. This was clearly a pleasure to her, and he was happy to enjoy it vicariously through her reactions.

Happy too, to study the pieces and see what forms and colours were causing this resonance in her.

Idly, she stepped back, giving herself more distance from the nearest picture, but this action put her in the path of a man she had not noticed hurrying down the street. He pushed her so roughly out of his way that she stumbled and Farine had to reach out a hand to steady her. He looked furious and shouted something unintelligible after the man.

She was about to ask him what he had spoken, as it was neither French nor English. But her words, thoughts and even her breath were suddenly splintered and blasted away in an instant, along with the shop window that had been in place fifteen feet away from them.

7

The world appeared to be on its side. This was puzzling, and she was trying to make sense of the people moving backwards and forwards, or up and down as it looked to her. Something was obviously wrong. There was snow falling. No, it couldn't be, surely it was summer? Paper then? No, well never mind. What was that man doing bending over something? Someone perhaps? Another man came towards her and bent down to speak to her. But then he didn't, he just mouthed at her and she was even more puzzled. Another face appeared, she knew this one, definitely. Who though? Farine! That was it; they'd been walking up the street, hadn't they? He sat down on the pavement next to her. Oh, she was lying on the pavement! Then he too started mouthing something to her, but stopped and put his head in his hands.

Beyond the people, she could see ambulances and police cars pulling up. Odd, she hadn't heard the sirens. Probably because of that bell or alarm or whatever it was, ringing away. Soon a man in green came towards them, she recognised it as a paramedic uniform. He started the mouthing routine and she wished they would all stop and leave her in peace, this was really tiresome. She was glad he was here though, because she had noticed Farine was hurt, there was blood on his legs, and his beautiful, beautiful skin was covered in cuts. She lifted her arm to point this out to the ambulance man, and discovered that her own flesh too was bloodied and slashed.

In the hospital, things slowly started to make sense. With a combination of pointing, mouthing and even written notes, the doctor and nurses checked her over, removed what felt like hundreds of glass splinters and dressed her many cuts. Jennifer arrived suddenly, looking rather white, and rushed to take hold of her. This was a relief, as communication could improve; they started signing to each other.

"Is your mother deaf anyway?" asked a nurse.

"No, I did a British Sign Language course one year, mum picked up the basics. We use it sometimes, like across a noisy room or something."

"I thought not, but it made me wonder seeing you sign to each other. Oh well, it will come in handy now. There's no way of telling if the deafness will last hours or days."

They were a bit worried about the blow her head must have received when she hit the pavement, but there was no apparent concussion, just a developing lump and bruise as evidence. They eventually agreed to let her go home; Jenny would stay with her and watch out for any problems.

By now, Lucy was concerned about Farine. They had been separated for treatment and there was no sign of him when they were discharged. As Jenny drove, Lucy found there was already a text from him saying he was home. He had been patched up pretty quickly, but had been sent off without being allowed to see her, as she was still being treated. Jenny was desperate to hear what had happened, but Lucy couldn't tell her very much. Back at home, they put the local news on the television. The explosion was reported but there was only conjecture as to what was the cause. An assistant inside the shop had been injured, but not too badly. Several passers by had been hurt, mainly of course by the glass. It seemed she and Farine were among the lucky ones, as several others had to stay in hospital.

It was a strange evening. The deafness persisted. When it wasn't infuriating, it gave them something to laugh at, trying to ask and answer questions. Jenny feared that her mum might well be in shock, but Lucy maintained plenty of tea and hugs was the best remedy. She was worried about Farine though, as he was alone. Several messages came and went, calls being pointless, and he reassured her that he was fine. Apart from the same loss of hearing, he insisted his injuries were slight.

Lucy could hear reasonably well again by Monday afternoon, which was just as well because the doorbell rang. She went to answer it and found Farine on the step embracing a large bunch of lilies. They went through to the kitchen, where she found a vase and dealt with the flowers as they chatted.

"I was really worried about you; you seemed to be very disorientated."

"That's hardly surprising, is it? I'm not terribly used to being blown up!"

He nodded and agreed it was a new, and preferably singular, experience. He commented on the smell in the kitchen, she explained she'd made some olive bread.

"It gave me something to work out my frustrations on, kneading the dough. Would you like some? And I've got some red wine open; Jen's coming for dinner after work so she can check up on me. Go on, try a bit. You could probably do with a drink."

In the end he accepted both, and relaxed more, taking off his tie and rolling up his sleeves, she was pleased to see most of his cuts were small, and already healing.

"What about your head, is it very sore?" he asked her.

"I had a monumental headache yesterday; today it's just a bad one. The bruise is pretty tender though, it makes combing my hair a challenge. I think the worst thing is this ringing in my ears. I started hearing again this morning, but everything has to compete with the ringing sound. 'Phone calls are the worst, I've been letting them cut to the answering machine then I can listen to them a few times to try and make it out. If I reply to what you say with something ridiculous, I've probably misheard you. Anyway, what about you, what have you done to get over it?"

"Well, I only had two cuts that needed stitching, everything else was minor. It looked much worse than it was, I think. Somehow I didn't crash my head into anything. And I could hear again yesterday, so I just lay in my flat listening to some Bach, very peaceful. Then I went to mass at the cathedral, it seemed," he paused, "appropriate."

"Why the cathedral, and not the mosque?"

He grinned, "It's closer. You remember our conversation from earlier then?"

"At first I couldn't remember anything I'd been doing, I mean all morning, not just immediately beforehand." He nodded in understanding. "Then bits started coming back, rather randomly, which has been confusing. I think I've got most of it sorted now, but I won't know if I haven't, will I?"

She thought of moments through the day when pieces of memory had lurched back into her mind, or her hands. She'd found herself drawing a long foreleg and foot dangling a flip-flop, and it was only after that she'd remembered them having coffee.

"I do remember the man bumping into me and then you spoke in another language, it was quite startling." She sat down at the table opposite him, "What was it?"

"Ah yes, I remember that. I was furious, he was so rude. So I swore at him in Arabic. I can swear tolerably in English, and French of course. But for serious imprecation I use Arabic, my father spoke it, and he taught me the essentials!"

She smiled at that but then looked serious, "I've thought about that several times. If he hadn't pushed me, we wouldn't have been looking down the road, we'd have been turning the other way towards it and taken the blast face-on." She went pale and put her hand over her mouth; he reached out and squeezed her shoulder. "I know you shouldn't do 'what if?' but at lunch-time they said one man has lost his sight. That could have been us, and it makes me feel sick!"

He reached for her hand and held it tightly for a while. Gradually the colour came back into her face and she took her hand away.

"I'll be fine really, don't worry. I guess it's bound to take time for the shock to wear off. Have you heard any more about it? Why they think it happened?"

"Other than it definitely being a bomb, you mean? No. I called a friend of mine in the crown prosecution service, I asked him to keep his ears open with the police and let me know if they come up with anything. It cannot be terrorism, not enough widespread carnage for that."

"Then what?"

He shrugged, "Who knows?"

Lucy looked at the clock, and declared it was time to start the cooking ready for Jennifer's arrival. She asked Farine if he would like to join them, but he declined saying he had some files to go through for a court appearance next day. They parted with various exhortations about taking care and a promise to check up on each other later in the week.

When Jenny arrived, she was pleased to find that her mum had improved a good deal, and was persuaded, finally, that she need stay only one more night. There was another telephone call from Tom during the evening. The one on Sunday morning had been frustrating as Lucy couldn't hear a thing so Jenny had had to talk to her dad. Lucy had kept interjecting with instructions that he was on no account to cut short his trip. At least this time, they were able to talk for a while, and she could reassure him that she was doing fine. After a while though, the effort of sorting out the sound got too much and she put her daughter back on.

During the few days that followed, Lucy was extremely glad that she had made the progress she did on her contracts the week before. Her head and the tinnitus continued to be annoying, but she was at least able to work for a few hours at a time. This was enough to do the organising and tidying she knew was needed. Even so, every so often she would find herself reliving the scene that met her eyes as she had lain on the pavement. It would cause her to shiver and tremble for a while, and she would have to find something else to do to nudge herself out of it. Eventually she decided there was only one cure. She would have to go back and stand outside the shop. She needed to prove to herself that she could survive this intact.

The street itself was, of course, very familiar. But approaching the gallery started an involuntary clenching of her stomach. "Come on," she growled at herself, "this is why you're doing this, get on with it." Her feet were obeying, but reluctantly. By the time she passed the gallery and stood outside what was now a boarded-up shop front, name unrecognisable, her heart was hammering and her throat felt constricted. She stood still, trying not to peer inside through the open door, and trying also not to turn and run away as quickly as possible. She gave a start when something moved within the dimness beyond the doorway. It quickly resolved itself from nameless terror to man straightening up. She watched him, hands on hips, looking around, up and down. There was something familiar about him, but his stance and toss of the head failed to identify him in her mind. Suddenly he turned towards her, aware of her presence.

"What is it? What can I do for you?"

His words were much more a challenge than an offer of assistance. He took two rapid strides and filled the doorway. The voice had started the domino-fall of her thoughts, his face looking sharply down at her completed it.

"Oh it's you!" she said, without thinking.

His frown deepened and he leaned forward even more, looming over her. "What d'you mean by that? And who the hell are you?" He stepped out from the shop, pulling the blank wooden door to behind him, locking it and then returning his stare to her face. "I said what did you mean?"

"I, I'm sorry. I didn't realise this was your shop, not that I would know, but anyway, I just came back to see if I could - and I didn't expect, and - I'm sorry."

He started to complain about the babble of nonsense she had offered him, but quickly realised it was pointless, as she was on the point of fainting. He grabbed her arm, and leant her against the wall, there being nothing else available in the way of support. "Are you okay lady? Are you ill or something?"

She had dropped her head down, now raised it slowly as the swimming sensation faded. "Not ill, no. Shock, or delayed reaction. Maybe just pure fear, being back on this spot."

He looked at her eyes narrowing, suddenly widening again. "You were here you mean, when it went off?"

She nodded, "Yes, we were standing in front of the gallery there when it happened. I felt I had to come back and get over the incident. I can't avoid this street for the rest of my life."

"Ah, I see." He gave a quick smile, "You had me going there for a minute. But you said something - do I know you?" Again he looked closely at her face. "Wait, I do, I've seen you before somewhere."

"The restaurant, with Farine du Blez."

"Oh yes, that's right. Sorry, I didn't recognise you." His frown returned, "Was he with you, when the blast happened?"

"Yes, we'd just come walking up the street, stopped to look in that window for a moment and next thing we know we're on the ground."

Repeating it, and finding she was actually still upright was gradually easing the shock. Slowly she felt her legs solidify underneath her and her breathing settle. She looked up at his face, the green eyes somehow softer in daylight, the features less sharp than seen just in profile. "Is it badly damaged, inside?"

He shrugged, "Superficial mainly. Obviously the frontage has to be replaced, temporary job at the moment for security, stands and fittings blown to smithereens." His rapid assessment almost made her smile, his mental list ticked off visibly before her. He picked up on it and smiled back. "Thought I'd left all that sort of thing behind me years ago, but I've seen enough to know the procedure."

"Northern Ireland?"

"Aye. They're enjoying a more civilised way of life over there now, but I've been here quite a while. It's history to me. Don't suppose you know what it's like."

"Not really. I've seen Belfast, and the most bombed hotel in Europe, I have friends in County Antrim. If my one small experience is anything to go by, they deserve the peace; I wouldn't want to have lived with all that."

He just nodded, eyes wandering back over the front of his assaulted shop.

"Do you know why it happened? Will you keep going?"

His eyes darted back to her, his mouth hardening, then a shrug, "You either go back or you go forward. I'll get it repaired and open it again as soon as I can. At least my signwriter is well practised now, this was the tenth shop."

"What was it called?"

"I took the name from the old business; that was Jubilee Cards. But that sounded outdated I thought, so I changed it to

Jubilations. Has a happier ring somehow, what do you reckon?"

"More modern, definitely."

"Yeah, exactly. Look, are you okay? Can I get you anything?"

"No, I'm fine, really."

"Good, good. Well, I must dash, got to see a man about a shop front!"

He had been looking up and down the street as he spoke. He turned, gave her a hasty salute with one hand as he walked out round a BMW parked on the yellow lines, got in the car and was gone.

By Friday, both web-sites were done, and happily the clients were pleased with the results. She felt that she had battled through something to get that result, and now she deserved a reward. It was halfway through the afternoon, so she sent off a text to Farine asking how he was, and if he felt like doing anything to cut loose. He had called her a couple of times in the week, but she just hadn't felt like going out anywhere. She was guessing he might be glad to hear she was feeling more like being sociable now.

She had a reply some time later suggesting they meet at a wine bar when he got out of the office. Yes, she thought, why not? So she took her time getting ready and walked slowly up to meet him, enjoying an afternoon warm enough to require no extra layers on arms or legs.

She found a table outside in the sun and picked up a copy of the local evening paper someone had left behind. The bombing still held enough interest to be on the front page, but in truth there was no further news. The Chief Superintendent had given a press conference, reassuring the public that terrorism was not suspected. She had gone along to the incident room they had set up earlier in the week, along with many other casualties. Unfortunately none of them seemed to have anything very helpful to offer, other than their own painful tales of shock and injury. Presumably these had been as uninformative to the police as she imagined, as a Detective

Chief Inspector Bonnington was repeating his appeal for witnesses. The expressions on the two men in the press photo looked harried, she thought. Trying to show concern, or hide frustration?

The wines were served and waiting by the time he arrived. She watched him go through the tie off, collar loosened and sleeves rolled up routine, realising it was already familiar. It was another little sign that going through the bomb incident together had strengthened the friendship they had started. Nothing like shared adversity, she thought. They would be filling sand buckets and comparing ration books soon.

They chatted about how they had got on through the week, and he was pleased for her that the design jobs had both been successfully completed.

"You do realise what this means, don't you?" she asked smiling faintly. He looked mystified. "Time to start your web-site. I need to know what your requirements are now."

He smiled back, "Aha, you think I will have forgotten. But you are wrong. Justine and I spent one lunch-time going through it this week, we have made the decisions."

"You didn't say anything!"

"I didn't need to. You said nothing would happen for a fortnight, I was going to e-mail them to you next week." He paused and looked across at her, "As long as you are feeling okay, there is no hurry."

"I'm fine! I feel a lot better today, particularly as the other two got finished on time. It's made me feel I must be back to normal."

He frowned slightly, "What is it? Something still bothers you."

She pulled her mouth to one side and gave her head a quick shake, "Just this ringing in the ears, it's in the background now, but it's irritating. That's all, honestly!" She returned his stare with a glare of her own then they both smiled.

"Would you like to come to a concert tonight? I am going with a few friends to listen to some Schumann by quite a good local chamber orchestra. Would you like that?"

She smiled, "No, thank you it's a lovely idea, but I think not."

"I know you're not enthusiastic about classical, but I expect you could get to enjoy it, you know."

"I expect I could. And your desire to educate me is very commendable, I'm sure. But maybe when my ears have stopped buzzing perhaps?"

He squeezed his eyes shut briefly, "Of course, that was stupid of me, wasn't it?"

"Uncharacteristic, let's say. But then, less than a week ago you got blown off your feet too. You are excused on this occasion."

"Very kind of you, thank you. But I want to take you out and cheer you up. Where shall we go? What do you feel like doing?"

She closed her eyes now, and leaned back in her seat, "What do I feel like?" she thought quietly for a while, her face peaceful under the light falling on it.

"I feel like having wide open spaces around me, walking a long way and feeling sunshine on my bare arms. A long empty beach, that's what I feel like."

"Good, where is one?"

She laughed loudly, opening her eyes and looking at him in disbelief, "You don't know where the nearest beach is?"

He looked puzzled, "No, should I?"

"Well, I suppose I can't imagine not knowing, that's all. And to be fair, the nearest beach isn't what we need. If we go further south, to Brean Down there are big stretches of dunes and flat sand, that's more what I had in mind."

"Okay then let's do that. Tomorrow?"

"We could. It would be best to go early in the morning, it gets busy, and then the nice empty spaces are no longer empty," she looked at him seriously, "I mean really early."

He shrugged, "That's fine, this concert will not go on late tonight. I'll come and get you in the morning, just say what time."

"Six o'clock? Can you cope with that?"

"Of course."

"Good, we'll do it properly then. A day at the seaside, marvellous!"

They chatted on for a while, Lucy felt relaxed and happy, pleased with the thought of her day out to come. Eventually, they both agreed they ought to be moving on to their respective evenings, and parted cheerfully.

'So, as you can tell, I'm feeling quite chipper again. So much so I'm dragging the tame solicitor off to the beach tomorrow – we'll see just how tough he is. I intend to have a proper picnic. I hope you don't feel too left out, I just can't bear not to make the most of this good weather. Although I expect sunshine doesn't feel like a commodity you have to use every fraction of over there. Is the heat still bothering you? At least from the sound of it you're over that stomach bug properly now. Don't catch another one of those! And (boring wifely question) are you eating properly? Answer expected to that one.

I've just realised, by the time you get this, you might well have the next one waiting too – so it will all be history. Never mind, you won't have to wait in suspense to hear how the seaside activities go and whether or not I drown the Frenchman.'

It occurred to her that talking about a picnic was not enough, action was also needed. She finished her e-mails quickly and headed off to see what exciting things she could find for an al fresco breakfast. Ah, that was a good idea; did she have any of that left?

8

As promised, he arrived outside her house at six the next morning. When she answered the door, she handed him a large box and brought another one with her,

"What is this for?" he demanded, at a loss.

"It's for going in the boot, come on get it open, there's a good chap."

They stowed her baggage and got into the car. She should have known, she thought, that it would be a top of the range model. What else? A beat up little old car like Nick's? She hadn't a clue about letters and numbers after car makes, but she didn't need to. Electric everything, and very swish interior with superbly comfortable seats said it all. The soft top was down, which was chilly in the early morning like this, but definitely good fun, she decided.

They were soon on the road heading out of the city. Her navigation duty was an easy one for this trip, and with very little traffic around he was able to put his foot down.

As soon as they were under way he asked her about all the stuff in the boot.

"You'll see, don't worry."

He couldn't get anything else out of her other than the sort of smile a cat produces when it's pulled one over on its humans. He turned the stereo on, some inevitable classical piece was in there, and she listened for a while without complaint.

"Are you okay with this?" he asked after she had gone quiet for a few minutes.

"I don't mind the Brandenburgs for a bit."

"Oh! You know these concertos?"

"Well, I'm not a total ditz you know. I can recognise the top fifty most-played classics! Probably not much more though."

By now they were at the motorway, and he put up the hood, at the touch of a button of course, against the noise.

"Can I change it?" she asked pointing at the CD player.

"Of course, there are some more discs in the console there."

She just smiled again, and reached down to the bag at her feet, pulling out a CD of her own. "Actually I think it's time we educated you, get an earful of this."

She put the disc in and after a few moments guitar riffs burst out of the speakers. Another minute or so and he turned to her, "This is the song you were singing – at the café that day!"

She nodded, "Yep, if we listen to it a few more times I'm sure you'll pick it up. And there are some other good ones on here too. By the time we're on our way home we can do this properly, top down, music blaring, singing our heads off. A real day out. What do you reckon? Are you up for it?"

He was lost for words briefly then nodded, "Why not? I can have singing lessons from you, no problem!"

"Ah, well I'd follow the CD if I were you; my singing is pretty bad actually. That's why we'll need the music up but I'll help with the words, the ones I know anyway."

They played the first track a couple of times then went through the rest. He listened with interest, fascinated by what she found a good song and not. Some tracks they both rejected as too mournful, but he was surprised by the range of things she liked. One track in particular, her real favourite, they played three times and he was already singing along, which seemed to please her a great deal. He had a good voice, which helped.

"So do you sing a lot yourself?"

"Well, I wouldn't say a lot. Jen and I sometimes have a bit of a laugh, when a good song comes on the radio we like to have a boogey round the kitchen. And the current favourites usually get us pogo-ing round the house."

"What is pogo-ing?" he asked mystified.

This made her smile, "You need teenagers for all this; it's jumping up and down waving your hands in the air to the music. Nick thinks I'm a total embarrassment, which just makes Jen and me do it all the more. Same goes for singing along. He thinks he's the only one that can get it right, but he's just as bad as us really."

"Why should you not sing if you enjoy it?"

"The worst thing you can do to a teenager is embarrass them. I've done it to Nick all his life, he's a bit miffed with me about it, but he'll get over it one day."

After the motorway, they put the top down again and had their first practice singing loudly along the country lanes until they got to the small town just before the beach. Lucy decided it was only human kindness to leave people there peacefully asleep in their beds. Down to the sand dunes it was still delightfully quiet, in fact when Lucy looked at her watch she declared that if she'd known how fast he drove, they could have had another half an hour to lie-in.

Walking along the hard-packed sand, particularly in bare feet, and even more particularly in this early morning sun, Lucy felt like she was in heaven. She wandered along eyes barely open, just feeling. They didn't even talk for a while; both of them seemed content to enjoy the space and the near silence.

Finally he made a comment, "The sea is very far away here."

"Yes, the sand is very flat so a small rise or fall in the tide causes it to change over a long distance. It means it can come in very quickly. People are getting their cars stuck here all the time. They drive down onto the sand in an evening, all they need is to get in a soft bit, they can't move the car easily and suddenly the tide is coming in and they're stuck."

He pulled a face, but didn't say anything else.

One or two early morning dog walkers were out on the beach, and polite good mornings were exchanged. However, by the time they had walked for twenty minutes or so they had the whole expanse of sky and rippled sand to themselves. They sat down on the edge of the dunes where it was drier and tried to decide whether the distant glint of water was getting any closer or not.

"I didn't think to check the tide times, so I can't tell you what stage it's at."

"You British seem very taken with the seaside, it's a big thing here."

"Well, we have a lot of it. Island race and all that you know. Have you ever been down to Cornwall?"

He shook his head. She wondered if he even knew where it was.

"Well, you should go. They have some spectacular beaches in Cornwall, South Wales too. And while I think about it, the very far north of Scotland. You definitely ought to go and see those places."

"Quite the travelogue, do you get a fee for sending people all over your country?"

"No, but if you like something, it's a good feeling to share it with someone else, isn't it? Especially if it's something they haven't done or seen before."

He looked into her face and smiled widely, "Yes it is. Is that why you are teaching me the songs, to share them with me?"

She nodded, "I guess so. Besides you like just doing something, live for the moment and all that. We can't sing along to Beethoven, but we can belt out anything from Led Zeppelin to The Zutons. You seem to want me to have fun, that's one thing I consider fun."

"Is it the sort of thing you do with Tom?"

There it was again. That uncomfortable feeling when he asked about Tom. Was he doing it to remind her that he knew she was married? Or delving into the more personal parts of her life to see what he could fish up? This was silly, he had been a complete gentleman to her so far, and they had both taken comfort from each other's company since the shock of last week. Nevertheless she gave him a cautious look.

"No, why?"

He shrugged, "You seemed to find it so amusing, I thought that was strange if you did it all the time."

"Tom doesn't find singing enjoyable; he wouldn't understand the desire to make a lot of noise like that."

She wasn't sure if that sounded disapproving of her husband's attitude or disapproving of Farine for having asked the question. Without the susurration of the sea, too distant to contribute, there was only awkward silence to lap to and fro between them. Saying anything else would only make it feel worse, best to let it go.

The lack of words gradually eased back into the realm of comfortable again, and as they rose to return they both agreed the water definitely looked closer now.

This time she asked him more questions about himself, and was shocked to find that he'd lived in England for twelve years.

"What, you think my English should be much better by now?"

"No, I think you should have seen more of the country by now. That's terrible."

They talked about the sights of England, then France, and drew up a list of essential places to visit for each other. By the time they had finished, they were back at the car.

"Ready for some breakfast?"

"Yes," he said.

"Right then, boot time."

She emptied the cool box, which contained sandwiches and champagne. They sat on the sand, and he opened the wine, looking at the label.

"It's cheap stuff, I've told you, I can't stand the other. But I did think we deserved a bit of a treat so smoked salmon and champagne it is!"

"You are very organised, when did you do all this?"

"Yesterday evening. Besides, domestic is my natural territory, don't think a small picnic is going to give me any problems."

"Of course I am not used to domestic. I am a lord and have an army of servants."

She smiled at this and then felt duty bound to up the ante. She leaned over to him and said, "Don't worry, different is fun, when you are over your fear."

She went back to the car and rummaged in the other box, bringing back a camping stove and her small coffee pot. She set all the equipment out on the sand, getting the stove level and fiddling with water and matches. She sat back down next to him again while the water heated.

"We could have just bought some coffee; you didn't need to take all this trouble."

She made a gargling noise in her throat "Where do you think you would have got any drinkable coffee round here? I don't advise you try it; your fine tastes would be seriously compromised. Besides, it's fun. Playing at camping is always good fun, unless it's raining of course. No; even then."

Again they sat quietly, she was sifting sand and letting it fall on her toes when she asked "Why do you always want to stop me taking trouble over something or making an effort? Do you regard me as a bit pathetic?"

"Good God no! I'm being ..." he was unable to finish the sentence.

"Polite?" she offered.

"Oh dear, now I am in trouble, I can tell."

She flashed him a quick smile, "I'll let you off this once, don't do it again" then reached forward to pour the coffee.

"So, you like to make an effort for people, do things for them?"

"Don't we all? For your friends, your family, people you like."

He thought for a moment "Yes, that makes sense. But it would be a good idea to be demonstrative with them too."

"Oh, is this about British reserve?"

He nodded, "I'm afraid so. I still find it odd. At home we kiss each other, touch each other a lot. Everybody here stands away from you, just in case you touch them by accident. It feels cold, and goodness knows, the climate is cold enough. What are they all frightened of? Even you, you get edgy if I touch your hand too often, or put my arm round your shoulder. I would do it to my brothers even, as well as my sisters or their children. God forbid I should do it to a man here!"

He sounded quite passionate, even hurt. She looked at him and wondered how much he missed his family. She lay on her stomach on the sand and pulled at the odd blades of grass sticking up.

"Yes, it must be very strange. Even when you learn the language really well, there are things that don't translate, I suppose, because of the history behind the words. Culture is quite difficult to absorb sometimes, even subtle differences from your own can be very isolating, I guess. Does it make you feel alien?"

He shrugged, rubbing his face, "I'm sorry, I didn't mean to be miserable. This is a very nice picnic, don't let me spoil it."

"You can say if you are miserable, I thought we were looking out for each other. I wouldn't like you to be sad by yourself. Wouldn't have anyone to sing along with me, would I, if you go off in a sulk?"

He rolled onto his front too, and they lay side by side for a few minutes talking about things that seemed very different to him. After a while he appeared to have got over his negative mood. She asked if he'd like more coffee, and he insisted that he have a go at the camping stove. Eventually he got the hang of it, and apart from nearly pouring boiling hot coffee over his foot, all was well. She maintained she didn't want any more though.

"I'm wired enough. I'm not used to mainlining it like you."

He could only manage a stare in response and she snorted.

"Don't think glaring is going to get you anywhere. I grew up with dirty looks, my whole family glares. In fact, I was in the British Olympic glaring team for several years."

She let out peels of laughter at her own joke, and his expression, and then rolled back on the sand gasping.

He leant down on one elbow by her side "Why are you making so much fun of me?"

"Well, it's a change from you making fun of me. Don't you like me doing it?"

"Yes, I think I do. It means you're not frightened of me any more."

"Ha, well watch out then. You don't know what I'll do next."

He looked at her silently for several seconds, before sitting up facing away from her to reach for the coffee. She raised her hand and rested it gently against his back.

"Are you really okay now?"

He turned to look at her over his shoulder, "Yes, I'm fine."

"I thought you might be annoyed with me."

He straightened out again, putting the coffee cup between them on the sand.

"I think you will know if I'm angry. Maybe sometimes I'm scared too."

She shook her head, lips pressed together "Can't imagine that, you being frightened of anything. You do all that honour and nobility stuff, but I've never seen anything like fear on your face. Still, I suppose everybody gets scared sometimes."

He nodded, lightly tracing a line in the sand by her side, "Yes, everybody, by different things though."

"What about last week? Did that scare you?"

"I was very worried when I saw you lying there. You were really dazed, and of course there was a lot of blood, it was impossible to tell at first if it was serious or not. I could only think that it was my fault, I took you there and got you into danger."

"Oh come on, D'Artagnan, that could hardly be your fault. We've been through this, 'what ifs' are no use to anyone. You can't take responsibility for me; I'm not a child or an idiot. We're supposed to be friends. I think that has some element of equality about it. It's a touch feudal at the moment you know."

He performed a particularly Gallic shrug.

"Yes I know," she interrupted whatever he'd been about to reply, "you've been brought up to take that attitude, but you live without it in large areas of your life. Just relax a bit with your friends as well. Or am I the only one you feel constrained to protect?"

He considered her face for a moment then turned on to his back and looked up to the sky. "I think it is ingrained in a gentleman to care for any lady he is with. Because most people seem to have abandoned gentlemanly ways, or care for other people in general, does that make it wrong for me to do it?"

"You are feeling out of place this morning, aren't you?" She considered his expression and went on, "I know how you feel; I always seem to be at odds with my surroundings. Whatever anyone else is thinking I seem to automatically take up the opposite viewpoint. Don't ask me why I'm like this, I always have been. And the older I get, the more the world seems determined to remind me of it. I find it impossible to go with a crowd."

"That's because you have a strong personality, but you don't just trample over every one else with it. You care for people too."

"Well that's alright then. We'll go off and be noble together, shall we? How about Don Quixote and Sancho Panza? Who are you going to be?"

He caught her eye and changed tack before he fell into her trap, "I think I will be the donkey."

"Good casting!" Then she sat up suddenly "Hey, we could have a donkey ride along the beach couldn't we? I wonder what time they start."

He propped himself up on his elbow again to look at her, "You can, I think I will not."

She frowned back at him "Why not?"

"Because if I sit on one of those small animals, my feet would probably trail on the ground. Comparisons with the good Don have gone far enough, I think."

She just nodded, smiling to herself, "I bet you ride though, bound to have done that too, I suppose."

"Yes, I ride. Do you?"

"No. I wanted to, when I was young. That and play the piano, but I didn't get the chance."

"That is a shame. Do you not play any instrument then?

"No, well, strummed a guitar a bit in my youth, but not really. Go on then, amaze me."

"I play the cello. I was thinking of taking up classical guitar, but I haven't got round to it yet. Maybe we could learn together."

She laughed out loud at that, and lay back down, turning her head to him.

"You're determined that I should be as polished and accomplished as you, aren't you? I don't see it happening. I can't even read music, and I think at my age, I would be very slow learning. Are you not content with me amusing you by making gauche remarks?"

"I don't think I'm any more determined than you are to point out the differences between us. I have the attitude that you can do what you want, you seem to prefer setting limitations on yourself."

She frowned, before looking abashed, "Yes, you're right. I think I do. But please can we stop being so serious? I thought we'd come out for some fun."

"Certainly, what do you suggest?"

By now, a lot more cars were arriving and different voices wafted to and fro across the beach. He glanced at her and caught her expression.

"Too many people for you?"

"Mm hm. Well, it's not too bad, but the best is definitely over. What about you?"

"I am happy to move on if you want. We have had a good time here. More singing practice?"

She smiled, "Definitely!"

He was content to follow her suggestion of driving back over the Mendips and visiting Cheddar, she seemed to know all this part of the countryside very well. She insisted they visit the caves, and he was surprised by how impressive it was; admitting that he'd expected to be bored by damp holes underground.

She shook her head. "Every time I go, I just love it. All those shapes and colours, it's amazing, just from one mineral being deposited. I always look forward to that pool at the end and seeing the stalactites reflected in it. It becomes a fairy landscape for me. I can't help populating it with fantastic creatures and miniature people riding up and down calcite ridges in chariots."

They went in one of the smaller caves next, with possibly even more spectacular deposits, fluted and coruscated into beautiful formations. This time it was more awkward for Farine as the route through was confined and twisted, not to mention well below the natural height of his head. Emerging into the light again, they shed sweaters and reapplied sunglasses.

With drinks in front of them at a café she knew, he looked across at her, "Happy?"

"Mmm. Very. How about you? Have you enjoyed being dragged round my day out?"

"Yes, but I wasn't dragged. I came of my own free will, remember."

"Actually if you think back, you insisted, but we'll let that pass. I'm glad you enjoyed it, it makes it more fun for me."

"Thank you. Did you like seeing me surprised by beautiful caves? "

"I did. That's the best part of my job, well the part I enjoy most, showing the design to the client for the first time. There's always the tension of whether or not they'll like it, and when they look happy it feels great."

"I think I can understand that. Sadly, not many people have a look of supreme joy on their faces at what their solicitor tells them."

"That's because of the bill!"

He smiled at her continued teasing. "Would you like to go somewhere else tomorrow?"

She shook her head as she swallowed some tea, "I'll be at church in the morning, so thank you but no."

"Church? I didn't think you approved of them?"

"I didn't say that. Besides it doesn't belong to a denomination, just a bunch of lovable lunatics together."

"What do you mean?"

"We don't belong to any big group or anything; we don't even have a building. We just hire a local school hall."

"Why do you refer to them as lunatics?"

"Seems safer than thinking of them as the people who've got it right," she shrugged. "Besides, I expect most people would think we were lunatics."

He looked inquiringly at her, but she maintained it would be hard to explain.

They drove home and whenever the traffic slowed, they made heads turn with the volume of their singing. That was certainly more probable than it being because of the quality.

9

Without much in the way of other current work, Lucy was able to make a start on the designs for Farine first thing Monday morning. She hummed cheerfully to herself for a while as she started manipulating shapes and logos on the screen in front of her. After a while she got up and went in search of a CD, bringing back the one they had played so much on Saturday. With that turned up on the hi-fi, and seated back at her desk, she soon lost herself in an alternative world of sound and images. By that evening, she was able to forewarn him that she was likely to ring through to his office in a day or two to arrange a viewing.

On Tuesday afternoon she was already calling Maureen to ask for the appointment. At first, she was told there was nothing in the current week, but after a quick referral, Maureen declared there was an hour available on Friday afternoon.

Happy with that, Lucy turned back to the keyboard, this time to write another e-mail.

'You'll never guess what. I am about to respond to a new enquiry I've had in from a big firm! It's something of a surprise, they aren't big enough to have in-house designers, but I would have expected them to go to a specialist design firm, rather than a little freelance like me. I'm not even sure at the moment how they got my name or where they saw my work. Anyway, it's exciting to be going up in the world. Well, until I find it's a job I don't fancy. I know, no use jumping to conclusions, I'm sure you'll tell me to wait and see. All this excitement has sent what other news I had for you clean out of my head!'

Before the end of the afternoon a text arrived from Farine, suggesting they meet for a drink that evening after fencing practice. She replied with the idea that they go for a drive out of the city again, and end up at a country pub she knew.

She took some different CDs with her this time; he said he was ready to learn a few more songs. They frightened natives in several villages before having a drink overlooking a reservoir and fighting off mosquitoes.

"Have you heard any more from your friend in the CPS?" she asked as they swatted periodically.

"I called him today; Angus said that a Detective Chief Inspector Bonnington is in charge of the case."

"Yes, he was in the paper last Friday. Is his name significant?"

"No, but apparently they have been consulting the Organised Crime Unit at the Met." He pulled a face and shrugged, "I know nothing about this kind of thing. I don't work in the criminal sector at all. It means no more to me than to you."

He then told her about a play he wanted to see, and she agreed to go with him on the Thursday evening. They spent a long time chatting about various productions they had enjoyed and it was quite dark by the time they headed home, still with the top down and trying to get the words right to one particular song.

On Thursday evening, she was aware very quickly that he was in charge again. It was the city. This was his natural element, whilst she had been more comfortable out in less populous areas. Perhaps she genuinely was developing a physical inability to be in a crowd, maybe as a reaction to the bombing, but then shrugged off that idea as silly. With the evening still warm, on the way home they decided to stop at a small bar and have a drink outside. They were sat relaxing when some very familiar music started and they both, without thinking, joined in, "Well, sometimes I go out by myself, and I look across the water..."

The stares from others round about caused them to stop, Lucy covering her face with her hands to hide her cheeks and the giggles she could not suppress. Farine said he thought they were doing pretty well, and shouldn't be embarrassed, but she preferred not to stay there for another drink and risk a second outburst. As he walked her back, he was apologising for not being able to meet for lunch next day before she brought her work in.

"Hey, that's okay, don't worry. I don't expect you to entertain me at all points of the week. I do have an independent life still. Maybe I ought to remember it more often."

"What do you mean?"

"Well I'm sure my friends would think it was a bit odd, us spending so much time together. Not that I've done much to tell them about it. They probably think I'm sitting at home being miserable with Tom away, not out on the razzle with a good-looking Frenchman. I know Jenny's a bit concerned."

"Why?"

She drew in a deep breath and blew it all out in a loud sigh, "I guess because, from her point of view, I'm acting strangely."

"Being friends with me?"

"You can't blame her, she doesn't know who you are; she's never even seen you. And with her dad away, me making friends with some unknown exotic bloke might not seem terribly appropriate."

He didn't say anything for a while, just looked thoughtful, then started to tell her how much he was looking forward to seeing the designs next day. When they reached her house, they parted with the usual 'au revoirs' and the double-cheek kiss.

'Tom my love, I was horrified at what you said! For goodness sake, there must be somebody who can sort this out. I'm sure you're only refraining from kicking up a fuss because it's you that's being inconvenienced. Your next e-mail had better give me details of how it's being resolved, otherwise I'll have to come out there and give everyone a talking to. Oh wait, that's not an incentive, is it? Well, I'm assuming my arrival would be a cause for delight rather than sorrow. Although the thought of me being the one to snap everyone to attention must, at least, make you smile.

Actually, on the subject of my trip, I am managing to amass a reasonable slush fund, but after the job for my pet solicitor there isn't a lot on the horizon. Let's hope business picks up, or the job for the big firm, Luckers, is a good one.

Business and pleasure are becoming blurred though. I met up with Farine tonight at the theatre, yes another evening out! If this carries on, when you come home I will be thoroughly used to having a social life and expect you to take me out at least three times a week. I daresay that's got you shaking in your boots!

I keep trying to work out if you would get on well with Farine, I just can't tell. He's odd enough to intrigue you, but rather more polished and sophisticated than your usual chums. I will have to keep you amused by recounting our cultural visits, which look set to continue, he's keen for me to go along to some dull classical concerts. Perhaps I should suggest a trip to the ballet. Does that sound like suitable revenge?'

She looked away from the keyboard and at the framed picture on the bookcase. Tom's smile beaming out at her gave no indication of what the flesh and blood face would look like in reaction to the forming e-mail. Had she said too much about Farine? Did it look like she couldn't think of anything else to talk about, or that she was happy for him to know what they were spending time doing? A heavy sigh did nothing to blow those questions away, not least because she couldn't answer them for herself, never mind her absent husband. Absent. Bloody absent! It was just as often a source of irritation these days, she noticed, as it was one of misery. When they had discussed the idea, six months had sounded manageable. Was she weaker than she realised? Or maybe it was bad timing. A shake of the head and a clenched jaw sent a message back to the beaming smile that whatever the reason, all was not as smooth as they had hoped. Alas, the electronic letter would not be able to relay the expression as the words went down the wires. She turned back to the keyboard, amended a few phrases, added her endearments and hit 'send' before going off to bed.

"I've brought some basic designs. If you look through these three sets, they give you a rough idea of how the different versions would work"

They were in his office, seated as once before, on the same side of the desk, with the designs slowly spreading out in front of them.

"Don't get the sets muddled!" she admonished him, automatically collecting some pieces of paper back together. "Just look at that set to begin with, we can always compare equivalent pages when you've had a quick browse through each lot."

"I think you are being very bossy."

"Yes I am, just do as you're told and all will be well."

He laughed; she wasn't even the slightest bit repentant.

"Okay, this will take time then. Would you like some coffee?"

"Mmm. Yes please." She bent over one of the pages, adding an extra note to herself.

He picked up the 'phone. "Ah Maureen, yes, could you bring us some coffee please, English style for Madame Cottonwood. Thank you."

She looked round at him, smiling to herself for a moment, thinking how long it was since he had last called her that. Funny how things moved on sometimes.

They started to work through the designs methodically now, and Maureen arrived with the coffee a few minutes in to their discussion.

He was pleased with what he saw, and they went through it twice before he decided there was definitely one he liked less than the others, but between the remaining two he wasn't sure. She gathered up the unwanted sheets, and they were able to spread the others out better to compare them. She lined them up in respective order, chewing her bottom lip in concentration as she tried to get them level. She reached for her coffee, taking a drink as she straightened the last one.

"I wish I could do that," he said on a slight sigh.

"What?" she asked in between sips.

"Nibble your lower lip."

The sharp intake of breath this caused, unfortunately coincided with the latest mouthful of coffee, and the resulting reaction left Lucy choking and several pages sprayed with regurgitated drink.

He had to slap her on the back a few times to help her clear her lungs, and she scrabbled in her bag for some tissues to mop up first herself, then her work.

He'd picked up the 'phone again, "Maureen, do we have some kind of cloth? Yes, a slight accident with the coffees."

Lucy was still coughing sporadically when Maureen appeared once more, bringing paper towels. The secretary gave the now wheezing Lucy a strange stare as she watched her trying to blot streaks of liquid from the designs. She wanted to shout, 'It's my work we're ruining here, you know!', but lack of breath didn't give her the option.

Left to themselves again, Lucy was still fuming, and turned to Farine with eyes blazing. "What was that for?"

He looked rather sheepish. As far as she could recall, it was the first time an expression anything like that had made it onto his normally composed features.

"My apologies, rather bad timing perhaps."

"Bad timing? Bad timing? I think we can go a little further than that, surely. How about entirely inappropriate?"

As far as she was concerned, sheepish wasn't nearly enough. She was waiting for contrite.

"Is the work very badly damaged?"

"That's not the point is it?" She now crossed her arms, a bad sign.

"I rather thought it was."

"Hardly! We can just print off more copies of that as we want."

"Good, that's okay then, isn't it?"

They were staring each other out, and Lucy's problem was, that as the heat of anger subsided, she knew he would he get the upper hand again in any exchange. She made one last effort. "What did you think you were doing, saying that?"

She knew straight away that was a mistake. Why give him an open door to rush through, sophistication and charm at the ready to disarm her once more?

"Don't answer that!" she snapped, annoyed with herself now, as well as with him.

He held up his palms in surrender. "I'm sorry. I wasn't trying to be louche, I just said what I was thinking."

She was definitely losing now, the fire of being affronted was dying and she knew, any moment she would be left with only basic embarrassment.

"Well, you shouldn't be thinking it. Oh, for goodness sake!" she muttered, turning away and back to the desk. She sat down in front of the designs and tried to put them in order again.

He came and sat down beside her, but she stayed coldly stiff and straight in her chair. He asked one or two questions, and she answered them with sparse replies. They managed, with an effort, to cover all the major features that needed to be discussed. Finally they agreed he should think about the designs for a day or so, and then let her know the final choice

"You could always show them to Justine, she might have an opinion to offer."

"Yes, I think I will; she is likely to express her interest."

They sat in silence for a moment.

"Will they have heard, out there, what went on?" asked Lucy softly, angling her head.

"What I said? No, of course not."

"I was thinking rather more of the raised voices afterwards," she explained with strained patience.

"Ah! I don't think so. They are quite heavy doors. People like to feel they have privacy with their solicitor."

She nodded, breathing carefully through her nose.

"Right then, I'll get off."

"Are you still upset with me?" he automatically reached his hand out to her forearm as it rested on the desk.

She looked at his hand pointedly, and then up to his face with an eyebrow raised. "I'm not quite sure what I should think at the moment."

"It's what you do think, not what you should think that matters. You described my words as inappropriate, not hurtful or annoying. Do you know that it is one of the words you use most often? It seems that 'appropriate' is very important to you."

"So, it's my fault now, for using the wrong word?"

"Don't be silly, I didn't say that. And I apologised for offending you. In France we really don't think there's anything wrong with paying a woman a compliment."

She picked up her handbag and case. "I think you're stretching it a bit there. You can't cover everything with the excuse of my British reserve. You wouldn't have said it to your sister."

"But you are not my sister." She was at the door now, hand on the handle. "Besides," he added, "I think you are making too much out of nothing. It was just a remark, you can always tell me to forget it, if the idea doesn't appeal to you."

She was feeling far too undermined by now to make any sensible reply to this. With her face flushed she left his office in silence, and swept past Maureen to get out of the building as quickly as possible.

Walking the long way home, she decided, was the best possible thing she could do. Feet in rhythmic motion, hands pushed down into her trouser pockets, she could let the scenery of buildings, vehicles and people blur past her eyes and allow her mind to roam. Her body was perfectly capable of navigating the route by itself; she was content to let it. Other things were demanding her attention. Annoyance mainly. She was annoyed with Farine for spoiling the friendship they had developed. Annoyed too, with Tom for being so far away and leaving her to get into a mess like this. And, of course, annoyed with herself for … for what exactly? For finding his suggestion a tempting one? There, she'd thought it. She had to admit she found him attractive, not just in the abstract, but personally. She had enjoyed all the attention he'd been paying her, but had chosen to ignore the fact that it was fun to be treated like a woman again. So, now what? Only two choices really. Put a stop to it, or stop being so bloody prissy about it and deal with it. The thought of a large glass of wine came to mind, pity her friend Mel was away this weekend. She suddenly felt very much in need of at least two glasses. Maybe she would chill out in front of the TV this evening with a bottle of Shiraz and a favourite film. She could indulge this current self-pity properly then, might as well do it right. This made her smile at last and she looked up to take in her surroundings. Good, nearly home.

She was laughing herself into a heap at the part where he offered to pay with a swan when her 'phone rang. "Hi," her answer was still bright from the laughter.

"Hello, Lucy. Are you ok?"

"Yes, fine. Hang on I'll just turn the TV off. Okay, what can I do for you?"

"You sound very cheerful. I thought you may still be angry with me."

"Well, I might be, but it won't do me much good will it?"

There was a pause, then, "Lucy, have you been drinking?"

"Oh yes. Judging from what I can see left in the bottle, quite a lot I'd say."

"Okay." He sounded nonplussed; this was obviously a new scenario for him.

"We can all do 'stupid', Farine, even me."

"Does that mean you're forgiving me?"

"Well, I might try and eke out the part of 'wounded friend' a bit longer, see what mileage it has, but essentially yes."

There was no reply for a few moments. She thought maybe she had overdone it. "Am I sounding dreadful?"

"A bit unusual, certainly."

"Sorry if I'm scaring you, I've had enough of trying to work everything out right for a while. Giving my sense of virtue a night off just now, no doubt I'll have chance to regret it tomorrow. You can take comfort in the fact we will both have said something we shouldn't, and I won't be able to do 'offended' any longer. How's that for a deal?"

"Acceptable, but… Lucy,"

"What?"

"Take care of yourself, okay?"

"Yeah, sure."

"Goodnight Lucy."

"Goodnight."

10

Lucy opened her eyes and checked the clock, not nearly as late as she had expected. It didn't work of course, like it did for youngsters. A late night and a lot too much to drink didn't seem to induce near-comatose conditions when you got past a certain age. Her body was far too used to getting up early to be duped by a cheap trick like last night's. Actually, she didn't feel too bad. Thirsty of course, but she'd drunk at least two glasses of water through the night, so not to a sickening degree. She drank some more water and turned on her back to contemplate the ceiling, laying bets with herself on how long it would be before she couldn't resist the call of the kettle any more. Not that long. She threw back the cover and swung her legs out of bed. Lie-ins didn't work like they did for the young either.

With a cup of tea in her hand, she wandered out to the bench to enjoy the peace and the sunshine. She found herself, drawn by an obvious thread, thinking about Nick, and how often he drank too much. She knew it was part of the university 'thing', not to mention the whole young male 'thing', but she believed him to be basically sensible. Surely, with the job he was doing up there over this summer, he wouldn't have the chance to go out drinking too often. Although, Friday nights were bound to be a prime chance. Maybe he was sleeping one off right now. In which case he certainly wouldn't be sat out in the sun, and thinking about her like this. Unless, of course, he hadn't actually made it to bed yet, that was possible. Well, he wouldn't be on his way home, she'd had no contact from him about this weekend. She ought to send him a text later, just check he was okay. He had said he would be driving down to see her a couple of times, but been vague, as usual, about when that might be.

A second cup of tea had her feeling most of the way back to normal, though she expected by this afternoon she would have overshot and reached exhausted and lifeless. Well, did it matter? Not really. Apart from some gardening that kept getting ignored, there was nothing happening. Unless Farine rang of course. She had to rate that as 'likely' these days.

What had Jenny said about this weekend? Oh yes, be nice to have a coffee together, and go shopping perhaps. That would be good; she hadn't spent so much time with her lately. Because of Farine, she had to admit. Maybe coffee could turn out to be a bit awkward, she wasn't sure what Jen was going to ask or say on that subject. So apart from that small problem, and the shopping, it would be nice to be with her daughter. Oh dear, this was all going downhill fast. Perhaps some physical exertion was required. If she had a quick shower, she could get out and tackle some weeding before Jen rang. Good idea.

Her time with Jenny passed relatively painlessly. There had been a good bit of reorganising at her work, and she was busy, for a while, bringing her up to date on who had left and who had arrived. Farine had made it on to the list of subjects covered, but Lucy had managed to concentrate on the amusing aspects of having a sophisticated Frenchman as a friend. Using this as a distraction, she was able to gloss over just how much time they were spending together, though she had the good grace to feel uncomfortable about the conscious subterfuge. They did not spend long at the shops; Jenny was going climbing for the afternoon with friends. After a quick lunch she hoisted bags of kit and coils of rope into her car and set off with a wave.

His mobile rang, good, he'd begun to think she was ignoring him. "Bonjour Lucy. How are you? I've tried to ring you several times. That's good, I thought you may still be sleeping off your indulgence. Yes, I've been to lunch with an old friend and I'm just walking home. Not far from you, about five minutes away actually. I thought I could call and see how you are, if you're still speaking to me. Well, I wasn't sure. Is that okay? Good, I'll be with you shortly."

As he walked, he wondered how awkward she would find his arrival. But he did want to make sure she was alright, and he didn't want her putting off making contact because of embarrassment. It could be quite amusing though.

When he reached the house she opened the door before he'd even reached up to the bell, and asked him straight through to the garden."

"How are you?"

"I told you already, I'm fine. Well a bit jaded, but I didn't drink that much you know." He was shaking his head. "Honestly, you'd think I'd committed a crime! You can't report me to the behaviour police, I've got information on you, remember."

"Ah yes, I do remember. It seems you did not drink enough to obliterate your memory anyway. So? Are we friends again?"

"Yes, yes,"

She waved this away, moving on quickly past the obstacle over which they had stumbled. That was a relief.

"Coffee?"

"Yes please."

When both of them had drinks organised they went outside. It was the first time he'd seen the garden, so they spent some time looking round, Lucy explaining how they had changed things over the time the years, and why she liked certain plants. She kept exclaiming over how much work she felt was not getting done.

Farine laughed. "You should come and see the château; you could give us some ideas. Much of the grounds are overgrown, I think there used to be many fruit trees at one time. I don't even know if they are still there."

"Depends on their age, they don't last forever. And I'm not a gardening expert. I say what will look good, in terms of form and shape, but Tom's always the one who knows if a plant will do well in a spot, or how to build something we need."

His gaze swept right round what was before him, "So everything here is what you have made between you, a combination of your talents?"

She paused, considering, "Yes, I suppose it is. We've had very little done by professionals, we've always just set to and had a go ourselves. Sometimes yelling at each other along the way, but we normally manage to achieve what we want."

He looked down at her, "Yes, I expect you do."

"Yep, if you want some totally bodged-together woodworking done, I'm your woman! I never let lack of expertise stand in my way."

She said she wanted to get on with some of her jobs and knelt down to tackle some weeds. He looked around to see if there was any way to help, feeling at something of a loss. He tried asking twice if there was anything he could do.

"Just sit down and talk, will you! I need restful right now, and watching you destroy my plants wouldn't fit into that category."

He shrugged, but complied without argument. She worked her way along the border, as he sat on the grass near her chatting lazily. He tried to ask questions about the garden every now and then. She glanced over occasionally as she answered him, or to explain something, and he wondered why she stared so when she did. Perhaps he was asking stupid things, or maybe she liked looking at him. That was an interesting thought after yesterday. She had never actually said she didn't like his suggestion.

"I have some official news for you, by the way," he said suddenly.

"Oh! What's that?"

"Yesterday, after you left, there was a 'phone call from your adversary."

"Les Wilson of purloined web-site fame you mean?"

"Yes, the man himself. I now have my own evidence regarding his intellectual capacity. It is impressive." She looked at him, bemused. "He has no idea how to go about dealing with this. First of all he tried to deny everything; then he tried to tell me there was nothing I could do about it."

"I'm guessing that was a mistake."

"Of course, I will double the compensation claim immediately." She smiled, no doubt thinking that was the solicitor's answer for everything. "He was not a happy man by the end of the call; I closed our interview by advising him to get a solicitor!"

The afternoon passed peaceably, and they ended it by having a glass of wine together at the top of the garden where the sunlight still fell. He had been invited to a party, and tried to persuade her to go with him.

"No, I think this one glass of wine will be enough for me tonight. I'm definitely too old for a whole weekend of overindulgence. An early night for me, I'm afraid."

They chatted then about the week ahead and she told him about the interest from the big firm, and how they wanted her to go over and see them on Friday morning. He tried to encourage her; already he could see she was unsure.

"Well, it's a much bigger job than usual for me. I'm glad I've got time to finish your designs off before I have to get my head round that one."

A moment's awkwardness ensued, that memory being revived again, but it passed without bother. They decided she would go into his office on the Thursday to install the web-site and get it running. He was away for a meeting, but he was quite happy for Justine to be the one who learnt how it would all work anyway. He asked her about the evenings, but apart from Jenny's climbing night, she said she was going to help her do some decorating in her flat. In the end they agreed they would meet on the Wednesday. He left soon after that to head home and then on to the party.

What he couldn't see, as the door closed behind him, was Lucy going to get out her sketch pad. She had been planning to check the e-mails and tell Tom the latest news, but somehow she was feeling reluctant about that. The sketch pad had a distinctly stronger appeal. She had spent some moments fixing in her mind the image of his arms stretched out, passing either side of his knees, hands clasped in front as he sat on the lawn. She would have to draw that now. Really, she would have loved to go and get her sketch pad at the time, but somehow it didn't seem right. Besides, people rarely stayed that relaxed once they knew they were being drawn.

Despite not being willing to see Farine, Lucy did have some company on the Monday of that week. She was helping Jenny with some painting in her flat, it was true. But an old friend like Mel was not going to be put off talking to her just because she was up a stepladder.

"Do you want a wine yet?" Mel asked, carefully placing a duster over the spattered stool before she perched on it.

"No thanks," came the slightly strained reply, "wouldn't help me get these edges straight. Coffee would be good though. Stop me falling asleep on the top step."

Mel pulled a face and left her seat to wander back out to Jenny's tiny kitchen. She returned with a brimming mug, and spilled some of its contents down the sides as it was handed up. Back to the stool and the careful arranging of her gypsy style cotton skirt away from brushes and rollers. She frowned slightly at her friend's back.

"How come you're painting and Jenny isn't? You do too much for her."

"She's got a meeting tonight. And don't pretend you wouldn't do it for Malcolm, if he lived near enough." Lucy threw a grin over her shoulder, down to Mel. "We did some together yesterday, and we'll both have a crack tomorrow evening. I do get Wednesday off, though."

"We could go out to a film if you like," offered Mel.

"Ah, sorry, no can do. Promised to meet up with my solicitor friend. You wouldn't approve of me standing up a guy like him, I promise you."

"Yes, he sounds intriguing. Tell me more."

Lucy moved the steps along, taking another swig of fortitude before she climbed back up. "Terrifically sophisticated. Geographically unaware. Refined tastes. That do for starters?"

Mel sighed through her nose. "How about interested in cuddly divorcees with large hearts and bigger boobs?"

"Couldn't say, though I think you may be in with a chance on account of the frontage. He is very French."

This resulted in several snorts of undisciplined laughter from both of them. Lucy complained it was making her paintwork erratic. Mel asked what on earth could be erotic about paintwork and Lucy replied that she had a one-track mind.

Mel winked, "Well, I was under the impression that was what Frenchmen had. How come you're getting on so well with him?"

Lucy stopped, brush hovering near the wall, "He's a bit lonely I think, I certainly am at the moment, we're good company for each other. There's nothing wrong with that, is there?"

"Nothing at all," replied Mel after a thoughtful sip of wine. "It's a great trick if you can pull it off." She got a stare from Lucy for that. "Come on, you know how it is. Sooner or later one or other of you will want more than the platonic stuff."

"Mel, do you begrudge me another friend?"

"No, just a handsome, sexy one that's all! I might have to come with you on one of these jaunts, check him out and make sure you're safe with him."

"Yes, it's a long time since I was allowed out on my own, Aunty Mel."

"Mm. Don't forget I'm away to see Malcolm for a few weeks. I don't want to get back from my wonderful holiday to find you in tatters. Promise me you'll be careful."

Lucy turned to her, eyes wide, "Whatever do you think I'm going to get up to?"

"From the look of it, painting your hair shocking pink!" She bellowed with laughter, and then spilled wine down her skirt. She swore and mopped at herself with a tissue intermittently.

Lucy couldn't help smiling, then had to turn her attention back to the paint, she wasn't far from the corner now.

"Anyway," said Mel, "what I don't understand is, how come he can work over here as a solicitor if he's French."

"Copyright and intellectual property is very much an international issue these days. Even you're aware of the world-wide web! He could work anywhere he can cope with the language."

"Does he, cope with the language well? Or does he speak like Inspector Clouseau all the time?"

Lucy spent a moment trying to quell the combination of images this brought up. "No! His English is superb. I asked him if he was one of these people who just pick up other languages naturally."

"What did he say? I suppose he's a polyglot or something."

"No, he said:" she tried to imitate his voice and accent, knowing he wouldn't have been flattered by either, "grammar has laws just like copyright, if I can get my head round the one, I will manage the other. And English is an interesting challenge, because you can bend the laws so far."

"He sounds a bit of a ponce, if you ask me. And if I had the choice of the South of France or here, I know where I'd be."

"You'll be in Canada shortly, so stop moaning. And he isn't a ponce, just – different. Tell me what you've got planned to do while you're over there."

They moved on to Mel's itinerary while the painting was finished and brushes were washed. Somehow that turned into a decision to make a quick foray to a wine bar nearby. They needed to cover a lot of ground if they weren't going to see each other for several weeks.

Wednesday, evening, like many of late, turned out warm and sunny again. The cool cotton top she wanted, needed to be ironed, so she put the local news on while she got the ironing board out. There had been a stabbing, unusually not down in the city-centre, but up in Clifton. A night-club owner had been found dead this afternoon when his staff arrived for work. She shivered, despite the temperature. What was happening here lately? It no longer felt such a civilised place to be. Would she report that to Tom when she e-mailed tonight? Not the kindest thing to do, giving him another thing to worry about at home, he would be bound to see it as something of concern and fret about being away.

Perhaps the latest crime story influenced their decision to walk down to the harbour side for a change. They ambled down through the university area, the elegant old buildings forming a classy backdrop for the noisy, laughing youngsters out with their friends for the evening. She envied them the apparent carefree nature of their lives, realising though that given the choice, she wouldn't go back to that stage with its uncertainties and self-doubts. She asked Farine how he saw it, but he did one of his habitual shrugs and said it was a pointless question. He was here, now, he couldn't go back in time, why think about it? Instead he turned their attention to the pleasant wide streets and their comparative beauty compared to the main shopping area only yards away.

After touring the new buildings, the ships anchored in the harbour, and watching a bridge-swing for a yacht just entering, they decided to walk away from the busier areas and head for a pub on the edge of one of the docks.

They chatted about various things; she regaled him with tales of decorating mishaps, all of which he believed, due to the tiny spots of colour on her hair and arms. In response, he told her about an awkward case he had been dealing with over the last few days.

"Makes my little problem seem nothing at all."

"No, it is not difficult, your case. Just be patient, it will be fine."

"Oh, while we're on work subjects, I've finished what I need to do with the designs you chose. I should get it all up and running tomorrow. Is Justine happy to spend some time with me and get the hang of it?"

"Yes, I think she is relieved it will not be me in charge of it. She thinks I am a dinosaur. That's great Lucy, thank you."

They moved on to talking about her visit to the new clients on Friday, and she finally agreed to meet him for lunch afterwards to tell him how she'd got on.

'So, I shall be intrigued to see how this interview with Luckers goes on Friday, Tom. I really miss having you around just to chat these things through with, I can't see your expression on e-mail! Actually, I've agreed to meet Farine afterwards, so I've got somebody to download all my thoughts to. He's bound to have different reactions to yours though, and won't recognise my panic lights going off the same way, will he? At least he's logical. Hopefully that will help.'

She sent it off, yawning. It would be very interesting to see what she would be able to write after that meeting on Friday.

11

He was already at a table when she arrived. He greeted her as usual then she slipped off her jacket and sat down with a sigh.

"Difficult meeting?"

She was aware of his eyes sweeping over her, starting at her face, as she nodded, but then travelling on down. He was looking appreciative. Of course, she had dressed a little smarter for the consultation today, choosing to wear her favourite linen skirt, and a top more tightly fitted than usual. She could feel a blush rising to her cheeks and she leaned forward, elbow on the table, resting her forehead in her hand, to try and hide it. Why had she not thought of this when she dressed this morning? Because the other meeting had been on her mind. She had not given any thought to seeing Farine later and trying to remain demure. That word in her brain nearly made her laugh out loud. A nice tee-shirt and skirt, not even above the knee, was provocative was it? What planet was she on? So, she was trying to manoeuvre around him and steer his thoughts about her now, eh? Well that was a great idea wasn't, it? She shook her head and muttered to herself.

"Lucy, are you ok? Do you not feel well?"

She sat up straight and looked at him, faintly surprised, as though she'd forgotten he was there.

"I'm sorry Farine, my head's all in a muddle. I'm not being very good company, I'm afraid."

He touched the back of her hand as it lay on the table, "That's no problem, tell me about it. Why was it so difficult?"

She looked at him blankly, "Tell you about what?"

He looked really concerned now, "Your meeting!"

She did laugh then, and the blood rushed to her face once more. This time she grabbed her handbag from the floor and started rooting through it furiously to avoid his eyes.

"What are you looking for?"

"Er, my brain, I've obviously put it somewhere!"

She dumped the bag down again and smiled at him, "Start again shall we? Hi, how are you? How's your morning been?"

"Mine has been okay, yours has obviously been gruelling. I think maybe you need some food. Let's order, then we can talk."

She nodded, "I must be in a bad way, you're being more sensible than me."

"Yes choose something quickly, I fear for you."

They smiled easily at each other and moved on to the practicalities, heads bent to their menus.

"Maybe I could have glass of wine?"

He looked up at her momentarily surprised, "Yes of course. Whatever you want."

They gave their orders, and soon they sat back relaxing with glasses in front of them. She lifted her wine, took a sip and then rested the glass against her cheek, feeling the condensation cool and moist against her skin. Her eyes were closed and she sighed again.

"Okay, you had better start talking, I only have my lunch-hour, and you seem to have a lot on your mind."

"No, not that much. I was just in overdrive I think. Hence the wine. It's a bigger job than I appreciated from the first chat I had with them. They are quite a big outfit, and they want something with all the bells and whistles. You know how it is, you keep trying to go with it, and push yourself to think it'll be okay. But actually, I may have to tell them I can't do it. I think a small team would be needed to do it properly. Some actual computer experts for a start. I'll think about it, but I'd be better pulling out sooner rather than later. I'm sure they've talked to other designers too."

He nodded, relieved that she was making sense at last.

The food arrived, Lucy realised she was famished, so they ate in silence for a few minutes. Gradually she returned to normal.

"Oh my, that's better. You were right, sustenance was required."

"Yes, you see, I can be practical too. Do you want a dessert?"

"No, that's fine. Actually I've probably eaten it too quickly; it's all sat in a lump in my stomach now."

110

"Then let's take a stroll."

They got up to leave; she gathered her jacket and bags as he settled the bill.

Outside, the clouds had rolled in threateningly, and they were darkening fast. There was a moment's chaos as he sorted out getting on the correct side of her, and tried to take her briefcase to carry.

"Ah, the old 'noblesse oblige' eh?"

"Yes, of course, I insist madame."

"As long as you don't insist on 'droit de seigneur' too!"

He looked at her with one eyebrow raised, and she stopped, her hand flicking up To her face as it went bright red. She didn't know what to say or do. Finally she started stammering an apology and he burst out laughing.

"I love it when you say the things you think you should not. They are much more fun than what you consider appropriate." He got them moving again, though Lucy was still beside herself with remorse. "Oh come on," he chided, "just laugh about it."

They walked on up the hill and across the main road onto the downs, both in silence for a while, musing on their own thoughts. Suddenly the rain started, big heavy drops, the opening notes of a crashing symphony to come.

"Quick!" He grabbed her hand and pulled her along, trying to hurry her to his pace. "My car is a little further along; I will be going straight on to my meeting so I can run you home on the way."

They clattered to a stop by the car, threw the bags in the back and dropped into their seats, pulling the doors closed against the deluge which now thrummed on the soft top, and cascaded down the windscreen.

"Uh, you are all wet, here let me help you get your jacket off, you will be shivering."

He turned towards her as she wriggled in her seat trying to pull at the cuffs. He reached an arm across to grab the sleeve she was struggling with; she had to lean towards him to give herself enough room to pull her arm out. Their faces were very close, and he just leaned forward and started gently kissing his way across her mouth. She closed her eyes, thoughts tumbling out of their regular orbit. She was vaguely aware of them as they plummeted into freefall, and then they were lost, flaring into incandescence. He moved his left hand up to cradle her head; with his right he pulled off his tie and undid his shirt, then lifted her hand to his chest. By now he was biting along her jaw, and started kissing down her neck and round to her throat. She was sure she could hear somebody whimpering.

"It's okay, don't worry," he whispered in her ear, before kissing that too.

At the same time he slid his right hand under her tee-shirt and ran his thumb gently along a rib. She thought vaguely about now being a good moment to die, but then his fingers moved round to her spine and softly stroked up and down. Perhaps it would be worth staying alive for another minute or two then.

She was aware of the heat of his skin under her left hand and spread her fingers to take in more sensations. Oh that skin! As she felt it, she could see in her mind the colour of it, it always fascinated her so. He was pulling her closer towards him and she sensed the muscle tense beneath her fingers. He was kissing her on the lips again and …'What the hell are you doing?'

It had only been her conscious mind ending radio silence, but it may as well have been someone yelling in her ear. Her eyes flew open and she tried to speak, difficult when someone had found an alternative use for her mouth.

"No. . .don't. . .stop. . ."

"Don't worry," he was whispering again, "I won't stop."

She had her mouth free now, but it was busy gulping in air and gasping it out again. "No," she tried again "Don't. Stop."

"What?" he said, pulling his head back slightly, "Is that, don't stop? Or don't, stop."

She nodded, their faces still close enough to feel his breath on her cheek. She dropped her head forward until her hair was against his jaw and her forehead was on his shoulder. "That's definitely stop."

"Definitely?"

"Yes."

"Are you sure?"

"Yes" she whispered the last very quietly and said nothing when he rested his cheek against the top of her head.

"Why?" he asked finally.

"Because we shouldn't be doing this."

The hand she still held against his chest now applied pressure as she pushed him back and turned herself forward in her own seat again.

His voice was harsh, "Because of rules?"

"Because of decency, loyalty, promises. Pick whichever you like."

She was staring at the windscreen, but it was impossible that she saw anything through it, the water still streamed down the outside and condensation had formed on the inside. He noticed that another rain had also started to fall, quietly but profusely.

He reached for a handkerchief and gently wiped both her cheeks. He smoothed the hair away from her face; she did nothing to stop him, but remained silent as the tears kept flowing.

"Have I frightened you?"

"No," she said shaking her head slightly, "you haven't frightened me."

She had stressed the 'you', he touched her arm "What then?"

"Myself. My feelings."

She looked at him hot and dishevelled, "For goodness sake open a window before I suffocate!"

"Now what?" he asked her after a few moments of blank silence.

She was looking bleak again, "We say goodbye. You go to your meeting, I will go home."

He wasn't prepared to put up with that. He shook his head vehemently. "No, not acceptable. I am not leaving you like this. You will spend all afternoon hating yourself. Hate me if you must, but don't hate yourself."

She was crying again, "I can't hate you. I've so much enjoyed being friends with you, and now it's all a mess."

At that she put her hands over her face and gave way to real sobbing. He felt at a loss for a while, and then became exasperated. "Lucy, that's enough, it's not the end of the world. Come now. We'll talk and sort this out."

"You need to get to your meeting."

"Oh damn the meeting! It's only boring men in suits."

He pulled his 'phone out of his pocket, "Ah Maureen, yes it is I. No I'm not there yet, actually I'm in my car, and I'm going nowhere right now. Yes, you're right the rain is not helping. Can you warn them I will definitely be late. Yes, I am concerned I might not get there at all. Tell them to cancel if they prefer, I can't say how long it will take me." He put the 'phone away.

"Sneaky," she said, through her snivels.

"I'm a solicitor, okay? It's how you say things as well as what you say. And what you don't say can be just as important."

She wiped her face again, "I'm not sure there's anything even you can say to sort this lot out."

"Please, you are being melodramatic now. We will talk, sensibly if we must. We will apply logic, but we will be honest with each other and we will come to an arrangement."

"What sort of an arrangement? I'll be a good person all week, but an adulteress on Saturdays?"

He snapped at her, "I'm not aware that we have committed adultery! Did I miss something? Pity; that was the part I was looking forward to."

She gave a slight gasp. Was she shocked? There was no point dissembling, still, she was obviously not used to being in this sort of situation.

"Okay, I'm sorry you are finding this difficult, but I think you are making more of it than you need to. Tell me, why is this so terrible?"

"Because I shouldn't be doing this!"

114

"Because of your principles? I thought you didn't live in fear of doing wrong! Is this the first time this week you have done something you shouldn't?"

"Of course not, but I don't want to hurt anyone. And I could have avoided this. You have to make choices all the time, and I could have made choices that would not have ended up with us here. . .in this. . .doing that. . .uh!"

He reflected for a moment. "You mean, you should have known exactly where you would go wrong and avoided it?

"No, but I could have spotted the things that I knew would be dangerous, not put myself in their way."

"I think you really mean, not put yourself in my way, don't you?" He carefully kept the smile from breaking out on his face, she was unlikely to appreciate it.

She closed her eyes and put her head back against the rest, "Probably."

"So, you should not be friends with me, in case feelings arise which lead to actions you regret? But then you shouldn't be friends with anyone. That sounds like living in fear; I thought you wanted to get away from that."

"I know, but I could have been more honest with myself about what I was feeling, and not put myself in a situation that I couldn't resist."

"There you go again! What did you not resist? If you had not resisted by now we. . . Well, perhaps better not to finish that thought at the moment. It looked like resistance from where I was anyway."

She rolled her head sideways to look at him, "I'm sorry if you feel I led you on, I didn't mean, I mean it wasn't - I don't know what I mean."

She was so perturbed by this, her innocence was charming, in a way. "That is obvious. And you are going round in circles. I think you should stop being quite so apologetic." He grinned swiftly, "Besides, you don't need to be sorry to me, I was enjoying myself. So were you for a while."

"That's my problem!" she shouted holding her hands out in front of her imploringly.

"Ah, I see. It would be ok if you didn't enjoy it! Now I understand. All will be well if only I make it unpleasant for you."

She looked at him exasperated. "Stop taking the piss."

At least she was getting beyond helpless misery. "Yes, okay. Shall I be practical instead?" She nodded, her mouth settling into a hard line. "Okay then, stay here. I will be back in a minute. I mean it, don't you dare leave."

With that he got out of the car. He was glad the rain had almost stopped.

He returned within a few minutes, and struggled with the door, trying to juggle something in his hands. As he was getting into the car, the mobile rang in his pocket, overstretching the situation completely. He thrust two coffee cartons towards Lucy.

"Tiens!" He retrieved his 'phone and slid into his seat. "Yes Maureen. Okay. No, I don't know how long to get back from here, still no real movement. Yes, just finish what you have and go home. I will call back at the office later." He put the phone away and ran his hand over his hair. "Well, that's sorted out, and I think the woman at the coffee stall has got over her fright of a dishevelled man rushing up to demand drinks in French. She will think I am a tourist."

She turned towards him in the seat, and started sipping her drink carefully, handing him back one of them.

"Very well. Let us make a start. Don't waste your time reacting, just think and reply, okay?" This got a nod, and a glare. "First, I assume you will not have an affair with me?" She opened her mouth, saw his face and closed it again. She shook her head instead. "Okay. Second, would you like to remain friends? No, I didn't ask you for three reasons why we cannot be." She did the mouth routine once more. "Just answer the question. Would you like to be?" Her eyes were lowered to contemplate the depths of the coffee carton. Answer enough, he thought. "Okay. Let's work on that one then."

"How can we be?" she asked very quietly.

"Lucy, people get into this situation all the time. They are friends, and then one day their feelings go a bit further. They find themselves too close and they must deal with it. They have to decide what they will do. You've already taken the hard decision. You have said we will not have an affair. I can't make you, it does take two. Now we know we are attracted to one another we don't need to play games. We can be sensible about what we do or don't do. In some ways it means it's easier." He received a frown, as she stirred the froth on her coffee with her finger. "I think, if you are honest, you will admit that what makes you feel so bad is embarrassment. You did not want me to know that you felt that way. Is that not so?" She didn't need to answer this one; she wasn't even raising her eyes. He put his finger under her chin and lifted her face. "Why should I think less of you for having the same sort of feelings for me as I do for you?"

She blinked a few times, "I don't know. It seems different, perhaps because you're single, so you can fancy anyone you like. But I'm married, so I should be faithful."

"That's very naïve, to equate being faithful with not desiring anyone else."

"Yes."

"Good, you're being honest again."

"You know, sometimes you really annoy me."

"I expect so. Like it or not, we have become quite close. We speak to each other like we would to few other people. We are bound to stir up strong feelings of all kinds; we just have to learn to cope."

"Or stay apart."

"That's denial."

"No, pretending this never happened would be denial. Neither of us is doing that. We're disagreeing about what's the best thing to do next."

They both drank coffee for a while in silence. He decided risk was the safest policy. "If you said you never wanted to see me again, I would be hurt."

"You might be hurt if we keep seeing each other. You might be hurt every time."

"You mean because we don't make love? Please, I am a man of honour, not a teenage boy!" She smiled at that. "What is funny?"

"Just you, doing the whole Count of Monte Cristo thing again. And I wasn't implying you couldn't keep your hands to yourself, I meant hurt in all kinds of ways. We would say certain things, then wonder if it could be taken the wrong way, wince at a every double entendre, all that sort of thing."

"But that is my point. If we know this, then we can take care. We can laugh at every double entendre instead, or say something kind. Friends hurt each other all the time, but they say sorry and try again."

She stared at him for several seconds before dropping her gaze, "Yes, that's true, or should be. But in practice many friendships fail because of hurt."

"And you're not convinced we can manage it?" She shook her head. "Why?"

"Because, this feels like more than friendship. There is a level of intimacy between us that goes beyond what I have with other friends."

"Are they all the same, these other friends? Do you feel the same about all of them?"

She picked up immediately on where this was going, "No, obviously I'm closer to some than to others."

"Then how do you know I am not your closest friend?"

The tears started again then, just slowly. "Close friends comfort each other. It would be hard for you to comfort me when you are currently the source of my discomfort."

"That is true. But maybe you think too narrowly."

He sat still for a while, put his coffee down, turned to her, brushed the tears off her cheeks with his thumbs and kissed her gently on the forehead.

"Did that feel like I was trying to seduce you?"

"No" she whispered.

"Was it comforting?"

"Yes."

"There, then you must decide if you want my friendship. It would be unkind of me to force you to say yes. And I can see it will give you problems, but problems are there to be solved. Will you think about it?"

"Yes."

He nodded, smiling, "Okay. Now I had better take you home. Then I'll go back to the office and pretend to be a solicitor for a while."

He drove her home and walked her to the front door. "Look at me." She turned her face up to him. "Promise me you will not sit there and go through it all in your head blaming yourself."

"Okay, I promise."

He held her eyes for a while, searching them to see if there was any chance she meant this. Finally he nodded, not convinced, but hopeful. "I will leave you to think about what we said. I will wait for you to contact me and tell me your answer. But I do expect you to make contact, not just avoid me. Yes?"

She nodded. He bent and kissed both cheeks, by now it must be familiar to her. There was no adverse reaction. "Au revoir."

"Au revoir," she replied.

Four hours later she was at the keyboard again, hoping by now, it might suggest what she could write. She couldn't avoid e-mailing him; he would think there was something wrong straightaway. No, not true, it was already Friday afternoon; she'd forgotten that in the heat of her dilemma. Even that phrase made her shudder. Stick to calm thinking! She had sent a quick message this morning, they were several hours ahead. He wouldn't be able to get to the e-mails again until Monday morning. She had time to think about this and decide what, if anything, she said. And that meant she could also think about how to handle it from here, and then she would be writing, having dealt with it already. Yes, that was the way forward.

Walking round the room, touching objects at random and looking out of the window, she thought back to the previous Friday. Easy steps to adultery? She certainly felt she could accuse herself of taking them, even if she hadn't trod the last few paces. After all, to think it was as bad as to commit it. Was it, though? Was there no lightening of the sentence for having stopped short, let's be honest, a reasonable way before the end? And she hadn't set out to do that. Had he? No, she didn't think so. Obviously the whole idea wasn't as repellent to him anyway, but it hadn't been a trap. It happened to other people all the time, he'd said. Just an inevitable progression of where they had found themselves going. But she wasn't other people, and this sort of thing did not happen to her, not until now. She was angry with herself for having been so stupid, but realised she was angry too with men, yes quite possibly all men, for their part in this mess! She dropped into the chair again in front of the computer, staring at the dormant screen, seeing instead the re-run of this afternoon's flight over enemy territory. How could she look either man in the face again? Tears started, she let them flow unchecked until she realised they were dripping into the keyboard and she leapt up with an expletive.

Throughout the weekend, she vacillated between stern annoyance and seeping self-pity. The end result was a blanket misery for which she was forced to find a string of semi-credible excuses when in company. She was avoiding the latter as much as possible, but found the alternative almost as trying. And still she didn't know what to tell Tom.

After lunch on Sunday she found herself out in the garden, struggling with one climber that grew like a monster. She needed to cut it back every couple of months and it was due again now. Its growth was prodigious and so was the energy required to tackle it. The day was slightly overcast, if not she wouldn't have attempted it, but even so she was sweating with the struggle. At least there was satisfaction in hacking off whole branches and chopping long unwanted stems out of it. Therapeutic, she decided, working some of her misery and frustration out. Even when branches slipped out of her sweat-slicked grasp to slap her in the face, it felt better to have a physical struggle than the mental one she'd agonised over. A straightforward simple task seemed relaxing by comparison. By the time it was tamed and put firmly back in its place she was able to sit and enjoy a mug of tea and turn her mind back to the e-mail she needed to write.

'I have to say the meeting with Luckers presented me with as many challenges and questions as it did answers. It's extra money of course, but it's also at the edge of my capabilities. I may well tell them it's just too big a job.

Yes, I did see Farine afterwards. His reaction was different to mine; he's used to operating in a different league though. Actually, as we've spent more time together recently, one or two radical differences in our approach to life have become apparent. Well, that shouldn't surprise me, should it? Anyway, I do find myself wondering how this friendship will go; maybe it will peter out soon.

Is it still terrifically hot? You always used to manage the heat much better than me, but I've been enjoying the sunny days we've had recently, perhaps we're changing places. Although I suppose it's not the same kind of temperatures that you're experiencing.'

She paused, reading back over the critical section. Fraud, she was being deliberately circumspect, but that couldn't be helped. Now was not the time to tell him what had transpired. His last couple of e-mails had sounded wistful. It wouldn't help him to read about a situation he could only wonder about from afar. She went back to typing cheerful and domestic things.

'And I wrestled with that brute in the top corner this afternoon. You should have seen the mess I made! I won though.'

Her fingers carried on reporting, her mind strayed to the next struggle she had to face, time to get to grips with her dithering thoughts. Perhaps a bit of vicious pruning was just the treatment they needed too.

12

By Monday morning she was ready for action again. A different kind of action, it was true. Finally, she had convinced herself of what she must do, and then spent another two hours debating how to communicate it. She couldn't risk contacting him by e-mail, as far as she knew that was open-access within the office. Any text message would be too terse, but she felt the need for more distance than a personal call. Chances were, he would be with a client. If she called his mobile she should get his voice mail. Providing she had a message ready, she could deliver that and run. Finally she snatched up her 'phone and called him, heart thumping. She was in luck, the beep came, and she started her message.

"I think you're right, we need to talk. I would suggest neutral ground, but I don't feel any bar or café would be private enough. If you're happy with the idea, I think it's best for you to come here this evening for an hour or so, just so we get things straight. How about eight? If this arrangement doesn't suit, please let me know."

She clicked her phone off and sat down, letting go of the tension that had crept into her arms and neck. After that she attempted to do some work, but it wasn't very successful. Her heart started racing again when she heard a text arrive later in the afternoon; it said simply that he would be there. She was relieved, but also terrified. Not of him, but of the effect he had on her. Everything was quite clear in her mind right now, but inevitably he would take charge of any argument and reduce her to a feeling of inadequacy or triviality. She swallowed, what was the matter with her? He wasn't going to beat her over the head, was he? Thoroughly annoyed with herself, she went out to vent some frustration on more weeds. They, at least, couldn't answer back.

Pouring water into the kettle and the espresso pot, she went over again in her head the things she really wanted to say. Stay calm, she told herself, you're an adult, you can do this. Strangely, she felt her daughter, half her age, would tackle it better than she would. The doorbell rang; she wiped her palms down the side of her shorts once more, before opening the door.

They sat on either side of the kitchen table, drinks placed neatly in front of them. Lucy looked uncomfortable, but he hadn't expected anything else. She looked as if she were gathering herself ready for some great leap.

"I have thought about what you said, and I want you to know that I have really enjoyed your friendship..."

He raised one eyebrow, and she faltered. He prompted her, "But. . ."

"But I think it is more sensible if we don't see each other, socially, any more. Obviously we both have professional obligations to each other, and I would have thought that we are capable of fulfilling those."

"The professional is not in question, only our personal involvement."

"Yes, well, now you know what I think about that."

"Because?"

She bit her lip and then looked back at him, "Because I don't see how we can carry on as friends after what happened, and I'm not prepared to carry on as anything else."

"You have already told me the latter; I think you should give me your reasons for the former."

She looked at him bewildered. Had she expected him to nod quietly and leave?

"I'm sorry if this isn't sophisticated enough for you, or very well presented, I don't do it very often." Her tone had sharpened as her eyes narrowed.

"Lucy, one of the things I like about you is your honesty. There has been something very warm and open about it. Right now you sound as if you are reading a script someone has written for you. What are you really thinking?"

"I've just told you."

"No. You say you are not sophisticated, but you're trying to be, trying to hide what you really feel. To be urbane is to present a front to the world. Why do you think I like you so much? I have become closer to you in a few weeks then to some people over many years. You let me into your world, not just the parts you think are public. I have few friends like that; can you blame me for wanting to hold on to you? I have not had such closeness except with lovers before, not surprising that I automatically think of that as the next step. For me anyway, the boundary between friends and lovers is more fluid than for you. You want a fixed line, that's the difference."

"I can't help that. I know my morality seems outdated and unrealistic to you, but that's part of me."

"I have no objection to it. But you cannot ask me to think the same."

"I don't expect you to! I've never said that. All I'm asking you to do is accept that those are my values and allow me to act accordingly. That's why we can't be friends."

"Can you not be friends with me because you will molest me all the time? As flattering as it is to think I am irresistible, I hardly think that is the truth. And if you are so frustrated by the lack of your husband, you had better stay away from all men, or you will be in constant trouble."

She looked as though he had struck her, rather than merely remonstrating. Tears were already wetting her cheeks. She leant forward putting both hands to her forehead, soon he saw drips fall from her wrists and spill onto the table.

Her voice, which had been winding higher, now came out low and indistinct. "How dare you speak to me like that?"

"What, you mean speak honestly? I thought that's what you preferred."

"Why are you doing this? Do you get some kind of kick out of it? Do you enjoy seeing me reduced to tears?"

"No," he said very quietly, "I am not willing to give up something I value without a fight. Do you not value our friendship?"

She banged her palm down on the table, "Well, how do you know what it is? If I'm in the state you suggest, I might just be using you to fill in while Tom's away? Lonely, frustrated, what else can you think of?"

"I think that would worry you more than me, if it were true. You have taken very little from me, but you have been willing to give me a great deal. All friends, or lovers, are for a given time. Of course, if your husband were here you would not spend time with me like this. In that case we would have enjoyed a few meetings over work and that would be the end of it. But we do have this time. It is up to us what we do with it."

She said nothing. He got up to bring her a glass of water and something to wipe her face. She accepted them automatically. She blinked several times and tried to look at him, but ended up with her head in her hands again.

He sat down, speaking more softly now. "I think you torment yourself. You keep trying to work out how to get everything right. Instead of just seeing what happens and dealing with problems when they arise."

"Well, of course. If I don't take care to see where the dangers are, I'm just going to walk straight into them, like on Friday," Her words started strong, but tailed away.

"I disagree. By worrying, you get all tense, and you try to take responsibility for my feelings and actions as well as your own. It's not possible. Please just deal with your own self and what is actually happening, not what you fear might happen."

"You always manage to turn my head inside out. I knew exactly what I thought before you came. Now I don't know what I'm doing."

Good, she was giving ground, time to press home the advantage. "Have we had fun together? I mean before this upset."

She nodded, "You know we have."

"Have I made you do anything you didn't want to?"

She shook her head, "Apart from this."

"Has being together made life more or less enjoyable for you?"

"You know the answer to that."

"Then let's get on with it. We don't need to agonise about it."

"But how can we? When we might...." She wafted a hand, giving up on vocals.

"Stray over your line?"

She nodded.

"You just have to say, that's all. It's as easy as that. I don't find it embarrassing or difficult. You can say when you are not comfortable with something. Really."

She rubbed her hand back and forth across her forehead.

"Well, that's okay as long as it's you crossing the line, but what if it's me?" Her face flushed and she closed her eyes, groaning slightly. "I can't believe I'm having this conversation. I hardly know you, yet we're discussing the rules of engagement for a relationship. What next?" She managed to open her eyes again.

"I think you do know me, otherwise you wouldn't feel comfortable saying that."

"Right now I'm so far out of my comfort zone I've forgotten what it looks like. This is like no friendship I've ever had before."

"Nor I. Exciting isn't it?"

"Scary."

"Is there anything exciting that isn't also frightening? There is always risk with excitement."

"I'm not good with risk."

"But you said you wanted to be adventurous."

"I knew I'd regret that!"

"Yes, very probably. Too late I'm afraid." He had resisted quoting back to her any more of her declarations from a braver moment. It paid off; he was rewarded with a tentative smile. Very fragile, not one to treat carelessly. He waited.

"How did we get here? To this I mean."

He shrugged, "Does it matter?"

"Only to my sanity, and that appears to be an expendable commodity at the moment."

After a pause, Lucy said she felt the need of something stronger than tea. She got out a bottle of Pernod, and they both had some, taking it in the native style. He felt that was a good step forward and picked up the momentum.

"While we are dealing with these matters, I need to be honest with you too."

She looked up at him over her glass, with some apprehension. "Yes?"

"If we are staying friends, then I don't want this English distance between us. We greet each other properly. I don't want you flinching every time I touch you, wondering if I will do something wrong. If you don't feel something is right, or it makes things awkward, you say so, okay?"

She nodded.

"And you can always tell me if things are getting difficult for you."

Her eyes widened and she almost choked, breathing in the fumes of the pastis too fast and stinging her throat.

He gave her a moment to find her composure again. "Anything else? You might as well say now anything that is troubling you."

She shrugged. "I still think we might be kidding ourselves. If I could talk about this to any of my friends, I know they would say I was being stupid. I would say I was being stupid."

He replied slowly, "It is interesting that you do not tell them then. You think they would disapprove. So I think you have kept silent because you know already that you do want to remain friends with me."

"Or, I haven't told them because I'm ashamed of what I'm doing! And we're going round in circles. You know I like to spend time with you, I doubt the wisdom of it, that's all."

Match point. "No," he smiled broadly, "It is not sensible. Not at all. Will sensible Lucy Cottonwood dare to be with a dangerous character like Farine du Blez?"

"Now you're making fun of me."

"Oh yes."

He took a long look at her, almost as fascinated by why he found it so hard to let her go as by why she struggled so much. It was definitely game over, but sometimes at this point he became aware that the winning had been the prize he wanted. She was going to do the reasoning it out now, he could see from her face. That was okay, this odd combination of rational and passionate was quite appealing. Something women usually found difficult in him. She looked up.

"There are lots of things about this I can't get my head round. I can't promise that I won't go all wobbly again. You say just get on with it and see what happens, but actually that might involve me having fits of self-loathing, or times when I really don't want to see you. Or, in a week I might tell you to get lost altogether."

He gave another shrug, "None of us can say what things will be like a week from now. I keep trying to tell you, everything is a risk."

"I really don't understand why you're doing this, what's in it for you?"

He sighed, "I thought I had explained that. You are not dull-witted, why do you wish me to go through it again?"

"I don't know; I'm just struggling to make any sense out of it all. I'm used to being the one who's solving problems, not creating them. And I'm certainly not used to finding out I'm an object of desire! You're several years younger than me for heaven's sake."

"What has that got to do with it? It's only a few years; besides, I once had a lover twice my age. She was certainly older than you are now. Older than my mother in fact."

"Aaargh! Way too much information," she groaned, putting her hands over her ears.

He laughed, "You're such a peculiar mix of naïve and wise, that's certainly part of why I like you."

She got up and ran another glass of water. Then she started spluttering into it and had to sit down again, coughing.

"Are you alright?" he asked.

"Yes, just overcome by hysteria, I've run out of reasonable reactions. I'm reaching for the distinctly unreasonable now."

"There you are, another reason, I like the way you make fun of yourself."

"I'll bear it in mind for when I next have to write my CV. 'Can laugh at dire circumstances' – that should be a winner."

128

She put her left hand up to her head and rubbed it. "And that's something else that annoys me!" she announced suddenly.

"What?" he was mystified.

"You can see very easily when I'm embarrassed; I can't tell when you are. That's not fair."

"Well, if you want to know you'll have to put your hand to my cheek and feel if it's hot. But it won't help you much."

"Why?"

"I don't get embarrassed every five minutes like you do.

"Uh, great!"

He regarded her calmly, one reaction she hadn't mastered yet. She looked at him and away again several times.

Finally she sighed, "Well then, are we going to sit here looking at each other all evening monitoring my embarrassment or what?"

"I think," he replied quietly, "that is up to you, non?"

"Let's go out then, at least for a walk or something."

"Together?"

She pulled a face, "No, you go first and I'll follow you in five minutes. Of course together!"

He stood up smiling to himself and within a couple of minutes they were walking up the road and heading for the downs.

'Hi again. The hot weather has continued here – had a look on the internet to check yours, certainly more consistent than ours! Are you feeling any more comfortable with it yet? Jenny's getting quite a tan. I think they're making the most of the sunshine; they keep going over to Cheddar to climb in the gorge. I suppose it's a bit of a treat after climbing indoors all winter.

You're right I'm still friends with Farine, my predictions were wrong there. I think my French would horrify him, so not sure your suggestions about getting some tuition would go down well. He did once comment on my accent – not impressed for some reason! Can't think why.

How long is this extra trip going to take? Is it predictable anyway? Or will it depend on what you find when you get there? I suppose you're going to tell me you will have no e-mail access for a while, I looked it up, seems pretty remote. But feel free to put me right and tell me they have a well-equipped base. Haha. Chance would be a fine thing.

Is it getting frustrating? The unpredictability I mean. You sounded pretty fed up with it. You may be used to working out in different countries, including developing ones, but don't forget you're also used to having corporate bucks behind you. Any charity just isn't going to have that clout is it? Take some comfort in the fact that they're doing a good job with what they've got (I'm quoting Tom Cottonwood there, by the way!) and that you're helping them to improve. Sermon over. What else can I tell you?'

She read through, wondering what other bits of news there were, and decided the latest story of a shopkeeper being beaten up on his own doorstep was better left out. Maybe he would feel more cheerful after his fact-finding tour. She couldn't deny the feeling of guilt that crept round the back of her mind when she compared his current life with hers. In one sense, he'd signed up for these difficulties, but by definition the unknown always took you by surprise. In the same way, her decision to continue her 'extra-mural friendship' as she called it, gave rise to some fairly unusual challenges of her own, some of which she certainly hadn't been expecting.

Over the course of the next two weeks she discovered that Farine had been right. She was tempted to hate him on those grounds alone. However, it did mean things were easier than she had expected. They had met for lunch several times and continued to meet for a drink after work occasionally. They were out on a walk again together now, something else that happened regularly. She had felt tentative at first, but they had both been perfectly civilised and had kept away from situations that she might have considered inadvisable. They had got so used to having each other's company that she had to admit, it would be very difficult now to cease suddenly. And it was a friendship they both seemed to have settled into with ease. It was at those precise moments though, when it started to feel comfortable and normal, that she would suddenly get a rush of nerves and pull back from him in her mind.

They had wandered onto the suspension bridge, and were leaning on the parapet looking down at the evening lights coming on in the city. Suddenly Lucy shivered and looked down at her feet for a moment.

"Are you cold? It is quite warm."

"No, not cold, just remembering."

"What?"

She looked sideways at him and tried to shrug it off, "Our Mad Five Minutes. It has to be said with capitals I feel, although the abbreviation MFM is acceptable. Every now and then it haunts me. It's getting better, gradually." She felt very pleased with herself for being capable of referring to it without disappearing down a vortex of horror and remorse

"Oh I remember it too. Though probably, I think about it differently to you."

The smile stayed on his face, and she grimaced to herself. Okay, not all that capable then. "Yes, well, forget I mentioned it, that's quite enough of that."

He was enjoying the chance to tease her too much, and turned towards her, leaning on the stonework.

"For all you know, I'm saying penances for it."

"Good, that makes me feel better," but she said it with her eyes closed.

"Do you do that a lot?"

"What?" she asked, startled into opening her eyes again.

"Make designations for things, like the MFM."

"Oh yes, all the time. And people."

"Tell me some."

She pulled the corners of her mouth down, "Well, it's quite hard to think of any on the spot like that." After a moment she asked, "Do you remember Mr Featherstone, the awkward client?" He nodded. "Well, I think of him as Our Little Problem, although the 'our' in this case is the royal plural. And then there's Vanessa of course." As soon as she'd said it, she blushed, although she couldn't think of a reason why.

"Do you mean my friend Vanessa?"

"Mmm."

"Well, what is she?"

"Nothing horrendous, but I have to call her The Magnificent Vanessa in my head."

"Yes, that's good, very fitting. And Carl?"

"Afraid he's stick-man, not very kind, is it?"

"No, but understandable. I don't think he's so featureless when he talks about his music. What am I?"

"You're you, no designation needed."

"Is that good or bad?" he asked quietly, reaching out to tuck her hair behind her ear.

She shrugged, "It just means I know you too well to package you like that, and leave my hair alone." She gave him what she hoped was a pointed look, and he turned back towards the river.

After a few moments' quiet he spoke again. "Would you like the chance to come up with some more little titles? For my friends, I mean." She looked inquisitive and he went on, "I have been invited to another party tomorrow night. Why don't you come with me?"

"I don't know your friends."

"That is because you have not met them. If you did, then you would! Faultless logic, hein?"

She gave a little snort, "I'm not terribly good at parties, especially when I don't know anyone."

"I don't believe you, and anyway you know me. Probably The Magnificent Vanessa and her Stick-man will be there too."

"Don't you dare say that to their faces!"

"Of course not. What do you think I am? Honestly Lucy." He paused, "Although, of course, I might find myself saying it and getting you into trouble. If you were there, you could keep an eye on me." She narrowed her eyes and glared at him, but failed to come up with any smart response. "You know, you are out of practise with your glaring. You had better

132

spend more time with me; I will give you plenty of opportunities to use it."

He was laughing loudly by now, and she was wondering what she'd done to get him in this mood. "What on earth has come over you? You're always so cool and impassive. This is a Farine I don't know."

He stood very close to her, "Always cool and impassive?"

"Okay, not always," she said it through gritted teeth and frozen lips.

He leaned down until his forehead just rested against hers for a moment. Next second he'd taken her hand and turned her round. "Let's move."

They walked quickly for a while, so quickly she was almost jogging, and consequently out of breath.

"Will you come with me then?"

"What sort of party is it?"

He shrugged and pulled a face, "Just a party, the usual sort. In someone's house. Probably quite a lot of people and quite a lot of wine. Loud music, dancing. What else is there to say about parties?"

"Well, there's whether it's a smart party or not. The kind of things people will be wearing. Important stuff like that."

"Oh, important to women you mean."

"Funnily enough, it's a woman you've asked to go with you."

"Okay. Not smart, not evening dress or anything. Just wear something you like wearing, that you feel good in."

"Alright then. What time?"

"I'll pick you up at eight-thirty. We can walk; it's not very far from where you live."

She nodded. In truth, she was fascinated to meet more of his friends and see what they were like. Maybe it would be worth putting up with the agonies of being somewhere she didn't expect to fit in for the interest value.

13

She had spoken to Vanessa, who was actually quite amusing to talk to, but definitely still Magnificent. She was surprised that the other woman had been so friendly towards her, like they were old friends, and had drawn her in to the conversation with some other friends. By now though, she was feeling a bit out of it again. Vanessa and the latest arrivals became deeply engrossed in a discussion regarding some music. Lucy allowed herself to drift away and by default gravitated towards the drinks table.

She could see dark hair moving above and beyond other heads. It caused the pressure of recognition in her mind, even before the face emerged into a gap between two people leaning apart to laugh. The dark head bent to examine the bottles on the table, but Lucy had already let out an involuntary gasp. The features, still easily recognisable, bore the evidence of an attempt to rearrange them. One eye must have been fully black; it had now faded to green-yellow. Various cuts and grazes were scattered across the rest of his countenance, half of the mouth was still swollen.

Forgetting dislike, and probably manners, she pushed between intervening bodies until she was next to him.

"Mr. Brogan, whatever's happened to you?"

His head turned, "Oh hello, up you pop again, eh? I had a little disagreement with someone, nothing to worry about."

"It doesn't look like nothing. Are you sure you're alright?"

"I will be when I find something worth drinking. Pass me that one, will you? The Barossa, yeah thanks."

Lucy complied but continued to stare. He took a long pull at the wine he'd poured. "You're very concerned for my welfare. Wouldn't have thought I was your type, darlin'. Not if you're with the ever-so-suave Mister du Blez. I take it he's here too?"

Her face darkened. She wished she hadn't come across. It seemed this was not the first drink he'd enjoyed, and it was following on fast from whatever had gone before.

"Well, I'm sorry to intrude. You'll have to forgive me for appearing nosey. I just thought I would commiserate on your appalling bad luck, first your shop, now this." She turned to go, irritated at having wasted her sympathy on such an undeserving individual. But something clicked in her brain and she turned back with a sharp whisper, "It was you!"

"There you go again. Enigmatic statements every time. What was me?"

"The nameless shopkeeper found beaten up in his own doorway. It isn't bad luck, is it? It's a vendetta! Whatever's happening?"

He looked at her, eyes shining like pebbles under shifting water, "What do you know?" He took hold of her elbow, so tightly it caused a sharp intake of breath.

"What?"

"How do you know about this?"

"It was in the paper! It doesn't take a lot of working out, does it?" Her own voice had been a low growl in reply to his, and she summoned a look black enough to match.

People were turning slightly, frowns on faces at the animosity being transmitted. He eased his grip and put his wine glass down. Slowly, he leant forward taking his weight onto his hands.

"I'm sorry. That was disgraceful of me." One hand went up to rub across his brow. "Forgive me, please." The hand was extended now to touch lightly the arm he'd gripped so fiercely. "I confess to being a little paranoid at the moment. And I have to assume you're right about what's happening. But I would prefer you to keep that to yourself. I'm trying to resolve it."

She nodded, silent in incomprehension about such matters.

He pushed the wine glass further away, "I'm tired and I'm drinking too much. Not quite the polished gentleman you're currently keeping company with. Where is Farine? Maybe I should say hello. Some of his polish might rub off on me, eh?"

She wasn't sure what to reply, but never got the chance. A man she had never met before suddenly interposed himself between them.

"Sorry for butting in, hope you don't mind." He turned with a beaming smile to Brogan, who shrugged, and then back to Lucy, hand offered for her to shake.

"I'm Guy, one of Farine's running friends. I've been trying to get hold of you all evening to say hello. He's told me so much about you."

By the time she had mustered polite responses to the cheerful man stationed right in front of her, Brogan had slipped away. She tried to focus on Guy instead of the man he had occluded.

"Told you what exactly?"

"Not a lot, to be honest. But it looked like your previous chat needed interrupting. I apologise if I spoiled a deep and meaningful conversation."

"No, you didn't ruin anything of value. He is somewhat baffling."

"From where I was standing, it looked more like threatening."

"Odd, definitely. I don't know him well enough to judge beyond that. Are you really a friend of Farine's?"

"Yes, that and the running are genuine. We usually get together four or five times a week, along with Angus."

"Oh, is he the one in the Crown Prosecution Service?"

"That's right. We try and spur each other on with training. Now we're no longer young studs, it helps to keep off the flab."

"Well, I haven't met Angus yet, but neither you nor Farine hardly qualify as podgy!"

"Ah good, it's working then. I'm glad to know we're getting something right."

She allowed her smile to fade before asking, "So, is this the once-over?"

"Good Lord, no. I'm hardly his minder, just interested. He's one of a kind, sometimes I think he ends up a bit lonely. It's fascinating to see who makes him happy."

"I'm thinking of making a placard. It might say: I'm someone else's wife; this isn't what you think; we get on well."

"That's up to the two of you, really, isn't it?"

Just then Farine joined them, apologising for getting caught up so long with another group of long-absent friends. As he was chattering, Lucy found herself scanning the room for Brogan, but he seemed to have disappeared totally. The crush around the drinks table increased again and Lucy pleaded for some air. The three of them moved outside, picking up Angus en route. Introductions were made, and Lucy found herself facing a ginger-haired Scot with tiny metal-rimmed glasses and a cheeky smile. Somehow it made her smile too.

"You're a long way from home."

"Not lived there for over twenty-five years."

"You've kept the accent though."

"Oh yes, part and parcel. You were with Farine when that bomb-blast occurred, weren't you?"

"Yes, I was. Pretty damn scary I have to say. Have the police got anyone in their sights for that yet?"

"Not that I've heard. I'm sure word would have gone round if they had."

"The guy who owns the shop is here tonight. Did you know?"

"No, I'd no idea. You'll have to point him out to me."

"As he's sporting a fair number of fading bruises, I don't think you can miss him."

Angus made a face and was about to ask more when Guy's wife appeared asking after Angus' family. There was general talk for a while and Lucy found herself fading away again from all these people who were very pleasant but meant nothing to her. Their only connection was through one man, who for a little while allowed his trajectory to stray between their differing orbits. She was feeling herself an observer of these other worlds, standing apart and peering down a telescope of faint connection. Through its lens she saw Farine talking to his friends, laughing and joking with them. She felt strangely pleased, glad that he had like minds to share at least some of his life with. Currently, Angus was complaining that he, being the shortest by a long way, actually ran twice as fast to cover the distance in the same time as Farine. Laughter faded and they moved on to discussing the week ahead, concluding that before work running sessions would be more desirable while it was so hot.

"Where do you go?" asked Lucy.

"Just on the downs, like most people," put in Guy.

"Yeah, that's where I jog too," she said.

"Join us then," offered Angus.

She shook her head, "No way. You lot sound serious, I'm just a bumbler."

"I'll be lucky to make it at all this week." Everyone looked to Angus at that. "I have a big case coming to court, a murder. And I have some less than ideal witnesses to prepare."

Naturally, the others were keen to hear what details Angus could safely share. People round about, including a small group perched on stools nearby, turned to listen, their interest caught by the word usually restricted to headlines. Lucy noticed straightaway that this was where Chris Brogan had been hiding, albeit unintentionally. He had rendered himself invisible by the simple means of sitting down. Angus, aware of the extra audience shifted topics quickly. His eyes had swept over the surrounding throng listening in, opened fractionally when traversing the battered individual, and then tracked straight to Lucy. She had given a tiny nod and his attention went back to his friends, responding to further height-related teasing. He must be used to censoring what he could talk about in public, she thought, like Farine. Except of course, murder was generally more salacious than purloined designs. Suddenly she felt tired. Tired of the ridiculous human habit of hurting others to get what you wanted. Tired of standing and talking, when she'd rather be walking or resting. Just tired. She looked around, no empty seats. It was as busy out here as it was in the house. But there was some sort of raised flower bed at the end of the terrace. The wall around it looked eminently suitable as a perch right now. She wandered along, glad to withdraw from the throng, and take a rest. She closed her eyes, shutting out this world of alien company; breathing their air required extended politeness and she was tired of that too.

Farine looked around. She'd done it again, disappeared. Trying to dissociate herself from him, or just stay away from people in general? Maybe she was making a point that she felt out of place here and would rather be somewhere else. Well, she could have always hung on to him more, stayed glued to his side. No, that wasn't likely. Suddenly guilt tinged his thinking. He didn't mind what people thought was going on between them. But she was married, and despite their dismissal of other people's expectations, it would matter if word got round that she was being free with her affections. Perhaps he should find her and see if she would prefer to leave. Find her: that was the first part. He set off to weave a course between bodies but his passage was suddenly interrupted by one unfolding from a seat in his way. He was taken aback momentarily by the by the state of the face, but before he could comment the other man was initiating engagement.

"Hello there, Farine. You don't mind if I use your first name, do you? This is a social occasion after all."

A slight inclination of the head was all Farine was prepared to give; he didn't even want to waste breath on this individual.

"I get the distinct impression you don't like me. That's not very friendly, is it now? What have I ever done to you?"

This last question was posed very softly, somehow loading it with even more import by its very lack of emphasis.

Farine felt himself drop automatically into work mode, face stilling to immobility, mind racing on to get ahead of his mouth. "I'm sorry you feel that Mr. Brogan. I can only say in my defence that I work with hundreds of clients. I tend to assume they will not all wish to be close companions when their cases are closed." He gave a smile, as insincere as the one on the face opposite.

"But they don't all turn up at parties and restaurants where you and your girlfriend are, surely? It wouldn't hurt you to pass the time of day now, would it?"

"Of course not, and I apologise if you think my manners have been lacking. I wasn't aware I was avoiding you, I didn't even realise you were here. Perhaps we just don't have enough in common to overlap very frequently."

"Oh I don't know. Maybe we have too much in common. Maybe that's a problem to you, one you've decided to knock out of your way."

The man must be off his head. "I'm sorry Mr. Brogan, you've lost me. I can't say I'm aware of any area of conflict between us. We're not in the same line of business. We can hardly be competitors.

"Well, who can say? I guess that depends on exactly what you're involved with and who your associates are."

"You know exactly what my business is, having had the benefit of my services. If there's something bothering you, I think you should make it plain. I wouldn't want it to cause the kind of trouble you've obviously been in recently."

"Don't think I can't look after myself. You're not the only who can dole out the strong-arm stuff. I suggest you think about your own safety. Clifton doesn't appear to be quite the civilised area you'd imagine."

What was he referring to? At the restaurant? Brogan moved to push past Farine, knocking in to him pointedly. He took a step sideways, robbing the gesture of its force and creating a space for the Irishman to depart.

He found her on the low garden wall and she waited while he brought her another glass of wine.

"Mmm, lovely, thank you. Farine, who do your friends think I am?"

"You have heard me introduce you to them. You are Lucy, my web-site designer with whom I have become friends."

"Hmm. I get the feeling a back story has been written, and I'm beginning to think I'm an idiot for having come here with you."

"Why do you say that?"

"Come on! You know very well what they're all thinking. Coming to a party together like this is pretty much a 'couples' thing."

He shook his head, "I can point out several people who have come together very definitely not 'in a relationship' as you would say."

"How come I'm being scrutinised so carefully then? They all seem fascinated by me. And I'm fairly sure it's not because of my glittering personality."

He shrugged, then leant forward resting his arms across his knees, "I thought we were concerned with what we know, not what other people think."

"Easier said than done! People talk, they don't always take a lot of care about what they repeat."

"Well, this isn't the first time I've been to a party with a woman that I'm not having an affair with. On the other hand I have to be honest with you and say that it is the first time that the secret I'm keeping to myself is that I am not her lover! That is a novelty."

"Mmm, thought it was something like that."

They stayed put and drank their wine in silence for a while. The light was beginning to fade. Lucy adored these summer evenings and was happy to stay outside and watch a few stars appear while she cooled off. Others continued to drift in and out of the house, coming out to get some air for a while and then return for more wine or food. Suddenly one of Lucy's favourite songs came on, her feet started tapping automatically. There was a reasonable amount of space at this end of the patio and Farine pulled her to her feet saying, "Let's dance then!"

She was not in the least bit surprised that his sense of rhythm was excellent. From what she remembered of the Somali people, dancing was a huge part of their culture, so his mother would have passed that on by genes and by practice.

He had absolutely no trouble coping with the informal sliding, shuffling variety of dance she had learnt in her youth. Neither did a cha-cha present him with any problems when she moved into that. Suddenly another woman, Guy's wife appeared, begging him to give her a dance too, as Guy had refused. Farine looked at Lucy enquiringly; she nodded and left them to enjoy a particularly energetic song. She took the chance to sit down again for a breather and to indulge in a spot more observation.

A well-manicured, well-dressed woman came and sat down close to her. Lucy looked round in surprise; they hadn't been introduced. She had no time to even think of a soubriquet to substitute for her unknown name.

"So, you're the reason our lovely Farine has had such a spring in his step lately. Quite literally at the moment, I see. I must say we've all been dying to find out the cause." ·

Lucy felt colour rise to her face, and she thought it best to say nothing.

"What's your special input into his life then, hm?"

"I think you're under some kind of misapprehension. Farine and I are good friends, that's all. We met through business." She spoke quietly, and was careful to pronounce his name properly, something the other woman seemed to struggle with.

"Oh, how quaint! Well, you can play miss innocent if you like, but that metallic noise you hear behind you is the sound of knives being sharpened."

Lucy could do nothing now but stare.

"I'm warning you for your own good. Take a look around sweetheart. How many of the women here who haven't been in Farine's bed, wouldn't fight tooth and claw to get there? There are very few, I can tell you!"

Apart from affronted, Lucy was also aware of a volcanic mix of fury and derision building inside her. When she opened her mouth, a froth of incredulous laughter was blown out ahead of the words.

"Really? Strange, but I've never thought of any man as an object to be fought over. And I'm sure Farine is more than capable of making up his own mind about what he wants."

The woman lowered her lashes and tipped her head back to sneer down at Lucy.

"Oh yes, you can be sure Farine will take what he wants, and he'll leave what he's not interested in. His tastes run to the refined, that's well known."

With that she stood up and walked away, although when Lucy thought back to that moment later on, she had to describe it to herself as 'sashayed'. She wasn't sure if that was accurate or not, as she had never had to use that word about anyone before.

She was still feeling somewhat stung, and hollow, following her brief eruption, staring after her visitor, when Farine came and flopped down beside her.

"Now I am really hot too. My heart is beating much too fast, I thought I was fit." He looked at her, "Lucy, do you not care I have danced myself out of breath?"

"You've still got breath, Farine. You wouldn't be talking so much otherwise." Then she seemed to reconnect with the world, "Sorry, I'll get you some water." She headed to the kitchen, hoping that she wouldn't meet The Tigress, as she'd had to name her, on the way. The Importance of Being Earnest came to mind once more. To have one unpleasant encounter at a party was unfortunate – two definitely smacked of carelessness. She grabbed two glasses and was filling them at the sink, when a familiar voice came over her shoulder.

"Hi Lucy! Having a good time?"

She turned her head to see Mark, and a girl she didn't know, by the drinks table.

"Hi Mark. How are you?"

He tried to reply, but was interrupted by his partner determined to drag him away.

"Sorry, Lucy; got to dance. I'll have a word with you later."

Lucy nodded, hoping that later might be too late, and took the water outside.

"Are you alright? You looked very strange a minute ago."

"Fine," she said with a fixed smile. He looked at her enquiringly.

"Maybe I've had enough for tonight."

"No problem, I think I have no energy left either, after my dancing lessons!"

He looked up at her expecting to get a reaction from this, but again was offered a flat mouth pretending to be a smile.

They worked their way round the people he felt they ought to take leave of, Lucy half-heartedly so, until they got to Lisa and Anthony. The three of them exchanged genuine hugs; that left them with only their hosts to find and bid goodnight. As they were leaving Lucy caught sight of the Tigress watching from further down the hall, but she made no move to speak to either of them.

Walking away from the party Farine asked Lucy if she was very tired.

"No actually, I'm not. I do feel very restless though. I don't really want to go home, if I'm honest."

"You'd just had enough of the people?" She nodded. "Okay then what shall we do?"

She pushed her hands through her hair. She didn't like to say, but the party, or rather the incidents there had left a nasty taste in her mouth, quite literally, she felt.

"How about going for a coffee and a dessert? I feel the need for something sweet. Is there anywhere at this time of night?"

He consulted his watch. "We could go to Hubert's. He will be tidying customers away by now, but he will allow me to presume upon his hospitality."

"That would be great. Do you mind though?"

"Not at all."

He had been right. Most tables were empty, and were also being cleared. A few other customers lingered however, which prevented them from feeling too conspicuous. When

144

Farine spoke to him, Hubert seemed entirely at ease with their request. Shortly, a waiter brought them coffee and some kind of pear and almond tart. Lucy set to, and declared it to be just what she had needed. They had said very little so far, as she sat back with her coffee she toyed with the spoon and wondered what, if anything, she ought to divulge.

"Are you going to tell me what is troubling you?"

She sighed and fiddled with her cup, "It was my own fault, I was busy out in the garden, then didn't have much time to eat before the party. Probably just low blood sugar, but that dessert should sort me out."

He waited patiently for her to say more. All he got was: "I think your friend may like to go home sometime before dawn. Why don't we walk some more?"

They thanked Hubert, and left him to close up.

Outside, Lucy decided she was still restless, and revived by the food, said she would like to walk around a while longer and maybe watch the sun come up. Farine was surprised by this, but quite happy to indulge her. As they walked through the streets in what remained of the night, he could not see her face properly. The lines were brought out sharply by the monochrome street lights, but this gave away none of the subtleties of expression that he needed to read her mood. For her part, she saw slabs of dark and light reflected from the smooth planes of his face, but the deep shadows and angular bone structure made it more inscrutable than ever. They were almost beyond the streets now, soon there would only be moonlight, and that just a sliver, to see by as they headed inevitably towards the downs.

14

They had reached the open spaces, leaving any other human activity behind. It was by now, thankfully, too close to morning for the undesirables that frequented the place at night. She sighed, as if trying to exchange the whole capacity of her lungs.

He looked down at her, "Well, you still have not said what was so unsettling at the party. Obviously there was something."

She shrugged and pulled her face into a grimace, "I'm not sure I can define it."

"I still think you're not very happy about everyone assuming you are my girlfriend."

She gave a snort, "That makes us sound like Lisa and Anthony. But then, that's the problem isn't it? In Lucy-land adults are allowed to have innocent teenage crushes. Married women are allowed to spend their time with handsome sophisticated men, while their friends look on indulgently. Everybody likes everybody else, and no-one has a nasty thing to say to anyone. Real life doesn't quite match up though, does it?"

"You're back to thinking you are behaving badly then?"

"Not badly, just unrealistic. I'm so far from sensible that words like 'lunatic' are now in view."

"Ah, I'm leading you astray again. Perhaps I should have made a large sign to wear at the party."

"No. Sorry, it's not you, not your fault I mean. I was having a lovely time actually."

"So, what spoiled it?"

She shook her head, "I didn't want to say anything, but I can see we'll end up in another argument if I don't explain. A woman came to speak to me. She never told me her name so I can't enlighten you."

He was quiet a moment, "You could describe her."

"Yes, I could. She had very blonde hair, very long nails, a very even tan and a very tight smile. She was a 'very' kind of person."

"Sounds like Eloise. I did see her there; I think she was in the hall as we left."

"Yes, that's her."

"And what did she have to say?"

"I don't think I'll repeat her exact words. Suffice to say she tried to frighten me off you, then for good measure she tried to make me frightened of you."

"I see."

They had reached the downs now, and it was deserted. He strode along hands in his pockets. She looked at his face for a moment but it was distinctly unreadable.

"How did she try to make you frightened of me?"

"More or less implied there was only one way in which I could provide any interest, I lacked the sophistication for anything else, after that I'd be tossed aside."

He stopped in his tracks and looked down at her, making his face completely in shadow, whereas hers was angled up to look at him and caught fully in the available moonlight. He took her hold of her by the arms, gripping them tightly, almost lifting her off her feet. "Did it work?"

She shook her head slowly, "Given that I'm not currently providing any of that kind of interest, that's not the reason you're spending time with me. If it's the idea of the conquest you like, then you'd be excited when I'm scared or angry. None of the above apply. Whatever you're after, it isn't that."

He huffed slightly through his nose, eased his hold on her and smoothed her arms. "And how did you work all that out?"

"How do you think? By observation. I've worked out what turns you on, at least with me anyway."

"Oh! That sounds very interesting, and what is it?"

"When I make you laugh."

He pulled her to him suddenly and wrapped his arms tightly round her.

"Her we go again, just when I'm meant to be the scary one, you terrify me. Did you send Eloise away thoroughly frightened too?"

"I hardly said a word to her, partly because some of what she said was true." She was struggling to speak, as she was more or less clamped to his chest, and pulled her head back to get the words out.

He looked down into her face again, "And what was that?"

"That we're having an affair. I denied it, but I knew I was on shaky ground."

He released her and gently took hold of her chin to tip her face up. "Here we go again. What affair is this?"

She pulled away from him, exasperated. "Oh, come on Farine! You know very well this is a sort of affair, just one without sex, that's all."

"Is this something else that exists in Lucy-land, sexless affairs?"

"Clearly. Well, maybe not from your point of view, but I'm involved in an untenable relationship. And when the real world hits it, well. . ."

She turned and started walking on again, after a moment he followed.

"Are you going to finish that last part?"

She glanced up at him again, wishing she could make out more of what he thought, but then perhaps it was easier to say all this without that knowledge.

"When the real world hits, then there's trouble. Someone speaks to Tom, or things just become too complicated, or you get. . ."

Again she failed to finish the thought.

"I get what?"

"Fed up with all the messing around or my convoluted behaviour circuits." She stopped and faced him once more. "I know what I'm getting out of this, but I still don't understand what's in it for you. I'm naïve and gauche, and thus quite possibly amusing. But you're used to full-blooded, high octane relationships, apparently. One thing I won't ever do is willingly hurt Tom. You could argue I'm over the line now, but not in my mind. We've never believed one person can totally satisfy all the needs of another, we've both got independent friends. I'm stretching the definition with you for sure, but no way will I ever sleep with you. I'm not sure I could, it would be a complete denial of who I am and what I believe."

She caught an expression flitting across his face, and laughed derisively. "Yes, yes, you could make it happen one way or another. I'm sure seduction is an art. We already know the temptation exists. But we've been through that, just getting your own way isn't what you want, is it? Well, if it is, you need to know that you'll destroy me."

"Why? Because adultery is an unforgivable sin?"

"No. There's forgiveness for that. But I'm not prepared for the human fallout. It's so messy and painful. Like I said; I won't cause that much damage. That would be what would destroy me, hurting people I loved."

"I don't want to destroy you. I rather like you, I think you know that."

"So why keep playing this game?"

He looked quite blank for a few moments, as far as she could tell in this light. Then he shrugged, "Perhaps I'm not sure myself. We keep saying our friendship is different, maybe that's what I like. Most people protect themselves. You keep being open and vulnerable, I think you see it as a weakness, but it's one of your greatest strengths. I can't help the fact that it's very attractive, and I don't mean just physically. Perhaps being with you makes me feel a better person."

"Huh! Don't bother with the St. Lucy idea. I don't regard it as particularly holy to be enjoying one man's company while my husband's too far away to give me his. Or to be scheming about how long I can keep it going."

"Really?" He sounded pleased. "Now I am surprised. I thought this was heading for another 'we can't carry on like this' speech."

"No speech. It's a fact, we can't. But I'm in too deep to stop it myself. You're much too much fun, I'm afraid. Nevertheless something will; stop it, I mean. We will crash and burn at some point." She suddenly added vehemently, "Stupid bloody woman!"

He frowned, trying to fit the last comment in with the rest of it all. "Eloise? I don't understand. I thought she tried to put you off?"

"Yes, she did. One of my less admirable traits is obstinacy. She pretty much guaranteed I'll keep going as long as I can."

He draped his arm round her shoulder and turned her to walk on again. "Well, that is good news. There is no-one I would rather have a non-affair with. We can have endless fun making arrangements to meet in secret, pretending that we are not having an affair, when all the time only we really know that we are actually – not having an affair! This is completely new territory for me, excellent!"

She was shaking her head at his idiocy, but then pulled her mouth into a line. "I don't know what kind of a crazy friend this makes me; you know you have every right to walk away. I think you're mad, and I know I'm mad. Why do it?"

"I keep telling you, because of the fun." He kissed the top of her head. "Shame about the other kind of amusement we're not having, but there we go. You know I could make it a lot of fun for you, really, if you wanted."

She pushed him off and moved so that she was walking about three feet away. "I've said my piece on that. If you can't accept it, I'd rather you leave me alone."

He put up his hands in surrender, "Okay, okay. I was just making my position plain too. I promise I won't do anything I shouldn't. Well, nothing dangerous anyway. I will see if I can track down some of that stuff they put in the water for prisoners."

"You mean bromide?"

"If that's the name of it, yes. Then I can go back to treating you like one of my sisters, almost."

By now they had reached the top of the downs, and the middle of the wide open space. Already the sky was turning grey, with a hint of light at the eastern edge; it wouldn't be long before the sun rose. They decided it was a good place to sit and wait for the spectacle. After a few moments Lucy

150

started shivering, without movement there was nothing to keep her warm in the pre-dawn chill.

He got up and moved saying, "Don't panic I'm not attacking you, but you need some heat."

He sat down behind her, or rather around her, putting his legs alongside hers. He rubbed her arms vigorously for a few seconds, then wrapped his own around hers.

She said very quietly, "Look, that's so beautiful."

"What?" he asked, resting his chin on her shoulder to try and see what she was referring to.

"That," she nodded downwards. "Look at the symmetry we make."

His limbs were longer, but by sitting behind her he had compensated for the extra length. The result was two pairs of legs bent in unison, knees level, arms resting on them together, her elbows inside his. His dark shape perfectly echoed the form of her paler limbs.

"Don't take this as an insult," she spoke softly and paused for a moment, "but in some ways this is more satisfying than any illicit carnal pleasure on offer." She gently opened out his fingers to a slight curve, and rested her hands inside his. "There, that would make a marvellous picture. If you can bear to sit still for a few minutes, it will get even better."

He sat obediently, and waited. The first rays of sunlight appeared, and shortly, what had been a pleasing black and white arrangement became suffused with warmth. Her skin took on pink tones, and his came alive with the complex range of colours that Lucy so longed to paint.

"When this present madness is over, however it comes to an end, this moment will be the one I choose to remember. I'll close my eyes and see this, and I'll think of how special it was."

He said nothing, just sat with her, even his breathing was quiet.

After a minute or two, Lucy lifted one hand and ran her fingers down her other arm and his next to it, "I find the sight of these two skins together utterly entrancing. I could look at it for hours, the textures and the colours are so absorbing."

"I have never been part of a work of art before. Thank you," he said it quite simply, without any hint of sarcasm.

"Farine, you're a work of art in your own right! You're a gift to anyone who can draw."

"Do you still draw and paint then?"

"Yes, well sketching mainly. I got fed up with painting because I'm just not good enough. That's why I swapped to graphics."

She had turned to look at him over her shoulder, and the symmetry was broken. They stood up, feeling the need to move and get warm again.

"You should keep doing your art. I expect it is better than you think. I would like to see some of it."

"Oh dear me, why did I say anything? Another one for me to regret."

"You are so strange. If I had a gift like that I would make use of it."

"I do, I'm a designer, remember."

"Yes, alright, but I'm sure your friends would appreciate your drawing. Surely they would like to see you use it?"

"I don't know. I've never thought about it. I just regard it as something I do as a diversion now and then. It helps me to unwind, to put on paper the images I carry in my head. Sometimes, when my mind feels too full of things, I just have to draw some, to get them out of the way, if that makes sense."

"Yes. I feel like that about the cello. There are times when you lose yourself in a piece of music, and it gives the thinking part of your brain a rest."

"Yes, that's it exactly."

They had wandered over to the edge of the gorge, and looked down to the small ribbon of river at the bottom. The sun was not yet high enough to shine down into it, and it looked grey and miserable compared to the warming greenery around them.

Lucy yawned, "Oh, I need a cup of tea. I'm getting too old for this all-night stuff."

They decided they would head back to her house, having been mentioned, a hot drink took on an irresistible appeal.

15

With the kettle on, Lucy felt the world had a chance of returning to some semblance of normality. She was struggling with the espresso maker, when Farine took it out of her hands.

"I can manage," she said shortly.

"Yes, but if I do it, it will taste better." He insisted, so she let him get on with it.

Sitting outside, in what was now quite warm sunshine, she tried to apply her mind to the day ahead. Every thought seemed to be interrupted by a yawn though.

He brought his coffee out, "What next?"

"I was aiming to carry straight on with the day, but if I'm honest, the thought of getting three or four hours sleep before I go to church is becoming ever more attractive. It's still early enough to do that."

"Will I see you later?"

"No, I think I have to shoe-horn some sense and practicality into my increasingly ludicrous lifestyle. Spending all day every day together would be asking for trouble."

She sat for a moment and then started laughing, doubling over and having to set her mug down. "Because spending the whole night walking round the downs with you was such a sane thing to do! As if!" She calmed down, "Sorry, hysteria setting in."

"Then you are overtired, n'est ce pas?"

"Oui, certainement."

He grinned behind his coffee cup, she didn't even seem conscious of replying in kind. "Okay, then go to bed for a while. I'll call you tomorrow, maybe we meet for lunch?"

"Maybe, or Tuesday perhaps. At the moment I can't even remember what work I have. Or what I'm supposed to be doing. I'm sure there was something."

He said goodbye, and left her with a stern admonition to go and sleep while she could.

"Okay then, what's he look like?"

Lucy gave a sigh that originated somewhere near her toes. "Difficult to say."

"You can do better than that Luce! Try again, or draw him for me." The ensuing silence caused Mel to look at her friend with a large grin on her face. "I think that's fairly clear the answer is good looking."

"You know as well as I do, that's entirely a matter of taste."

"Yes, and from your reluctance to give me details I conclude he's very much to yours!"

"You know me, I get fascinated by people, that doesn't mean he's a pin-up."

Mel tucked one leg underneath her and reached for the large wine-glass, "Before I went off to see Malcolm you were happily jabbering away at me about this new chum of yours with the interesting background. And you said he was handsome. Now I'm back, I can't get a word out of you and you're sighing like a lovelorn teenager. What else am I meant to think except that something is afoot? You look so uncomfortable anybody would think you'd been having it away with him." She was laughing at her own goading of her friend. Having originated on opposite sides of the Pennines, they were used to speaking plainly with each other. By the time she was taking another mouthful of the wine though, Lucy's lack of response registered and Mel spluttered on her drink. "Oh my God, you have! I can't believe it!"

"Mel! Don't be stupid. Of course I haven't."

"What then? Something's obviously been going on, tell me."

Lucy could manage no more than an embarrassed muttering accompanied by dark sideways glowers at her old friend.

"Has he made a pass at you? Have you been in a clinch with him? Oh yes, you have! Look at your face! Come on then, details."

"No, you've got this all wrong. Well, not really anyway, well hardly at all. Only almost, a bit. Sort of."

Mel was shaking with laughter, her more voluptuous curves rippling in the silent intervals of her mirth. "Get you! If I wait a bit longer you'll have worked up to full-scale blue-movie. Do you want to tell me now, before it gets any worse?" Still just the denial of silent head-shaking. "Go on. I want the details. Do I have to work through all the anatomical possibilities, while you do the yes-no interlude?"

"Mel! You're being completely revolting. Stop it. Just 'cos you were brought up on a farm."

This was the nature of their ritual banter, and hadn't altered appreciably in the twenty-eight years since they met at university. Mel reached for the bottle again, helping herself and topping Lucy's glass up at the same time.

Regarding her friend more quietly, Mel voiced a further opinion, "Whatever happened, you haven't found it creepy. You feel guilty about it, so I have to conclude it was pretty good." Suddenly she smiled again, "Of course the real problem is your Luce Morals." This too was an old joke, but it always served to lighten the tension of their more heart-searching discussions.

Lucy smiled, "Yes it is, partly. And he says that too, except not in your words." She got up from where she'd been sat on the floor, draping herself sideways across an easy chair instead, legs dangling from one side. "He seems to think it's perfectly acceptable to keep yourself amused with another man while your husband is away for six months. But you know I couldn't do that. I like this guy, I'm delighted to have his friendship, and I couldn't keep it if I was playing fast and loose with him. He thinks it's possible, but I know I couldn't do it. And no way do I want to hurt Tom. Adultery is out of the question."

"Do you not think, Luce, that's why you're finding him so attractive? Plain, straightforward, lack of sex. Tom's away, you're not getting it, in walks Sexy Longlegs and bingo! If Tom was around, you'd be friends with the Frenchman, end of story. I can tell you, when Todd ran off with the petrol-station girl, I hated all men for two months, then I couldn't get enough of them! He might have been a shit, but Todd was good value in the bedroom department. This guy sounds rather like him."

"No, he isn't." She was aware she was defending Farine, but couldn't help it. "I don't think he's the kind to cheat. I mean, obviously he has different values to mine, but he's very honest about it. And since I've said all I want is to be friends, he's been a perfect gentleman." She contemplated the depths of her Merlot for a moment, "He said my friendship was more important than having an affair."

"Yeah, right!"

"No, he was very sensible, said if being attracted to each other gets in the way then we don't put ourselves in risky situations, stick to what doesn't cause us any trouble."

"It all sounds terrifically noble."

"He is, unbelievably so."

"Exactly. He's just smoothing you along until you slide between the sheets with him."

"Oh Mel, for crying out loud! Take a look at me. Do you think he can't find someone younger, more glamorous, more willing to jump into bed with him? I don't know why, but he likes my company and I like his. It's really hard to contemplate doing without it at a time I most want it."

Mel leaned across, squeezing Lucy's arm. "I know, babe, I know. And he probably likes you for the same reason we all do, you're good fun. I just don't want you to get damaged or messed around. And you will be if you hurt Tom."

"I know, I do keep thinking about that. I also know you're right about the deprivation thing. But he's also exciting to be with. Tom is reliable, dependable, all those wonderful things you want in a husband, but not very romantic. This guy is so much fun, it's intoxicating."

Mel leant back, reclining at an odd angle now on the sofa, "So he's happy not to seduce you outright, but he's still determined to charm the socks off you."

"I think it oozes out of his pores. One of his involuntary actions, like breathing."

"In that case, make the most of him or hand him over!"

This set them both off wheezing with laughter until Lucy gasped out, "You're as nissed as a pewt! As usual."

"I don't know what you put in that bottle."

"It's not what's in it; it's how much you've had out of it. Dreadful woman."

"So I'm an alcoholic and you've got a toyboy. I've told you I'm willing to swap. Anyway, you still haven't told me what he really looks like. Give us a clue."

"Actually, I was wondering if you might get to see him."

"When? How?" Mel had sobered remarkably quickly.

"You are coming to Chepstow, aren't you?"

"Sure, is he?"

"I thought I'd ask him when I see him tomorrow."

"Great, then I can give you the benefit of my exhaustive experience."

Walking down the street to the café, she was in something of a dream. The company she had tried to withdraw from were offering her more money and more time to do the job they wanted. She was still a bit unsure, but having spent a day roughing out what needed to be done, she had a better idea of how much work was really involved. Her deliberations prevented her from spotting the figure approaching her with a purposeful look on his face.

"Lucy, you're not escaping this time!"

She stopped short, flustered and looked up into Mark's face.

"Oh hi. Sorry, I was miles away."

"So I see. What are you up to?"

"Erm," she hesitated looking around her, "Nothing," she finished lamely.

"I was surprised to see you at that party the other night. What did the Harpy want with you?"

"What?"

"Eloise, or the Harpy to most of us. Was she giving you a hard time?"

"Well, I don't know if, I mean. . . Why do you call her the Harpy?"

"Hah! If you'd had much of a conversation with her, you'd know. Not the most endearing of women. Usually, if she's not got it in for you, she's got it in for someone else and wants to let you know about it."

"Oh."

"Anyway, can't see what she'd have to say to you, unless it was about Farine."

"Farine?" she asked faintly.

"Yes, well she's always carried a torch for him, not that it's done her any good. And I hear you've been spending a lot of time with him lately. Enjoying a fling while Tom's away?"

Lucy turned bright red and stammered something incoherent.

"Oh don't worry Lucy, I know that's not the sort of thing you do with your time. Just pulling your leg. Besides, you're hardly Farine's type, are you?"

Again she was reduced to virtual gibberish. Before she could martial any kind of proper response, he was moving away.

"Well, got to dash, I'm due elsewhere as of five minutes ago. Take care."

Sitting down opposite Farine, she exhaled forcefully and shook her head as if to clear it. Then she reached for the water he had waiting for her. "Can you explain this conspiracy amongst your friends please?"

"Comment?" he looked at her mystified.

"I've just run into Mark, who made a point of telling me I'm not your type for an affair!"

"Mark? Who is Mark?"

"They guy who gave me your name!"

"Oh yes, him. But I thought he was your friend, I only know him a little."

"He seems to know a lot of the people you know, and he was there on Saturday night."

"Was he? I did not see him."

Well, he's another one stepping on my obstinacy pedal. I suspect collusion."

He smiled then narrowed his eyes, "So, you have discovered my evil plot to get you driven into my arms, hein? I must remember to send him his fee."

They smirked quietly, avoiding each others eyes, while the waiter brought the food.

"Also, it seems I'm not the only one who comes up with names for people. He knows Eloise, and referred to her as the Harpy."

They spent a minute sorting out what a Harpy was, and Lucy hoped she might then get a bit more on Eloise and the reason for her attitude, but he was still unforthcoming on the subject. Instead they moved on to work and other mundane topics.

"So, do you think you will take this contract from the big company?"

She sat back and looked out of the window. "Mm, I think so. Having worked out what they want, I reckon I can do it, but it will be a challenge. They are offering me a good fee, and to be honest, there isn't much else on the horizon at the moment. I couldn't do it if there were other jobs waiting though, so it seems to fit in well."

He nodded, "Eh bien, that should be a good step for you. Maybe you will get more large contracts after this one."

"Not sure I want them. I quite like short jobs I can get my teeth into quickly. I'm not keen on the feeling of things hanging over me, which a bigger job tends to give. Anyway, there was something else I wanted to talk to you about." She sat forward, leaning her elbows on the table; he looked at her, eyebrows raised. "How would you like to come out with me on Friday evening? No, slow down, you may not be so enthusiastic when you know what it is! I'm going with a group of friends, to an open air theatre company. We usually go and see them each year when they come to Chepstow Castle. It's a lovely venue, a natural amphitheatre inside ruined castle walls. Highly atmospheric. We take picnics and generally a good time is had by all. They're mostly church friends, but I wondered if you'd like to try it."

"Yes, of course I'd like to come. You're not ashamed of me meeting your friends then?"

"No, why should I be? But the church people would find our friendship pretty much outré. So, I might not be entirely

160

sure how to introduce you. Probably have to run the gauntlet a bit on Sunday and risk a certain amount of disapproval."

He frowned, "They would disapprove of you having new friends?"

"No. They would disapprove of me spending a lot of time on my own with an unattached man, when I'm not an unattached woman! With good reason, I remind you," she muttered the last, aware that her voice had been gradually rising.

"So," he said slowly "your associates don't want us to be friends, and my associates want us to be lovers. Are we damned then?"

"Not damned, just doomed." She said this matter-of-factly and looked at him levelly. After a moment she spoke again quietly, "I can't help feeling we've stepped off the main road onto a pretty risky path, you know. Possibly because the rebel in my head is tired of keeping a low profile."

"Well, you said you wanted to risk things. You also said that keeping to the rules is religion, and you hate it. Here we are, doing what other people say we can't do, you should be happy."

"Keeping to the rules for the sake of it is religion. I suspect some rules are there for safety. I have a feeling I'm flouting the wrong ones, and probably taking the wrong risks." She shrugged looking out of the window absently, "The trouble is, it can be difficult to tell until it's too late."

"Well, that's the nature of adventure, you tend not to know where exactly all the dangers lie."

She nodded and drank the rest of her coffee, "We've got very serious all of a sudden."

"I'm reasonably certain that's your fault, although being a gentleman, I won't point it out."

She laughed, and they moved on to the arrangements for the Friday outing.

"Am I not going to see you before then?"

"No, I want to crack on with this contract. Besides, it will be good for my soul to deny myself your company for a little while," she saw his expression and grinned. "It also means I don't have to feel so guilty when you meet my friends."

He had run three out of the required five kilometres this morning. Alone though. There had been a short call from Guy the evening before, explaining about a sudden meeting called in Plymouth which would need him to make a start even before running time. He hoped to join Farine the following day.

He had pushed up his speed for the last kilometre, now he eased back, letting his breathing settle. Not many other people were about at all, just the two youngsters he'd seen the last couple of days. Here they were again in their hooded track-suits, slowly lumbering towards him. Obviously beginners. No, not even that, no running shoes. Suddenly this gave new meaning to their presence, in the split second the leg was extended, he was responding to it. Not in time to hop over it, but his mind was already organising his muscles to bunch for the roll. As well as expending the momentum of the fall, the roll took him further away from his assailants than they expected. They now had more ground to cover before they could start the planned kicking. He used that slight delay to prepare himself. On his back, right leg bent to protect vulnerable organs and take the kick, left foot ready. As soon as the attacker swung his boot, Farine lashed out underneath it, foot straight to the knee bearing the man's weight. He went down screaming. Presumably that was the ligament gone.

Check out attacker number two. Coming from the other side. No time to rearrange legs, watch for which foot was raised, grab the ankle and pull hard. This one went down onto his back, winded. Farine now got to his feet and went straight in with a solid punch straight down into his nose. Blood spurted. Farine ignored it and finished him off with a couple of quick jabs before stepping back. He looked across, checked number one was definitely out of it and walked some distance away. Then he took the time to extract his 'phone from his shorts' pocket.

"Yes, I'd like to report an attempted mugging."

He gave brief details of the attack and the location as he watched the two casualties stagger to their feet and help each other to hobble away.

"No, I don't need treatment, just grazing and minor cuts. Actually, I would prefer not to hang around here in case they come back. It will be easiest for you to contact me at my practice, I'm a solicitor." He gave his address as he looked at the wrist-band he was wearing. "I'm not sure how good a description I can give you, but I can provide you with some DNA."

His gaze swept around the downs, now empty of unsavoury characters. He started to run. Two kilometres left, then he could see to his shoulder, it was beginning to sting. Some antiseptic would be wise.

"What happened to your face? Not another one beaten up?"

His fingers flew up to the cut over his cheekbone, "Ah, I took a dive when I was running on Wednesday. It's fine."

"Oh, I thought someone's bill hadn't been to their liking."

"You would assume that." He smiled, "I will have you know that solicitors deal with things in a very civilised way. We're here to take the fisticuffs out of disputes, not put them in."

Her eyes swept him up and down. "You haven't skinned your knees; did you land on your head?"

"Where I would feel no pain? Shoulder, I managed to roll into the fall."

She grabbed his arm, turning him, and pulled up the sleeve of his shirt, "Ooh, that's quite nasty. Are you looking after it?"

"Yes." He waited a moment while she checked all exposable damage. "You know, any thoughts I've had about you undressing me are being rapidly rearranged in my mind. Sadly."

"Nice try, but you're not putting me off that easily. When we get back you can come in for first-aid. I think I've got some stepladders in the garage."

"It will have to be second-aid. I did the first part. And are you sure you want me in your house late at night taking my clothes off? Who knows where that might lead?"

She should have found that annoying. Or possibly provocative. But she didn't. As they loaded the car she tried to analyse it. There was something there. She couldn't quite put her finger on it. He was teasing, but it didn't sound like usual. More like he was laying a trail to something. But what?

By now, they were ready to set off. She stared out of the window in silence, letting him navigate the tight suburban streets undisturbed. When they reached the main road out of the city, she turned.

"Odd then, that you went for a way to end the fighting."

His head flicked round to look at her, before being pulled sharply back to the road. "What do you mean?"

Yes, definitely something he was touchy about. But why? He'd talked about it openly before. "What you said about solicitors. And the fact that you spent your youth apparently in one form of combat or another."

His face relaxed into an open smile. "Still combat. Just bloodless, hopefully."

Something there had amused him. And he sounded very pleased with himself, she had done what he wanted. What had she missed? She would have to try again later, probing mind and shoulder at the same time maybe.

Cocooned in the small world of the car again, now with only the lights from the dashboard display outlining their faces, they talked about the evening.

"Yes, it was very enjoyable, very amusing. As you said, it was a good time for all."

"I'm glad you liked it, and you seemed to get on with everyone you spoke to."

"Why not? They were friendly people, most of the time anyway," he was grinning to himself, "When they weren't staring at me with disapproval."

"Well, what did you expect? Particularly when you kept draping your arm round me during the second half."

"I have long arms, what do they think I should do with them? I can't keep them folded up all the time. Besides, they all kissed each other when you met and when you parted, I was just joining in. That's normal."

"Ah, but not on both cheeks!"

They both spent several seconds laughing at the woman who, being taken by surprise at the French style of greeting, had leapt back startled.

"And you already know what I think about this English view of not touching each other. My God, you're all so terrified. If I took Etienne and Gloria out, I would be ashamed not to hold on to them and take care of them."

"Who's Gloria? You haven't mentioned her before."

"Etienne's sister, she is nearly fifteen, just becoming a woman and very pretty. They are what you would call 'good kids'. I am very close to them," he sighed, "but maybe I should go home and see them more often. Their parents don't spend enough time with them; they are left too much to their own devices. And Etienne will be Count one day; his father should be doing more to prepare him."

Lucy had watched his face as he had said all this, intrigued. "You know, you go on about how little you want to be Count, but you care about all of this very much."

"I care about my family. They just drive me mad sometimes, that's all. But I wouldn't dream of being distant with them, and in the same way I have no intention of being distant with you."

"Droit de seigneur, you see. No, wait, let me explain! You've come up with a modern version, that's all. As far as you're concerned I'm part of your realm, or estate, or whatever Counts have. You consider me in the same category as Gloria and your sisters, for some reason. I'm under your protection, and you have territorial rights. You don't like anybody else dictating what you should do. You can't deny it, can you?"

He was very quiet, finally giving a small shrug and a muttered, "C'est possible."

Lucy felt very pleased with herself for this piece of exposition, and sat back smiling.

"So, you will explain all this to your friends will you, on Sunday?"

She stopped smiling and wrinkled her nose. "Probably not, now you mention it. I'll just have to go for the 'well, he's French you know' option; that should cover most of it."

They continued to chat about the evening, laughing again over some of the things the theatre troupe had done in their production.

"I did not think Shakespeare could be so funny. It always was very hard to read for me, with the ancient language."

"Not quite ancient, but I know what you mean. That's why we like going to see that particular group; somehow they make it very accessible, even though they speak at a rate of knots!"

"So what about tomorrow? Have you any plans?"

"I promised Jenny I'd go shopping with her. She has a friend's wedding to go to soon, and she needs an outfit. I might be lying on the sofa with an ice pack on my head for the evening. Or, drinking my way through a bottle of wine muttering feebly to myself, shopping takes me that way sometimes. You?"

"I will do some cello practice, I have been very lax lately. Probably a concert in the evening. Call me if you get bored, you can always come with me."

The evening had been delightful. Her enjoyment at his participation in it was so strong it shimmered around her in the atmosphere. The easy way they could talk like this added to it. Held within the car they breathed it repeatedly in and out, miniscule scintillating particles wafting from one to the other. She could feel the headiness of it affecting her. By the time they reached home, she knew she had to get out and breathe cool city-evening air before she was lost.

He put his arm along the back of the seat and turned to speak to her. She reached for the door handle hurriedly, "I need to get out of the car."

"Do you feel sick?" he asked after her disappearing form.

"No, just weak at the knees," she muttered when she was out of earshot.

They unloaded the chairs and picnic things from the boot and dumped them in the hallway. They exchanged the usual farewell.

"Bonsoir, cherie," he said, turning to go.

She smiled after his retreating back, forgetting completely about the promised first-aid and what it was she meant to find out.

16

He stepped through the doors, from the sound of it this must be the place, yes. Through another set of glass doors was obviously the hall where the music was coming from. He went in, looking round carefully, spotted what he was after and then hesitated. Difficult to interrupt at that precise moment. He walked forward a short way, keeping to the side, and stopped at the end of the row of seats in which she stood. He leant against the wall, crossing one foot behind the other, checked his watch and pushed his hands into his pockets. He could afford to wait a minute or two.

He glanced at her again; she had her eyes closed as she sang; one arm in the air. They appeared to be singing the same song over and over again, but the people all looked very intent on it. He checked again, she was still in the same attitude. Just then a young woman emerged at the front of the hall, she had two large brightly coloured flags and started to turn and twirl, making the fabric follow her movements. There had been one or two others standing at the back, where he came in, wafting flags, but their movements were nothing like this. She flowed with the music, and instead of a simple backwards and forwards motion, the flags she turned cascaded and tumbled, one after the other up and down, around her, over her head and then out like wings. It was mesmerising. A second girl joined her, there was something familiar about her, but he didn't think he'd met her anywhere. She used her flags in a similar way, and they echoed each other, yet without orchestration. The singing changed, moving from the repeated words to something he couldn't understand, apparently in several parts, and gradually building up to some sort of climax.

"What are you doing here?" a voice hissed at him from just below shoulder level.

"Ah, I need to see you, urgently," he looked down at her imploringly.

She took his arm, and turned him round smartly to propel him back the way he came.

He spoke back over his shoulder, "Don't be annoyed, for all you know, I have come here to get saved."

"Good idea, I'd finish the job if I were you. I'm probably going for your jugular in the next few seconds."

She muttered all this as she marched him out of the hall, keen, it seemed, to escape before some kind of usher, heading their way, could intercept them.

Out in the foyer, she turned to him, "How did you find us?"

He smiled, "Well, there are these very useful things called websites." Her expression stopped him, and he glanced at his watch again. "Seriously, I must speak to you, I haven't got long."

Just then the door opened again and the second flag girl emerged.

"Mum, what's going on?"

Lucy pursed her lips very briefly, "Jenny, this is Farine, about whom you have heard such a lot. Farine, my daughter."

He reached out his hand to her and she shook it, but her expression belied her feelings as to the safety of doing so.

"Pardon this intrusion, mademoiselle, I must speak to your mother. I promise I will not keep her long."

Jenny shot Lucy a questioning glance.

She gave her head a brief shake. "It's okay, I'll be back in a few minutes."

The girl turned to go back in the hall, glaring slightly over her shoulder at Farine."

"Merci ma petite."

Lucy snorted and dragged him to the entrance. "Now you will be lucky to get out alive! Come on, before she changes her mind."

"Does she not speak French?"

"No, but she understands enough to know you called her 'my little one'. That really is living dangerously."

Outside he looked around, "Is there anywhere we can talk?"

She pulled a face, "Nowhere private. What's the matter?"

In the end they went and sat in his car. She looked at him frowning; he was obviously agitated, rubbing his hand across his head and face.

"Well?" she tried again.

He looked at her, his face miserable, "I must go to France, my plane leaves in less than two hours. Francine called me in the night."

"What's happened?"

"It's Maman, she is in hospital. Very seriously ill, but we don't know what's wrong. I have to get there as quickly as I can, she is in intensive care."

"Oh, Farine, I'm so sorry," her tone changed automatically from annoyance to concern, "Is there anything I can do?"

He shook his head, "No, I've been into the office and left what instructions I can, apart from that nothing is needed. Well, you can pray for Maman."

"Of course I will; and for you." She reached out and took hold of his hand, he held on tightly for a few moments. She wished there was something she could do to relieve the anxiety and shock he was feeling. "By the time you arrive, she could be out of danger."

He nodded, but was obviously thinking of the possible alternatives. "Well, I must go. I will drive straight to the airport now. I'll call you and let you know what happens, how she is…"

He was unable to finish, Lucy got out of the car and went round to his side to say farewell. As they made their 'au revoirs' she bent down and hugged him briefly.

"Take care."

He nodded and then was gone, out of sight in seconds. She turned back, aware of several pairs of eyes swivelled in her direction and staring out through the large glass windows of the hall.

*

She looked down into the small face; big eyes turned up to her, smile wide and warm as he reached up his arms. She lifted him and he wrapped the long arms round her neck and clasped his legs round her waist.

"Hello my lovely boy."

170

*She had spoken in Somali, it was one of the few times she
still used her native language. Her greeting to him had become
almost a nickname. He seemed to like it, something held
uniquely between the two of them.*

"How was school? Are you tired?"

"Hungry."

*She walked into the kitchen and sat him on the table
while she reached for some food and a drink to give him. "You
are not saying much, did you not enjoy school today?"*

*He shrugged, swinging his legs from the edge of the table
and looking towards the other two children playing together.
They were giggling as they took it in turns to pile up blocks
and books and toys in pursuit of a giddy tower. The inevitable
happened and the small boy wailed, blaming his sister for
spoiling it. Everyone ignored the noise and the little girl
started to pick up blocks and begin a new construction.*

"Were you in trouble again?"

*He put the glass down on the table and held out his arms
to her once more. She took a seat by him and pulled him down
onto her knee, singing something over him for a few minutes
which he didn't understand.*

"Did the other children tease you?"

*He shook his head. Maybe she would have to leave it and
come back to the subject later, "Well, fetch me your reading
book, let me see what you have today."*

*He stayed still, closing his eyes. Odd, he usually loved
this part of the day and was keen to show her the latest book
and tell her how pleased the teacher was with his reading.*

"Do you have a new book?"

*Another shake of the head. This was puzzling her deeply
and she frowned, sitting him up straight to look into his face.*

*"My son, tell me what is the trouble. What happened
today and why do you not have a book?"*

*"I told the teacher I don't want to learn to read anymore.
I won't bring home any more books. My teacher was angry."*

*She was stunned, and perplexed. He had been so quick to
pick up this skill, and loved every book that came into his
hands. What had caused this sudden obstinacy?*

"I want you to tell me why. That is what children do at school, they learn to read; you can't be surprised if the teacher is angry with you. I will be angry with you if you don't tell me."

He picked at a thread on her dress and looked at her out of the corner of his eyes once or twice. Another outburst from the far end of the table came and went as before. His mouth wrinkled into an odd line and he whispered his answer. "Because you can't read."

He leant back against her and she rested her chin on his head, "What makes you say that?"

"You never notice when I get the words wrong. And I heard Grandpère and Grandmère talking yesterday. He said how pleased he was that I could read so well. She laughed and said 'it's more than his mother can do'. I want to be like you, I don't want you to be the only one who can't read."

She pulled her arms tightly round him, "Do you know what I would like to do about it?" He shook his head. "I would like to read. I have learnt some words, from your books and you reading them to me. If you keep learning, I can learn too."

He looked up at her face, his quietness forgotten, "Truly?"

She nodded. He started to wriggle on her knee, "I can learn and teach you!"

"Yes," she said solemnly, "You can be the teacher, but not if you are very strict with me."

"I won't be Maman, I'll be kind. I won't make you read out loud in front of everyone else."

"Is that what your teacher does?"

"Yes," he shrugged, "But I don't care because I can do it. There are some children in the class who can't and they hate it."

"Well, you can teach me in secret. But you will have to tell your teacher tomorrow that you are sorry for being rude and that you would very much like to take a new book home."

He nodded, now all animation and restless limbs, "Can I go and play?"

"Of course, but don't be too rough with the others."
Before she could loose him from her arms there was a noise
nearby. "Sylvie is waking from her nap, let me get her, she is
on the window seat and may fall."
"I will bring her for you"
He was down from her knee and across to his baby sister
instantly, picking up the toddler who clung to his shirt with
fingers still chubby from babyhood. He looked over the top of
the fine blonde hair, automatically cradled against his neck,
"Why is Sylvie much prettier than Francine?"
The small girl at the far end of the table stuck out her
tongue at him, very pink against her dark skin. He replied in
kind, handing the baby to his mother.
"Francine is beautiful too; you are all beautiful, and all
different. Pass me Sylvie's cup from the side please."
The tower on the table fell down once more, the little boy
wailed again, this time slapping his sister's arm in annoyance.
She turned and pushed him, he fell from his chair and hit the
flagged floor with that particular sickening thud known to all
parents. Just as familiar was the two-second silence, followed
by the start of an almighty scream. She was already on her
feet, baby balanced on one hip, cloth snatched up in the other
hand as she ran to him. Francine started to cry, fearful of what
she had caused. Sylvie too, tuning in to the general upset,
began to grizzle. Blood was running from Henri's mouth and a
quick burst of Arabic came from her own as she held the cloth
to his face.
"You tell me it is wrong to use rude words Maman."
"It is wrong also to be cheeky to your parents, Farine,
now run and find Papa."

*

"Etienne, where is Etienne?"

"She's asking for Papa! She's still delirious. I thought
she would be better today."

The woman's voice was brittle, the tautness of anxiety
stretching it thin. A voice much further down the register
sounded in reply, "Stop panicking, she's just coming round.
Give her time to find her senses."

The woman in the bed opened her eyes and located the source of the deeper voice, smiling as recognition came, "Hello my lovely boy."

He squeezed the hand he was holding and bent to kiss her cheek softly, smiling for the eyes which hovered between open and closed. "Are you feeling better?"

"Yes," the reply was still quiet, but clear, "And you can tell Francine her mother has not lost her sanity yet. I can't help dreaming about her father occasionally."

Farine allowed his sister to replace him and have her own reunion. As she did so, she returned to the calm orderly woman he knew better. He stood with his hand on her shoulder as they both offered morsels of family news, to be digested slowly and one at a time. Soon their mother was sleeping again, having been reassured that the two youngest siblings would replace them at the next visiting time.

Francine looked down at her then reached out for her brother, "I'm so relieved!"

"I know," he said holding her tightly, "So am I. None of us are ready to lose her yet."

"Where's the Sexy Frenchman then?"

"Back in France, his mother was taken ill and he had to rush off."

"Oh, that's not nice, poor guy. Well, I mean if it's genuine, if he's not done a runner after meeting your friends."

"Mel! You're so suspicious. No, I don't think so. Anyway, why would he have to do a runner? He's not obligated to me in any way."

"Mm."

"What does that mean?" She handed the first glass of wine across. "Besides, he called me this morning to let me know she's got meningitis. But they can use antibiotics and she's on the mend. There was someone else there talking French."

She nodded, "He's pretty fond of you, that was obvious, very attentive."

Lucy shook her head, "I think that's his manner. If he takes you out then he looks after you, that's how he is. But you see what I mean about charming?"

"I certainly do. And I can see why you think he's gorgeous." She waved away her friend's protestations. "Yes you do. I bet you spend hours drawing him. I used to share a room with you, remember? He's a bit thin for my liking, but frankly I could get over that. If you're staying on the straight and narrow, would you put in a few words on my behalf?"

"Ah, well you're off to a good start. He did ask me who was the friend with all those nice curves."

"Uh, he thinks I'm fat!"

"No, the way he said it led me to believe it was an appreciative enquiry. It was Jane who offended him."

"What, when she had a fit at being kissed twice?" They both laughed as Lucy nodded. Mel put a dreamy look on her face, "I would have had hers; I did my best to hang on to him for a second go."

"I noticed!"

They settled themselves comfortably across various pieces of furniture. Mel looked at her friend affectionately, "What are you going to do?"

Lucy shrugged, "I don't have to do anything, he's not here."

"And when he comes back?"

Lucy took temporary refuge in the Shiraz, "I don't know. You obviously think I have a problem."

"I know you do. You're infatuated with him, and you can't handle it."

"Of course I can't! For goodness sake, how can someone my age have a crush on a man?"

"Poor love; it's not a function of age, only condition. I've had dozens. None of us get what we want. I've had lots of short-term exciting men friends, and I'd gladly swap for something warm and predictable like you have with Tom. In your case, it's the other way round."

Lucy pulled her mouth down, "No I don't want to swap. I acknowledge the excitement value, but I know better than to think a bit of fun and games could replace a decent long-term relationship."

"Then why are you still seeing him?"

"Like you said, I'm lonely and I miss having a man around."

Mel twisted, putting her feet up and laying her head on an arm-rest. "Well, in that case you have three options."

"Go on then."

"One, you go at it like rabbits for a few weeks, get it out of your system. At the end you wave him goodbye with a fond tear and some steamy memories."

"Not an option," Lucy growled.

"Two, you pack your bags and tell him you're all his. If he likes you that much, you can ride off into the sunset together."

"Oh please!"

"Three, you continue your present course of trying to pretend you're just good friends and when Tom gets back, everything will be fine."

"See, I'm doing the only possible thing. You were no help at all."

"Idiot! The last one was a joke. Nobody with half a brain would believe that would work. The only realistic third option is to wave bye-bye now." A few moments went by. "Does he shave his legs?"

"What?"

"The other night, I couldn't help noticing how smooth his legs were. Does he shave them?"

"I can't say I thought to ask, but a lot of African races have much less body hair. His. . ." she bit her lip, grimacing.

"His what? Oh my God, Luce, you have to finish that sentence! If you don't, I'll imagine you in all sorts of scenarios you'd rather I didn't."

"Don't be ridiculous. All I was going to say was, his chest is smooth. Hairless that is. There's nothing unseemly about knowing that, is there?"

"I don't know. You didn't want to say it – for some reason."

"Because I knew you'd make more of it than you should."

"Hnhh." Suddenly Mel laughed out loud. "I don't think I know anyone else who uses the word unseemly. You are priceless." Just as suddenly as the laughter had started, it stopped. "I don't know. I'll grant you he's attractive. But he seems very aloof and arrogant. If you're not going for his body, I can't see he's that much fun to be with."

"No, he is honestly. His arrogance is like a jacket he puts on to look stylish – it's just an outer layer. Underneath he's really fascinating."

Lucy had taken refuge in the wine glass again. Mel had her head twisted round to watch her. When she spoke again it was very quietly, "Luce, Tom's one of the good guys. Whatever you do, you can't mess him around. If you can't cope with a bit on the side, about which you keep your lips sealed forevermore, then you have to decide who you're going to hurt." There was no reply at all. "I never took you for a greedy woman, but you don't get them both!"

"And I never took myself for a stupid woman, but that's what I'm being. I've never been in this place before, Mel. I always thought I'd be strong and good. But. . ."

"The spirit is willing."

"And my flesh is a whole lot weaker than I realised."

"I know pet, I know all about that one." She thought for a moment, "Tell you what."

"Hmm?"

"If you decide Sexy Longlegs is too hot *not* to handle, let me know and I'll make sure I'm around to comfort Tom when he gets back. He's much too good to go to waste." Mel smiled, thinking Lucy would enjoy that one. Her eyes didn't join in with the general merriment though.

Walking up the road, deep in thought, Lucy failed to register in her mind the voice that was falling on her ears. Considerations of the project in hand, sometimes eased by the action of legs swinging, rendered the sound one with the background noises of the street. Until the voice changed tactics, raising itself to a level hard to ignore. And using words guaranteed to engage her attention.

"Hey! Mrs. Du Blez, over here."

Lucy was literally stopped in her tracks, swivelling her head to find the origin of the words and their intended recipient. It did not take long to locate the grinning face of Chris Brogan. More scanning, however, failed to place anyone else he could be hailing. His grin widened to face-splitting proportions.

"Yes, you. Don't tell me I've managed to mystify you this time."

Lucy walked slowly across to him, standing near his shop. She hadn't even been conscious of being in its location, thoughts focussed intently on her work.

She regarded him coolly, "Mr. Brogan, I'm sorry to tell you that I'm not Madame du Blez."

"No? Well, it got your attention. Can't say you looked very pleased though. No doubt the girlfriend wouldn't be happy to run into the wife." Her gaze lowered from cool to icy. He laughed, "Ach, don't be taking it so seriously now. I tried a politer approach, but you were ignoring me."

"So, what do you want?" She was unwilling to give him further scope for provocation and hoped he might come to the point.

"Just wondering where Farine had got to these days. I wanted to consult him about something."

"Why don't you ring his practice?"

"I did. Some old bird just kept telling me he was currently unavailable, not taking on any new cases. Ring back later."

"So what are you expecting from me?" She ticked off on her fingers, "I'm not his wife; I'm not his girlfriend; and I'm not his secretary."

"But you do know where he is?"

"Only to within about fifty miles."

He looked extremely confused, "You mean. . ."

"I mean, he's in France. A family member is seriously ill, he's needed there." Somehow she felt reluctant to tell him anything, but bare facts might prevent more prying.

"Oh!" Brogan looked genuinely surprised, wiping his hand across his mouth.

"Is there some problem?"

"No. No, that's fine. I didn't expect, no, it doesn't matter." He was all smiles again. "I thought he was avoiding me, that's all. I'm sorry about the Mrs. Du Blez thing. What is your name anyway? Farine never did introduce you."

Again there was that creeping reluctance, the rising of hairs on the back of her neck, but she could hardly refuse to answer, "Lucy."

"Well, Miss Enigma, at least I have a name for you now."

He looked set to start on another session of unwelcome banter, but was interrupted by his mobile 'phone ringing. Lucy took the opportunity to leave him with a nod and a raised hand as he turned his attention into the instrument. Excellent timing, as far as she was concerned.

Having more time to herself held advantages, she was able to press on with the large contract, and on Thursday accepted Jenny's suggestion that they go out to the cinema together. On the journey back home, her daughter couldn't help making use of the time to probe a little into the Farine situation.

"How come he had to tell you about his mother? Doesn't he have other friends?"

"I'm sure he does, maybe he told them first."

"Well, do you suppose he went and dragged them away from whatever they were doing? He seems a bit stuck on you."

"If you were upset, wouldn't you go to someone you knew would be sympathetic?"

"Yes, well he should have other friends besides you. You've only known him two months or something, how come you're best buddies?"

Lucy shrugged, this was definitely awkward, "We get on very well; that just happens, some people you click with."

Jenny was still grumbling, not entirely satisfied, ut said nothing else.

When they got home, they had a cup of tea together. Lucy decided she had better do a little bit more exploring on just how worried Jenny was about her unlikely friendship. "So, you're obviously concerned about me being such good friends with Farine. Have you spoken to dad about it?"

"Jenny nodded, "I e-mailed him, asking if I needed to panic."

"Taking your 'looking-after mum' responsibilities seriously then! And what did he say?"

"He said he didn't think you were suddenly going to be a different person to the one he's known for the last twenty-five years. He also said I should cut you some slack."

Lucy smiled down into her drink. How very sane and typical of Tom. Well, it was certainly much easier to live up to his good faith in her with Farine also at a distance.

Jenny left soon after that. Lucy clicked on the answerphone to check for messages, and was glad she hadn't tried it while her daughter was still there. There was a call from Farine, who sounded reasonably intoxicated, which was something of a shock. After a few phrases switching between French and English, he suddenly launched into one of the songs they'd sung in the car together, but there were some other voices providing backing sounds too.

"'Cos since I've come on home, well my body's been a mess. And I miss your curly hair and the way you like to dress. Why don't you come on over, start making a fool out of me? Why don't you come on over Lu-ucy?" The call ended with giggling and gales of laughter from someone. She couldn't help smiling, despite herself, at the nonsense, and chose to see it as everyone relaxing after an improvement in things at the hospital. She wondered what to do, and decided that if she rang his home number she could leave a message there, he would probably be picking up any messages on his mobile every so often. She didn't want to disturb him if he was with his family.

"Got your call. I'm guessing Maman has improved today by the general air of jollity. I must say though, you obviously need more singing lessons, quite a few of the words were wrong. Never mind, I won't tell the Zutons you're murdering their work. Take care."

She hoped that would make sense to him, though he might not make sense of anything for a while if he had a hangover to match how he'd sounded.

On Sunday evening she had a call from him at the office. He must have gone straight there after he got back, to start catching up with cases. They chatted for a few minutes about how his mother was and then he broached the subject of when they might meet up. He sounded very tired and apologetic about not being able to see her, but she was adamant that he should worry about himself.

"Okay, but I want to see you soon. I will be in touch."

17

On Tuesday morning Lucy got a text with a plea to meet
Farine for a very brief lunch. She replied accepting, but
suggested they meet up on the downs; she would pick up some
sandwiches on her way to save time.

She was there first, sitting on a bench when he arrived.
As he greeted her she could see the lines around his eyes and
wondered how many hours he'd been putting in to catch up.
She handed the food and a coffee across in silence, deciding it
might be best to give him a few minutes before they talked.

Eventually he sighed and looked at her, "Are you
speaking to me?"

"Yes, of course. I just thought you looked like a man
who needed to eat and rest rather than be dazzled with
conversation."

"You're probably right, I'm sorry."

"Now then, you tell me off if I do unnecessary
apologising. Don't you start."

"Okay, but I am genuinely sorry we haven't had any time
together. You can believe me when I say I would rather be out
with you than catching up on tedious cases."

"Well even I don't find that incredible. You chose to be a
solicitor though I'm afraid." He nodded and applied himself to
the coffee. "Anyway, if we're going to talk, let's not waste the
words on work. How is your mother getting on?"

"Mm," he swallowed, "Very well, they say she will be
out of hospital by Friday. Apparently she will be very weak for
some time; a lot of, what's that word for getting better?"

"Convalescence?"

"Yes, a lot of convalescence will be required. I think
Francine will have her at her house, Henri and Delphine
wouldn't have the first idea about looking after her. Suzette
would be sensible but she wouldn't stop Henri from being a
nuisance."

"Who's Delphine?"

"Henri's wife. She spends most of her time in the
gardens. At least that's slightly useful and generally harmless."

"Dear me, what's the poor woman done to deserve such a damning summary of her existence?"

He pulled a face, "I am being unkind, take no notice of me. However I cannot pretend she is in any way practical, apart from with plants. I get annoyed because she pays little attention even to bringing up her own children. She certainly wouldn't be any use looking after Maman."

"But Francine will?"

"Yes, she is more like you. She sees a problem, simple, she fixes it. She doesn't always say a lot, but you can rely on her."

"Ah well, she's got me beaten there then. I can rabbit on for England."

"Would that be at Olympic level?"

She smiled at him, pleased that he had enough capacity to tease her. But then he looked at his watch and deflated a little once more.

"I will have to go. Thank you for making the effort to have lunch, I'm glad you are my friend right now."

She felt herself blushing, rather more because she thought the compliment unwarranted, than the possibility of it being anything other than entirely innocent.

"I don't think I'm doing an awful lot to help you out. If there is anything I can do, let me know."

Very briefly his eyelids lowered a fraction and one end of his mouth curled in a half smile, anything but innocent. Then he ran his long fingers across his face, effectively wiping the expression away. Lucy determined not to react at all, as though she hadn't even been aware of it, but she was unable to do anything about her heart rate which increased of its own accord. He kissed her on both cheeks at that point and stood to leave.

"I will be working this evening again. And tomorrow. Maybe Thursday we could have lunch."

She looked up at him, concerned about just how tired he did seem. No doubt the whole shock of his mother's illness and having to dash home was taking an inevitable toll on him. She was always amazed by how exhausting emotional upsets were. On top of that he now had cases to bring up to date and meetings to reschedule.

"Only if you want to."

He reached out his hand and rested it on her shoulder, "You know very well I want to."

"Yes, but I meant if it fits in too. Don't fret about seeing me; we'll get together when you're free."

"I need something to keep me sane. I can only be a solicitor for so many hours in a week."

"Well, I can definitely understand that bit. Ten minutes would be my limit. You know where I am anyway. We can easily do something like this again on Thursday if that's any use."

He nodded and smiled as he left. She stayed on the bench and watched his long stride cover the ground swiftly, despite his relaxed pace. She recognised the automatic response engendered by seeing a friend suffer, and wondered just how much of a tug on her emotions it would turn out to be. Something else that was increasing the strength of the bond they had formed. Even when she was trying to lessen it, her efforts seemed to be either overwhelmed or undermined by external forces. She didn't have any answers, only more questions to sigh over.

"Won't be able to meet for lunch – sorry," arrived on her 'phone late Thursday morning. Obviously he was still struggling to clear his desk and she felt frustrated on his behalf. She was surprised, therefore, at a call from Maureen later on in the afternoon, and when she was put through to Farine his voice was very flat.

"Lucy I have had a call from a Mr. Prendergast, he's acting for Leslie Wilson."

"Oh that's quite quick, isn't it?"

"Yes, it is. And he wants to meet us as soon as possible. I tried to suggest some suitable dates, but he wanted to make it next week. I've refused, but said we can make the following Friday afternoon, provided it is a brief session, I have a meeting here at three. Is this okay for you?"

184

"Yes, no problem."

She had a horrible feeling that if it was someone else's case, he would have refused point blank to be railroaded into a meeting so hurriedly.

"Okay then, we will do that. I'm sorry, cherie, I need to be in the office again for the next couple of evenings and on Saturday."

"That's okay, don't worry but ...." She trailed off hesitating.

"What is it?"

"Well, you're going to need food at some point, why don't we meet up for a quick glass of wine and something to eat later. You can get back to the office afterwards and work the rest of the evening."

He paused for a moment, "Yes, I would like that. It would need to be early though, maybe six, otherwise I just won't feel like coming back in here. Would that be okay for you?"

"Yes, that's fine. Why don't we go to that place nearest your office; that would be okay wouldn't it?"

"Yes, I'll see you there. Lucy, thank you."

It was nearly six-thirty when he arrived, full of apology about losing track of the time. She shushed him.

"I'm not annoyed, stop worrying. However, I have already got through a whole glass of wine on an empty stomach so don't be surprised if I start being loud and badly behaved."

"Good, as long as it is amusing I won't complain. I could do with a change from work."

"I can't guarantee amusing, but I can promise not to talk about suing anyone."

"Tell me what you have been doing then; still the big contract?"

"Yes, it's coming along well. Often, when I think a job will be really difficult, by the time I've got to grips with what actually needs doing, I find I've done a lot of it in the process. That's always a nice feeling, suddenly looking over it and realising you've got the different bits done, it just needs careful assembly from there."

"Yes, that must be satisfying. Not at all like casework which just grinds on slowly."

They paused while the food and more wine arrived then Farine asked what Lucy was smiling to herself about.

"Well, it's the opposite way round to usual. People reckon that men have brains that are task oriented and women cope much better with continual casework, but you and I seem to be bucking the trend."

"What did you expect? Surely you didn't expect either of us to be normal?"

"No, certainly not. That wouldn't do at all, would it?"

They smiled at each other and ate in peaceful silence for a little while.

"So, have you heard any more? Is your mother coming out of hospital tomorrow?"

"Yes, it seems so. And I was right; she will go to Francine's."

"I though she lived at the château anyway."

"On the estate, but they have a house at the vineyard. I don't think Francine and Henri would survive for long in the same building. As far as she is concerned he is the little brother and should know his place. Whereas he thinks he is in charge and has no intention of listening to her advice."

"The more I hear about your family, the more I understand why you live over here!"

"Thank you, I told you it wasn't easy."

"Do they all fight like this?"

"No, I think Francine, Henri and I fight a lot because we were all born so close together. Somehow the others seem a lot younger and the gap made it easier to get along more peacefully. Actually it is very interesting for me when I go home, because I'm still getting to know Tomas, my youngest brother. He was only just in his teens when I left, so I haven't really known him as an adult. He seemed so much more mature this time; he probably dealt with things best. Well, he and Francine between them."

By now he was looking a good bit more relaxed; she scanned his face carefully and nodded to herself.

"What is it?"

"I was just thinking that's better, you were looking rather worn out when you arrived."

"I felt it, but now you are sounding like my mother, concerned for my welfare."

"You keep telling me we're friends, that's what friends do isn't it?"

"I suppose so. I would prefer the amusingly bad behaviour though, which I'm still waiting for."

"Ah, I think the floor show has been cancelled. Probably due to lack of inspiration, or interest. One of the above."

"I'm sorry; I'm not being very good company, am I?"

"Please don't use that line. I can still clearly remember the last time we had a scenario like this."

He did laugh then. "Now that is bad behaviour, reminding me of that. Would you like another glass of wine? Things could get interesting perhaps?" He brought out his wolfish smile to accompany the last comment, but it only served to amuse her.

"No chance. And you're going back to work, remember? So toddle off to your office now and I will escort myself virtuously back home."

They moved outside and turned to each other for their farewells.

"Thank you for cheering me up. Alas, I have meetings all day tomorrow. I expect I will have to work through the evening too. I'm hoping that if I work Saturday, that should get me up to date. I'm sorry this is all so dull."

"Don't keep apologising, and don't overdo it, get some rest!"

It was always a waste of time, she thought, saying it to a man, but still she couldn't resist saying it.

Farine was walking down the street, his head low, mind still entangled with cases being brought up to date. Lucy had been right last night, it was better to get out for a quick meal and then do another hour or two. Thirteen hours of continuous work made for poor spirits. Would tomorrow see the backlog cleared? He lifted his eyes to sweep the street ahead of him, jealously watching the busy progress of those heading for home and their weekends. Then he saw him. Damn! There was still that to deal with too, but he would have preferred not here. Somewhere with more space and distinctly less people would have been to his liking. Still, the opportunity was presenting itself, and after all, may it not be better in the public view of many eyes?

Not one to waste time on indecision, Farine moved quickly from the shady side of the street into full sun and directly into the path of Chris Brogan.

"Good afternoon." There was a feral reaction. His lip curled into a silent snarl. The scent of the man increased as adrenaline flowed. No matter. "I would like to talk to you. It won't take long, and I'm sure it will save us both a lot of bother."

Brogan's eyes darted quickly side to side, checking the surroundings. Farine tipped his head in query. "You are worried this is some sort of trap? I just want to talk. Look," he pointed to some light metal tables and chairs placed outside a coffee bar, profiting from the good weather, "let's take a seat here, we can both see the street and each other clearly. What do you say?"

Brogan nodded and sat down warily. Both of them chose to sit well back from the table, line of sight clear to each other's feet. The Ulsterman then slouched back, regarding Farine with interest.

"I think we need to clear up some misunderstandings. I have no idea why you sent two incompetents to assault me, but I don't regard it as clever or excusable."

"Who says I did?"

"We were at a party three days before, where my friends and I openly discussed our running routines. You took the trouble to warn me about my safety. It hardly requires a great mind to link the two. I want to know the reason."

"I would have thought that needed no Sherlock Holmes either." Farine narrowed his eyes and shook his head slightly. "Oh come on! Don't act the innocent. What about the pressure you've been putting on me?"

Farine felt as if he'd stumbled into another universe; one that didn't match his usual one in enough details for recognition. "The restaurant? That was hardly anything."

"I'm not talking about your party trick. I'm talking about the hiding you sent for me. Like for like, that was all."

"You think I was responsible for the beating you got? But why?" Suddenly he laughed at the ludicrous scenario being outlined for him. "That's nonsense! Besides, Mr. Brogan, I can assure you, if I wanted you to suffer, I would attend to it myself. Why do you think I would have hired men to attack you?"

Brogan again flicked his eyes around, checking or searching for something. He opened his mouth to speak, but before he could, an overweight man in a large apron emerged from the shop and loomed over the table.

"You gents going to order? Or just using my furniture for a rest?"

Farine looked at him darkly, "Two coffees."

Brogan looked up with a quick smile, "I'd prefer tea."

The waiter grunted and returned to the interior.

Brogan turned back to Farine, "Are you going to deny all knowledge of the bomb as well?"

"The bomb!" Farine sat back and his hand rubbed repeatedly over his head. This was going from ludicrous to maniac. "How do you know I was there? And what has that got to do with this?"

Brogan was beginning to look uneasy. "My shop, it was my shop that was blown up."

Farine shook his head, "I had no idea. You told me you had opened a place in Clifton, that was all. How could I know it was your shop? You think I'm responsible for that too?" He was monitoring the other man's face closely. "Apart from anything else, I was injured, why would I blow myself up?"

"Bombs can be tricky; they don't always go off according to plan. Especially for amateurs."

"I'm not an amateur, I'm a non-starter. What would I know about making bombs? I'm a solicitor for God's sake!"

"Well you seem to know about brawling. You don't look badly damaged from your encounter. You have some experience there obviously."

He gave a pronounced shrug, "I've done combat sports since I was a boy, I know about balance and force and moving well. The two you sent after me were obviously used to tackling unwary targets, not someone who could respond. But I'm guessing your experience is somewhat different to mine, from what you've said."

They held each other's eyes for several seconds. The waiter reappeared in the silence, his tray deposited on the table with enough force to slop liquid into saucers. Two coffees were put in front of Farine, a tall glass with pale water and floating tea bag in front of Brogan, the bill was tucked under the small milk jug.

Brogan stirred his tea. "Aye, I've had some experience of conflict. You can't grow up in Belfast without. But that's the past. I'm concerned with the present." He looked straight at Farine now, "When I said pressure, I meant pressure over the business. I took it you were part of something that saw me as a threat."

"I can't imagine what." He stroked his lip reflectively. "You mean some kind of protection racket, don't you? If you're experiencing this sort of trouble, it has to be. But why would you think I was involved?"

Brogan's turn to shrug, "You made it clear that night we ran in to each other that you didn't like me around. And at the party, you referred to my attack with some relish. Adding that to your presence when the shop went up, it seems obvious."

"To you perhaps, not to me."

"If it's happening to you, it tends to be on your mind. Know what I mean?"

Farine nodded, "Yes, I suppose it would be." He reached for the coffee and grimaced when it reached his mouth. "Well,

I had already regretted my rather physical means of ending our first conversation, but I had no idea it could lead to this. I assure you, I am nothing but a solicitor."

Brogan looked thoughtful, "I have no proof of that, do I?"

"Apart from the fact that we are having this talk? If I was involved in some form of extortion, I would send round another heavy reminder, I suppose. Or at least threaten it. As I said, I'm a man of the law, and as such, I must ask, have you not reported this problem to the police?"

The tea stopped partway to its target, "Maybe I'm dealing with it my own way."

"Mr. Brogan, we are hardly friends, but I have no wish to see you as a casualty. If there is some kind of gang running a racket here, the only way to deal with it is through the authorities."

Maybe this last sentiment helped to tip the balance; certainly the other man now looked more relaxed. "Thanks for your advice, but let's stick to sorting out you and me. Are you saying we have no need to carry on a feud?"

"I can see none. I'm not thrilled to have been a target for violence, and I certainly don't condone it. But from your circumstances, I can understand your conclusion that I was a threat to you. As I am not, surely it makes more sense for you to suspend hostilities with me. You appear to have enough to deal with. Although I must say it never occurred to me that greetings cards could be such a cut-throat business."

"Oh aye," he smiled, "terrible thing paper cuts. I get them all the time." The joke seemed lost on the taller man, but Brogan obviously wanted to part with a friendly gesture, as he held out his hand. "I think you're right. Let's shake on a gentleman's agreement. We'll call it a very unfortunate misunderstanding, which we're happy to put behind us."

Farine reached out and shook the proffered hand, not with any great relish, but at least satisfied that reason had prevailed. Brogan started to rise, "And give my regards to Mrs. du Blez, no doubt she's glad you're back from France."

The recently levelling universe tilted queasily once more. Instead of a lifeline, Brogan threw him only a smug grin.

Farine shook his head, "I have no wife, what do you mean?"

Brogan flapped his hand dismissively, "You know, the woman, Lucy. I admit I teased her with that title, mainly to needle her and find out what I wanted. Your absence seemed to tie in with avoiding me after the attack, more corroboration from my point of view. She told me you were in France. And I had assumed she would have told you about the shop."

Farine could do nothing but stare. What was Lucy doing engaging this man in conversation? His bewilderment was obvious enough to heighten the other man's amusement. He gathered himself to leave this time.

"Girlfriend not tell you about our little chats? Women, eh? You can't trust them, can you? She's not my type of course, I like them younger and warmer, but I can see she'd appeal to you. More cerebral I suppose."

"That's enough." Farine's voice was very low, and very purposeful. The grin on Brogan's face was in danger of meeting in his hair. "We may have put one problem behind us, but I warn you not to start another. Stay away from Lucy. If you don't, I will come after you myself, and you will regret it."

Brogan raised a hand in lax salute, "Just a solicitor. Aye, okay. I told you, she's not my type. Don't worry Mr. du Blez, she's all yours. I take it you're happy to settle the bill here."

With one more determined leer, he turned and picked up his previous route along the street, walking quickly and soon disappearing from sight.

Farine tried another sip of the coffee, but it was still undrinkable. He leaned forward, arms across his knees. Now what was he supposed to think? Why had Lucy not said anything about meeting Brogan? Surely she hadn't been sucked in by his sickly coating of charm? She had been convinced on one inspection that he was not to be trusted. Now he had another mystery to delve into. He rose, checking his watch to see if there was any time left to go and eat. As he took his first stride towards Hubert's there was a furious

192

banging from the café window, behind which the proprietor glared, pointing at the table. Farine retraced his steps and went in to pay. He said very carefully, in French, that he wouldn't have given such boiled cat's piss to his worst enemy, and he hoped the man choked on it himself before he could poison any other poor customers. The man nodded, Farine smiled benignly as he left.

She was sitting reading a book she had started for the weekend, curled up in her favourite chair, when the doorbell rang. She peered through the window before going to open the door.

"Hello, I thought you were working again."

"I've had enough for today. If I'm going to work tomorrow I think I need to get out for a while. Come for a walk? And a drink perhaps."

She nodded, reaching for her thin jacket in case the evening cooled later. They headed, as usual, for the downs, but instead of the normal comments on the evening, the weather and the surroundings, he was silent.

"What's the matter?"

"What do you mean?"

She would have to say he sounded cagey. "With you. Unusually quiet. Something's bugging you."

He shrugged, "Tired maybe."

She had been married long enough to know when a man was avoiding the issue. Fine. He wasn't her man; he could avoid whatever issues he wanted. Nevertheless, she was irritated. Why ask her out to keep glum company with him? She could manage that by herself. She slowed her pace, the reluctance to be in this situation played out through her feet. He had wandered on ahead, unaware of her lagging behind. He stopped under a tree, looking up into the branches above him. Suddenly he jumped, grabbed a branch and swung for a moment before starting to execute pull-ups. Now what was he up to? More like something young men did to show off their muscles. What had got into him tonight? She walked on, ignoring his odd behaviour. She heard him drop to the ground again behind her and felt rather than heard him catch up.

"I want to ask you something."

"Ask away."

"Why did you not tell me you'd been seeing Chris Brogan?"

She stopped ambling in order to face him. That one question contained all the right elements to spontaneously combust. She was incensed on so many levels that she didn't know where to start.

"Seeing him? Seeing him? Would you care to define that? Are we talking about the physical use of my eyes here? Or perhaps a different connotation is implied, one that seems to disturb you. Are you expecting me to justify something, the existence of which you have not bothered to verify? Correct me if I'm wrong, but I wasn't aware I'd signed my soul over to you. Do I need your permission now to speak to the inhabitants of this city? Would you like me to take the veil? Or maybe carry a placard with the address of your practice and the advice: 'consult my solicitor'?" She ran out of steam as quickly as she had boiled over, blinking suddenly at the tirade which had flowed from her.

He allowed no more than a faint look of surprise onto his face. "I seem to have struck a nerve. No matter, it was just a question."

She breathed heavily for a moment, trying to find equilibrium. "No it wasn't just a question. It was a loaded one, and it took you some time to work up to asking it." They stared at each other for several seconds. "Ask what you like, but don't pretend you haven't got some kind of agenda here."

His eyelids descended slowly. He nodded, "Okay, okay. I was worried. I don't like him."

"I know. Neither do I."

Eyes back up to her face. "Then why have you been seeing. . ." he ground his teeth, "chatting to him?"

"I take it that you've been talking to him yourself, in order to find this out." He nodded. "So how did that happen?"

A shrug, "I ran into him, in the street."

"Exactly. And that's just how I've bumped into him. As one of his outlets is in the main shopping area, it's easy to do."

"But you said nothing! You didn't even tell me it was his shop that blew up."

"Considering your reaction when we first spoke to him, I didn't dare."

He spoke very slowly, "What do you mean?"

"You looked in danger of breaking his arm because he held us up by talking. What would you have done if you knew he was being distinctly creepy?"

One hand was in his pocket, the other went up to his head. He appeared to be holding his scalp in place. He turned this way and that, not knowing what to do with himself. "And you said nothing! Did he threaten you?"

"No-o." She turned her head to regard him from the corners of her eyes. "Are you expecting him to?" There was no answer and she carried on in a more even tone. "Apart from the party, I've had three conversations with him. Every one of them has been odd, but I felt that he was trying to get information out of me more than threaten me."

Now Farine let both hands hang loose at his sides, staring at the ground. "I can't believe you didn't tell me."

"What would you have done?"

Fists, suddenly bunched, were thrust down into his pockets again. "Found him, and made him tell me what was going on."

"Mm. Precisely. Given that you told me he's a vindictive man, I'm not sure that would have been a good thing."

He reached out for her, taking hold of both arms and shaking his head. "Lucy, he might have hurt you. How would I have forgiven myself?"

"Do you know him to be a violent man?" Her voice came out almost as a squeak.

"I've found out that he is. I didn't know that until recently."

"Some clients you have! And do you also know what is going on?"

"I think so."

"Then perhaps we should share our information. As a lawyer, you can decide if I've transgressed terribly."

"No, you haven't." He pushed hair back from her face. "You will have behaved very properly, I'm sure. It will be me that has been the sinner."

"We'll 'fess up to each other and find out shall we? Your faith in my goodness is touching, but possibly misplaced. I promise you, I'm capable of most human failings."

"Hmm. That sounds encouraging. Worth getting my hopes up?"

His ability to move from black mood to soaring charm never failed to amuse her. But she shook her head, "Let's move on. We can walk properly now and talk."

They worked along the edge of the gorge, looking across at the dark trees growing up from precarious footholds on the other side, and glancing back along the curve of the nearer limestone edge. As they walked, Lucy related her Brogan incidents. Farine made various exclamations, most of them in horror at all this happening without his knowledge. By the time they reached the steep path down through the woods it was his turn. When he got to the attack, Lucy's outcry eclipsed any he'd made.

"You told me you fell running!"

"I did. But it wasn't an accident."

She was close to apoplexy. "I don't see how you can be annoyed with me, when you said nothing about this.

"What would you have done? I don't think you'd make a very good bodyguard."

She spluttered incoherently, muttering words like 'sexist' and 'patronising' before subsiding on a sigh, "Fair point. Fighting is your department, but I'd rather you avoided it."

"I'm not seeking it out. And hopefully I've dealt with the problem. But I do want to know if you have any more encounters with him."

They emerged from the path onto the road, crossing over to look at the river. The tide was in, allowing the muddy banks to be demurely covered. For once, the water managed to look attractive. The normally brown silt-laden flow was camouflaged by a golden glow from the low sun, its parting gift for the brief absence about to begin.

He leant on the railings, "So, will you tell me, if you come across him again?"

"Yes, agreed. Do you think he will go to the police?"

"I doubt it. It's not the impression he left me with."

"No, he doesn't come across as the type, does he?"

After strolling along for a while they had to regain all the lost height and work back up the hill, but used the road, which was slightly less arduous. By the time they were in Clifton again they were ready for a drink and found a table outside at their 'usual' wine bar. He closed his eyes, leaning his head on his hand.

Her compassion circuits fired again, "You look really tired."

"Yes, I am, but my eyes feel better, and my head. I've been indoors too much since I got back. It's been difficult after being outside so much back in France."

"So you enjoyed being at home?"

He sat back in his chair, "I suppose so, but then it was an odd visit really, the drama of Maman being so ill was something new. I think we all acted strangely for a while."

"Talking of which, I never asked you about the 'phone call. I assumed that was due to a certain amount of delirium."

"Oh yes, I'd forgotten that. I'd half expected you to tell me off about it."

"Well, it was quite funny. I'm not sure what you intended by it though, you obviously had an audience. Goodness knows what they thought you were doing."

"Ringing my girlfriend, probably."

"Mm, well it hardly sounded like you were addressing someone you think of like one of your sisters!"

"No, I couldn't say that. I might have agreed to treat you as I would my sister, but you can't expect me to think of you that way."

He reached his hand out, gently running his fingertips along the length of her forearm and resting his hand there while he stroked her skin with his thumb. She swiped at his hand with her own, a sharp flick across his fingers the result. Her face was settling to stern, but his eyes widening in shock made her laugh instead.

"Behave yourself then. That's not treating me as a brother would."

"You can't be so cruel as to deny me the occasional expression of frustration. It isn't my natural choice of the way to go, after all."

"Frustration accepted. Seduction denied."

He ran his hand across his head and smiled.

"Okay, I accept the reprimand. But that means you find the contact seductive, something else I can't help liking."

She closed her eyes and shook her head fractionally, the frown robbed of its power by the slightest of smiles hovering on her mouth. He leaned his head closer, his voice emerging deep and quiet when he spoke.

"Tell me what you're thinking."

Her smile widened, the head shaking increased in tempo.

"I hope that means it's something you would find very embarrassing to admit to, and over which you would feel guilty for at least two days."

The smile turned into a teeth-bared grimace and she opened her eyes to glare at him, cheeks darkening, "What's got into you tonight? Are you on something?"

He took a mouthful of his drink, "On the contrary, I have just forgotten to put the bromide in my coffee recently."

She spluttered with laughter and his face opened into a broad smile as he put his glass down.

"How do you do that?" she asked smiling in return, "How come you find it so easy to deal with all this female emotional stuff?"

"I am big brother to four girls, and my mother has had no husband for twenty years. I've had a lot of practice, believe me."

"I thought you lived away from them to avoid it all."

"They can still use the 'phone, and they tend to save things up for when I get home. I always arrive to a chorus of people calling my name and pouring out a long list of trials."

198

"Then why are you taking on another sorry case, one you have no obligation to?"

"Perhaps I miss it." He looked away from her and into a distance she could not see, "Yes, perhaps I do miss them more than I realise. Interesting."

On Sunday he rang after lunch, his voice very subdued.

"Lucy, I want to see you. Please will you come?"

"Is anything wrong?"

"No, well, just. . .please come."

"Okay, I'll be there in about half an hour."

She had to change back out of the gardening clothes she'd just assumed, and she sighed, frowning to herself, wondering exactly what was amiss.

18

When she got to his flat, he let her in and padded straight through to the lounge area, saying hardly anything. He sat down on the huge sofa and held his hand out to her; she took it and sat down next to him.

"Thank you for coming, I knew you would."

"Are you okay?"

He nodded, then closed his eyes and leant his head back, "Well, no. I don't know. I'm tired and miserable. I need your company."

She wasn't really sure what to say next, but that became irrelevant as he pulled her down onto the settee and wrapped himself round her.

"Stop fussing, I'm not doing anything to you. Just be still."

She wriggled to get her face free and tried to look at him, he had his eyes closed again.

"Can't you be still?"

"Well, I do need to breathe."

"Yes, okay get comfy; then be still."

"What is this? I mean do you want to talk?"

"No I want you to be quiet. I just need to be."

She tried to say something else, but he shushed her. She was being given no choice but to lie there, wondering what this was all about. Part of her wanted to be very obstreperous and demand to know what he thought he was doing, but then he wasn't doing anything. After a few minutes she realised that's exactly what was happening, nothing. For a while she found it very difficult, simply to rest and not speak or move. After some time though, she realised the tension she'd had from the surprise of being engulfed was ebbing away and her mind was drifting from thought to thought. She even fell asleep briefly; it was warm and a bit stuffy for her liking in the flat, although he was probably finding it rather cool after his trip to the south of France. When she woke, she managed to sneak a look at her watch, and discovered they'd been lying like this for over an hour. There was definitely a crick developing in the small of her back. The more she tried not to think about it, the more insistent it became. She must have reacted to it, as he suddenly spoke.

"What is the problem? You're wriggling again."

"Too long in one position, my back's aching."

Like wire uncoiling he unwound his arms and legs from around her without opening his eyes. "Okay, go and move around for a few minutes, then come back."

She got up, and trotted round the flat, taking the opportunity to open the balcony door for some air. When she returned, she brought a cushion and made herself more comfortable. Straightaway, his arms and legs went round her again and she was once more in his peculiar embrace.

This time, it was easier to relax, and she found herself remembering odd things and planning some drawings she would like to do. More time passed, and she felt less bothered about counting it. She was taken by surprise therefore when he spoke.

"This reminds me of Sylvie and me when we were children."

She had a feeling she needed to stay in the background, so all she said was, "Oh?"

"Yes, we would go and hide when we were in trouble, we just lay holding onto each other and keeping quiet so they wouldn't find us. When we heard them go away, then we lay and talked. She is four years younger than me, sometimes I would tell her the stories I had been reading, and then we would be in the stories in our minds and plan going off for adventures. I was always a famous swordsman of course, and I would promise to save her and be her protector."

He stopped, and she risked a question, "Were you in trouble very often?"

"Oh yes, all the time. Grandmère hated me remember, so there was always something I'd done wrong. From about three years old Sylvie would defy her. She would stamp her foot and say, 'It's not fair, it was Henri, not Farine,' then Grandmère would be so angry with her she would forget what I had done. So when I was in trouble we ran away, when she was in trouble we ran away just the same.

She was the first one after Henri, so that was his chance to bully somebody smaller than himself; he couldn't do it with Francine or me. Of course, if he was unkind to Sylvie then I beat him, and I was in trouble again.

As we got older, Sylvie would make me listen to her favourite stories. They always involved horses. We were going to run away and train wild horses on the Camargue, or run away to America and become cowboys, either seemed attractive."

He stopped again; she was utterly fascinated by now, "Where did you hide?"

"Ah, a crumbling château is very useful for some things. Odd places to hide is one of them. Strange cupboards, attic rooms; if we had the time to make our escape, we would get out of the house and go up into the stable loft. Also she could climb trees very well by the time she was six."

"You must love her very much."

"Yes we are still very close, though I don't see a lot of her, she lives the furthest away. She married a man who breeds horses, not really surprising. Matthieu is a good husband I think, she seems happy. Mind you, when they got engaged, I promised him I would break every bone in his body if he didn't make her happy."

"Some incentive then."

"Well, we got on very well, before and after the threat. I wish we saw more of them, but of course it is not easy to leave the farm for very long. Maman usually goes down to stay with them for a month or so each year. When she is stronger I think they will take her down."

She looked up, and discovered he had his eyes open. He smiled at her, before rubbing his face against her hair, then unwound himself once more. "Thank you."

They both sat up, she wasn't sure quite what to do or say now. "Do you feel better?"

He nodded taking hold of her hand again, "Sometimes I just need to be, and I couldn't face 'being' alone. I had forgotten about me and Sylvie doing that, well not thought of it for a long time. I hope it wasn't too scary."

202

"No, as it turned out. You could have explained perhaps, at the beginning."

He shrugged, "How do you explain that? And you would have said no, it doesn't sound like 'appropriate' behaviour, does it?"

She didn't need to say anything, so she sat back in the sofa and closed her eyes for a while. "Did you get to spend some time with Etienne? Did you do any fencing practice together?"

"Oui. I think the children were very glad to see me, it frightened them having Maman taken so ill. She tries to look after them quite a lot. They didn't want me to return so soon, but I cannot abandon my office at will. Anyway, I managed to have a couple of sessions with Etienne, he really has some promise. I must make sure I go home again before too long. Or maybe they could visit me here. You would like them, and they're dying to meet you."

She sat bolt upright, "They're what? They know about me?"

He turned his head to look at her, puzzled. "Of course. Who do you think was singing with me on the 'phone call? They think it is hilarious that you are teaching me modern songs."

She was trying to speak, but for a moment succeeded in producing only gargling noises somewhere in her throat. "I can't believe this! You've told your family about us, about our, I mean… "

"Stop panicking, they know we're not lovers, I've told them you won't leave your husband."

She thought she might be about to expire, and flopped her head down onto the sofa, moaning into it.

"Why are you being hysterical?"

She raised her head again, "Oh let me think. What could I possibly object to about being discussed by your entire and peculiar family? Not to mention having my morals scrutinised and my sexual preferences considered. No, can't think of a single thing I'd mind there. That's all fine then."

"You're being ridiculous. They think you look like a very nice English lady."

"I look like! How do they know what I look like?"

"From the pictures I have on my 'phone. How else?"

"What pictures? Show me, show me now, or I swear you'll regret it."

He went to get his mobile, and brought up the pictures he had.

"When did you take these?"

"Well, obviously that one is on the downs, and this one is an evening we went out for a drink, at the wine bar I think. And of course this is you dancing at the party."

"You can't do this. You can't just take and keep pictures of me like this. It constitutes stalking or something!"

He raised an eyebrow and looked at her for a second, "Shall I recommend a good solicitor?"

"Don't try and be clever with me. You know this is unacceptable."

"And have you drawn me?" he asked very quietly.

Her face reddened, and she sat very still, "It's not the same."

"Why? Did you ask me if I minded?"

She got up and walked out onto the balcony. She wasn't sure whether fresh air would make anything better, but it seemed worth a try. After a little while he came and joined her.

"I'm sorry you're upset about the pictures. Why is it so bad?"

"Well, it's not just that. It's the fact that this whole stupid game, the secret non-affair you seem to delight in, is hardly a secret when you go home and discuss it with the entire du Blez clan. And supposing someone here sees those pictures? What then?"

"What if someone sees your drawings? Do you pretend it's some stranger? Do you think your drawing is so bad no-one will recognise me?"

"I don't do faces, but no, I can't pretend you wouldn't be recognised. Anyone who knows you would see it as you. But I don't carry them round, showing everyone."

"Well, maybe the difference is that I am not ashamed of our friendship. And I thought we were behaving ourselves impeccably so that you didn't have to be either."

"We've been through this. We are closer than ordinary friends, or do you wrap yourself around anyone who happens to be here at the time?" She pointed back to the sofa, as if he might be in any doubt about what she was referring to.

He looked stung and turned away. "I asked for your help because I thought you cared about your friends, and I thought you cared for me. I'm sorry if that has trespassed too greatly on your respectability."

"I do care! And don't try and make this about my view of right and wrong. I haven't got a problem being with you, but I can't pretend it doesn't cause problems in how I deal with other people. When I go home I'll be writing e-mails to Tom, what do you suggest I tell him? Oh Farine says it's okay, his family all know I won't leave you. By the way we had a lovely time cuddling up for several hours in his flat. Hope all is well with you. Does that sound about right?"

He turned back to her and took hold of her arm, "I'm sorry, I don't mean to forget you're married. My life is without that kind of commitment, it doesn't automatically occur to me how what I do affects someone else. You are right, I'm expecting too much of you."

They stood looking at each other, saying nothing.

He put his hand on her shoulder, "Come and have a glass of wine, let's make peace."

She followed him back in, and flopped down on the sofa. He brought them both wine and handed her a glass, then sat down on the floor by her feet, his back against the furniture. They sat in silence for a little while.

"So, you have told Tom about me then?"

"I tell him most things. I don't want to keep it a secret from him that I've been spending time with you. It's better if he hears it from me than from someone else." She paused, "I suppose I'm somewhat circumspect in what I say and how I say it, I don't want to make it difficult for him so far away.

Probably, I'm leaving out some stuff I should put in and vice versa."

"Did you tell him about our Mad Five Minutes?"

"No, I thought that would be too cruel. It's possible that I will tell him eventually, when we're together again, but I don't know yet. It's not fair of me to say it just because I want it off my chest, I could go to confession for that, couldn't I?"

He turned to look at her, and found she was smiling slightly.

"Yes, it's very useful for that."

Walking home, he asked her again about the drawings, "Have you told Tom that you've been drawing me?"

"I haven't made a point of it; I don't regard that as particularly inflammatory. I draw lots of people without having been in a clinch with them. I told you, it clears my head out. He's used to me drawing all and sundry."

"I would like to see them one day. Will I like them?"

"How can I tell that? I never do, I can always see what's wrong with them."

They walked on, discussing the whole realm of not liking their own work, whether music or art, and decided that other people had to give an opinion, but even that couldn't be relied upon. Finally they reached her door.

"I will call you; I should have more time this week. Hopefully things will be a bit calmer now. And of course, we have the meeting for your case soon."

She nodded, "Do I need to do anything for that?"

"No, we might run over one or two points beforehand, but don't worry I will have everything ready."

They said au revoir, but he put his arms round her as they did so.

"Thank you for this afternoon. I mean it, and I'm sorry for annoying you. I, well, just thank you anyway. Au revoir, cherie."

He was right about his work, it was only a couple of evenings later that they went for a walk along the top of the gorge and decided to stop for a drink; the evening was still very hot. As they arrived, a group of people were in the act of vacating one of the wooden tables outside, giving them the chance to grab it. During the discussion as to what Lucy wanted to drink, a voice cut across the general babble of the pub terrace.

"Luce! Luce! Over here."

Farine and Lucy turned to see a hand being waved frantically in the air. Mel was sitting several tables away, she turned and said something to her companions before extricating herself to come across.

"Hi guys. Couldn't ignore you. Sorry for making a spectacle of you though."

Lucy gave a small expulsion of breath, "Liar! You take every chance you can to embarrass your friends."

"True," grinned Mel, perching on the same bench as Lucy. "But Frenchy here doesn't know that."

The Frenchman in question appeared to be unmoved by the insult, insisting instead that Mel join them for at least one drink.

When he left for the bar Lucy turned to her friend. "Who are you with?"

"Work colleagues, it's Brian's birthday and we promised him a drink."

They chatted about various things, including, of course, Farine, until he returned with wine for Mel and a lager he set down in front of Lucy.

"You on the lager, Luce? You know you'll regret it."

"Does it make her behave badly?" asked Farine.

"Bad luck, nothing makes her do that." Mel gave a belly laugh as she replied.

"I'm just so hot and thirsty; you can't beat a cold lager for that."

"I know," said Mel, looking at her watch pointedly.

Farine could make nothing of their amusement and started to talk about the play they had all seen. Mel in turn asked how his mother was getting on. Some time went by in pleasant conversation until Lucy rose.

"It's no use."

Mel started laughing again, "Thirteen minutes! That's pathetic even for you."

Farine was looking bewildered. Mel explained as Lucy left, head shaking. "Lager goes straight through her. She never could hold it."

The laughter stopped, Mel was still looking straight at Farine. His eyes had wandered away, but when he spoke there was no doubt where his words were directed. "Say it then, now is your chance."

"You're going to hurt each other."

He did look at her now, "I expect the concern for your friend, but for me too?"

"She's too good a judge of character to take up with a total scumball. She won't leave Tom. If that means you get hurt, she'll be damaged too. Just so you know."

"Thank you for the warning." A short silence hung between them. "No advice to go with it? Like, stop it now. That's what all her other friends think, no?"

"Well, I'm not one of her Holy Joe chums. My advice was quite different." She gave a charming smile before saying, "I told her to shag you senseless and move on."

"I see. Are you telling me that so I encourage her?"

"No. Wouldn't work. If you haven't noticed yet, Lucy is remarkably immune to what anybody else thinks she should do."

"I had noticed."

"Well, there you are then. The purpose of this talk is for information only. And," she drained her wine before finishing, "to let you know that whatever happens between you, she has at least one friend who will stand by her."

Farine could see Lucy emerging from the pub. He murmured a soft 'thank you' before she could reach them. Mel nodded and got to her feet as Lucy arrived.

"Why is there always a queue for the ladies? Mel are you leaving us?"

"Yes, I've ditched my party long enough. It looks like I don't want to be with them. Be good. Or at least careful." She walked away chuckling.

"Sorry," said Lucy climbing back into her seat. "She's a total embarrassment most of the time. I dread to think what she's been saying to you."

"Yes, but you are very fond of each other."

Lucy nodded, wondering what they had passed between them. Without doubt, there would have been something.

19

The pub was almost empty inside, most people preferring to stay out even though the temperature was dropping now. The speakers were blasting out an old Blondie number. Lucy, as ever, was sucked straight into the song and joined in, the empty tables around her allowing her to crank up her own volume, "…cover me with love. Roll me in designer sheets, I'll never get enough."

Of course Farine was on his way back to the table with the drinks, she didn't give it any thought until he made minute changes to his expression, giving her cause to do likewise and stop singing. She lifted the drink to her mouth instead and tried to look at him from under her eyelids as she tipped her head back. Annoyingly, she could never manage that nearly so well as he seemed to. He was staring down at the table in silence, beyond that she could not discern.

"Sorry," she said shortly.

He looked up, "For what?"

She closed her eyes and huffed out a sigh. He frowned.

"Do you mean you're sorry for your singing, or for drawing my attention to a forbidden pastime?"

She was rubbing her hand over her left cheek and eyebrow, "Just, sorry!" She sighed again, "I suppose I mean I wasn't trying to wind you up."

"Lucy, I'm not bound by your constraints. If I can't handle the frustration I don't have to live with it. I don't see you every night of the week."

She sat very still trying to work out why he had said that, or just what her reaction was. His tone, as he continued, made it obvious he took it as a negative one.

"What, are you jealous? Or just disapproving?"

She found herself searching his face for her own answers to both questions. Then she dropped her gaze to keep her expression to herself, "That's rather harsh. Are you saying that to shock me or make a point about something?"

"Neither. You told me you prefer honest to polite. Did you not really mean that?"

"Well, I certainly didn't expect you to tell me all about your propensity for using women casually."

"Now you're being harsh. I never *use* women. Plenty of people are happy to share straightforward physical pleasure. As long as you both know what the score is, I can't see the harm. Believe me, I never pretend to offer more than I'm really willing to give. My relationship with you is of a different nature, for various reasons. You want fun of a different kind, but you're not disgusted with me for being willing to provide that."

"Obviously I'm just a hypocrite after all. About everything it seems."

"Look, we don't need another argument. I said it because you constantly feel uncomfortable about putting me in what you see as a difficult position. However, from your reaction, I surmise it's done nothing to allay your guilt."

Her head came up, "I'm not used to someone who can out-honest me! And besides that, we've been busy saying what good friends we are. We established on Sunday I have a concern for you. Well, I don't like to think of you putting yourself at risk, or into unnecessary situations because of the game we're playing."

Her eyes had burned with feeling and her speech was a verbal rolling up of her sleeves to fight. They seemed to be doing that more and more frequently at the moment.

He smiled slightly as he responded, "Don't you think I'm old enough to look after myself? Are you the one to instruct me in the ways of the big bad world?"

"You don't have to sneer. I'm sure you can manage the obvious risks of modern life far better than me. But we're all more vulnerable than we like to admit, or are even aware of. As a friend, I can't stop myself caring what happens to you, emotionally or any other way."

He put his hand over hers on the table, "I wasn't sneering. Lucy, I hope you will always be my friend. You're much more interesting than any I've had before."

He was trying to sweet-talk her now, was he? She tried to swat it away, "I find that hard to believe."

"Why would I want to be with you if you weren't interesting? Your logic is strange sometimes. You've asked me over and over what I get out of this, but it seems to me you're the one who gets nothing. You feel bad for denying me your body, and you feel worse for contemplating the pleasure if you didn't! I can't begin to understand how you cope with it. If I were in your position, I would go for the pleasure and sort the rest out later. Why don't you?"

She smiled, shaking her head, "Ha, got you there, I'm good at thinking long-term. And I know The Pain Equation."

"What's the Pain Equation? Is that real? Or something from Lucy-land?"

"Real; to me anyway. It's how you balance out whether something will be worth doing or not."

"So, tell me, it sounds useful."

She tried an explanation, waving her hands in the air, but he looked lost. Giving way, she reached for a pen and found an old receipt to write on the back of.

"Look, if I make a graph, this axis is the present pleasure of an action. This one is the resulting pain when you get to it, not perceived pain from where you are now, but what it will feel like when it happens. Then you draw a line where the value of the pleasure equals the value of the pain, anything above the line is worth doing, anything below it isn't."

He shook his head, whether in disbelief or confusion she wasn't sure.

"How do you know what the pain really will be like? You said 'not what it looks like from here', what else have you got to go on?"

"I told you: that's the part I'm good at, recognising things from a long way off."

"So you're implying that I get it wrong, that I undervalue the future pain of my actions. But you could just as well be underestimating the present pleasure of something. Maybe you see ahead well, but not what's right in front of you."

"That's possible. But something here and now is easier to evaluate surely?"

"It could be. Anyway, it's different, I'll give you that. Are you honestly telling me that you plot everything on a graph before you do it?"

"No! Not at all. But I suppose intuitively, that's how I think of it, how I make my decisions. We all do it, though maybe not with a graph."

He was quiet for a while, looking at the scrap of paper and musing.

She watched his face, "What are you thinking?"

"Just wondering, on your graph, where sleeping with me falls."

She put a small 'x' on the paper, "Just so you know."

"I'm gratified to see the pleasure value is high, alas you have assigned it an even higher value on the pain axis. I have no way to argue with your assessment of the resulting agony, but as you haven't actually done it, how do you know just how pleasurable it is? You could be seriously underestimating."

"Are you always so arrogant?"

"Almost always. Besides, I am French. It is recognised that we make the best lovers, justifiably so. From what I've seen of British men, your axis in that direction has never needed the sort of values we would reach."

Her palm didn't make it as far as connecting with his face; he was right about the speed of his reflexes. He held her wrist tightly for a moment before loosening his grip and looking straight into her eyes, their normal bluish light replaced by flinty grey opacity. He lowered his lids to cut himself off from their glare,

"Okay, I'm sorry. That was too far, I admit it. No personal disrespect was intended. I was following your mathematical process and got carried away. I never knew equations could be so risky."

He turned her hand and kissed the back of it gently before lowering it to the table again. She sat back in her seat. Was there anything about this man she could make sense of? He was gentler, ruder, more provocative, more fun than anyone she had come across before, and she was utterly exhausted from trying to work out how to handle him. Well, handle herself was more accurate. There was no option to manage him. Like him or leave him alone was all that was on offer. She put both hands up to her face, massaging her forehead and tuning out of her surroundings momentarily.

"Are you not speaking to me now?" His words arrived at the same time as his fingers teased out the hair trapped between her face and hands, making her jump.

"Don't!" she snapped, lowering her slender barricade.

"I didn't mean to hurt you."

"No, I don't expect you did," her voice was cool, conveying both distance and weariness, "I don't expect either of us means to cause all the damage we're wreaking on each other. We both ought to know better than to fool around with somebody else's feelings. What will it take before we see sense?"

"You make us sound very bad. Are we both being so awful?"

"I don't know, I'm too tired of messing around to think straight. One minute we're perfectly good friends, the next we're acting archly and winding each other up. That's not very considerate on either side is it?"

He paused for a few seconds, "No, it isn't. Shall I walk you home?"

"Yes, I think that's probably a good idea."

'Well Tom, I'm cracking on with the Lucker's contract. I feel quite pleased with myself at the moment for managing such a big job. Probably be a different story tomorrow!

No, I haven't seen as much of Farine lately. He was very busy for a while when he got back, and the couple of times we've met up, he's been in an odd sort of mood. I suppose the poor guy was pretty shaken by his mother's illness, I get the impression they're very close. On that theme, Rich is back; apparently his ailing parent has rallied too, though he seems to think it could be something of a long-term scenario.'

She paused, going to open the door, only to find no-one there. Odd, somebody had rung the bell. There weren't enough young children living in the road these days to be bothered by

214

that game. As she turned, she spotted the flowers resting against the side of the step. Of course, it should have been obvious. In mitigation, it was only a small posy, but as she bent to pick it up the scent hit her straight away. She loved the smell of pinks, so much stronger than florist's carnations. These were spicy, smelling of nutmeg, and their small petals, white frills edged with dark magenta, looked like tiny ballerina skirts. Simple enjoyment of these sensations carried her back through to the kitchen before she spotted the card tucked inside the paper. That too was small but, again, had been carefully chosen. The picture was of a scruffy dog, head down forlornly, his lead stretched out and tied to something indeterminate. Inside it read: I am missing our walks, will saying sorry not be enough?

It was much later during the evening that she was able to think of a reply. She sent a text: flowers lovely, dog cute, man forgiven! When she turned on her phone next morning there was a message on her voice mail, which had been sent late the night before. "I will finish the days of my penance and see you soon." She wasn't sure exactly what he meant by the penance part, but the general drift was clear. A thin pang of guilt, like a long slim blade ran through her, had she just passed up a perfect opportunity to put a stop to this nonsense? It didn't feel right to capitalise on an accidental misery, she would be happier dealing with it properly, providing she had the nerve to do it. Whatever dealing with it properly might entail.

Shining steel sent reflections of sunlight skittering across the kitchen walls as she spun the pan by the handle, before tightening her hold and slapping it down onto the hob. She threw both hands in the air and did a quick wiggle before spinning on her toes to samba across the floor and collect spatulas and a knife. The music was loud and she was singing and swaying, her eyes closed in between reaching for implements. A quick jump up and down was followed by side-stepping to the 'fridge, elbows out. She extracted a jar of olives and shuffled backwards swinging her hips, "Come up and see me, make me smi-i-i-ile. I'll do what you want, running wi-i-i-ild."

She pivoted, arms out again and head bobbing side to side. The singing was abruptly cut off and replaced by a scream as she dropped the jar at his feet.

With one hand to her heart and the other to her head she stood aghast for a moment, both of them looking ineffectually at the smashed glass and wasted olives strewn between them on the floor. Then they both tried to move and speak at the same time.

"What do you think you're doing scaring me like that?"

"I'll clear this up, mind your feet on that bit."

"How long have you been standing there? No leave it, I'll do it!"

"Have you got a cloth and something to put this in?"

Again in unison, they stopped babbling and looked at each other, by now both crouched down either side of the wreckage.

"I'm sorry, I didn't mean to startle you," he bent his head and started to collect the larger pieces of glass into his cupped hand.

"Why didn't you ring the doorbell, instead of sneaking up on me?" She passed him an empty pot for the debris.

"I did; no answer. But I could hear the music and your back door was open. Cloth?"

Now she passed him kitchen towel, simultaneously issuing an instruction, "Stop. Stay exactly as you are."

He froze, but looked up at her face after a few seconds, wondering what he was supposed to be waiting for. Her eyes were intent on something, but he couldn't tell exactly what. He waited a little longer for her to find whatever it was she seemed to be searching for, nothing happened.

"Is there a purpose to this?"

"Yes, that's okay now," she reached forward as she spoke and gingerly lifted off his hand the last piece he'd picked up. It was from the bottom of the jar, where it had broken into part of a ring. An arc had formed, terminating at either end in razor sharp horns. She carried away this piece carefully and set it on some cardboard on the window ledge. After that it was back to the practicalities of cleaning.

They straightened up; she took the pot of fragments from him, absently squashing into it a slimy piece of the kitchen paper.

"Ow!" she pulled her hand back sharply and 'tutted' in annoyance at the blood dripping down her finger.

"Plasters?" he asked, taking the pot back into his possession.

"Cupboard over the microwave," she held her finger under the tap to rinse away the blood, then wrapped a fresh piece of tissue over it and squeezed to stop the flow. He took her hand, examining the finger to check there was no glass embedded there before wrapping the plaster tightly round and over the cut.

"Fine, emergency over."

"Yes, but it's a nuisance. I've got all those onions and things to chop. This is right in my way, and I think it's still oozing a bit to be honest."

"No problem, I can do that for you."

"You don't have to, I'm sure I can manage."

He gave her an austere look, "No need to worry, I'm not a blundering male in the kitchen. My youngest sister is a cook, we all get ordered around in her domain as unskilled help. Chopping vegetable is one of the tasks she hands out regularly."

Unsurprisingly, he wielded the knife like a pro and was soon passing across piles of slivered onions which hissed into the frying pan. With the peppers added in and everything spluttering away gently, she declared it was time to have a coffee. Again he took the mechanics of it out of her hands.

"What was all that about with the broken glass, and why have you saved one piece?"

"It made a really good composition. I was fixing it in my mind, but that shape is too hard to remember, I'd never get all those angles right from memory."

"What about my hand though?"

"I've seen those quite a lot, I'll remember that."

Even as she said it, she bent her right hand into the curve his had made under the glass, rehearsing the shape. He looked distractedly at her for a moment then closed his eyes slowly and leaned his head forward to rest against a cupboard door.

"That's why you stare at me so much!"

"Yes, of course," a smile broke across her face, "Did you think I was admiring your manly form all the time?"

He shook his head, "God, I really am arrogant, aren't I?"

"That might count as vain rather than arrogant actually. Either way, I'm used to observing people covertly, but you don't mind being watched, so I suppose I've made the most of it."

"But you let me tease you about how you felt; you never said it was art! You had every chance to, to …" He waved his arm, attempting to compensate for the eventual failure of his voice.

"Take you down a peg or two?"

"Yes, that's the phrase!"

She shrugged, "I can't see the point. It's not harmful arrogance, most of the time anyway. Why would I need to score off you? You do that when you feel inferior to people, and actually I don't, not even about you being a Count. I might feel awkward, not sure how to conduct things, but I don't feel less than anyone else."

His hand was running over the back of his head, obviously trying to readjust his thinking and fit it into this newly-discovered framework.

"So, have I spoken like a complete idiot all the time?"

"No, not all the time."

His eyes turned to her face, trying to take in what went with the words. Now she closed her eyes and he saw her mouth the word 'shit!' as she turned away.

"I came to make peace between us again, not make things worse. Don't disappear off into some realm of shame and guilt. You might as well enjoy having wrong-footed me for a few minutes at least."

She held up one finger, "Overstating there, probably just embarrassment."

218

"Good. Drink the coffee. And I think the onions are burning."

The frying was rescued, more coffee made, along with tea for Lucy and then they sat outside under the shade of a tree, away from the heat of the kitchen.

"Are you cooking for something special?"

"Some friends are coming round tonight. I thought I'd get it prepared early before the day gets too hot. I can just stick it in the oven later."

He looked at her in surprise as she sighed and pulled her mouth to one side.

"Are you not looking forward to seeing your friends?"

"Well, it's a bit awkward at the moment. With Tom away I feel a bit of a spare part in our usual crowd. They all try to be very kind and supportive, but somehow I end up feeling like I'm receiving a hospital visit. 'How are you dear? Not long now. How are you coping?' that sort of thing." She pulled at some long pieces of grass, "And I'll be given a careful grilling, very tactfully of course, about this chap I've been spending a lot of time with."

"Oh. The big bad wolf again."

"Yep. As though I can't see, or may not have noticed, that it's a bit questionable. The way they think it will help for them to carefully draw my attention to it, is a sign of the fact that they have no idea how I really tick."

"Another foot on the obstinacy pedal?" She nodded. "Why ask them round?"

"They sort of asked themselves."

"You could have said no."

"Would look like I had something to hide, don't you think? I've put them off twice already. Besides, they're nice people really; I'm just out of sorts with everyone."

"How do they know about me?"

"Well, if you think back, you turned up at church one day. You can't deny you're a noticeable kind of person."

"Ah, yes. Did I occasion a lot of questions?"

"A fair few. All very polite. I considered saying you were my mid-life crisis and great in bed, but decided that was too cheap and predictable."

He smiled at her, signalling his pleasure that she was back to treating the whole thing as allowable humour and hence off the 'highly emotive' list.

"You said you were missing the walks, how do you fancy a real one tomorrow?"

"Fine, are you not going to church?"

She shook her head, "Probably enough soul-searching will take place tonight, I reckon I'm allowed a day off for that. I thought, if you like, we could head for the Mendips again and I can take you up to a spot with a great view."

"Yes, I'd like that. I'm having dinner with some friends in the evening, so as long we're back by late afternoon it would be fine. Another dawn start?"

"No need, four hours for travelling and walking is plenty. But earlyish maybe."

"Okay, I'll come for you about eight shall I?"

"Yes, that's fine."

He lay back on the grass staring at the sky. After a few moments calm she asked quietly, "Just how long where you standing watching me earlier?"

"I don't know exactly, I didn't check my watch. You didn't do anything too ghastly, if that's what worries you."

"Well, I won't know, will I? Our definitions of 'ghastly' might differ. It always seems to me that I end up embarrassed in any exchange. You get the upper hand every time."

"No, don't think of it like that. I was simply enjoying the sight of you so relaxed. I wasn't stalking. Anyway, I thought you'd evened the tally a bit today."

She turned to lie on her front, leaning on her elbows, "Yes, I must hang on to that one for a while, you probably won't give me too many chances like that."

"Not now I know what your game is. I will be en garde!"

"Don't go all D'Artagnan on me, not unless you're prepared to wear the hat."

They both smiled at that image, words ebbing away as they relaxed into the quiet of lying peacefully. She put her head down on her arms and chose to let this oasis of calm contentment claim her totally for a little while. All she could hear was the birds proclaiming their territory within her own, and feel the gentle rhythm of regular breathing. He was right; simply to 'be' alongside another human was very comforting. A pity it was even more treacherous than any of their recent highly charged interludes.

20

Once again they were heading off, Lucy navigating and music playing loudly as they rode along with the hood down. Today, she was slightly surprised to discover, they were back to classical.

"Have you got fed up of singing lessons?"

He shot her a quick glance, "It seemed that we ran into too many difficulties occasioned by over-friendly lyrics. I was playing safe."

"I see," she sighed her response. "You probably have a good point there. We won't have any of that trouble with good dependable classics at least." Her tone of voice seemed to carry more meaning than she'd intended and she mentally kicked herself, but he smiled lightly and let it rest.

Before long they had nosed through the country lanes and stopped at the bottom of the combe she was heading for, pulling into a stony lay-by to park the car. She changed into her walking boots and swung the small rucksack onto her back.

"I can carry that," he said holding out his hand for it. She raised an eyebrow by way of reply. He pulled a face, "Don't worry, I'm not implying you're pathetic, I wouldn't dare."

She smiled, shaking her head, "There's very little in it. If you want to be noble though, you can carry it on the way back."

She led him across the road and onto a narrow track that wound its way along the side of the combe, into a stream-cut for a while and then steeply up to emerge on a plateau of short grass and intermittent mixed woodland. All sight of the road and its traffic was lost within minutes, and they were soon walking in easy rhythm under a wide morning sky, glorious, it seemed, entirely for their benefit.

"I do like being here early. You get so much more peace, and a feeling of the place having secrets to share with you and no-one else. Am I horribly anti-social do you think?"

"Not horribly, just a little bit. I suspect you cope better with people if you get right away from them sometimes. You like room to move freely."

"You're right. Having an open horizon seems to let my mind out of its cage too. I don't like a walk that's all under trees; it makes me feel too hemmed in. I like this limestone scenery because you get the wide spaces. And it's easy walking!"

"So where is this, and where are we going to?"

"We've walked up from Burrington Combe, and we're heading for Dolebury Warren. It's a high point and there was an Iron Age Fort here. You get good views across the Bristol Channel and into Wales. We certainly should today, the sky's very clear, as long as there isn't too much of a heat haze."

"I like walking in this kind of landscape too, it reminds me a bit of our estate, but then we also have tracts of much denser forest."

She looked at him with interest, he said very little about the place usually, and she'd given no thought to how much or little land he owned. Since his sudden trip back there he had mentioned his family a lot more, now he was obviously thinking about the whole set-up again. Something about it puzzled her.

"There's one thing I don't get, probably a lot actually, but one thing certainly seems odd."

"What's that?" He looked a little wary.

"You always seem such a city guy, no real idea of the countryside outside Bristol, but your home must be rural. Surely you grew up away from big towns?"

He nodded, "True, and I do like it, but I was at university in Paris, then worked in Toulouse. In fact I've lived and worked in cities ever since, so I've got used to it. Sometimes, at home, I've felt constricted because it is so rural. But actually I think I'm getting to the point where I appreciate it again. It was really good to see the place when I was there, although I suppose it could have been relief at Maman's recovery."

"It's your age."

He gave her a withering look, "Thank you so much."

"Any time."

He couldn't maintain his disapproving stare in the face of her amusement and gave up as they tackled the next uphill section. They were soon through the stubby trees and crossing a stile to emerge on the next parcel of more level ground. As they did so, a flock of small birds rose from the grass at their feet, flickering away from them, dipping and rising through their curved trajectories as they headed for refuge at the field margins. Lucy identified them for him, chattering about the different wildlife that could be found here. It didn't seem long before they had crossed the last stile and met the steep banks that made up the remains of the old fort. As they leant into the final short slopes, Lucy found herself explaining the basic construction of the site and what it would have been like when it was inhabited.

"How do you know all this? You seem to have very wide knowledge."

"Can't take a lot of the credit, I'm afraid. It's Tom, he's the kind of man that absorbs information. Geology, geography, archaeology, history. If he lives in a place, or visits it, he soaks up what there is to know about it. Eventually some of it works its way through to me. I resist, but the inevitable happens sooner or later."

"What do you know for yourself then? What do you absorb?"

"Apart from graphics?" she paused, wrinkling her nose, "Cookery I suppose, such as it is, terrible old songs, odd facts that I can't imagine being of any use. Bits of language or dialect that help me to communicate. That sort of thing."

They stood on top of the hill and let silence take over for a while as they enjoyed the panorama. Soon though, Lucy was once more using her osmotically gained information to point out what they were seeing in different directions. She waved her hand towards the other hills nearby, "We're on the Mendips as you know, these hills, all limestone humps, are what's left of stuff thrown up in an ancient mountain-building episode. There's Crook Peak, that's towards the end of the chain, and its last gasp is that little lump sat out in the channel, the island of Steepholm."

She went on to talk about the Bristol Channel, with the dangers of the tidal race and sandbanks that made it notorious.

Suddenly she smiled up at him, "And you have been such a good pupil for this morning's natural history lesson, that teacher says you can close your books now and have some coffee."

She turned aside into a hollow below the mounds of overgrown stones, more to be away from the course of other human traffic than because they needed shelter from the usual piercing wind that blew up here. The rucksack was opened and a flask was produced, along with some decent biscuits.

"You've been domestic again."

"It happens. Problem?"

"No, very pleasant. And I didn't feel you were lecturing me. It was interesting to hear about where we are. I think you must have been a good teacher."

"That's the problem, I can't stop. It does just happen, like being domestic and drawing. They're background things and they sort of fall out of me when I'm not looking. A bit like you speaking solicitor-ese; when you're in the situation, it comes by default."

He smiled as he took the coffee she handed him, and they both let their eyes rise over their drinks to sweep across the view in front of them. After a little while he noticed her gaze had shifted. A lazy little smile crept onto his face and one eyebrow lifted slightly as he enquired softly, "Planning another drawing?" She shook her head slightly and a faint smile ghosted its presence on her mouth. "Don't tell me, you're admitting to admiration!"

"No, I won't. If you want the truth, I was wondering what it's like to have shin bones that long."

He laughed, nodding towards her legs, "It's very much like having shin bones that short! You get used to them."

"Mine are not 'that short' as you put it, I'm average height. You're tall, without question. How tall are you anyway?"

"One metre ninety-five, tall but not exceptional."

She did a quick calculation, "Yep, six foot four in old money, about what I guessed. Were you very clumsy as a teenager?"

"No! I don't think so. Why should I be?"

"Because when they go through the growth spurt, a teenager's long bones grow so fast they literally don't know where the ends of their limbs are, hence they become clumsy. I thought it might have been very noticeable for you."

"Is this one of the useless facts you've picked up?" She nodded. "Well, maybe it's true, but at that age I was doing fencing practice every day. I had to know exactly what my reach was, so I probably adapted quickly."

"Maybe all teenagers should take up fencing then. I can see that going down a storm on the National Curriculum!"

"Well, it's good exercise. Like every sport, the fitter you are overall, the better you perform at your own discipline. I have quite strong arms still, even though I don't fence as much as I used to."

"Do you need strong arms then? I thought fencing swords weren't heavy."

"The sabre is the heaviest, and just you try holding anything out at arm's length for a period of time."

"I suppose so; you've got the length of the arm, in your case quite a lot, plus the length of the sword. Yes, that must take a fair amount of effort to control."

She couldn't help herself, her eyes travelled all the way up from his wrist to assess first his forearm muscles then his biceps. Of course, the length of his limbs masked the muscle bulk. Presumably he would have good pectorals too. Yes, the tee-shirt he wore allowed the evidence of that to show through, but then she knew that anyway, from that few minutes they'd - mm, better find something else to look at! Otherwise she would be forced to answer further awkward questions. And she wouldn't be happy to answer honestly this time. Drat! She'd thought for a moment she'd got away with that one, but as she looked away, she caught sight of a smile too wide to be hidden behind his coffee cup. The awkward question he asked, however, was not the one she expected.

"How did it go last night? You haven't said."

"Oh, fine really. You're enjoying some of the benefits now actually." She indicated the biscuits, "Not quite sure why

I need food parcels, but they're nicer than any I would buy myself."

"Perhaps they fear you will starve yourself without a husband to live for."

"Now then, don't you go encouraging me to be cynical; I'm good at that on my own. You're supposed to tell me off for under-appreciating my very kind friends. Which they are, and they did their best not to make me feel like a scarlet woman."

"A scarlet woman? Hardly!"

She waved her hand, with biscuit, vaguely in the air, "Well, you get the drift."

"Did you manage not to say anything cheap and predictable?"

"I did quite well I thought. Although," she paused and bared her teeth in a quick grimace, "I did hint that you had been helping me with my drawing by sitting for me. That left them with something of a worried frown, I think."

He was laughing, "Very good."

"I just told you, you're not meant to incite me to be so horrible. I'm ashamed of how subversive I can be. Can't you come up with even a hint of disapprobation?" She wondered for a moment if she was expecting too much of his vocabulary, but her worries were unfounded.

"Certainly not. I'm afraid incitement to trouble is one of my many talents, and always has been."

"Oh, what are the others? Obviously apart from fencing, law and the cello."

"Ah, I thought it was my other talents you did not wish me to discuss."

He had said it evenly, with a light voice, but she still had to close her eyes and take measured breaths through her nose for a few seconds.

"Sorry, too much of a temptation. Am I in trouble again?"

She emerged back into light and sound, shaking her head, even smiling slightly, "I think I opened the door for that one all by myself."

"Yes, I would say so. Thank you for admitting it."

She looked at him to see if he was being sarcastic, but he seemed relaxed. He was putting the cup down, and laughter started to sound inside her head. He found it amusing when he thought she was checking him over. As if she needed to see much of his body to feel the attraction! He had no idea the sight of that elegant hand and long fingers could do the job by themselves. She'd always been fascinated by hands and feet, hence most of her drawings involved them, but his were so beautiful. The ludicrous nature of the situation hit her and the laughter took hold properly, forcing itself out of her mouth. Soon she was wrapping her arms round her middle to steady ribs aching from trying not to shake, and doubling over to hide her face.

"What is so funny?" She shook her head, incapable of speech, struggling to draw enough breath now. "Something has amused you. Can I not share it?"

She was biting her bottom lip to try and bring the fit to an end, but his expression of bewildered annoyance simply fuelled her mirth, and she had to wipe tears from her eyes. Finally she made it to the gasping and moaning stage, trying to apologise.

"It wouldn't be so bad if you would tell me what you were laughing at."

"Couldn't possibly explain, sorry."

He was frowning and grumbling vaguely. To distract him she threw the rucksack across, "Here, as I'm incapable, you make yourself useful and pack that up. You wanted a turn anyway." She took the chance to scramble back up on to the path ahead of him and compose herself for the rest of the walk.

By now the temperature had risen, and so had the number of other walkers. As they descended back through the levels they saw a group of young men on mountain bikes too. They were whooping and shouting as they rattled and juddered their way swiftly down a dusty, rutted slope.

"That must be a bit bone-shaking when it's dry like this. Quite the opposite to what it can be like over winter. But getting muddy seems to be the object of the sport."

"I gather you wouldn't want to take part then."

228

"No! Far too much testosterone needed. More your kind of thing surely?"

"Actually I would prefer one of those," he pointed to the skyline where a string of horses and riders appeared in silhouette, "But down the bike route, not nose to tail at a steady plod."

They dropped down the final section and arrived back at the car. She was very appreciative of the fact that it was open-topped, and they didn't have to sit in something resembling a kiln to start their journey back. As soon as they were under way she fished a CD out of her rucksack.

"Can I put this on? The day's too sunny for classics, and I think there are no unsafe lyrics on here to get us into trouble."

He nodded, but after a few bars gave her a sideways look, and when the tambourine started he curled his lip. "I'm surprised you like this. It's a bit rough and peasant-like for you isn't it? Not rock, not clever, quite naïve in fact."

"Do you think so?" She smiled to herself and asked him a couple of questions on an entirely different subject before letting the conversation drop. She left the CD playing though, and by track five, when he was tapping the wheel and unconsciously singing along she turned to him, the smile no longer disguised.

He caught her expression and nodded, "Yes, okay, I'm hooked, it's very good. Actually Etienne would really like this, who is it?"

"A band called Beirut. If I analyse the components, I should dislike it, but I find it irresistible, and totally joyful. He's a great singer, don't you think?"

He nodded, too busy joining in with his own voice to spare it for a reply.

By the time they reached her house, they were on the second run through and were both surfing happily on the cheerful swell it had created. She asked if he'd like to stay for some lunch and he accepted readily. To continue the good mood, she put more music on in the kitchen while they made sandwiches, then she had to hike the volume up so they could hear it from the garden where they chose to eat.

"Did you enjoy the walk?"

His positive response was somewhat muffled by the sandwich he made it round, but he managed to convey his enthusiasm. When his mouth was free, he admitted that it was a shame he hadn't explored more of the area and seen some of the sights before this. Again he referred back to his family, reiterating a wish to bring the children over and see them enjoy it too.

She seemed to be losing interest in his plans, abandoning her polite enquiry as already dealt with. He looked at her, eyebrows raised.

"I have something to tell you!" Her eyes danced, tawny flecks glowing.

"Well you've had plenty of opportunity. Why have you waited until now?" She shrugged, too keen on divulging what she knew to explain the delay. "Go on then," he said, inclining his head.

"About Chris Brogan, well, his company."

"Lucy, you promised me you'd stay away from him." The food was lowered, as was the timbre of his voice. It was also hard, as if he was admonishing a child. It arrested her flow for an instant.

"I promised to tell you anything that happened, which I'm trying to do." She treated him to a glare, just in case he'd missed her vocal umbrage. "Besides, he wasn't there. I checked carefully." She lapsed into silence, a fitting punishment for his lack of appreciation. He was forced into urging her on with a gesture. "I went out with Jenny after you left yesterday afternoon. We felt like a mooch, so we went over to visit Portishead. There we are trundling down the High Street, when suddenly I realise there's a new card shop and it's Jubilations." Her conclusion elicited no matching excited reaction.

"I take it that's the name of his chain."

"Yes, he told me he wanted something more modern and lively."

Farine's eyes searched over her face, "So? That tells us what?"

She tutted, "I went in, to see what his stuff is like. I had a good look at all the stock, and it seems really dated. There was nothing that looked remotely modern."

"Surely not everyone wants trendy designs. Some people like the traditional."

"Yes, of course, but even that gets re-interpreted with colours that are in fashion. And as well as that, the name on the back of everything I picked up is still Jubilee Cards. If he wants to take the business forward under a new name, surely he'd make certain what's in the shops gives the right image and has all the right logos on it. I didn't say anything to Jenny, just watched for her reaction. She turned her nose up at it pretty quickly, I can tell you. And there weren't exactly hundreds of people in there buying masses of cards. How is he doing so well with something that looks so much like a dead duck?"

Finally, her point seemed to have penetrated. He stared at the ground, face sombre and forehead puckered. He shook his head. "I don't know anything about the commercial operation of a card company, but it sounds odd, certainly."

"There you are then!" This was, apparently, some form of triumph, according to her expression.

He ruined it all by indulging in advice. "Lucy, please don't start playing the detective. I do not trust this man. I want you to stay away from everything connected with him. Promise me you won't go anywhere near his shops again."

"I think you're being just a little bit ridiculous. And I don't belong to you, in case you'd forgotten."

He stretched his head up and tipped it back, closing his eyes. For several seconds he appeared to be making mute appeal to the heavens. She was beginning to wonder if he was entering into a vow of silence when he let out a long breath and looked at her again. "I have not forgotten, you make sure of that. But you would have no contact with this man if you hadn't been with me that evening. I don't want his dislike of me to spill over into any harm to you. And as you don't belong to me, I can do nothing about protecting you for the majority of hours in a week. I am asking you not to do anything that could provoke him, or be misconstrued as interference in his affairs. Do you understand me?"

"I'm not an idiot."

"Then please don't act like one."

She turned away. She had no desire for him to see the sudden tears which threatened to form. Why? Why was she so hurt by his words?

He reached for her shoulder, voice softened to accompany the touch, "Lucy."

She shook his hand off and got up to walk away. A lost cause, his legs were far longer and he overtook her before she got more than three paces. He put his arms round her, ignoring the protests she issued and held her tightly to him, letting her rant ineffectually until it passed.

"I don't care." He kissed the top of her head. "I don't care if you're angry with me or offended. I'm not willing to let you bring trouble on yourself. I won't let you go until you promise me."

She was sobbing now, desperate not to, failing that desperate not to let him see. All useless, as she was shaking against him. "Stop this. Stop it now. Let go of me."

"No."

She looked up at him, anger emerging through the welter of emotion pouring through her. "You have no right!"

"Yes, I do. You said we are friends. What would you think of a man who let his friend walk into danger without doing all he could to stop them?"

"I think we've moved beyond that issue, don't you?" Her voice was quiet and shaky, but she held his eyes."

"You mean I have no right to care for you, to want to protect you?"

"You have no right to stand here reminding me that the man who should be doing this isn't."

In answer he pulled her closer and put his head against hers. "I'm sorry," he whispered. Again he left a soft kiss on her hair, then released her.

She was utterly miserable, uncertain what to do or how to proceed. After a few desultory movements she turned to him, "I think you'd better go."

He shook his head. "No. We're beyond the polite and the proper as well. You're lonely and upset. I'm not walking away to leave you crying by yourself. If it was Mel here instead of me, you'd have a good wail and pour out all your troubles on her. What's the difference?"

She opened her mouth to explain in detail exactly what that was, but no more than a strangled cry of frustration emerged. With that out of the way, she was back to racking sobs, folding into a heap on the grass. He sat down beside her and took one hand, which he wouldn't let go of, leaving her to mop her face intermittently with the other. Gradually she calmed. When she got as far as staring bleakly into space, he rubbed her back.

"How about some tea?"

She nodded, too exhausted to complain or argue any more at his assumption of command. In the kitchen she rubbed her hands upwards over her face and then outwards, pushing the hair back from the sides of her head. She reached for the now boiled kettle and made them both drinks. He was leaning back against the work surface; legs stretched out and crossed at the ankles. As she sipped at the hot tea, he put his hand up to her shoulder, "Feeling better?"

She nodded; eyes closed and silent. Take refuge in the tea, much safer.

"I'm sorry if I upset you."

"No," she squeezed out a small smile, "Really, not just you. I think I'm tired." She noticed that she didn't say tired of what. He might have noticed too, he was scanning her face carefully. Think of something active, she instructed herself. She put the cup down. "I've got something to show you, I nearly forgot."

With that she left the kitchen, returning moments later holding a piece of paper about seven inches square, which she handed to him. It worked, his face lit up and after a few seconds he lifted his eyes to hers.

"It's good, I really like it."

"You're welcome to keep it, if you want it that is. I can quite understand if you have no desire for a drawing of yourself holding a piece of broken glass!"

"No, I would like it. Are you sure? How can you have done this already?"

"I wake up very early in summer, that didn't take long." She didn't mention the two failed attempts and the fourth one she'd already put in her portfolio. He was still inspecting the one in his hands, fascinated.

"I think Maman would really like to have this. I will send it to her."

Somehow, she'd been expecting him to say that, and she went off again, this time to fetch some card and an envelope so he could get it home intact. When they had slotted it safely into its housing, and finished their drinks, he said he needed to go, but it took a few moments to convince him that she was recovered enough to be left. One or other of them was busy for the next two evenings, so he left her with a reminder to be at his office on Wednesday afternoon.

"Oui, monsieur le Notaire, I won't forget."

21

On Wednesday afternoon Lucy arrived promptly for her session with Farine. She had to concentrate on keeping her face straight when Maureen announced her arrival in the usual formal terms. Once in his office, she let the grin she'd been keeping under control spread right across her face. He glanced up from the files in front of him and looked at her enquiringly.

"What is so funny?"

"Well, for all that you say about our friendship and not being ashamed, I notice I am still very much Madame Cottonwood here, M. du Blez!"

"Of course, this is business. Besides, Maureen would probably shoot us both if she thought there was the slightest impropriety like using first names."

"Oh? Does she want you for herself?"

"Certainly not, but the poor romantic lost wife should not be wronged. Whilst I am this tragic figure, I must maintain my lonely vigil, hoping against hope to reclaim her."

Lucy was sniggering at his performance and he had to reprimand her about her lack of attention to the matter in hand.

"I don't know this man, he is unfamiliar to me. His offices are not far away, so I have insisted that we go there, I want to see what kind of practice he has, maybe that will give me an idea of who we are dealing with." He was almost talking to himself, looking pensively at the folder in front of him. "Also, I am surprised by how quickly he has asked for a meeting. He seems to have dispensed with the usual flurry of letters first."

"Isn't that a good thing, a sign he wants to get on with it?"

"No, it is a sign of haste. We need to know why."

"I thought this was a simple case?"

"It is, or should be, so why is he so concerned to deal with it quickly? Go through the contact you had with your client again," he looked down the file, "yes, Mr. Lesley Wilson."

"He rang me, said he'd just opened the car firm, a new venture for him. He thought a web-site would be useful. We made an appointment. When I went, I thought it was in a bit of a rough area, but the two cars he had in the garage both looked very new. There were a couple of trucks there as well, more like delivery vans. As I told you before, he persuaded me to do an outline design, but then said he'd decided to use another designer."

"You only saw him the once?"

"Yes, I e-mailed the work in. Two weeks later I got the cheque that he'd promised. End of story, as I thought."

Farine sat back in his chair and stared at the ceiling. Then he put his hand across his face rubbing his forefinger back and forth along his cheekbone. Lucy wondered if she dare reach for a pencil and paper. Probably not, that must constitute impropriety.

"Well, we know he is not very bright. But we don't know why he is so keen to deal with it quickly now. I'm assuming the haste is his, rather than his solicitor's." He frowned at the file again, "We will see on Friday."

Suddenly he looked up at her, "Okay, I need to tell you a few things. Let me do the talking, try to remain calm and even. If they say something outrageous, bite your tongue. Sometimes they like to ask the client directly, to undermine things. If so, we use this code. If I want you to answer yes, I turn to you and ask you what you think. If I want you to say no, I don't look at you, and say my client must speak for herself. Do you understand?"

She nodded, trying to keep her face straight. She felt very glad it was a simple copyright issue, and nothing more serious.

Business was concluded at that point, and Farine reappeared as himself, asking her to go to a jazz club with him that evening. "I am told there is a new young pianist playing this week. Would you like to go and hear him?"

"That would be nice. Thank you. I'll meet you there, shall I?"

Out in the foyer they shook hands formally again, but Lucy found it very hard not to say something flippant and watch for Maureen's reaction. She settled for turning back just as she was going through the door and Maureen's head was

236

bent over her desk again. She raised her hand to make a shooting action at him with her fingers, whilst blowing him a kiss. She laughed all the way down the stairs at the glare this had produced.

"Farine? I'm really sorry, I've had this rotten headache come on. There's no way I can face sitting in the jazz club tonight. No, you go and see him, it doesn't matter. No, it's probably the heat; it's been so humid all week. I'm just going to bed early. What, Friday? Are you sure? Well okay, I'll see you Friday afternoon anyway, we can sort it out then. Yeah, you too. Au revoir."

He sat up. His heart, thumping out the rhythm of sudden fear, pushed him to move. There were words echoing in his ear, and it was a few moments before he could fully accept they had been spoken in a dream and not by someone nearby. He rubbed his forehead, trying to wipe off the disturbed feeling just as he cleared the sweat beading there. He swung his legs out of the bed and reached for water. Hot and stuffy, that was the problem. He rose and walked through to the lounge, opened the sliding door wide and stepped out on to the balcony. No thought was given to his naked skin, now quicksilvered by moonlight. After a few moments the tom-tom beat of his pulse had calmed and he had cooled enough to want at least a thin layer between him and the night breeze.

Returning in a robe and carrying a glass of pastis, he was in the action of sitting when the words sounded again in his head and he remembered what he had been dreaming. Mathilde, he'd dreamt of Mathilde. Why now? He shook his head, who could understand the workings of the sub-conscious? But as the aniseed aroma spread up through his nasal passages, warmed and released by his tongue, so too realisation spread into his mind. Lucy. Yes, he could see similarities. As well as huge differences. A derisive sound escaped as a breath over his teeth, very obvious differences. He couldn't imagine Lucy sliding her hand up the back of his thigh to squeeze him provocatively before they had even sat down to lunch together. A woman, twice his age, Mathilde had completely astounded him with her business-like approach to sex and emotion. Especially surprising when it was a result of heartache. No, maybe not a surprise. Everybody tries to find control somewhere.

He could remember the growing feeling of being out of his depth as they had eaten that first meal together. He had thought it was in regard to some case she had brought in to his boss that morning. He hadn't questioned it when Dubois had asked him to go to lunch with her. The odd looks that had passed between the older man and the woman, he had put down to determination on his part, and exasperation on hers, at being fobbed off with the junior. From this distance he could feel amusement at the awkward exchanges he had made, thinking he was supposed to find out about her legal problems. But it had become clear he was the one being interviewed, and for something else entirely. He had set the wine glass down carefully, hardly having drunk any of it, and looked at her calmly to ask what. The movement of her hand up his leg was accompanied by a direct gaze and the question of whether it was an unpleasant idea to make love to woman so much older than himself. A slow smile accompanied the memory of his answer; he'd thought it so clever at the time, now it sounded arrogant and brash in his memory.

"If I considered it unappealing, madame, I would have arrested your progress some ten centimetres ago."

He hadn't made it back to work that afternoon. She had taken him to the small flat she kept and promptly blown away many of his preconceptions. In all sorts of ways. He had considered himself experienced, particularly after fencing trips abroad and living in Africa. Indeed, Mathilde expressed her appreciation for his skills as a lover. But she had a depth of experience in more than the physical.

It had taken some time for her to tell him anything about herself. He still believed she wouldn't have shared that with everyone. By her own admission, some young men were purely for her release. Always young men. She explained they reliably accepted the arrangement of sex without complications; suitable older men generally thought a lot more and tended to want greater emotional involvement. Dubois, it turned out, was an old friend of the family and knew all about her circumstances. He had been merely accepting the inevitable when Farine had seen them taking leave of each other and caught Mathilde's attention.

He had been seeing her for over three weeks when he had asked outright if affairs were a constant feature of her life. As he twirled the liquid in his glass now, he saw not the cloudy miniature whirlpool, but her face as she had replied. She had asked first that he keep everything done or spoken within the flat confidential. Then she had turned to him.

"Farine, I am married to a man I still love intensely. He has a degenerative disease. Slowly he has lost control of bodily functions. He can no longer speak, although currently he can still make inarticulate sounds."

"And so you seek consolation elsewhere?" He'd taken her hand to let her know he felt no condemnation for her actions. She had merely shrugged.

"Yes, of course, partly. But more than that. While his mind still worked well, he made me promise that I would not be dragged down into this stinking hell-pit with him. He said he hated it, but could bear his life being cut short, as long as he didn't have to go down carrying the knowledge that my life was twisted beyond recognition too. He loved to buy me nice clothes and jewellery, take me to the theatre. We are wealthy, and we have enjoyed much. He wanted me to stay the woman I had been for him. He made me promise that I would put him into nursing care when he deteriorated too much."

"And have you?"

She had shaken her head. "Not yet. He is still at home. As far as I can tell, or convince myself, he understands quite a lot of what I say. I pay for attendants so I can go out to the places I always did, and come home to tell him about them. I buy new clothes and show him. I put on perfume for him. Even," she'd looked at him, chin out, "tell him about what I've been doing here. But not about the men. I tell him that I'm remembering times he and I had together. When I look at him though," her voice had faltered finally, "I can't remember when his body did those things. I can no longer see him doing what we enjoyed so much together. I use you, and the rest, to take me back to that in my mind."

"What did you tell him, the day we first had together?"

"I told him that I could remember an afternoon when we made love and lay together for hours. That we had watched the sun trace lines across our bodies as it turned the shadows like hands on a clock. Whether he and I ever did that or not, I can't be sure. I expect so, it's what lovers do. But you and I had done it, so I could talk about it with passion and joy for him."

They had sat quiet for a while before he turned and kissed her cheek. "I think you are a very loving wife."

"Do you prefer to stop seeing me now?"

"No, not at all. I am giving something to you; you are giving something to me. If, from that, your husband gains something as well, who can resent it?"

"It's not what people normally expect from an affair."

"I don't think I care about that."

"I don't want emotional involvement."

"I understand."

And he had. Even now, looking out over the lights of Bristol, instead of Toulouse, he could feel nothing but compassion for Mathilde. He stood, leaning on the rail for a few moments and trying to recall the scent of her perfume, the feel of her fine hair in his hands as he used to let down the chignon she kept it in. As his thoughts slid from the past, through the present and then on into his immediate future, his frown deepened. He pushed himself upright, held his finger with his thumb and then flicked the rail making it 'ting' loudly as he turned away, something must happen soon. One way or another.

He stepped back inside the flat, taking a seat on the sofa and tipping his head back. Seven months it had lasted with Mathilde. With ups and downs, like the time he had bought her a silk scarf because it was the colour of her eyes. She had handed it back, face cold.

"Give it to one of your other girlfriends. I won't be taking it home to wear. You're a sweet boy, but I don't want your affections."

And then the time she had been so angry when he'd arrived. Wanting immediately to get into bed, and then pushing him away. Then she'd cried and asked his forgiveness. They had made love, but she'd broken down, sobbing out her husband's name even as he'd taken her. He'd held her in his arms and soothed her for a while, trying to offer comfort where he knew everything was pain.

Two weeks after that, she'd said it was over.

"Because I saw how you really feel?" he'd asked.

She'd looked at him, thoughtful for a moment, reached out and touched his cheek. "Because I felt safe letting you see. I can't do this, we've become too close."

"I don't mind, I know why you're doing it."

A quiet shake of the head, "Farine you are a family man. Yes, yes, you've had your divorce and you don't think you can marry for love anymore. You've done some wild things out in Africa and believe you'd ruin a good woman, but you'll mature. You're not thirty yet. Men take longer to grow up than women. From what you've told me about your background, I know you will end up wanting the same. You shouldn't be investing your energies in me. You are a man waiting to get married. The only question is how long. And I want to keep things simple. So go."

He sat up, rubbing his face again. Sometimes, like now, he wondered if he should have been more insistent. He could have argued more about the marrying part. They would not have stayed together, but maybe they could have had a little longer. He had valued her. She was the only person he'd ever told about the incident out in Somalia. She had been extremely calm about it, asking him a few practical questions and then summarising it into what he'd always thought.

"You had no choice, it was him or you. Maybe if you'd known his life you could feel sorrow that he was forced into being a bandit. Or maybe he was always bad. It doesn't matter; you had to act on the situation you found yourself in. You seem to take no pleasure in it, other than in the ability to survive, why worry?"

She had been right. There was no pleasure in the memory of the knife-thrust between the ribs, only satisfaction at the efficiency of it. No pleasure when the living man became a limp body in his arms, merely relief at being the one still alive. Also a strange feeling, but a welcome one, that his father would be proud he'd learnt well from him. He knew clearly he wasn't at the level of a trained soldier, but his father, and the fencing, had taught him enough to make him a harder target than the average traveller. He was thankful for that.

He put the glass down on the side table and walked softly back to the bedroom, shedding the robe and sliding under the sheet. Yes, certainly something familiar in the strong ideals and the determination to live by them that he could see in Lucy. He enjoyed her friendship a lot. But she was naïve compared to Mathilde, and probably less resolute. Was there any comfort in that? He drew his hand across the empty space beside him in the bed. Not so far. Was he waiting to marry? Surely not with his talent for wanting unavailable women. On purpose? That was too deep a question. Depth, that was the problem. Easy enough to find a fellow occupant for the bed, but most of the women happy enough to pass through it, he wanted to keep that way, passing through. He turned over; perhaps he did want something more permanent. He was no longer a wild young man. Maybe Lucy was right. No, that was Mathilde. Now his thoughts were muddled, he needed to sleep.

The appointment on Friday was for the early afternoon, so Farine collected her in his car and they drove there in good time. She noticed he had classical music playing again, either avoiding inappropriate lyrics still or leaving the raucous singing for off-duty times. She was smiling to herself about it, and he must have noticed.

"You keep grinning like an idiot again, as you did the other day. Why am I so funny all of a sudden?"

"Not really funny. I suppose I'm just amused by seeing you as a solicitor again, I've got used to seeing you in relaxed mode. It's usually you pushing me into outrageous behaviour, but I realised the other day in your office I was being the rebel and winding you up instead."

"It's been like that from the beginning, surely you realised?"

She shook her head, not feeling any need to reply, instead allowing her mind to drift back over recent events. Things had see-sawed up and down several times lately. Correction, her feelings had, and her behaviour was unravelling fast. This needed resolving. After today, there wouldn't be any handy excuses for continuing contact. She had to face the fact that it was from pure choice if she continued to see more of him than was in any way necessary. Of course, it had been choice all along, but it was amazing how one's mind could obscure things for guilt or convenience. Her thoughts were interrupted.

"Ah, I think this is the place."

He slowed the car and peered along the fronts of the buildings, in what looked like a very well-to-do business area. Lucy was surprised; she had been expecting somewhere rather more run down, to match the garage of the original contact.

They walked in through the main entrance to consult the polished steel directory board. Tilley, Thompson and Prendergast had the first floor to themselves. Upstairs, they found the offices to be very smart and thickly carpeted. Having given their names to Mrs. Henderson, as her desk plate denoted her, they were bidden to take seats and wait. They indulged in waiting room behaviour, looking around them at everything, without apparently taking in anything

After a little while another man entered from the stairs and looked towards Mrs. Henderson.

"Go straight in please," she said briskly to the arrival, whom Lucy recognised as Les Wilson. He vanished through the appropriate door. Farine sighed heavily, looked at his watch again. Several minutes went by, in which she would have said Farine looked at his watch at least six times. Was he genuinely concerned about running late, or acting that for Mrs. Henderson's benefit?

Finally the desk 'phone buzzed, and they were told to go in.

Everyone shook hands, Les Wilson had trouble meeting their eyes, Mr. Prendergast stared directly into them, but his bland expression was unreadable. Lucy noticed that Farine had lowered his lids slightly, which made it difficult to tell where he was looking or what he was thinking. It reminded her of a hunting hawk, leather cap over its head. But you still knew it was ready to fly and drop onto its prey, given the chance. So, let the battle of the solicitors begin.

Both men opened files and Lucy braced herself for a tedious exchange of detailed arguments regarding proof that her work had been plagiarised. It came as something of a shock when Mr. Prendergast gave a broad smile and made his opening remark.

"My client is extremely sorry to have caused you so much inconvenience Mrs. Cottonwood. He apologises unreservedly, and hopes we can conclude this matter to your satisfaction with all speed."

Farine wasted no time in disbelief, "So, your client admits culpability?"

The solicitor swallowed, as if trying to keep down something unpalatable. "Yes, indeed. Mr. Wilson is er, inexperienced in these realms and simply acted in ignorance, not realising what he did was an infringement of your client's obvious copyright of this material."

The repentant Mr. Wilson was sweating visibly, and under the brief attention of three pairs of eyes nodded vigorously, but refrained from speaking. Lucy concluded he'd been given his instructions too.

"I see," said Farine. "Are you agreeing to meet our claim for compensation in full?"

"Well, it seems to me, having perused the case, that we could suggest a course of action mutually beneficial to both parties."

"And what would that be?"

"As Mrs. Cottonwood went to the trouble of preparing designs for my client, why doesn't he purchase those designs as he should have done at the time? Obviously he accepts that the fee will need to be substantially more than was originally quoted to offset any time and inconvenience caused by his actions, and of course your own fees." Through this, his eyes had darted several times to the man at his side.

Lucy's head was reeling. They weren't even proper designs, it was a quick mock-up on a standard template; what was he talking about? She had to tune back in quickly, Farine was speaking now.

"What sort of fee had you in mind for purchasing the designs?"

"Well, that could be negotiated obviously, but let's say three times the original quote for the work. Would that seem reasonable?"

"I think my client needs to speak for herself on this matter," he said keeping perfectly still.

'Oh thank you!' Was Lucy's first thought, quickly followed by 'now what do I say?' all of which she fitted into the space of wriggling in her seat and clearing her throat. "Well, it isn't just a question of the money. My reputation has been damaged, and I don't see why my designs are acceptable now when they weren't earlier. I don't feel inclined to agree."

She tried to glance at Farine, wondering if she was saying the right things or not. Mr. Prendergast didn't seem too thrilled, she thought, confused if anything. Also Les Wilson was looking anxiously from one to another of them repeatedly.

Suddenly Farine was closing the file up and looking at his watch again.

"I am very sorry; I have another engagement back in my offices. As we were a little late in commencing our discussion that is all the time I have available at the moment. Why don't you put your proposal in writing, and send it to me as normal. My client and I can discuss it thoroughly, and we will contact you in due course."

By the time he'd said this he was on his feet and had shaken hands with the two men opposite, Lucy had to jump up and do likewise. They left the office in silence.

On the way back down to the lobby, she started to speak to him, but he just shook his head.

22

As the car turned out of the archway and onto the road, Farine glanced at her.

"So what did you make of all that?"

"Rather a surprise. You weren't expecting that either, then?""

"Not at all. And I'm not sure Mr. Prendergast was very pleased with his client."

"Why did they change their minds and offer me so much money? They weren't even proper designs I sent him, I never did any!"

"An extremely good question. Clearly there is some reason that Wilson wants the case closed. If you ask me. . ." He stopped and Lucy had to urge him to share his thinking. "I'm disobeying my own rules here."

"Not really, it is my case; you are supposed to advise me."

"Yes, but I don't normally divulge what I think is going on behind the obvious. I stick to the facts."

"You're in way too deep for that."

An odd curve formed on his lips, but he nodded. "True. It is my guess that Wilson changed his mind. The original intention was to contest the issue, or at least work towards a minimal payment. Prendergast would have accepted the case on those grounds. But today, Wilson was very eager to get you satisfied and out of the way. I think he's changed his instruction to his solicitor, leaving him very annoyed!"

She grinned, "Awkward clients, eh? And now what, that we've refused?"

"We haven't technically. We said we would think about it. That means we'll accept, but take our time to annoy them, or drag it out and hope for an even bigger offer."

"Does it? Oh. You speak the lingo, of course."

They were nearing Clifton by now, and Lucy said: "Don't bother going to my house, just go straight to your office if you're late. I wouldn't mind a walk to clear my head from all that nonsense anyway."

"Are you sure? Okay, thank you. What about tonight? Do you want to try the jazz club again?"

"Yes, if you'd like to. I'll meet you there. What time?"

"How about nine? I have a feeling I will have to work a little late."

"Fine. I'll see you at nine."

He parked the car and they took leave of each other speedily before Farine dashed off.

Sitting in front of the keyboard, she was picking restlessly at a corner of some paper. This afternoon, instead of being a tidy end point to the whole business, had opened up a whole slew of questions. She sighed and rubbed her head, hopefully the threatening storm would lighten the air. Maybe there needed to be something similar with Farine, something that would wash all the heat and heaviness out of what was going on between them. No, she knew what needed to happen. She struggled to find the resolve to do it; that was all.

The problem was, the only person that would be capable of giving her that resolve was so far away. Geographically, if not in other ways. Had they let things slide over the last few years? Was this current insanity symptomatic of a separation she had been unaware of? Perhaps physical proximity had masked a deeper, tectonic drift that had been going on. A few centimetres a year, that was all it took to end up on different continents.

But she knew, even if that was true, she couldn't hurt him. She just had to find the right moment to end this game. Things had been very strange with Farine lately. One moment best friends, the next infuriating each other and causing hurt on both sides. That wasn't redolent of dalliance, but something else entirely. She was jolted out of her reverie as lightning flashed across the sky and the following thunder-roll shook the windows.

They left the jazz club after a couple of drinks. Although the flair of the young man on the piano this evening was admirable, somehow neither of them was in the mood for sitting indoors where it was still hot and airless. Outside, it was warm, but the air was much fresher as the skies had cleared, and Lucy automatically turned to walk uphill towards the downs. Farine settled into his long easy stride next to her and they strolled along in companionable silence. Leaving the concentration of light behind them, and emerging onto the open spaces of the downs, Lucy looked up and pointed to the constellations she could recognise.

"Have you studied astronomy?" Farine asked, surprised.

She laughed. "No, not at all. Tom is always trying to get me to remember the main ones, but they just don't stay in my head. After Cassiopeia, Orion and The Plough I'm really struggling. My problem is I can't see the shapes they are supposed to make, they're pretty much random dots to me."

"I expected it would be easier for you to see patterns than for the rest of us. Surely, being a designer gives you an advantage."

"You would think so, wouldn't you? Doesn't seem to work though."

Just then a group of young men walked by, rowdy from drink, and Farine pulled her closer to himself. When they had passed she whispered, "Getting ready to defend me?"

"Of course," he said smiling down at her. Suddenly he stopped and took her arm. "Lucy, come back to the apartment with me. It is a beautiful evening; we can just sit on the balcony and look down towards the river. Let's sit with a glass of good wine and talk until we have nothing left to say."

She scrunched, then wriggled, her shoulders, indicating inner struggle.

"Oh for goodness sake!" he exclaimed, "What are you frightened of? Have we not been perfectly good friends and managed to behave ourselves for the last few weeks?"

"Yes, we have. And I'm not implying you've done anything wrong, it's just ..."

"Just what? Tell me."

"People would be bound to get the wrong impression, me going back to your flat late at night; you know what they would think."

"People? What people? Who are we announcing this to? Has your daughter arranged for us to be followed? Are you, or are you not free to do what you like?"

She stood in silence, breathing carefully through her nose, her mouth held in a taut line. Finally she nodded, "It sounds like a lovely idea actually." Her tone was weary, and Farine found himself feeling annoyance again with whatever it was that so assiduously stopped her following her impulses.

He took her hand and tucked it under the crook of his arm to help her keep pace with him, "Good, it will not take us long from here."

His flat was just as delightful by night as it was in the day. Possibly more so. He opened the French windows onto the balcony, and the noise of the city drifted in, but mutedly, like low background music. As he went to turn on a light, she noticed the drawing she had given him propped against the lamp base.

"Not sent it away yet then?" she nodded to indicate her subject.

"No, I thought I would enjoy it for a few days first. I spoke to Maman yesterday evening and told her I had something special to send her, but I'm keeping just what it is a surprise."

She moved outside leaning on the rail so she could see the ships down on the river, their navigation lamps winking red and green as they bobbed up and down on the water. He joined her and they stood together in peaceful silence drinking it all in through their eyes, while the air cooled slowly on their arms. They sipped their wine from time to time, leaning on the rail.

Suddenly he turned to her, "Lucy, why don't you stay? Let's enjoy the weekend together, we can go out somewhere tomorrow, just take off and go wherever we want. Say you will."

She was shaking her head slowly, "You know I can't do that."

He banged his hand on the rail, the vibrations transmitted outwards. "No, I don't know that. You keep saying it, but I don't understand it. You're still worried about your friends, and how they disapprove of your association with me."

Her eyes were tightly closed and her face strained as she replied. "It isn't that, we said we wouldn't put ourselves in awkward positions. A weekend together seems like a risky situation to me."

"But you know me now; don't you trust me when I promise not to seduce you?"

"I do trust you. But. . . I don't know, I think I'm losing track of what's right and wrong."

"You're doing it again, worrying over someone else's definitions and standards. It never does you any good; you should just be true to who you are."

She sat down in one of the wicker chairs again, placing her wine on the table next to her, "So who am I?" she asked in a tiny voice, "I'm even losing track of that, I think."

He came and stood beside her, "Don't be so hard on yourself, you don't have to answer all the questions. Decide what you want to do, that's all. It makes me angry that you spend so much energy trying to balance out what you think is right with what you feel inside. Is it such a sin to be friends with me?"

She looked down at her hands for several seconds, trying to weigh his challenge. She looked back up at Farine and shook her head. "No, not to be friends," she whispered. A broad smile spread across his face; she shook her head again more decisively, "But that doesn't mean everything I say or do with you is okay. I think sometimes I just abandon propriety when I'm with you."

He sat down in the other chair. "What is propriety? Rules for people who don't know when they are being offensive. I thought you had learned how to tell me when I stray over your line now."

She was laughing. "I don't know how you do it! You always seem to turn things on their head."

He stretched his legs out; they almost covered the width of the balcony. "No, I do not turn things on their head; I just make you work out what is in yours. You get yourself in a muddle because you always try to please somebody else. Why don't you please yourself, or yourself and God if you must?"

"Ah well, that's the downside of being a wife and a mother. You always have someone else to please too."

He made one of his French noises, "Your husband and son are both far away; your daughter is grown up. Why can you not please yourself for two days?"

She did not seem to have an answer for that question, so they sat quietly for a few moments, looking out at the scene before them.

After a while he spoke again quietly, "Tell me honestly, would you like to spend the weekend with me? You have already decided we will not sleep together, so you need not worry about us committing great sins. Can we not just have fun, and enjoy each other's company?"

Sometimes his directness still took her breath away, and with it the ability to hide behind half-formed assumptions or fears. "Yes, I would like to spend the time with you. I can't get that squared away in my head with lots of other things, and I have a nasty feeling I will have to settle accounts at some point. But if I'm honest, right now, it sounds great."

"Eh bien! Good, that is all we need to think of for now. Let's be happy, and leave all your agonising for later." With that he poured them both more wine, and looked up, "Show me the constellations again."

"I can't here. There's too much light to see the stars properly. You'll just have to imagine them."

They started to talk about different places they had visited, and what sights they had seen there. She was not surprised that he had a wider experience of the world than she had, although he wasn't always clear about why he had been in various places. Several of them had been because of the fencing, and she realised that must have been a very exciting part of his life.

"Why did you move to England?" she asked after a while.

He shrugged, "You know that, to escape the family. Britain isn't the only place I've disappeared to. At first, I wanted be away from my grandmother. After my father died there was a lot of pressure on me to go home and take up my duties as le Comte. I did exactly what he did and ran away. Except I did it physically, rather than into a bottle. Henri was quite happy to live in the château and be in charge. If I'd stayed in France it would have been too easy to get dragged home for this and that. It was Henri's fortieth birthday this year. If I was in France, I would have had to go home for it, but Britain is another country, it seems much further and therefore easier to make an excuse."

"But your grandmother's long dead now, and I know you're close to your mother and the rest of them. Don't you miss them?"

"To go home for a visit is fine. Living there would be different. My mother would start to suggest various women I could marry. Francine would ask me what I want done with the vineyards, Henri would worry I would take over the château, and Tomas would think up endless schemes I ought to support, which Henri has already vetoed. They do much better without me."

"Yes, but sometimes it must feel too far. When your mother was ill, it was really difficult for you."

He nodded, not saying anything, just leaning forward, arms on his knees and hand moving across his face.

"What will happen eventually though? About the succession?"

"If I stay single and have no children, Henri really will become Count; that would please him very much. Although, if I live a long and happy life, which is my plan, he will not get to enjoy it for many years. I've told you already, Etienne will succeed him, and the du Blez family will be satisfactorily noble again."

"But you always make Henri sound more of a businessman than an aristocrat."

"Well, to be honest, in the modern age, that is more useful. I have all the sophistication; he has the ability to make the estate solvent again."

"Can't you sell off the estate and solve the family finances."

"Selling the estate is not an option. In France the title goes with the land, and cannot be transferred. To sell the estate would be the end of the noble line."

"Well, you always say that you don't care about being Count, what would it matter if it ended?"

"It wouldn't matter to me, but I can't make that decision for the generations before and after me, can I?"

Lucy couldn't help thinking that she wasn't the only one constrained by other people's expectations. She said so, as gently as she could.

"Ah yes, of course. But this is a different matter, isn't it? We are not talking about my personal life, but my position as head of an estate."

Lucy couldn't see the difference herself, but after they had been round it a couple of times they left it and moved on to less contentious subjects.

When they had finished the wine, and the city was quietening, Lucy said she was tired, Farine showed her to the guest room, which seemed to contain everything she might need. She was surprised at how relaxed she felt, despite all her earlier self-doubt, and as she slipped into sleep she realised her heart felt lighter and more settled than it had for several days. A final weekend together; that would be a good way to end the whole affair.

23

A glorious smell of coffee was the first thing she was conscious of next morning. She peered over the edge of the bedcover and discovered Farine stood in the doorway looking down at her. He was wearing pale shorts and a light-blue linen shirt. He looked great, as usual.

"Good you are awake."

She lay back and pushed her hand through her hair, "Do you always come and stare at your guests before they've had chance to make themselves human?"

"I came to see if you would like some coffee."

"Although it smells fabulous, my system does not recognise anything at first except a nice cup of tea."

"Ach, your English tea," he exclaimed turning away, adding wearily, "I will put the kettle on for you."

She smiled at his reaction, and sat up looking round for the extra bath-robe. She walked through to his kitchen, where the sun was streaming in, and he held out a mug towards her.

"What's this?"

"Your tea," he said, frowning.

"No, Farine. This is hot water." She took it to the sink, where she poured it away and turned towards the kettle to make a 'proper cup'.

"I suppose you want milk in it too," he said reaching into the 'fridge.

"Yep, definitely."

She stirred the drink, and as she lifted it to her mouth, he made a face.

"What a colour! How can you drink that?"

"Hey, what about the stuff you drink? It's not coffee as the rest of us know it, more like something you'd drain out of your radiators."

He didn't understand the comparison and she thoroughly enjoyed his perplexed expression as he tried to work it out. They carried their preferred drinks out onto the balcony again, where the day was already under way and warming fast.

"Oh I do love this. I would sit out here for my breakfast every day." She sat back in the chair, and tilted her face up to the sun, while it was still bearable.

"Where shall we go do you think?" he asked, setting his espresso cup down.

"Well, my house first, I haven't even got any clean underwear, have I? After that I don't know. I always find it really difficult when someone says we can do anything I feel like. Have you any ideas?"

"A gallery perhaps, maybe the theatre later? Or do you feel like going up to London?" She wrinkled her nose. "What then? Tell me what you'd like to do."

"It's such a glorious day. Can't we get out of the city? Something like go for a walk along a river or by a lake; that would be good."

"Yes, of course. The Cotswolds maybe, would you like that?"

"Yes, perfect. Let's do that. And you know where they are, do you?" She laughed at his disgusted expression, but then he was on his feet, startling her. "Are we going now?"

"No, drink your tea; I will go down to the bakery. I must get fresh bread for some breakfast. I won't be long."

Of course, she thought, the French would never dream of toasting a slice of day old bread for breakfast, would they? He was gone a little while, and she took the chance to pad through to the kitchen again for a second cup of tea.

When he returned she was still soaking up the sunshine with a mug in her hand. She could hear him humming to himself in the kitchen, so she went through to find him unpacking the fruit and bread he'd brought.

"Great, we can eat, and then I can nip home and get a few things I'll need."

He looked at her frowning, "You don't need to go home. You can get what you need from around here, there are shops."

"Why would I go to the shops? I don't live very far away. It won't take long."

He slammed the loaf down on the kitchen table, swearing she presumed, in French. He was more angry than she'd ever seen him, and instinctively she put her hand up and rested her fingertips against his chest. "Farine, what's the matter?"

He stuck his hands on his hips and looked down at the floor. Eventually he gave a shrug and a flick of his hands. "I don't want you to go back to your house, not for anything. We can find whatever you think you need."

"Why? What's the problem?"

"Because you will pick up your responsibilities along with the letters from your doormat. You will check the answerphone, and then maybe your e-mail, and your eyes will change. You will still spend the weekend with me because you have promised, but your head will have changed your heart, and you will not be with me the same way anymore."

She looked at him for several seconds then moved her hand up to his cheek. "Ok, we won't go home then. I will leave all sensible thinking until Sunday evening. I can't promise you what will happen after that, but for now we will just enjoy ourselves."

He took hold of the hand curved around his cheek, and softly kissed the palm. "Thank you." He pulled her to him to hug her. She muttered something into his chest. He held her away again so he could hear.

"What was that?"

"I said: put me down! And I can't face any more emotional contortions on an empty stomach. Can we please eat?"

He nodded as he brushed the hair off her face, "Sorry. Go and get your shower, I will put on some more coffee."

She headed back to her room muttering under her breath, "Does he have any idea how erotic kissing somebody's hand like that is? Does he know what he's doing to me? Yes, he probably does. And I'm complicit; what am I doing?"

She showered, and wished she could rinse out of her head all the confusion just as easily as the shampoo from her hair. She was talking to the walls, asking them why she had finally taken leave of her senses, but they didn't seem to think it was worth giving her an answer. She stood for a few moments with her eyes closed, letting the water run full on her face. She groaned slightly, thinking of Tom, and what she would say to him, for she would have to tell him somehow, about all, well, some of this. As she dried herself though, she did as she had promised, and put her questions and reservations on one side. She wasn't cancelling, just postponing any considerations of what would need to happen later, but first she needed to approach the day ahead. By the time she walked back to the kitchen she was ready for some of his strong coffee and his company.

They sat on the balcony with breakfast, as she had wanted. Then they walked down to the shops together so that she could pick up a few things to see her through the weekend. She found a little boutique selling mainly teenage wear, but they had some shorts and skirts she considered an appropriate length on the sale rack. It was a treat in itself, shopping with a man who didn't regard it as torture. Farine found it natural to comment on the clothes and help her choose colours. He vetoed the first pair of sunglasses she tried on and insisted she have some she thought rather too flashy, laughing helplessly at what she thought were the best ones. The morning was passing quickly, and they finished with a quick dash into a chemist's shop for sun-tan lotion before going back to his flat. She warned him to take shoes fit for walking, but he shrugged her concerns away. They collected the car, and set off with the top down to enjoy the sunshine.

As they drove along, she applied some of the sun cream, turning to him. "I don't suppose you have to worry about sunburn, do you? Does it make any difference?"

"I go darker," he replied "My mother always comments on how pale I am when I have been in England for a while. But then she also says I am thin, and look unwell."

258

"Ah, she's a normal mother then," laughed Lucy, "we have an irresistible urge to feed our children. I think it's hard-wired."

Just then her mobile started to ring. She fished it out of her bag, and dropped it into her lap until it stopped. "Oh dear," she said.

"What's the matter?"

"It's Jennifer. Obviously she's trying to get hold of me. She's probably wondering where I am."

As if to confirm that, a text arrived. She concentrated on dealing with this, chewing her lip for a moment before replying.

"What did you say?"

"I said I felt that I needed a break, and had decided to take myself off for the weekend. I also said I'll tell her all about it on Monday. That last bit might be tricky."

He nodded. There was a further text arrival, and she replied again.

"Thank goodness we're actually in the car, I could say 'On my way to the Cotswolds' without lying!"

They found a spot that suited them and started to walk up through woods onto a hill and along a ridge before descending to a stream, following its course for a mile or two. It took them a few hours, and it was late afternoon before they drove down into a small town to find a café. They wandered along arm in arm after that and spotted a small gallery that had work by local artists as well as the predictable tourist material. They both found themselves admiring a collection of paintings by the same man. Farine was particularly entranced by a small piece depicting a bridge over a river, executed in pastels. It was slightly unusual in that the scene had been rendered with geometric shapes and blocks of colour. They were discussing it, when the owner came over to offer information.

"Is that the bridge at the bottom of the town here?" asked Lucy, "We were arguing as to whether or not it is."

"Yes it is, but done from an old photograph taken in the 1890's."

"Ah yes," said Farine, "that is why it looks so different, there are none of the buildings you can see now."

They were left to continue their deliberations.

"Why don't you get it if you like it so much?" asked Lucy.

Farine frowned. "Yes, I do like it, but I do not think there is anywhere in the apartment where it would fit well. Maybe another time, hein?"

They left the shop and slowly worked their way back towards the car.

"What would you like to do next Lucy?"

"Well, I've had my wish, and made you walk further than you were expecting! What about you? Isn't there anything you would like to do?"

He ambled on for a few moments before replying, "I would like to go somewhere we can look at the stars again. Where would be best?"

"Anywhere away from street lights really. I know, why don't we drive back down and head for the Mendips? I know a decent little pub right on the edge of the hills. We could get something to eat and then drive up onto the tops, by then it will be dark and we can sit and look at the stars for a while."

"Yes, that would be excellent." She stopped and hesitated. "What is it?"

"Erm, if we're heading off again, I think I'll go and find a loo. I'm sure there were some back there, meet you at the car in ten minutes."

She was off up the street before he could reply. He frowned slightly, she was up to something, he was sure. Then a smile flashed across his face, well he could get up to something too.

It was dark, they had found an ideal spot, and with the top down still on the car, they tipped their seats back and stared upwards. They were rewarded by the sight of countless twinkling points.

"It's amazing isn't it? You normally see so few, just because of the light pollution. I can remember camping in a field in South Wales and seeing the Milky Way properly for the first time." He made her point it out and explain it to him. "Navigating by the stars wasn't part of the lordly education then?"

"No, strange because there was a lot of outdoor pursuits. I think it was assumed there would always be a servant to drive one home at the end. Perhaps my father learned in the army; that would be normal no? But he never taught me that."

They sat in silence for a while, and Lucy found herself thinking how he always sounded happy when he was reminiscing about times with his father and grandfather, but the shadow of his grandmother seemed to stretch over other memories like a black cloud. Maybe it had even had an effect on his short marriage. Suddenly he was getting out of the car. "Where are you going?"

"Nowhere, it's okay, I just have something in the boot I want to bring."

Within a few seconds there was a 'pop' and then he got back into his seat holding a bottle of champagne and some glasses.

"What? Where did this lot come from?"

"I got it all when you disappeared. Don't worry I made sure I sure I got the cheap stuff. Good idea, no?"

She could still tell when he was smiling, because his teeth always looked so white, even in the faint light here. Maybe my whole face shows up the same way, she thought. Then she forgot about it as they turned their attention back to the sky and sipped their champagne.

"Yes!" she shouted and pointed quickly, "Did you see it?"

"What was it?" he asked bewildered.

"Shooting star, I love seeing them. They're so ephemeral, just a second or less, that's all you get."

"I missed it, where was it?"

She directed him to the section of sky she had been watching, but although they waited for a while, they didn't see any more.

He started to sing quietly, "Catch a falling star, you'll go far in the pageant of the bizarre. . ."

"She turned to him, "So you like the Zero Seven CD I lent you then?"

"Yes, the first part of that song had a certain appeal." He sang again, "It's never gonna be, normal, you and me. What you're signing up for is a storm at sea."

"Ah, yes I can see why it caught your attention." She wasn't sure if she was relieved or not that he'd stopped singing before the rest of the song. Suddenly she shivered. "It's getting cold; I didn't bring anything else to wear, did I?"

They stayed still for a few more minutes, trying to ignore the fact that they were beginning to feel distinctly chilly. In the end they decided to head home and finish the champagne on the balcony.

She sat back again in her favourite spot and sighed deeply. "What a lovely decadent day. Thank you, it was a delight."

She had reached across and squeezed his arm. He was smiling and shaking his head, "Decadent? I think you must have led a sheltered life."

"I'm sure I have, but it was still decadent. We thought of no-one but ourselves, and did exactly what we felt like. Isn't that decadent?"

"Okay, I will let you have that as a definition. Do you feel guilty?"

Now she shook her head, "Not at all. Are you pleased with me for that?"

He replied softly, "Yes, very. You have done well."

Suddenly there was a lurching sensation in the pit of her stomach and her mouth felt dry. If he came across to her right now and put his arms round her, she did not know what would happen. She desperately wanted him to do just that, and at the same time felt like crying with dread of it. All she could do was sit very still and will it to pass quickly. Her eyes started to sting, and she closed them hoping no tears would leak out below the lids, if they did, she knew he would not rest until he found out what was wrong.

After a minute or two she got up and passed him murmuring that she wanted to make some tea. She went into the shower room and gave way to crying briefly, then washed her face. She was back in the kitchen and reaching for the kettle, when he appeared in the doorway.

"You're sad."

She looked up at him and nodded, deciding to forego the denials, which would be pointless. Then she held up her hand, "Don't ask me, okay. You have to trust me too. I'll deal with it. Give me a minute."

He just nodded and left her to make the essential drink. Somehow, that helped. It made her feel better that he allowed her to sort it out and wasn't fussing over her. She took a few deep breaths and then, picking up her mug, went out to the balcony again.

After a little while they started chatting. She was relieved that the strength of feeling that had overtaken her was diminishing. He was asking questions about her life, which brought Tom and the children back into the picture. That steadied her, and they were soon arguing over some aspect of human behaviour. Particularly her own of course.

"So why do you not have more days like this? Why do you constantly deny yourself the things that would make you happy?"

"Because you can't spend all your time on amusement. There is also a home to run, and there have been children to look after. If I constantly ignore the one to deal with the other, things are bound to get out of balance. I agree with you, I've probably erred on the side of being sensible for too long, and forgotten how to enjoy myself. But that doesn't invalidate the need to be committed to my family. You have a solicitor's practice, you're not telling me you only turn up when you feel like it. I can't imagine you keeping many clients that way!"

"No, of course, that is my job. But when those responsibilities are fulfilled, then I can do what I like. Is that not so?"

"Sure," she nodded vehemently, "but you also commit yourself to fencing practice, because it matters to you. If you have a family, then you have responsibilities towards them too, because they matter. Surely you can see that."

"Yes, naturally. I think you just give too much to them and don't leave enough time for yourself."

"Well that's a hard one to assess isn't it? It depends on many things to do with the kind of life you lead, your job, where you live and so on. You can only work that out between you. Sort out the long term and short term. That's another tricky one."

"What do you mean?"

"Well some people are good at immediate things, like you and enjoying yourself. You've made today a fabulous day, because you're really good at sensing how I feel and responding to that. You would buy me flowers then and there if I admired them, because you live for the moment."

"What's wrong with that?"

"Nothing, it's great. But that's short term. Once you settle down to a serious relationship you have to take a longer-term view of things. Like I said the other night, I'm better at that. You need it to cope with looking after the house, having children, dealing with them going to school and all of that stuff. You can easily say it's boring, but it's pretty important, if these things aren't dealt with, the family will soon suffer." He was looking very blank, so she tried another tack. "You must understand this. What about all the planning in your family? Generation to generation, your grandfather teaching you to be a gentleman; that's all long-term planning."

"Yes, but in a specific area. Not for everything in your life. It's not possible."

"Depends. That's what maturing is about, isn't it? Getting better at understanding the passage of time, and how things fit into it."

"I find that hard, to me the moment you are in is the only one you can do anything about."

"Well, maybe that's why you're a successful lover, but not a husband."

As soon as the words had been despatched from her mouth, she could have bitten off the tongue that sent them. Too late, she realised the look on his face she had taken for blank, had in fact been bleak; now it progressed to stricken. He got up and walked into the lounge. She put her head into her hands and groaned. What had she done? How could she have been so crass? For the second time that night, she wiped tears off her cheeks. This time it was someone else needing the comfort though. She followed him through and reached out to touch him.

"I'm sorry," she said quietly, "that was completely out of order. I would blame it on too much drink, but actually I just didn't think what I was saying. You have every right to be angry with me, and I apologise."

He looked down at her sombrely. "That does not stop it being the truth."

"No, it's not the truth. At best, it's an opinion, and we both know that my opinion veers towards the good but dull. Farine, lots of people think much more short-term than me. And they have good marriages. Besides you do plan for the long-term, what about Etienne? I was just on my high horse about Lucy Cottonwood knowing the best way to do everything. You must recognise that."

"That's the second time in ten minutes you have said I must know something, which shall I choose?"

He turned away from her and she felt desolate. Despite all their time together, she felt she didn't know him well enough to find the right words or actions now. Maybe there weren't any. Maybe she had just killed their friendship. That would serve her right for feeling the way she did about him. She shook her head, no, that was a stupid thought. This wasn't an equation, with bad things and good things having to cancel out; she refused to succumb to that temptation at least. "Is there anything I can do?"

He looked back at her over his shoulder. "No, you must be tired. Go to bed."

She had to be content with that; she lifted one foot and then the other, both now feeling as if they were held in lead divers' boots, to walk away from him.

In bed, she lay staring at the ceiling, tears sliding down either side of her face and soaking into her hair. She groaned aloud, "Oh God! I didn't mean to hurt him."

It was a while before she drifted off to sleep, face still damp and the sound of his cello seeping under the door.

24

When she opened her eyes, everything was quiet, so quiet she wondered if she was alone in the flat. She turned over and closed her eyes once more, despite the fact that it was late, hoping that would shut out the images from last night. It didn't work. She groaned, opened her eyes again and sat up. The day, and Farine, would have to be faced. Once more she reached for the 'guest robe' and trotted off to the kitchen.

Having made herself some tea, she looked around to see if he was awake too. He was standing out on the balcony, but he made no move to come and speak to her, although he must have heard her padding about.

She had a sudden urge and, after searching the coffee table and a desk in the hall, found what she was looking for. She sat in the corner of the lounge, partly hidden by the muslin curtain moving in the slight breeze, and quietly began to sketch. Gradually, on the paper in her lap emerged the pattern of the balcony railing and two long limbs, one foot tucked up behind the calf of the other. She shaded quickly, catching the light and dark of frosted glass and legs. Then she concentrated on the sole of his foot, paler than the rest of the skin, having to concentrate to capture the creases. If she overdid it, then it looked like an old foot, too little emphasis and it seemed unrealistic. After a few more minutes she was satisfied, and she went away to have her shower, being careful to take the pad of paper with her.

She went back into the kitchen and helped herself to some breakfast, or was it brunch? Farine was now in the lounge, sitting on the sofa engulfed by a Sunday broadsheet.

"Good morning," she said quietly as she walked through and out onto the balcony.

There was something of a grunt from behind the paper, which she chose to interpret as a reply. She sat in the wicker chair again, but found that this morning's offering tasted like ashes in her mouth, in comparison with yesterday's ambrosia. The sun did not feel so warm either. Maybe, she thought, if this carries on, it will be easy for us to walk away from each other and just forget the whole thing. She sighed and put the plate on the table, she knew exactly why everything felt so sour, but did not know what to do about it. She pulled her feet up onto the edge of the chair and wrapped her arms round her knees. She sat like that for some time, with eyes closed, allowing the sounds from below to drift across her hearing and letting her mind wander. Suddenly her eyes opened again and she stood up. This was getting them nowhere. Time for action.

"Would you like some tea?" she asked as she crossed the lounge again.

"Certainly not."

"Shall I make you some coffee then?"

"I expressly forbid it."

She made a face at the newspaper, which gave nothing away as to what was going on behind it. "Would you like me to leave?"

"No."

"Liar."

With that, he did move half of the paper aside so that he could look at her, but the only thing he sent in her direction was a glower. She simply raised one eyebrow, and he retreated.

"I'm terribly sorry if I'm annoying you," she said, voice sharply bright, "but it's hard to know what to do when someone's sulking."

"I am not sulking."

"No, of course not." With that she departed, made tea again, and returned to sit in the corner of the room, once more with pad and pencil. This time she was sketching the back of the sofa, the newspaper, his arm holding it, and the sliver of his head visible between cushion and page. Nothing of his face could be seen; but the edge of his eyebrow, his jaw line and cheek made interesting angles. She knew he must be wondering what she was doing. He sighed several times and turned pages every so often.

When she was satisfied with her sketch, she put the pad down and moved forward to take a section of the paper. She sat on the floor, with her back against a chair and started to read. Every now and then she 'tutted' or 'humphed' at some article, refusing to let him forget her presence. She even ventured a comment once, but neither expected nor received a reply. Finally, she stood, rubbing the base of her back. "Oooh, I've been sat on the floor too long. I'd better move around a bit." She picked up the mug she had used earlier and took it through to the kitchen, spending a few moments rinsing it out.

When she returned to the lounge, he was on the floor in front of the sofa, newspaper abandoned, and her makeshift sketchpad in his hand.

He looked up at her, "This is me."

"Yes."

"Do I really look so . . . so angry? And how can you show that, with so little of me in the drawing?"

"Well I'm sure a decent artist could do better, but that's how we know what people are feeling, isn't it? Body language I mean. You can hide a scowl behind a newspaper, but the tension in your body still communicates the mood behind it."

"I'm not angry with you though."

She sat down sideways on the chair arm, so that she could face him.

"I know that, well mainly not with me anyway. You're angry with the world, and your family and yourself, I just happen to be in the room picking up the vibrations."

"I have made the morning miserable for you, I am sorry."

"Well, I think I asked for it, in part at least. But I don't want you to stay unhappy, why don't we talk about it?"

He shook his head, "I don't want to talk."

"No, of course you don't, you're a man! Maybe it would be good for you though. Sometimes it helps to work things through."

He turned his head to her slowly, eyes looking into hers very directly. "I meant I don't want to talk it through with you. That wouldn't help."

She could feel her heart thud inside her chest. Conversely she felt as if all the blood were draining back to it, away from her head and hands. It was a moment before she could speak. "I see. I'm sorry. Then I really should go if you're that angry with me." She tried to shrug and make a small smile, as if this was all perfectly reasonable and she didn't mind. As she rose from her seat he caught her wrist.

"I don't think you see at all. You still have no idea what the problem is."

"It's what I said last night, surely."

He closed his eyes, leaning his head back, "Yes, it's what you said last night. And what it means. And the rest of it."

She was lost. He was contradicting himself now. Suddenly he pulled her down on top of him as he slid onto his back. He circled her with his arms and kissed her.

When he stopped she asked quietly "What was that for?"

He shrugged, "It seemed preferable to talking."

She put her hands to his shoulders and pushed herself off him. She settled herself on her side, leaning on one elbow, looking into his face.

"Well, I am going to talk and you are going to listen. You need to hear this."

He opened his mouth to speak, but she lay the fingers of her free hand on his lips. "Shhh. Just for once you are not in charge." Then she rested her hand, curled into a loose fist on his chest.

"Like it or not, your grandmother's attitude has affected you. She was a bitter woman, and that bitterness must have started before you came along. You don't get that mean without practice. Has it ever occurred to you to wonder why she was like that?" Again, he parted his lips to speak; again, she stopped him. "Rhetorical question. You assume it was because of your birth. But just think, Farine; think about what went on before you arrived. How many catholic families of that time do you know with only one child? Did your grandmother want that? And that one child turns his back on her, can't stand her. He walks out of her life, only to return having given his love to a woman she sees as inferior to herself in every way. Every way except one. What did you say your mother excelled at?" She nodded at him to indicate he could answer this one.

"Producing children."

270

"Exactly. Your grandmother, already feeling a failure and rejected now has this constant reminder of what she thinks she should have achieved."

He was silent for a little while. "Do you really think it was like this?"

"I don't know, obviously it's conjecture. But it seems to me highly likely they couldn't have more children for one reason or another. They may not have known why, people didn't have the same medical resources then we take for granted now. But she could have resented your grandfather, thinking it was his fault. You said she thought him weak in other ways. Or if she thought the problem was hers, she certainly would have felt she had let the family down. That kind of guilt feeling often leads to anger. And you know it's a classic thing when something important is outside of your control, the reaction is to try and control everything else."

He nodded, staring into the distance.

"She allowed that bitterness to come in, I'm not excusing it. But I think if you can accept there may have been reasons for it, it would be easier for you to forgive her. You don't have to carry it with you, nor accept that you caused it."

"It is hard to forgive something so despicable. She made a lot of misery for my grandfather, my parents and for me."

"Yes, she did. But if you understood it all, you wouldn't need to forgive, would you? For what you can't understand or explain, it's only that or resentment. I promise you, you will be doing more for yourself than for her if you let go of it."

He pondered a moment, "I think you may be right. Perhaps my mother knew something, she was always more tolerant of her, saying we should respect Grandmère. I just assumed it was from her background of venerating the elders."

"That's something else; you need to forgive your parents too."

"My parents, why? What did they do to me?"

"They didn't protect you. They were under her thumb, and they let her be cruel to you. Grandfather being extra nice to you away from her must have reinforced the idea that she had the right to treat you like she did. Tacit agreement."

He started to argue in a torrent of rapid French, but stopped in mid-sentence. "Yes, I suppose so."

"There you go; it's not just the English that repress things!"

"I need to think about this. It is a different way of seeing everything I grew up with."

"Yes, you do. Take some time, but don't put it off, face it."

He grinned at her, "Get my soul clean, eh?"

"I don't care how you see it. Just do it."

His face went serious again and he put his hand up to her temple, "Do you think then I will be able to marry a woman and keep her?"

"I think it will help. And I'm still sorry for what I said last night. I'm not always right."

"Really?"

She poked him in the ribs for that, and he winced theatrically.

"Mind my duelling scar!"

"Oh no, you don't mean it. Surely not!"

"Yes, I do, see."

He pulled up his shirt and there was indeed a scar running along one of his ribs on his left side.

She ran her forefinger along it gently. "Seriously, have you fought a duel? I thought it was illegal. And anyway, you told me fencing swords aren't even sharp."

"Of course it is illegal, but you know young men, they like to do dangerous things, better still if they are illegal. And I didn't use my fencing blade; I used my grandfather's duelling sabre that he left to me. It was while I was at the Sorbonne."

"What was it about?"

"A woman of course, the one I married."

"You mean you won? What happened to the other guy?"

"Of course I won; I am horrified that you doubt that. He had many more wounds than me; you should have seen how much he bled!"

She grimaced, "I sometimes think you've time-travelled from the Middle Ages!" Then she laughed, and patted his stomach, "Okay, put your body away now before I lose my self-control."

He sat up, "I know what you're doing. You are making a joke of it to hide the fact that you do want me. Very English."

"That's hardly news, is it? I thought we'd worked our way through that one."

He shook his head, "But I can't do it. I can't do this pretending not to feel something. For me passion is real, not a mental construct to be analysed."

She sat back from him a little. "But you're the one who's been saying we should enjoy being friends; that the lack of anything steamier is simply a choice we make."

He held a peculiar little smile on his face for a moment. "Lucy," he said softly, "you're so naïve. I'm not just talking about sex. I'm in love with you."

"What?" Her face contorted in horror. "But you can't be! You said - you did all that - you were all cool and sophisticated." She looked down into her lap, staring beyond what was there. Images and words running through her mind were turned over, examined and re-assessed. "You lied to me."

"No. I always told you the truth. I just didn't tell you everything."

"But you said," she stopped, trying to think of an example. "Yes, that night we argued in the pub, you said. . ."

"I said that I never promise a woman more than I'm willing to give."

She gave him a bleak look, "But you didn't say that sometimes you promise less than you're willing to give."

He nodded, "Something like that."

"You weren't honest." He pulled a face. "No, you weren't. You used the truth, but like a tool. You weren't honest with me. This is disastrous."

"I don't see why. It's a shame. I love you, but I'm not blaming you for it, I went into this with my eyes open. I'm an adult."

She was on the verge of tears, sputtering complaints still being issued like random gunfire. It was unclear whether anger or misery was the driving force behind them. Suddenly it erupted fully. "How long? How long have you known this? Why didn't you end it when you knew? I told you. I told you!" The words cleared the way for the tears which poured out of her. She curled up over her knees, arms crossed over her head and sobbed.

He reached out to rub her back, "Oh Lucy, Lucy, I am so sorry. I did not mean to hurt you, why is it so bad?"

"Idiot!" she hissed from inside her cocoon of limbs. "Why do you think?"

"Do you mean?" His voice wavered, then hardened." Lucy, are you saying you're in love with me too?"

She was rocking backwards and forwards slightly, moving her head in what could be a nodding motion. "Yes, you stupid man."

"But I thought that I was a distraction for you. I did not mean to risk your heart also. Please, don't hide from me; let me comfort you at least."

She allowed him to turn her towards him and cradle her against his chest which had the effect of muffling her voice. "Now you really know what a mess this is. I feel so stupid. I hate myself. Why can't I stop telling you everything that's inside me?"

"Shh, ma petite." He wrapped his arms tightly round her and waited for her sobs to subside. He stroked her hair and kissed the top of her head, "Why do you think you are stupid?"

"Because I shouldn't have fallen for you. I should have walked away when I could have. It was just excitement at first, well I think. I don't know. Why did you have to find me interesting and want my company? It made me feel," she sniffed, "special. It was too good to leave alone, so I played with fire." She squeezed her eyes tightly shut and more tears slid down her cheeks.

"You really thought I was just toying with you for my amusement? And now you are angry because I wasn't? That's not how it usually goes."

"But I thought I was safe because it didn't mean anything to you. If I felt more for you than I wanted to, it didn't matter because you would walk away with a smile at some point."

274

"And I thought you were safe because of your good husband and your loyalty and all those things you value. I should not have let you risk yourself, it is my fault."

"No. We're both guilty. We both assumed things, and neither of us was really honest. That's what I mean by stupid. We played around and now we're both hurt." She had quietened. It was so good to be close to him like this, and so impossible. The ache wasn't going to go away; it was no less because it was shared. "How long have you known?"

"I'm not sure exactly. That day on the beach made me feel we could spend a lot of time together. Soon after that, I think. You?"

"You know how slow I am on the uptake sometimes. It's really only been this last few weeks that I've realised how bad it is, we argued so much!"

"A strange way to recognise love."

"Do you think so? Only someone you love can annoy you intensely, yet leave you wanting still to be with them." Then she sighed, "I wish this had happened when I was in my thirties."

"Why? Do you think it would have been different, easier maybe?"

"Not emotionally, but I could have sat on the floor longer. My back aches!"

"Ah, we are welcoming back the sensible Lucy."

He got up onto the sofa and helped her up to sit beside him. She didn't make a fuss when he put his arm round her shoulders, but leant against him quietly. They sat like that for some time, both of them silent with their own thoughts. Eventually he suggested they have something to eat and they moved through to the kitchen. They said little, but stayed no more than a few inches apart.

They were on the settee again. Perhaps having said what had been hidden inside them, there was nothing else that really needed saying. Time went by unmeasured, he was enjoying having her close, and savouring the fact she cared for him. He had no idea how they would sort out the ensuing practicalities, but at least they could tackle them together now. He leant his face against her hair. He was really looking forward to making love to her and the unfolding of all the intimacies that would follow. She might be shy, if she'd been with one man such a long time that was very likely. It didn't matter, he had no intention of being hasty, but it was sheer joy to contemplate how close they would become. He gave a soft laugh.

She stirred, "What's funny? I could do with some amusement."

"You must have thought I was a complete Casanova. Assuming I was trifling with you."

"Well, you did leave me with that impression. Be honest, you did nothing to dispel it. In fact, I think you went out of your way to create it! So, what are you like?"

"I've been honest, or truthful at least. I haven't said anything false."

"So you do pick up women casually?"

"Yes. If that's what they're looking for."

"And you have drifted in and out of affairs with friends?"

"Sometimes. You can usually tell quite soon if there's any chance of it lasting. Since I came to England I've had two serious relationships. Well, three, I suppose. One was a bit on and off. Not for a few years though. What about you?"

"You know about me." She laughed, briefly.

"Just Tom, no-one before him?"

"No. Just the one man. This is the first time I've got anywhere near to betrayal. I still can't believe I've told you how I feel. It's going to be tough, dealing with it."

"But at least we have each other."

She looked up into his face, a mystified glaze across hers. "Hardly."

He could hear her words bouncing off the walls around him in the flat. The ensuing silence took on a texture. He felt as if he could step out of his body and look at everything, all the molecules in the air, the thoughts passing through their heads. He needed to. That hadn't made sense. "What do you mean?"

"Farine, what do you think we're going to do about this? Have a quick tumble in the sheets?"

"No," he smiled. "It would be much more than that now."

"Exactly. This ends here. We can't see each other any more."

He was at sea. Not something he enjoyed particularly, for the very reason that this up and down motion left him queasy. Someone had taken away the solid ground he'd been on and set him adrift and in peril, floating away from the shore.

"You can't mean that. We're in love with each other."

"Yes we are, but actually, I'm married to someone else. Bit of a problem there."

"But you want to be with me. You, you're sat here with me and . . ." He was shaking his head in disbelief. How could this be so contrary to everything he felt? Mel's words echoed back to him. He whispered, "You mean you won't leave Tom?"

"That's right."

"But you don't love him."

"What?"

"You never talk about him. You never say how much you're missing him. He's left you for six months, for God's sake!" He got to his feet and started pacing backwards and forwards in front of her, hand rubbing over the back of his head. "I can't believe this!" He stopped momentarily, turning to face her, hand held out in appeal. "You know, last night, I nearly asked you to run away with me. I didn't because I couldn't bear to hear you say no. And today you tell me you love me. But it seems that makes no difference. That's not enough."

She shook her head, "You're right, that's not enough. And just because I don't talk about Tom all the time doesn't mean I don't love him. Why would I talk about him to you? You don't even know him."

"So you don't really love me. You still love him. You lied."

"No, I don't think so. It's untenable to carry on a relationship with two men, agreed. But I assure you it's possible to love them both."

"So, you feel the same for him as you do for me, do you?"

Not just her eyes, but her whole face dropped. She couldn't look at him. Dumbness rose to take the place of her previous bold statements. He dropped to his knees, leaning on hers to bring his face close.

"Well, let's hear it?"

Slowly she met his gaze, "I love Tom. Right now, I'm in love with you."

He put first one hand up to her face, then the other, holding the eye-contact. "You mean what you feel for me is more passionate, more immediate?" She bit her lower lip. "Or more transient?"

A flicker of pain passed across her face, "Yes to the first two. The third? Who knows? Quite possibly."

"Or no, if you let it develop. Love isn't static, is it?"

"It seems not."

"Then why can't you accept what you feel for me and move with it?"

She gritted her teeth, forcing the words out through barely parted lips. "I'm married to Tom. That involves promises. And a legal contract. You, of all people, should respect that."

"Contracts are made and dissolved all the time. There are ways to end them."

"And usually one party is wronged. What has Tom done to deserve that? He's a good man!" She took hold of his wrists. "If he was cruel or unloving, I would walk away. If he didn't care, I could let go of him and choose you. But he does care! And he thinks he has a loving wife waiting for him. He doesn't deserve to be betrayed. I can't be with you."

He took his hands from her face; she loosed his wrists as he sat back on his heels. "You don't mean can't. You mean won't."

She opened her mouth, paused, licked her lips. "If you prefer that. I won't."

"You're the most obstinate woman I've ever met." She shrugged. "You'd better collect your things, I'll walk you home."

"That's not necessary, it's barely dark."

He stood, looking down at her, from what seemed a great height. "I insist. Pointless noble gestures seem to be the order of the day."

She went to the guest room to gather up the small pile of things she had accumulated. Movement felt difficult, as though someone had injected treacle into her joints. Her mind too felt slow, dully reverberating with the crash of emotional concertos they had played through. At one point she turned to find him standing silently in the doorway, hand outstretched with a number of CDs.

"Yours," was all he said before turning away.

She asked if he had a bag she could use to carry her things. He produced one in silence. As she loaded her bits and pieces into it, she couldn't help wondering if it was like this every time he broke up with someone. That caused a hollow laugh to escape from her insides. They were hardly breaking up – you had to be together first for that! And yet they had been together, in a way they had been incredibly close. Now they had to part, but she wished they could manage it without this flaying of each other's souls. Wasn't it hard enough?

She closed the bag; pointless question would be harder to zip up. No doubt she would be asking them of herself for some time to come. She stared at the bag with distaste, as if it was somehow to blame for this unpalatable turn of events. The chance to tell it what she thought of it was denied her.

"Ready?" his voice cut in, and he reached for the bag before she had even answered.

They left the flat in silence and set off on a familiar journey rendered strange by the prickly tension between them. Despite the lack of conversation, it seemed to Lucy that their steps got slower as they approached her house. The weight of the impending parting also pressed on her heart. She wanted to say something, if not to make it right, then at least better. It would hurt enough in any form, to take leave of each other so abraded and angry was almost unbearable.

"Farine, I'm sorry. We knew all along this was crazy, but truly, I never meant to hurt you." He was silent, nothing more than a quick flash of his eyes towards her and away again. This was ridiculous. "Please don't let's part hating each other. You once said we should enjoy the time we had together and accept it for what it was."

They turned into her path. The front door loomed ominously as the final barrier. Once beyond that, their connection would be severed.

"I don't think it's fair that you're being resentful now because it isn't more."

"Fair?" his voice crumpled the still air, silkily dark around them. "Is it fair to find we care so much for each other and turn your back on it?"

She reached for her keys, "No less fair than turning my back on a man who's loved and cared for me over twenty-five years."

His face was still. She unlocked the door and reached in for the light switch. The electric glow spilled from the doorway, picking out the severe lines of his expression. He handed the bag to her and she unzipped it to retrieve the contents.

He murmured, "You are being neither fair nor devoted. You are simply avoiding risk. Opting for what you know to be safe."

She looked up, flinching at the sting of what he'd said; tee-shirts and CDs slipping from her distracted fingers. Breathing heavily, she looked into the bottom of the bag, checking that nothing was left in there. Handing it back, she looked into his sombre face. "While you're prepared to be brave, I suppose."

"I'm prepared to do anything. I would give up my practice like that." His fingers snapped sharply under her nose. "I would go anywhere if you said yes, if you didn't want us to live together around here." She was shaken by the strength of his feelings, and she reached out for the simple solidity of the doorframe. "But you, what are you willing to do?"

"I'm willing to do what's best. Loving someone means wanting the best for them, not just enjoying them."

"Very noble. But I'm not convinced you're doing the best thing for your husband by staying with him when you've given your heart to me. And you're not doing me any good by foregoing the love we could share. You're willing to disappear back into keeping your tidy rules rather than deal with this."

"That's a cruel thing to say."

"Well, now we really do know each other. You're a small-minded woman and I'm a cruel man."

Suddenly her face softened. "No, you're not. You're a hurt and angry man. Actually, I do know you, and you're a good man." She reached up to touch his cheek, "And I forgive you."

He pushed her hand away, "It's not your forgiveness I want."

With that he turned and headed not for home, but up to the downs.

It was late, or early, depending how you counted. He was back in the flat. He'd walked and fumed, quietly hoping to run into trouble. But he wasn't a wayward youth anymore, picking fights to assuage his tortured fury. Now he sat in the dark, on the floor by the balcony door, a drink in his hand. Moonlight and streetlight blendeded to make odd patterns as they tumbled through the uncurtained windows together. He tossed the pastis back, swallowing quickly, hand tightening on the glass until it suddenly imploded. He carried on squeezing, and then looked down into fingers curled over glass shards smeared in alcohol, his skin seeping blood. Automatically his eyes went to the table, and the contrasting image of a calm hand safely balancing a potential danger. What a difference a few days made.

25

Farine opened the office door at the top of the stairs and stepped through. He wasn't feeling particularly alert after two or three hours of fitful sleep, which is probably why it took several moments for his brain to make sense of the scene that greeted him. He was still staring at the chaos of Maureen's desk, with its emptied drawers, when the secretary entered behind him.

"Oh, M. du Blez, you're in early. I was going to get started on the Johnson case for you before. . ."

Her words ran out of momentum, her attention turned by her employer's dazed expression to the disruption he was contemplating.

"What's happened? M. du Blez, what's all this?"

"I think, Maureen, we have been burgled," he muttered quietly.

"What? Why?" she cried bending to pick up the nearest pile of debris near her feet.

"No Maureen, you must leave it. I think we need to call the police."

The routine circuits in his brain were telling him the correct procedure, the conscious part of his mind was still struggling to get to grips with any action. "Let me see what has happened in my office and Justine's."

He checked both rooms, the same scene greeted him each time. Filing cabinet's untouched, desk-drawer's rifled. In his own office he leant against the edge of the desk and put his hand across his mouth, closing his eyes as if in thought. His mobile rang and he retrieved it from his jacket. It was Lucy, which caused a frown, unexpected to say the least.

He answered wearily, "Oui? This is not really a good time"

"Farine, this is Jennifer. Is my mother with you?"

There was one heartbeat of silence, "No, why should she be? We have, that is, I walked her home yesterday evening."

A similar microsecond's pause, "But she was with you this weekend wasn't she?"

"Yes, we went out on a trip together. Jennifer what is this about?"

"I want to find mum, she's not here. Do you know where she is?"

He stood away from the desk and ran his free hand across his head. What was happening? His thoughts started racing, automatically dragging his pulse along with them. "Have you checked the garden? You know she likes to be outside."

"Of course, I have! I do know my mum. And I've checked with the neighbours on either side. Do you think I'm an idiot?"

Throughout her terse replies, he had been holding the bridge of his nose and groaning under his breath, "Non, cherie, non. Ne fais pas cela. Non."

She was still speaking, but he could hear noises to indicate she was moving at the same time. "I've been in every room; there was some stuff dumped in the kitchen along with her 'phone and keys. Apart from that, the only sign she's been here is in the study. There's a lamp still on in here. Wait a minute," he could hear curtains being drawn, "I didn't see that before, there's a note on her desk, and things thrown on the floor."

"Oh, merdre! Non. What does she say?"

"It's not her, not her writing I mean."

"Are you sure?"

There was a sharp noise on the line, "My mother is incapable of writing anything without punctuation and proper spelling. This looks like it's been written by a six-year old." She went quiet, before saying faintly, "I think it's meant for you."

"What do you mean?"

"It says: very clever Frenchman, you forgot we'd have her address; but if she's not your girlfriend then it won't matter that we have her."

His head snapped up, "What?"

As she repeated it his head was turning, his eyes surveying the devastation before him.

"Farine, what's going on? What's happened to mum? What are you involved with? And who's taken her?"

His inaction was over; he took two strides to the nearest filing cabinet. "I don't know. There's only person who could think taking her would get my attention." He was rifling through the files, suddenly slamming the drawer shut again. "But it doesn't make any sense. I'm going to go there, If I find anything I will call you on your mother's 'phone, keep it with you." He closed his own mobile before she could remonstrate or delay him. Then he was moving out through the office to stand in front of the startled Maureen. "Old files, I need one."

Maureen was taken aback, but responded as the impeccable secretary she was. "Yes M. du Blez, which case?"

"Jubilee cards, possibly two years ago."

She moved along the corridor to where she knew she would find it. He followed, almost breathing down her neck as she moved, and twitching it from her fingers before she'd fully extracted it. He flipped the cover back and started scanning, stopped, and suddenly turned on his heel, back to his office.

He picked up and opened another file from his desk, one that had been left there last thing on Friday. His eyes were running over it quickly; there was something he had missed. Something that did make sense. He looked at the first file again and then back to this one. Slowly his eyelids lowered and he breathed heavily. "Idiot! Quelle imbecile!"

Maureen looked up in grave concern, she did not understand what was happening, but it was clearly something important. "M. du Blez, is there anything I can do?"

But he was already out of the door and dropping down the stairs in threes. He was running, and the route he had walked wearily a short time before, flew in reverse under his feet now. He dashed into the flat and snatched up a few items before collecting his car and taking off rather more quickly than the local speed limit would allow.

As he drove he started to speak in English, which seemed appropriate to him for what he had to say, "Lucy's God, I hope you will listen to me, please, for her sake. She doesn't deserve this. Please let me be in time, let me get her out." Then he switched to French, "Holy Mary, Mother of God, I promise I won't try to keep her, if only you'll let her be safe. If she's not then I promise you this, I will make them suffer." After that, he moved on to Arabic.

She had, of course, been crying on and off for several hours. Along with pacing the floor, making drinks and leaving them untouched, picking up her sketch pad and ripping the resulting efforts into shreds. The numbing, gnawing ache inside had been neither comforted nor alleviated by any of these activities. Several times she had dropped into the settee, surrendering to gravity and despair at the same time, only to rise and resume aimless wandering seconds later. On the final occasion she had dozed off, fitful sleep replacing sporadic tears. It was possibly this cessation of her outline passing to and fro across the curtains, that had been the signal the men outside were waiting for.

The house was not difficult to break into. As she hadn't gone to bed, she had not bothered to dead-lock the door. A light, still on in the room where she had temporarily quitted involvement with the world, was a useful guide to her location. By the time she was aware of anything happening, it was too late. Finding herself grabbed by a man on each side, one of whom clamped a large hand over her mouth, woke her and simultaneously rendered her helpless. To be roused by terror was not an experience she had ever had, nor was likely to want repeated. Trying to breathe, scream and resist were all completely unconscious actions, and largely ineffectual.

One of them spoke. "I'm not taking my hand away, so my advice is stop struggling. Breathing steadily through your nose is your best bet."

His hand was indeed pressed very firmly over her mouth, so firmly her head was pushed back with force against the settee. Her eyes, staring wide over the top of his hand, swung to his face and registered this information with a flicker. A few seconds passed in which she managed to get air into her lungs, and the idea into her head that she was in fact powerless. The face, not far from hers, was of a young man, thin and in need of a shave, nose somewhat bent. She tried to watch this face to gather any information about what was to happen next. He nodded to the man on the other side of her, who grasped both of her arms. The hand across her mouth was, contrary to indication, taken away. Involuntarily she gasped and screamed. This was cut off by a sharp slap across the face and then tape was applied in place of the hand. Panic threatened to take hold, she was trying to arch her back and pull away at the same time. Another slap and the voice again.

"I said breathe through your nose. The more you struggle, the worse it will gct."

It wasn't said kindly, or even threateningly. It was delivered as a fact, take it or leave it. Something she could take hold of, however unpleasant, was preferable to floundering in this sudden, drowning horror, and she nodded, willing herself to breathe in and out.

"Good. I'm going to tie you up, hands and feet. We can do it with a beating or without. Got it?"

She gave one more nod and then her hands were held together as the wrists were tied, followed by her ankles. Once this was done, the men seemed more relaxed and moved away from her. They stood in the centre of the room, looking around them. She wondered if they were sizing up what was worth stealing. Not that much. Would that mean more trouble? Then one thing slowly thawed in her frozen mind. She recognised one of the men, the one who had been silent so far. This wasn't a robbery, not anything nearly so simple. But why?

He had his 'phone to his ear, waiting for it to be answered.

"Aye, I know what the time is! We've had to wait, haven't we? What do you want us to do now?" There was a pause, he was obviously listening to some lengthy response and frowned accordingly. "Do you not just want us to get the address? That's what you said before!" He turned his back to her, one hand stuck into his pocket, shoulders tense. "I don't like the sound of that. Because it sounds like complications!" The hand was taken out of his pocket and used to scratch at his head instead. "Well, when will you be back? Are you sure that's best? How do we know it'll work anyway? What? Are you serious? Tell me what to say then." He turned back to stare at Lucy, before his eyes wandered off around the room again. "Yeah, yeah, got it." There was a nod or two, as he took in what were clearly final instructions and the 'phone was stowed away. He looked to Lucy, "Paper, pens? Point."

She lifted her hands and stuck a finger out to the desk behind him. He picked up a pen and grabbed a clean sheet of paper, then swept everything movable off the desk to leave an empty space. Lucy couldn't stop a noise coming from her throat at this wanton treatment of her work in progress. It was ignored. Instead he bent over as he wrote something, leaving the paper right in the middle of the blank table when it was finished.

He came across and knelt down to untie Lucy's ankles. "You're gonna walk out with us. If you struggle, I'll tie your feet back up, and being dragged is more painful than walking. Isn't that right Frankie?"

What she had to presume was Frankie, nodded. He went to take a look at what had been written. It caused him some slight amusement, but then he turned, "And if you give us any trouble, I'll be more than happy to make you suffer for it."

She was hauled to her feet and propelled towards her own front door. As they walked down the path she couldn't help hoping that at least one of the elderly neighbours was having trouble sleeping. She looked, but saw no hopeful signs of curtains twitching. There was a van parked nearby and she was quickly pushed inside, into the middle seat, one of them on either side again. As they drove away she was wondering exactly where the chance had been for her to make a brave but determined effort to escape. Funny, she hadn't noticed it at all. Somehow that made her almost as angry with herself as she was with these two thugs.

She tried to take note of the journey, as though that might help, but after the familiar streets close by, she felt she was losing all sense of direction and distance. They hadn't left the city, but they were certainly in areas she didn't recognise in the dark. There was not a lot of that left. Already she could see grey, low in the sky ahead; that must mean they were heading north-east.

The sun crawled up over the horizon, she glimpsed it through the castellated ups and downs of unimaginative sixties block buildings. They were definitely moving more slowly now, left and right turns alternating. This did look familiar. An industrial estate, rather run down, that she'd seen once before. There it was; a building she had even entered, and supposed she would be taken into now. A transport firm, small lorries parked up outside, all emblazoned with a name she knew well: Les Wilson. She turned to look at the driver of the van and the owner of that name, trying to see something on his face that would explain this. Then her attention was back on the road as they passed his own business and on to the next corner. A right turn was made and they pulled onto the forecourt of a small factory. She was yanked out and hustled quickly through a big metal-fold door which Frankie unlocked and pushed back a fraction, clanging it shut behind them. Even so, she had had time to read the name on the factory frontage. Somehow that wasn't a surprise. It dovetailed neatly into the rest of this surreal jigsaw. Perhaps it was all a nightmare. If only she could wake up. But it wasn't even daylight in here. The efforts of the dawn had not managed to penetrate the factory walls. Skylights allowed in vague illumination, but they were a long way up, and covered in dark detritus. She looked around and made out no more than the brooding humps of idle machinery crowding together at the back of the space they were in. The nearer section contained a scattering of boxes, some empty, some part-filled, along with rubbish and dust across the floor. The younger man suddenly took her arms and walked her roughly back. Her feet couldn't keep up and she sat down abruptly on the concrete, back banging against the wall. Tears stung her eyes, as much due to the frustration and horror of being gagged as the pain of landing on her rear. Frankie reached down and yanked the tape off her mouth. She gave a gurgling cry and then gasped in air.

Frankie bent to tie her feet again, then pointed his finger at her. "Now then, I don't want a racket. There's nobody around here yet, too early, so don't bother screaming. And if you get noisy, I'll tape you up again and then beat the living shit out of you. Understood?"

She nodded, lifting her hands to rub her face. Tears really came then, and she couldn't stop them. She had always suspected she was a coward, now she knew.

The two men retreated some distance, leaning against the bulky machines to talk in low voices. At first she was too distressed with her situation to take any notice, but as her heart-rate slowed she realised the only hope of getting out of it was to try and understand as much as she could. Not that the odd words she could catch made any sense, or told her any substantial facts. She already knew they were waiting for someone else, someone in charge. And she knew exactly who that was.

Some time had gone by; difficult to tell how much, but there was definitely more light filtering in. Both men had walked off through a small connecting door, and Lucy somehow felt freer to look around at her surroundings. There was something familiar about the machinery, and she realised there should be. They were Heidelberg presses, used in the printing process. No surprise there, she told herself, this was a card factory after all. But there was something not right. Trying to get her brain to function at all was an effort, but the thin thread of a familiar environment was a welcome trail to follow after her last few hours. Think, what was wrong with them? She had worked at a printing factory over one vacation while she was doing her degree. There were different sorts of Heidelbergs, depending on the particular process. Noisy, hot machines, they had all been uncomfortable to work with during the summer. She stared at these particular ones across the floor. They were covered in dust. That was what was wrong; they showed no signs of use. One in particular had suffered some kind of mutilation; parts of it lay on the floor. Not unusual to cannibalise an old one, but normally scavenged pieces were taken to replace broken parts on working machines. This one's innards were left spilled on the floor, no-one caring to mend or clear them up. So, he wasn't actually producing cards at all. Again, that wasn't really a surprise. The ones she had seen in the shop, she had thought dated from a few years ago. He was selling off old stock. But that wouldn't keep up with the apparent demand of a successful chain of outlets. What was making the money? And what had that got to do with Wilson? Her mind stalled at that point, flashing back to Friday and the meeting with him. He had been keen to get that business over with quickly. Was this a reaction to not accepting his offer? Over the top didn't cover it, perhaps he was a lunatic. No, he wasn't in charge. This was because Brogan had ordered it. So what did he want? Think. In Wilson's call to Brogan he'd asked about getting an address. Farine, obviously. Brogan had tried to get at him before. And now they'd chosen to do it – her thoughts were abruptly ended as the small door re-opened and voices flowed through. Instinctively she shrank down against the wall, wishing she could be somehow invisible. Two figures came in, arguing: Wilson and Brogan. Scowling replaced talking as they came across to her. Brogan looked down at her, smile automatically turning on.

"Well, madam Enigma, we meet yet again. You've been determined to get into this business from the beginning. Happy now?"

She didn't bother with a reply. Brogan squatted to bring his face nearer to hers. He reached one hand out lazily and touched her nose, speaking very softly.

"How long do you reckon before the boyfriend arrives? Don't bother with the denials, save time, eh? We can look forward to a nice little party all together. That'll be just grand, something to lighten my day."

Lucy felt sick. Even if she had something to say, she wasn't sure she could get her voice to work. There was some kind of numbing pressure from her throat all the way down inside. All she could do was stare, and she was aware of liquid brimming over her lower lids again.

"Now, now, darlin' too early to cry yet. Leave it for later."

He got up and walked towards Wilson, leaning against one of the presses and still scowling deeply. "I don't like this. Surely it's unnecessary."

"Too bad. You're in it now, and we don't have any option. The black bastard has had his nose in this from the beginning. I'm making sure he sticks it right in, then I'll push him out once and for all."

She could see Wilson's face crease even further. Anger was slowly emerging. "You told me to pay the bitch and get the case closed. That was supposed to be the easy way."

"Lesley, dear man, that was before I knew your stupidity had brought the world's most annoying solicitor into the game. If you remember, you never told me her name, why she was suing you, or the name of her lawyer, until Friday's mess." He patted the surly man on the shoulder. "We're not all blessed with brains, but for future reference Les, don't muddy the waters of your legit business with petty criminal tendencies." He looked around, then at his watch. "We've no idea when he'll arrive, it could be a while before he misses her. I'm going upstairs to do some proper work. Keep an eye on her until it's time to for the next delivery. Frankie's getting it packed up now."

He swept his eyes round once more and went back out through the wooden door to the rest of the building.

Lucy wanted to howl. It was not lost on her that Brogan hadn't cared what she heard, or that no-one had done anything to hide their identity. Whatever happened, he had no plans to release her. Her body reacted to this knowledge and she groaned.

"I feel sick!"

"So? What am I supposed to do about it?"

Lucy looked directly at Wilson. "For God's sake, it's not likely to be pleasant for you if I start throwing up! There must be a loo somewhere."

Wilson looked around him, possibly for someone else to answer that. She made one or two, quite genuine, retching noises. He came across, pulled the rope from her feet, hauled her upright and propelled her forwards in an amazingly short space of time. She was trotted through the door and across a small reception area, currently unmanned. A push through another door and she was into the washrooms. Just in time.

Performing basic bodily functions with a hostile man holding the edge of the inadequate door between them, would not have been on Lucy's list of life's unmissable experiences. Having finished the vomiting stage, she made no bones about using the facilities for further purposes. The stark alternative was the only incentive she needed. Some things proved impossible to do with hands tied together, but she managed enough to stave of the chances of utter shame for some time at least. His grumbles and hissed directives to get a move on did not actually progress to hauling her out by main force. She had jammed her foot behind the door to give her an extra moment, just in case. As soon as the noise of zipping shorts was heard, he forced the door back and yanked her out. This brought her up against the washbasin, and she leaned forward to get hands and face under the tap without asking. Again he remonstrated, but stopped short of physical intervention. This was not lost on her, she felt distinctly that either of the other two men would have grumbled less and interfered more. So, petty crook he may be, but she was right, he wasn't happy about the more severe crime Brogan was dragging him into. Maybe she could use that. She thanked him, meekly, and nodded to show that she was done. He opened the washroom door and looked out carefully. He was obviously afraid of Brogan, and of what would happen if it was known he'd allowed her any kind of courtesy.

"Thank you," she murmured again, as they went back across the lobby, with its tantalising glimpse of freedom beyond the glass panelling to the outside world. "I'm sorry, but I can't help being afraid." A grunt of response was all she got, and the door opened to go back to the workroom. "I do realise what's going to happen. You can't blame me for reacting to that." She was marched back to the exact same spot and sat down again. As he tied her feet, she tried a bit more. "This isn't really what you want, is it? Brogan's planning serious stuff here. You know it's not a great idea."

292

He gave her a withering look and moved back to his previous perch.

"Mr. Wilson," the politeness ridiculous, but she pressed on, "what you've done so far wouldn't be considered major crime. But if you go ahead with what Brogan's got lined up, what will happen to you?" He was frowning and she could tell he didn't enjoy being made to think about this, but she had no idea of how long she had. "There must be a considerable amount of evidence to point to you and Frankie. You've both been in my house. But Brogan hasn't touched anything, has he? If the police catch up with anyone, it won't be him. He gives the orders and you take the risk."

"Shut up, stupid cow."

"I'm only pointing out what you know anyway. Why don't you stop this before something terrible happens? The consequences could be horrendous. Please think."

"If you hadn't come chasing after me about your poxy bit of work, you wouldn't be here, would you?" He gave a sudden grin, no doubt delighted by this little ray of logic.

"No, but there's a hell of a difference between breaching copyright, and being an accessory to murder. I think the sentences are quite different too." She had spoken softly but they both knew her words had been clearly heard and understood. "You can put a stop to this. You could call the police, or just let me go if you can't face that. That would give you time to get out of the way."

He moved from his seat, turning. She couldn't see his face, or what he was doing. Hopefully he was considering, realising just what a hopeless mess he was in. He turned back and approached her, she looked up hopefully. He leant down and stuck more tape firmly across her mouth.

26

For some time, she could do nothing but lie in misery. She had slumped onto one side, tears flowing and pooling under her head. A lot of the time she just fought to keep herself breathing calmly in, and out. Any thoughts of further vomiting had to be squashed quickly and continuously, so they would fade and leave her able to focus on that all-important lung work again. She still had no idea of the time, her watch had stopped, the face cracked. There was no memory of how it had happened. Gradually something else did make it into her mind. Farine. What would he do? She really hoped he wouldn't come. Or was that: she desperately hoped he would? Reason told her it made no difference to her fate whether he turned up or not. She didn't want to die alone, here, abandoned. She didn't want to see him die, probably unpleasantly. Please God, let it be quick. Whatever happened, let it be quick. Don't let him come. Don't let Tom imagine her suffering. Tom! What on earth would he think? It would make absolutely no sense to him at all. She had no way to let him know she hadn't deserted him. No way of explaining to him or the children. Jenny, she was bound to come round today. She would see the note, sooner or later. Surely she would call the police. That's right, the police would come. Wouldn't they? Dear God, let the police come! But what if Farine did turn up? What would Brogan do? Breathe, just breathe, she told herself.

He had no trouble finding the address, and it was an obvious but welcome confirmation that the two buildings were so close. He didn't stop at either, but drove past Jubilee Cards and turned into the yard of a derelict warehouse he found round the corner. His eyes swept across the place, checking that there was no-one likely to come and poke into his being there. He left the car behind an abandoned, rusting container to be out of sight from the road. He wanted to provoke as little curiosity as possible. Now his attention turned to what was in the car. He ripped off his tie and smart lemon shirt, carefully smoothed on for the morning. A black tee-shirt was pulled over his head instead. Polished shoes also went and trainers took their place. He picked up the item he'd stowed under the seat, went round to the boot for something else. Then he locked the car, leaving the roof down for a fast exit. He hoped. He was about to adopt the hands-in-pocket shambling lope of a black man pointlessly wandering through a rundown area, when he realised the wall at the end of this unit, gave onto the back of the Jubilee factory. Better still. It took only seconds before he was on top of the wall and down the other side. He paused for a quick recce, and then ran across the weed strewn slope behind the factory, smiling. No windows on this side equalled no-one to see him approach. The worst moment was when he was at the top of the fire escape. The door there was the obvious means of entry, and he applied the tyre lever he'd brought to it. But there was no means of knowing what was on the other side. It would open outwards. If necessary, he could shield himself with that before dropping over the edge of the fire escape. Guns, he thought unlikely. Although more numerous these days, they were noisy. He imagined Brogan would not be utterly stupid, no guarantee though. By now the woodwork of the frame was beginning to splinter and it gave way with a final crunch. He held his breath, no sound from inside. He pulled the door back, risking a quick glance round the edge of it. He had to take a second look. An unexpected sight had met his eyes. Not the dim interior of a cold factory. And thankfully no welcoming party with lengths of pipe or baseball bats either. Instead, what greeted him and enfolded him into its warm embrace was something more like a greenhouse. He pulled the door to, as well as he could, behind him, because even in the sunshine, the spilling of bright light out through the opening would have been noticeable. He walked softly between the rows of plants and smiled. Not a card factory but a cannabis factory. The humid atmosphere soon caused sweat to break out on his forehead, that was irrelevant, but he was beginning to wonder how much of this there was and how to get to the rest of the building. He found the far wall; in fact there were three doors at intervals along it. This growing area seemed to take up the whole length of the building, and from what he could remember as he drove past, probably two-thirds or more of the depth. Presumably packing happened downstairs. No doubt that's where he needed to be. He decided to try each of the three doors in turn, and when he'd surveyed what was on the other side, opt for the most helpful. The first gave on to offices. Peering through the slightest crack he could manage, painfully aware of how bright the lights were, he could just make out glass screens over partition walls. He had to close the door again quickly; further investigation brought the outline of a man's head, just visible through a window off to his left. Best avoid this door if possible. The middle door gave onto a breeze-block wall, only a yard away. Nothing much could be seen to the left; to the right, some metal barrier, perpendicular to the wall. Time for the third door. This one opened into more of a space, terminated by railings again. But the view was wide enough now to see that the barrier ran around the edge of the floor, and the wall opposite was full-height. This must be the loading bay, and presumably there would be hoists or fork-lifts to lower goods to the despatch area below. Checking the door wouldn't slam behind him, or lock him out, he edged forward, crouching low, to peer down at the lower level. Yes, he was right, there was the large rolling door that would open to allow loading. He could see part-filled boxes on the concrete floor. The light here was dim, after the growing area, and he could make out no details of what was around the boxes. He couldn't see much else either; the majority of the downstairs was of course hidden under the floor he stood on. He was able to move to his right, and thus see more of what was underneath to his left. A small wooden door; more boxes; not much else. No, something to the back. More railings, by the look of it. At an angle - stairs! That was beyond where he could go on this level, his way was barred by another breeze-block wall. So, he if he went back to door number two, that may lead to the top of those stairs. Better to walk down quietly than risk making a noise by clambering down from here. As he slid back towards the door and the greenhouse, he picked up another piece of information. He heard voices below.

She had been left alone for some time, although she knew Wilson was not far away. Then she heard Brogan again.

"Frankie's nearly finished packing upstairs. The two of you can load up and then you get off to Nailsea. The wheels of industry must be kept oiled, eh?"

"What about the other goods?"

She guessed there had been a jerk of the head to go with that question, although there was little doubt to what he referred.

"Once you've gone, Frankie can take over." He paused. "Actually it's a waste of time having somebody stuck here baby-sitting. Before you set off, the two of you can tie her up to something too heavy to move, okay?"

"When you expecting the solicitor?"

A short laugh, "No idea. Depends how often they exchange pleasantries, I guess. Are you worried about him? Don't be. Frankie has a score to settle, and he knows what to expect this time. And I'm looking forward to wiping the polished smile off his smug features."

She saw his feet moving, receding across the floor and back towards the reception. Shortly after that she saw other feet, Frankie, arriving to organise loading. They came across to her and made her shuffle further back into the gloom, out of their way while they opened the large door and backed the truck up to it. Frankie then climbed into the fork-lift and lowered stacks of boxes from above. She had heard dragging movements from up there, but hadn't been able to see him accumulating his load. Now they brought down two pallets, and loaded them into the back of Wilson's van.

"You labelled 'em properly this time?"

"Yeah, yeah. You got a short memory or something"

"Watch your lip. Makes sense to do things properly; causes less suspicion that way."

Frankie burst out laughing, "Something you should bear in mind, Les. From what I hear."

Wilson spent a good minute swearing at him, and Lucy couldn't help wondering if this was to vent his frustration at being sucked into something he now regretted.

"Alright, alright," complained Frankie. "You've made your point. Shift your van out, I'll lock up. You might as well be off."

"We need to tie her up. Brogan said."

"Oh, so he did. Tell you what, move the van, I'll make us a coffee and we'll get her tied up before you set off, okay?"

He was trying to keep the peace, Lucy thought, sinking down to the floor again. Peace among thieves. No, that was supposed to be honour, and they weren't thieves. What were they? Well they had stolen her. It was cold on the concrete, and she was shivering uncontrollably now. What would they do to her? Surely they wouldn't kill her here, evidence and all that. Tonight probably, when it was dark, somewhere else, out of the way. What though? Faked car accident? Poison for a lovers' tryst? Oh, God no, what would Tom be left thinking? Tom, poor Tom, he would never see his wife again. He would feel so bad for leaving her. No, he hadn't left her, just gone to Africa. Someone else had been stolen in Africa, hadn't they? Who was that? Farine's mother, but that was years ago. Farine. Please God, she started again in her head. Don't let him come. Don't let him walk into this. What would they do to him? She realised her thoughts were being shaken together and tumbling out randomly, perhaps it was all this trembling. Could she get hypothermia in summer? Perhaps she could die of that, save them the bother of killing her. And save her from whatever horror they had planned. She felt so weak and listless; it was almost an appealing thought to just drift off and not have to face any more of this.

She saw them come back in, mugs in their hands, and Frankie was carrying rope or something. She'd love a hot drink. Then she felt nauseous again and she had to tell herself to breathe in, and breathe out, in and out. She watched them perch on boxes as they drank, talking over trivialities. Frankie put his empty mug down and leant on his hand as he asked about Wilson's delivery.

He had slipped through the middle door this time and turned right, moving quickly to get out of the confines of what was in effect a corridor. He was correct, these railings represented the top of a flight of stairs, which was hopefully the same set he'd seen terminating below. Every step felt noisy to him, but he had moved swiftly as well as softly to arrive at the bottom undetected. He was definitely well back in the factory, among large, heavy machinery, which sat idle. This gave him excellent cover and he made good use of it to work his way forward. Thankful that he now had the advantage of approaching out of the gloom, he slid from one piece of redundant metalwork to another. There was definitely a conversation going on, and he'd only heard two voices so far. He found a position from where he could see one man, who was using a box to lean on. From the angle of his head as he spoke, his companion must be further forward, slightly out of his line of sight. As he listened checking for other possible protagonists, he also looked around for some sign of Lucy. He needed to know where she was before he made any move. Finally, over to one side near the wall, he made out something like a bundle on the floor, but when he saw it roll slightly, he knew it was her. Good, she was out of the way. He pulled the knife out from behind his waist and settled it into his hand. He was taking a last look at the layout, to fix everything in his mind for movement.

Wilson asked idly "We got any more deliveries lined up?"

Farine sprang forward. The man's question was answered by a sudden gargling scream from his friend. This was due as much to the sight, as to the pain, of a large knife impaling his hand to the packed carton he'd been leaning on. He had no time to resolve the blur that passed him as the dark figure who had planted it there. Wilson did though, and bent to grab some kind of metal bar that was on the floor. He made a swipe at the tall figure advancing on him. Farine swung his torso back, barely having to move his feet to sidestep. Obviously, he was not up against a fencing man. Instead, he aimed a kick to his opponent's wrist, painful enough to ensure the makeshift weapon was dropped. His momentum carried him forward onto his right foot, allowing him to follow through with his left fist to the man's jaw line just below his ear.

Unconscious, good. That gave him probably twenty seconds to deal with his first victim, still gasping in panic and looking round wildly for some form of defence. Desperation lent the man resolve, and he grabbed the knife with his functioning hand, yanking it out of both box and flesh to free himself. The effort required caused him to sway back, off balance. Farine made use of that, kicking out to connect with the back of his knees. He collapsed to the floor, his head making a loud crack on the concrete, after which he lay still. Farine picked up his knife, wiping the blade on the man's clothes. He cast about quickly, and found the cord, conveniently brought in by Frankie, which he used to tie both their hands and feet before they could come round.

Finally, he was able to cross to the other crumpled form on the floor, the one that he wanted, and rip the tape off her mouth.

"Lucy, are you okay?" he asked, unable to refrain from the predictable question. Before she could even try and reply he had his arms round her and was cradling her against him. "I'm sorry, I'm so sorry. I didn't mean any of it." He stopped as suddenly as he'd begun and bent to cut through the ties on her ankles and wrists. He rubbed her arms and legs to get the blood moving. "You need to stand up, we must leave quickly. Here, lean on me."

"You need to get out, it's a trap," she croaked. With a swift tug, he had her on her feet, but she could barely move.

"Of course it's a trap!" he grinned at her.

"Brogan is here, he wants to, to. . ."

"Kill me?" He was moving her towards the door. "I aim to disappoint him. Are there any more?" He tipped his head back, "Besides those two?"

"I haven't seen any others. Brogan kept saying he was going upstairs to work." They had reached the reception area. "There could be people up there, but I haven't heard anyone else mentioned."

300

His eyes swept round as he nodded, "There are offices upstairs. Above where we are now. So keep your voice down. Although I think our friend back there probably made enough noise to wake the dead."

She reached out to the door; she was inches away from being out of this building and the worst nightmare of her life. Relief flooded through her, and she thought she might sink to the ground again, but outside would definitely be a good idea. Her hand pushed the door, pulled it. Equally ineffective, it was locked.

"Would these be any help now?"

She turned; Farine was already watching him carefully. He stood halfway up the stairs that led from reception to the offices, leaning nonchalantly on the hand-rail where the stairs turned. No doubt he'd been waiting out of sight. From his extended finger hung a small bunch of keys.

Farine started to speak, and she realised suddenly he was addressing her, not Brogan. "Lucy, whatever happens, don't get between us. Move yourself out of the way. Understood?"

He had spoken very calmly and quietly. She responded the same way, "Yes." With that, she started to inch away. The stairs where Brogan lolled were across the lobby from the exit. She moved to her right, towards the washroom and across to a desk where some erstwhile receptionist might have been stationed. It too was untidy and showed no signs of proper organised work taking place. Old-fashioned office paraphernalia cluttered the surface and the small pigeon holes above. She stood there, as if she was waiting to take a memo. The two men just seemed to be staring at each other.

Suddenly Brogan shouted "Here!" and threw the keys straight at Farine. He just put up his hand to deflect them, not even trying to catch them or move. They dropped to the ground. She wanted to rush over and snatch them up. But if he was ignoring them, then that must be what she was meant to do too.

"Very good!" sneered Brogan. He was wearing what Lucy had come to think of as the most annoying smile known to man. How she wanted to wipe it off his face for him. But she mustn't get in the way. Farine knew what he was doing in a fight. She didn't. She was beginning to wonder if anything was going to happen at all, they might all be locked into this ridiculous tableau forever. Well that was fine. She could leave all this staring each other out to the two of them. Her brain finally got the point that she was free to move and her hand went forward to pick up the 'phone.

There was some kind of hiss from Brogan and he was forced to move, leaping down the stairs to get to her. Farine moved too, and intercepted him with a punch. Surprise was not a factor this time and Brogan deflected it from its proper target. He was obviously used to physical interaction and a more considered interplay of jabs and kicks started. This swaying, thrashing dance they were strangely joined in was sheer mystery to Lucy, but she did realise that if Brogan was not contained quickly, her call to the police would be immaterial. She put the handset down and reached across the desk for something else. An outdated four-hole paper-punch; not elegant, but definitely heavy. She stepped towards the two men and took a swipe at the nearer head. It wasn't an accurate, or determined, enough blow to knock the Irishman out, but it certainly distracted him. Farine lost no time in getting his fingers either side of the man's neck. Lucy very much enjoyed his brief look of astonishment that faded into slack oblivion.

As soon as Brogan was on the floor Farine yanked at the telephone wire, ripping it out and finding a new use for it to truss his captive.

Lucy's jaw dropped. "I was going to call the police, I can't now!"

Farine looked up at her, faintly astonished. "Would you like me to untie him and plug you back in?"

She started to giggle, sat quickly on the edge of the desk and curled over as the laughter raced out of control. She knew it was hysteria but that didn't help to contain it.

Job finished, he came across and took hold of her. "It's okay; I promise you you're safe now."

She was shivering and shaking, stuck somewhere between maniac laughter and the possibility of more vomiting.

He pulled a chair across, sat on it and enfolded her on his knee. "Are you cold?" She nodded. He pulled his tee-shirt off and made her put it on, before wrapping his arms round her again. "Are you injured?" She shook her head, unable to stop her teeth chattering. "You have a bruise on your face."

She nodded, stammering out the bare details of being abducted. Several expressions went across his countenance, before he asked which one had hit her.

"The one you stabbed."

"Good, saves me going back to do it. I hope I got the correct hand."

"I couldn't say. Wilson was actually quite reluctant I think."

"Brogan? Did he hurt you?"

She shook her head. Then they both looked towards the man in question as he began to stir.

Farine turned back to her, "When did you last drink anything?"

She looked blank for a moment. "I've no idea. Last night sometime, when you left I suppose." For a sliver of a second, the memory of that came back, but was dispelled with less than a breath. That was a lifetime ago. A whole universe away. She was prevented from thinking any more about it by a string of invective issuing from floor-level.

"I'll shut him up," said Farine.

"No, please allow me." She got off his knee and reached up to the pigeon holes over the desk. She turned round, grinning like a madman again, and bent over Brogan with the parcel tape dispenser. "There. That's quite neat, I think."

"Lucy, find something to drink. You will be dehydrated and you're on the edge of hypothermia. Have water and then make tea."

They discovered the small kitchenette, which Lucy knew must exist, and Farine rooted around until he discovered some biscuits.

"Eat as well, if you can. But drink first. I'll go and check on Brogan."

She drank some water, somehow metallic and distasteful at first, but necessary, she realised. Next she fiddled with the ageing kettle, and looked sideways at the biscuits they'd found. She stuck her head out round the door to ask if he wanted a drink too. She nearly lost her composure once more, at the thought of this ridiculous, alien situation, in which they were now practising normal domesticity. But she found Brogan wide-eyed, Farine squatting by him. His knife was out again, held very still, point indenting the skin into a pale asterisk on the other man's cheek.

"Farine," she said softly, "torture isn't part of the deal."

His eyes came up to meet hers, and he nodded, removing the knife. He stood, "I'll just make sure the others are secure; then we really must call the police."

With a few terse sentences he reported the situation, or an outline at least, to the detective he'd finally been put through to. His mobile closed, he took her hand. "Let's take you home."

"Don't we have to wait for the police?"

"No. We're not being arrested for anything. We will be politely requested to go along and give statements at some point."

"But, I thought. . ."

"Don't be misled by television dramas. If we stress how ill you feel after your ordeal they may stretch to sending some detective sergeant round to interview you. Today, or tomorrow, or maybe next week. Unless you want to wait around while they deal with things here and give your name and address to a spotty young constable."

"I suppose you know all this from Angus."

He nodded. "I think we're better off getting you home."

Getting out of the place was delayed briefly by having to track down the front door key. The set Brogan had taunted them with belonged to something else, but the right one turned up in his office. Lucy breathed in deeply as soon as they were through the door. Industrial district air may not be the sweetest, but to her it was the best she'd ever had in her nostrils. That made her shudder at the memory of all her restricted breathing. Straightaway he put his arm round her shoulders.

"Are you okay, warming up yet?"

"Getting better thank you."

"You do know I didn't mean any of those things I said last night, don't you? I was being ridiculous, and you were right."

"Steady, too much humility and I'll think I'm dreaming. I would prefer the rescue to be real, not the product of my brain on the point of hypothermic collapse."

"Okay, but I am genuinely sorry. I should have never have said those things. I can't tell you how I felt when I found out this morning."

"How did you find out? Did you come round to apologise?"

"No, Jennifer found you missing and called me."

Lucy stopped in her tracks, recently regained colour draining from her face again. "Oh no, poor Jen!"

He passed her his 'phone, "Ring your number, she has your mobile, you're right she is probably sick with worry."

It was answered immediately.

"Jen, it's me! Yes, yes, I'm alright. Really. On my way home. How long?" She looked at him, "Maybe thirty minutes. Yes, I really am okay." After repeated reassurances she ended the call.

Farine reached for her hand and squeezed it. "You don't mind me holding on to you?"

"Mind? I insist! I still feel pretty shaky. Believe me holding onto some kind of action hero is the last thing I'd complain about right now."

They had reached the car and he helped her in. She sank into the seat, part of something familiar, known smells curling up to reassure her that she was back in safe territory. When he was in the car, she turned, taking hold of his upper arm with both hands then leant her head against it too. She closed her eyes for a moment then smiled. "I can't help noticing you took the chance to get your kit off."

"You can't blame me. And it was for medical purposes. Let me know if you need any resuscitation."

He started the car, but he was forced to drive with her hanging onto him. As they left the industrial estate she kissed him on the shoulder several times, "Don't worry, it's only hysteria setting in again. I'll be alright soon."

He smiled, "Well, personally I think it is safest to recover from hysteria gradually, I recommend taking your time. See, I will even drive more slowly than usual to help you calm down."

Lucy rolled her head back against the seat, covering her eyes with her hand.

"What is it?"

"Just a bit nauseous, the world keeps lurching out from underneath me every so often."

"Not surprising, it must have been terrifying for you."

"Strange, I'm already thinking 'did that really happen'. The last few hours appear to be in a bubble, sometimes I'm back inside it petrified, then it's at a distance from me looking very unreal."

"Shock makes your mind do odd things."

Suddenly she took hold of his hand again, and he glanced across to see her face streaked with tears. "I'm sorry, I just need to keep touching you and making sure you're real, and that I am here. I was so scared!"

"I understand; you had every right to be. I was scared too, terrified if you want to know. At least I could fight and make use of the adrenaline, you didn't have that chance."

"Yes, that reminds me," she said wiping a hand across her face, "I know about D'Artagnan, but where did Action Man come from? Is that some other little secret from your past?"

He shrugged, "Not really, you know my father was in the French army. He taught me some of his commando training, and I kept his knife. Given that I've practised fighting all my life, in one form or another, I'm not sure why everybody is so surprised that I know what to do."

She was thoughtful for a moment. "You mean Brogan?"

"Yes. He's an idiot. Just because he's terrorised people in a paramilitary setup, doesn't mean he's any good at hand-to-hand combat. Ditto the idiots he sent to attack me. If I had to face them all at once, then it would be a different matter. But in ones or twos?" He shrugged, "He just assumed I would be someone like him."

"Do you know that he was in the paramilitaries?"

"Not for sure, but I'm willing to bet the police find out that he was. He hinted at it when I spoke to him that time. And I believe it's quite a common thing. A lot of the guys who were involved with them turned to straightforward crime when the peace process got under way. They get used to the feeling of power and being somebody important. They like to make people afraid and think they can do it to everyone."

"Well, they managed with me. We don't all have fencing medals, I suppose."

"No." He was quiet for a little while, glancing at her occasionally to check her condition. After a while he asked softly, "Lucy, what did you mean when you mentioned the deal?"

"Hm? What deal?"

"That's what I mean. What deal where you talking about, when you told me not to do anything to Brogan?"

Her face contracted in concentration before she shook her head. "Don't know, don't remember what I said. Why, did I say something wrong?"

"No, no. Just wondered what you meant. It's, I mean, I ought to say, well. . ."

She looked at him, bemused. He was never the one stuck for words. Nothing was forthcoming, it seemed, so she decided to wait in greater comfort and rested her head against him again.

When he did speak it was in a very soft voice again. "It is a pity that we will never get to make love. I don't suppose just once would be acceptable, would it?"

She tried to tone down the smile, keen to avoid another expedition into the realm of hysteria. "I think it's very unfair of you to offer me a temptation like that when I've got all these euphoria hormones rocketing round my body. Now I know why you really took the shirt off."

"Oh, you've been admiring me, have you? I thought you were planning a sketch."

She moved her head against his arm so she could look up at his face. The curve of his cheek, the hairline running round his neck. Temptation didn't cover it. She closed the sight out from her eyes, sighing heavily. No going back, no changing horses in mid-race. Tom was her man; that was a fact. But she couldn't stop herself, and at the moment was not inclined to deny herself, enjoying the proximity of one who could be. Just for the ride home, until they got back to real life.

27

They pulled up a little way from her house and sat in silence, reluctant to move. After a moment she put her head in her hands, "I don't think I can cope with any more!"

Farine got out of the car and went round to help her. He shut the door, leaned against it and pulled her back gently by the hand he was still holding.

"It's very difficult for me to let go of you right now. I know we must, but after the various miseries I went through this morning, wondering what had happened to you, I just want to keep hold of you. Do you understand?"

She nodded and leant against him, letting him put his arms round her.

"It's not too surprising, is it? I feel much the same. Maybe we're allowed a twenty-four hour stay of execution – ugh! Bad choice of words," she shivered slightly and looked up at him. "They would have killed us, wouldn't they?"

He didn't need to speak; the way he lowered his eyelids and tightened his hold around her was enough.

She took a few deep breaths, then said in a serious voice, "Well, you know, I think that even the most sensible and virtuous of married women could be forgiven. For indulging in a brief emotional embrace with the man who'd just saved her life, I mean. As a practitioner of law, what's your opinion?"

"I think your reasoning is entirely sound, faultless in fact. You have convinced me."

"I've convinced myself too!" she said, her hand going up to pull his head down within reach.

They were engrossed enough not to notice another car pull up a little way ahead, or the young man that stepped out of the battered runabout juggling keys and CDs. He noticed them though, and frowned to himself, then angled his head in enquiry, then shook it and frowned again. Looking perplexed he turned away and walked up to a house where he let himself in.

"Nick! Oh Nick thank goodness you're here!"

He was somewhat taken aback by his sister rushing up to him and throwing her arms round his neck, even more so when she started crying.

"Erm, hi Jen. What's the matter?"

"Oh Nick it's awful! Mum's been abducted!"

"What? You're sure she's not just gone somewhere?" Her face stopped that line of enquiry short. "Have you called the police?"

"They didn't believe me! They said there was no real evidence of a struggle here. I wouldn't care, there's even a note, but they said there's no ransom demand and it's not clear that's what it means and. . ." Her incoherent repetitions of details served only to increase his bafflement. ". . .and she won't qualify as a missing person for forty-eight hours or something."

"That's ridiculous. But," he tried to point back through the door, "do you know there's a woman who looks just like her out there. She's snogging some half-naked black guy though. That can't be mum, can it?"

She gave a huge sigh, "You know this is what euphoria does, don't you?"

"Yes, all those hormones, but I'm not complaining."

"No, not right now. Although it. . ."

She was interrupted by what appeared to be a mob, all shouting at once. In reality it was only two people, each exclaiming something different. She turned to look at them, and had to let go of Farine to take hold of her distressed daughter instead and offer reassurance.

"I'm alright, really. Look, I'm fine."

Nick was glaring at Farine from under his dark eyebrows, turning to his sister he demanded, "Shouldn't we call the police?"

His already tortured understanding took a final blow when Jenny shrieked, "He's the one who's just rescued her!"

At this point someone decided they really would be better off in the house, and the street theatre moved on.

310

As they went through the blessedly welcome sight of her own front door, Lucy turned to her son, "Nick do you think you could get Farine a spare tee-shirt or something, please?"

He glowered a little, but stumped upstairs noisily and returned with a bright orange creation sporting a grunge band logo. He handed it to Farine without actually looking at him and disappeared into the kitchen. Lucy leaned towards Farine and spoke in a low voice, "I think that's another two years on my embarrassment account."

They went and took seats in the lounge, thankfully someone was making tea. Lucy had been starting to think she might commit murder herself if none was forthcoming, then shuddered; it was no joke any more. Nick and Jenny then started with the expected endless questions,

Between them they managed to reconstruct what had taken place over the last twelve hours or so. Lucy had trouble reconciling that with what felt like a week out of her life. There was a good deal of confusion and untangling to be done, particularly for Nick and Jenny, who knew nothing about Brogan.

"So," Nick asked, frowning, "what was the connection between this Brogan and Wilson who you were suing?"

Farine grimaced into the tea he'd been given, "He had a transport business; quite possibly he was used by Jubilee Cards when it was still a legitimate concern because he was so close. No doubt Brogan appealed to his somewhat dubious moral outlook by promising him more money for moving something else. What I don't understand myself," he put the cup down behind the chair-leg, hopefully out of sight, "is why Brogan thought of growing cannabis in the first place."

"I think I know," said Lucy, trying not to smile at Farine's tea problem. "One of the ways the police often track down cannabis factories is by the high electricity bills and heat output of the building. The presses would have had exactly the same effect. It would have looked, from that point of view, as though card production was carrying on as before."

"But surely, people couldn't just go into his shops and ask for the stuff outright?" Jenny put in.

Farine shook his head, "Of course not, but I would guess they were used as distribution centres. Somewhere dealers could come, and apparently take away boxes of cards. Except each box would have one or two cards on top and lots of something else underneath. The shops themselves, and the cards on sale, were just camouflage."

Lucy shook her head, "It doesn't explain why his shop got blown up, and what he thought we were after."

"I'm sure that was to do with a bigger gang. There will be some outfit running a lot of the drug trade in Bristol. It's unlikely that Brogan, having found a successful cover, wouldn't have wanted to move into harder, more lucrative substances. The people currently in charge of the market would want to dissuade him. What he said to me proves that, I think."

"Why did he think we were involved though?"

"That was my fault." Farine looked contrite. "Although our contact was accidental, by being somewhat," he pulled his laps back, "aggressive in the way I reacted to him, it made him believe I was an enemy. Once we got off on that footing, every interaction we had seemed to underline it. Until that chat I had with him in the street. But then when he found out it was us in the case against Wilson, it must have seemed to him that I'd lied, that we knew they were involved in something together and were pursuing them."

"Of course there's also the fact that he's an evil bastard."

Farine smiled at Lucy's in-depth analysis, "Yes, there is that too."

"Why did they take mum though?" Jenny asked quietly.

"That also is my fault. I don't know when they broke into my office, but there is nothing there to indicate where I live, I make sure of that. They had your address from the work you did for Wilson of course. They may have watched this house over the weekend," he paused and lightened the tone of his voice, "but cleverly, you weren't here."

She was already holding her hand over her mouth. Now tears started down her face again and her shoulders shook.

"If I'd been here, if I hadn't been with you. . ."

"Sshh, it's okay. You're safe."

Once more he put his arm round her, resting his chin on her head and looking quietly at the two youngsters, neither of whom seemed capable of speech.

Practical considerations soon started to re-establish themselves. After another round of drinks, it was decided they all needed to eat. Farine was then talking about going back to the office, but before he made any move, Lucy received a call from DCI Bonnington. He wanted statements from them as soon as possible. Farine took the 'phone and went into solicitor mode, insisting his client was in no fit state to leave the house, and someone could come to them.

Lucy decided she was putting off having a shower no longer, and went upstairs to try and make herself feel a little more human. Jenny came upstairs to join her after a while and sat on the bed, trying to work out if her mum was really okay, as Lucy dealt with her hair and face.

"I keep telling you, I'm fine. I was scared as hell, and I've probably got a few bruises, but I'm very much alive and in one piece! Seems like a good deal to me."

"Why were you with him all weekend?"

Lucy stopped in mid-movement and looked into the mirror at her daughter's face. "We've been really good friends for the last few months. We both decided we were in the mood for taking off and ignoring the rest of the world. That's it."

Jenny made a few facial contortions, not dissimilar to some of Lucy's own.

"You've got nothing to worry about, Jen, honestly."

"Really?"

"I promise. I don't expect you to like it, but it really is okay."

"I can't dislike it, can I? It seems he's saved your life."

Lucy closed her eyes and shuddered, feeling cold again despite the sunshine flooding into the room. They hugged, holding onto the safe outcome and each other until they were interrupted by the ring of the doorbell.

Eventually the police left, and exhaustion started to catch up with everyone in the house. There was some debate about where Lucy would spend the night. Jenny wanted to take her back to her own flat; she felt it would be horrible for her mum to have to stay in the house after what had happened the night before. Lucy thought that unfair on Nick as Jenny's flat wasn't big enough for them all. She could see Farine staring at her and knew he wanted to suggest she go with him. She gave her head the slightest of shakes and he turned away.

In the end it was agreed that both Jenny and Nick would stay in the house with her. She sent them off to sort out the spare room for Jenny, and bring in Nick's belongings from his car.

She went across to Farine, "Well, we've got about three minutes peace. Here we go again." They put their arms round each other and she whispered into his shoulder, "I'm really sorry."

"What, for getting yourself kidnapped? Yes, very thoughtless of you."

She smiled, "Have I made it all a lot worse, by being in danger?"

"No," he said after a moment, "somehow not. Perhaps I feel that I have done something useful at least, rather than just hurt you. But. . ." He bit his lip.

"What?"

"Well, I know we must part, and this is not logical, but will you let me know for the next few days that you are alright?"

She looked at his face closely, "Yes, I can message you. There's something else, isn't there? You said when we got out of the car 'various miseries'. What did you mean?"

He sighed, unusually for him, struggling to say what was on his mind. "When I got Jennifer's call, I didn't realise straight away what had happened. I thought for a moment that you, that perhaps…"

"Oh Farine! I wouldn't do anything like that. That would be so mean to everybody I care about, I can promise you I wouldn't."

"No, I didn't think so, but it was so scary for a few seconds."

"And me being abducted wasn't?"

"Of course it was, but I could play the Count of Monte Cristo for that."

She looked up into his face, smiling, "You know there's one thing you've made me change my mind about."

"What's that?"

"English distance. When we meet again, which I suppose we will with the police case and everything, if you don't greet me properly, I will be very offended."

"I wouldn't dream of offending you. I am a gentleman, you know."

"Yes, I do know."

They walked into the hall. At the door they said 'au revoir' and he left. Nick was coming down the stairs again, watching them with interest.

"He's very French, isn't he?"

"Farine du Blez, le Comte d'Ambouzac? Mais oui, vraiment."

"He's a Count? You never said; that must be really cool!"

For the following three days, Lucy dutifully sent texts to Farine reporting her wellbeing. On the fourth day there was nothing, on the Saturday she called him and said she wanted to meet him briefly for a coffee.

At the café he greeted her calmly, "First of all, I must thank you for the picture."

She looked at him with a frown, asking sharply, "What picture?"

"The one of the bridge in the Cotswolds. You organised it, according to the note. It arrived on Wednesday."

"Oh that, of course! Good grief, I'd forgotten all about it. That seems ages ago."

"I know. A lot has happened since then. In fact it was a week ago today."

She shook her head in disbelief, "I seem to remember you telling me once that we could never know what would happen in a week's time. You were right."

"Well, I've hung it in the corner over the cello, as you suggested on the card; it looks very good there."

They sat in silence for a moment, each watching the re-run of their own thoughts. She came back to the present, handing a small package across to him.

"What's this, another gift?"

"Hardly! It's just your tee-shirt, washed and returned."

"That wasn't necessary."

She smiled as she leant back in her chair. "Actually it was. I found myself keep picking it up and burying my face in it."

He sat very still, staring intently into his espresso for a moment. When he looked up he was smiling. "Thank you for telling me. But I don't suppose that means anything has changed."

"No. In a few days I'm flying out to Tanzania to join Tom."

He nodded. "That makes sense, I suppose." He stared out of the window for a moment then said quietly, almost under his breath, "It's such a pity. I really wanted you to come and meet the family. Apart from anything else, I regret the loss of you as a friend." His eyes came back to her, "I know you won't be keeping in touch."

Her lip quivered slightly, "No, I don't suppose I will." She took a moment then said more strongly, "You know, I still believe that by doing what is right, despite the pain, something good will come of this. Some kind of redemption."

"For you or me?"

"For us both." She shrugged, "For our families, who knows?"

They were both silent for a while, sitting still but moving apart. Like when a ship pulls away from the dock, a channel would open between them. Very narrow at first, but quietly and irrevocably widening, the gulf getting deeper and darker with each propeller beat. Soon they would only be able to wave in tearful farewell from opposite sides of it.

Suddenly she spoke again. "I wanted to tell you in person, about me going away. Tom, poor man, has coped with me being blown up, but abducted and threatened with murder is too much. He's right; the expense is nothing, is it?"

"Why that way round, rather than him coming home?"

"He had thought taking a wife out to Tanzania was a risk. Now he thinks Clifton is far more dangerous! If I'm honest, it's probably not a bad idea for me to get away for a while, and I would like to see what he's been working on."

"Don't the police mind you leaving the country?"

"Well, I spoke to DCI Bonnington. They know where I am; and he reckons by the time they've got the case together for court we'll probably be coming home anyway. If necessary we can fly back a little early."

He nodded and they sat quietly again for a while.

"What day are you leaving?"

"Tuesday, we got the first available flight we could."

"I will take you to Heathrow."

"Jenny and Nick were planning to do that, you don't need to."

He shook his head speaking vehemently, "My droit de seigneur, I insist upon it."

She was trying to suppress a smile, but couldn't quite manage. He didn't even make the effort.

28

"Okay this is a bit weird." She tried a laugh, but it came out rather staccato. His car, scene of so many different stages in what had happened between them, was now the setting for their final interaction, at least of any private kind. They couldn't rule out meeting in Clifton, or attending the probable trial together. But for those, they had an unspoken understanding about how they would behave. Slightly closer than professional greeting, bright welcome at old acquaintances long unseen. Nothing beyond that. He was very quiet and she found that unnerved her even more. There were one or two small things she wanted to say, but it was difficult to start with meaningful words when they were so obviously putting the issue with most meaning beyond reach. She could feel the miles disappearing behind her, aware of the journey ahead shrinking and shrinking until it would collapse to nothing. In the end she had to take a deep breath and just speak.

"You know you will find someone, even get married one day."

His eyes cast a look her way that belied any acceptance. "I've heard that before."

She wanted to touch him, soothe him, but that wouldn't help. She nodded, "I know. But you will. I can see that."

He gave an exasperated sigh, "You care about me; I understand you don't want me to be hurt. But don't say things just to try and make us both feel better."

"I'm not. I can see it. You're saying something about having to wait a long time, but that it's all been worth it."

He gave a flick of his eyebrows and breathed out through his nose. "I'm not going to fritter away my sanity on looking for someone. If you believe it, tell me where you see this taking place, France or England?"

"I don't know." Her voice held faint surprise, "But it's got long windows."

He gave her a look that could have been derision. After that he drove in silence.

*

*They were round the grave again. It seemed like no time
had passed, but it had. Many things had happened. A medal
won, a wife also won, and then lost. Standing here, it felt like
there had been nothing else, just loss and burial. Again he was
by his mother. This time he was, by necessity, the one giving
comfort and support. Although she was calm now, the wailing
and crying had been thorough. Not that it had been a surprise.
Liver failure had arrived as no shock to any of them. But it
meant no final peaceful family scenes this time, like they had
enjoyed with Grandpère. Instead hospitals and machines and
yet still death. They all stood in the same attitude, quiet
resigned sadness. Sad that it had happened, not in the last
week, but over the last twenty, perhaps thirty years. They had
never known him as anything but a drinker, and had been too
young to have seen him as anything but a heavy one. He
looked at his mother; he could swear she looked ten years, not
two years, older since the funeral before. She was still in her
thirties, and would no doubt recover after a few months, at
least physically. How she would fare in other ways, he had no
idea. She was strong, capable, practical, but her world had
revolved around Papa and they all knew it. He watched as a
shudder went through her, forcing from her a slight gasp, and
he tightened his hold on her as she swayed.*

*She nodded, "I'll be alright, just stand still with me a
minute, then we'll go."*

*His eyes travelled round the rest of them, Grandmère
looked as severe as ever, but even she could not pretend that
this hadn't exacted a toll on her. She was bent over
considerably now, and Henri at her side, looking so like their
father, must have been a poignant reminder of her last visit
here. Would he provide consolation for her? Also, he had a
feeling it would only be now Papa was gone, that realisation
would come of just how long ago Grandmère had lost her only
son. And with it, possibly regret. He could almost feel sorry for
her. They were moving, very slowly, Henri was attending to
her carefully anyway.*

As they passed, she turned her face to him, "No tears for your father?"

"I shed them before this day."

"You didn't love him as much as your grandfather then?"

He could feel his mother's hand tighten on his arm and soothed it with his own. "I loved them both, and they both loved me. I have no regrets at how I lived alongside either of them. Not a bad thing to be able to say at their gravesides, don't you think?"

She turned away and as they moved on, Henri sent back a look over his shoulder that seemed designed to convey disapproval, but succeeded only in registering worry and puzzlement. He watched as his brother turned back to steady the faltering steps at his side, and wondered how long before they would be here again.

He looked at his mother, "Are you alright now Maman? Are you ready to go? Say if you need more time."

She shook her head quietly and they too turned away from the grave. As they made their way down to the house, he received what he'd known would come, and dreaded.

"Monsieur le Comte, may I offer my sympathies…"

*

She was beginning to worry at how long he'd been silent, wondering if she had finally said too much. "You're very quiet."

"Sorry, I was remembering things."

"Oh." Her tone of voice was somewhere in between embarrassment and regret. "Farine, you know I wish it was easier."

"No, not those things. More ancient history than that." They were almost there, this was the last chance to give her his news.

"I have decided to go home to my family. I'm looking into selling my practice. When I've dealt with that I will return to the château and see if I can cope with living there. No doubt it will please some members of the household and not others."

She gave him a long considering look but said nothing. "Do you not think this is wise?"

"I think it is, if that's what you want. I don't like to think what's happened here has forced you into doing something you wouldn't have otherwise."

"I'm not running away because of you, if that's what you're thinking. Some of what you said to me is true; there are things I need to deal with in my family. I can't deal with them from here."

She nodded, "A new adventure then?"

"Yes, do you think this could be part of the redemption you spoke about?" He considered adding something but left it.

"Maybe, you'll know in time I guess."

"I would have liked you to meet them. I really think you would get on well with Gloria and Etienne, and I'm sure you would do them good."

"How do you reckon that?"

"With your good sense. Their mother is, how do you say, a little vapid. Gloria needs a strong woman to give her a good example. She can be a bit of a tragic heroine."

"Oh? I thought I'd cornered the market there, myself."

He laughed, "No, that's not how I see you at all." For the time left he talked about the different family members and sketched in their backgrounds. He wondered idly what he would tell them about her now.

After checking-in she turned to him, wondering how to say goodbye.

He put his hand in his pocket, and pulled out something. "I have a small gift for you." Her face pinched suddenly. "Don't worry; I don't think it's in any way compromising." He lifted her hand to fix what he held round her wrist.. "It's a watch, to replace the one that was broken in your adventure."

She could feel her eyes filling up and wanted to get it over with. "Thank you, and thanks for rescuing me. And of course for the glorious non-affair. I'll just disappear off into the distance now and be a good wife."

He pulled her to him tightly and said through gritted teeth, "I'm not letting you go to be a good wife. If you can't go and be a passionate wife then you shouldn't be going at all."

She felt the breath squeezed out of her, but managed to nod, "Okay, I'll bear that in mind."

He bent and gave her one swift kiss, then loosed her and they made their usual 'au revoirs' lightly.

They turned away from each other and she headed for the metal detectors and passport checks. It probably didn't matter, she thought, that she couldn't really see where she was going at the moment. There was nothing she particularly wanted to look at anyway.

It was only just before landing that she took the watch off, to adjust it to local time, and noticed that it was engraved on the back. It read: This silver medal in the Olympic discipline of hole-punch is presented to Lucy Cottonwood. She smiled at it stupidly until the rustle of people gathering belongings brought her to her senses.

The normal bewilderment of a strange airport was intensified by hearing completely unfamiliar languages on every side, without even the safety of recognised rhythms like French or German. Added to that, the mass of people jostling around her were black, with a few Caucasians here and there. This was the reverse of what she was used to. She had expected that to offer a shred of comfort somehow. But it was false, tricking her eyes into swivelling after any particularly tall man, only to find, within a fifth of a second, that he had entirely the wrong shade of skin. Then her gaze fell on something familiar, but the sigh of relief came along with a stab of shock. She knew, consciously, that he would look different. In the e-mails, he had rejoiced at the loss of his desk-bound flab, returning him to the wiry man she had first known. But he was positively slight. The tan suited him though. Before he left home his hairline had begun to recede slightly, it had since progressed to rapid retreat. The last time she'd seen that hair it had been grey too, now it was almost silver. The result was a graver, more distinguished man. She felt as though she were being greeted by a facsimile, rather than the real husband she had waved off five months ago. But he held his arms wide to embrace her, his smile narrowing the eyes above puffy skin. She wondered just how tired he was.

"Lu! It's really you at last. Here's my sweetheart, how are you?"

At least his voice was the same, and the smell of his skin, and the way her forehead fitted into his neck below the jaw line. She couldn't speak. She had to hold onto him and allow the normality of it back into her again as he spread kisses over her cheek and then the rest of her face.

He, at least, could be cheerful. "There, it's alright now. It must have been such an ordeal." He held her away from him to look at her face. Tears swam in her eyes as she nodded. "I know you haven't told me everything. I could tell you glossed over the scary bits. You were trying to keep it from me before I could see for myself you were alright, weren't you?"

Another nod, this one with a weak smile as an accompaniment.

He picked up her case and took her hand to turn them to the exit. "Come on, let's get you away from all this. Was it really horrible?"

Her lips started to tremble, nostrils flaring to in an attempt to control her features. Words were still too much, again all she could do was nod, tears now streaking one after another down her face.

"Good thing your solicitor guy is such a heroic type, although I wonder if it wouldn't have been safer to let the police deal with it." They were out of the terminal now, and almost at the pick-up he had waiting. He squeezed her hand. "It must have been so hard for you."

Finally she found her voice. "It was. You have no idea."

On Thursday, in the early evening, the door bell rang. When Farine answered it, Jennifer's voice replied. He let her up, wondering what this could be about. She got to his door with something of a struggle, carrying a large parcel, obviously a picture of some kind. He helped her in with it through the door and asked what it was.

"I don't know. On Monday when mum was getting everything ready to leave, she had this in the study, all done up in brown paper as you see it. She made me promise I would bring it round to you today. That's all I know about it."

They managed a few polite enquiries, including one covering Lucy's safe arrival in Tanzania, and then Jennifer left.

Farine carried the parcel through to the lounge but hesitated over opening it. In the end he brought scissors through, along with a glass of wine, and took a large mouthful before cutting the string.

He stood back considering the picture, now propped up on his sofa. He reached for the wine again. The drawing was larger than he had expected. Well, that is if he had been expecting it, he would have imagined it smaller. With the frame it was a good three feet high. That meant it was about life size. There, on the paper, were two sets of arms and legs nested together, the pale hands cupped tenderly inside the dark ones, his thumbs resting gently on top of hers. He stepped towards it and looked again at the label she'd put on the back. She'd signed and dated it, as well as adding a title: 'Symmetry in Transient Madness'. He put it upright again so that he could see it and took another sip of wine. His features were calm, he leaned forwards, closing his eyes, and rested his fingertips against the glass, as if, somehow, that would help him to feel the touch of the two skins portrayed beneath.

AFTERWORD

This book is a light hearted work of fiction. All the characters in it are fictional too. But not the places, not even Djibouti, where Farine's parents met and fell in love. It was finding out about this country that was the inspiration for Farine's mother, Azizi, as a character.

I came across Djibouti in a fact book of world countries. It consists of little more than a port and its only known industry is listed as people trafficking. The simple horror of that statistic stayed with me. What alternatives for employment do most people of that country have? I imagine almost as few as the poor souls passing through it have. They're all trapped.

It is not my intention to either glamorise or trivialise the trade in human beings. In the story, Azizi found rescue and happiness. In real life, countless thousands do not. We can raise our voices against such a trade, if we wish. After all, we are free to do so. For those who would like to, I mention here the web-site of an action group called Stop The Traffik, who campaign against slavery.

Visit www.stopthetraffik.org if you would like to know more. A percentage of any profits made by the sale of this book will go to support them.

Printed in the United States
210109BV00004B/40/P

9 781849 232449